# The Graystone Killings

An Ella Mills Mystery

CJ Horne

Copyright © 2023 by CJ Horne

All rights reserved.

No portion of this book may be reproduced in any form without written permission from the publisher or author, except as permitted by U.K. copyright law.

# The Gray Family

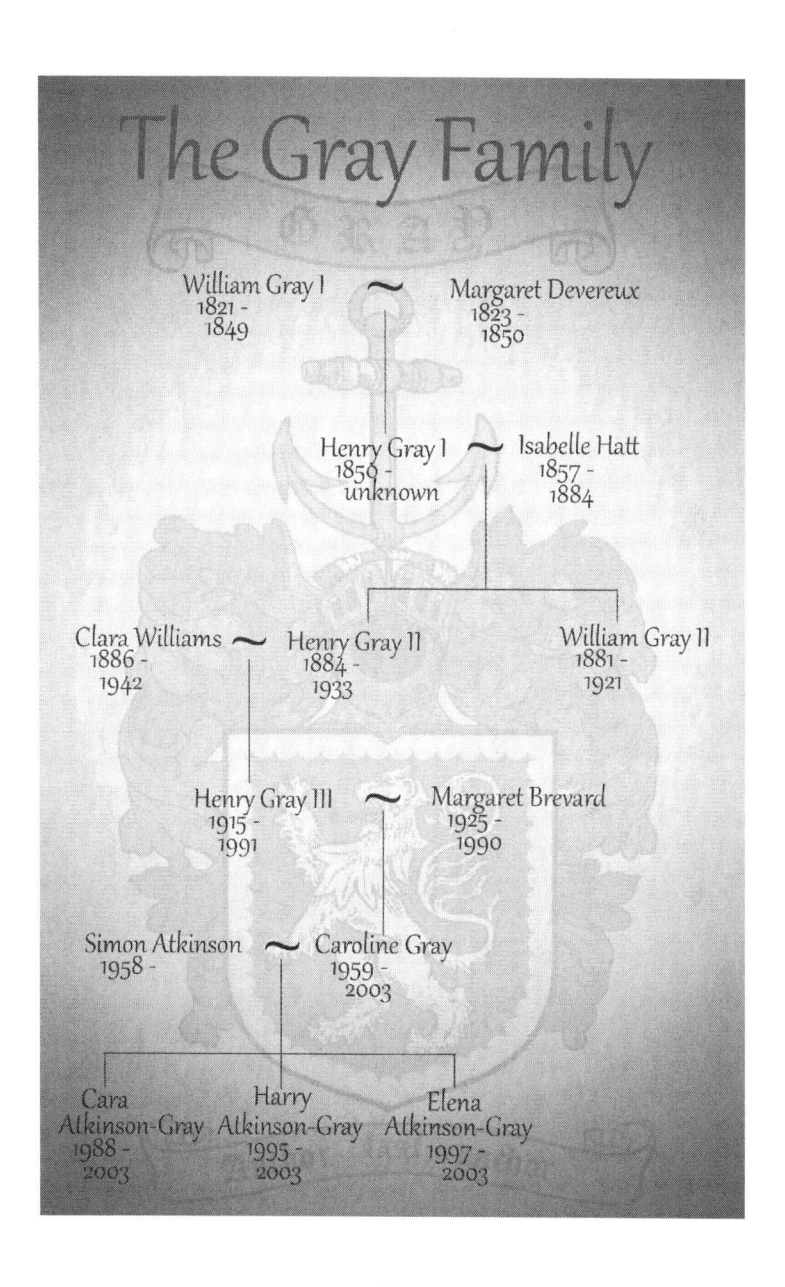

- William Gray I (1821 - 1849) ~ Margaret Devereux (1823 - 1850)
  - Henry Gray I (1856 - unknown) ~ Isabelle Hatt (1857 - 1884)
    - William Gray II (1881 - 1921)
    - Henry Gray II (1884 - 1933) ~ Clara Williams (1886 - 1942)
      - Henry Gray III (1915 - 1991) ~ Margaret Brevard (1925 - 1990)
        - Caroline Gray (1959 - 2003) ~ Simon Atkinson (1958 - )
          - Cara Atkinson-Gray (1988 - 2003)
          - Harry Atkinson-Gray (1995 - 2003)
          - Elena Atkinson-Gray (1997 - 2003)

# Contents

| | |
|---|---|
| Prologue | 1 |
| Chapter One | 14 |
| Chapter Two | 19 |
| Chapter Three | 24 |
| Chapter Four | 32 |
| Chapter Five | 41 |
| Chapter Six | 46 |
| Chapter Seven | 53 |
| Chapter Eight | 61 |
| Chapter Nine | 69 |
| Chapter Ten | 76 |
| Chapter Eleven | 83 |
| Chapter Twelve | 90 |

| | |
|---|---|
| Chapter Thirteen | 97 |
| Chapter Fourteen | 106 |
| Chapter Fifteen | 113 |
| Chapter Sixteen | 122 |
| Chapter Seventeen | 130 |
| Chapter Eighteen | 138 |
| Chapter Nineteen | 145 |
| Chapter Twenty | 150 |
| Chapter Twenty-One | 155 |
| Chapter Twenty-Two | 162 |
| Chapter Twenty-Three | 171 |
| Chapter Twenty-Four | 178 |
| Chapter Twenty-Five | 185 |
| Chapter Twenty-Six | 190 |
| Chapter Twenty-Seven | 196 |
| Chapter Twenty-Eight | 205 |
| Chapter Twenty-Nine | 213 |
| Chapter Thirty | 221 |
| Chapter Thirty-One | 229 |
| Chapter Thirty-Two | 238 |
| Chapter Thirty-Three | 244 |

| | |
|---|---:|
| Chapter Thirty-Four | 250 |
| Chapter Thirty-Five | 256 |
| Chapter Thirty-Six | 262 |
| Chapter Thirty-Seven | 271 |
| Chapter Thirty-Eight | 279 |
| Chapter Thirty-Nine | 287 |
| Chapter Forty | 294 |
| Chapter Forty-One | 301 |
| Chapter Forty-Two | 308 |
| Chapter Forty-Three | 314 |
| Chapter Forty-Four | 320 |
| Chapter Forty-Five | 328 |
| Chapter Forty-Six | 334 |
| Chapter Forty-Seven | 343 |
| Chapter Forty-Eight | 349 |
| Chapter Forty-Nine | 357 |
| Chapter Fifty | 366 |
| Chapter Fifty-One | 373 |
| Chapter Fifty-Two | 379 |
| Chapter Fifty-Three | 386 |
| Chapter Fifty-Four | 395 |

| | |
|---|---|
| Chapter Fifty-Five | 405 |
| Chapter Fifty-Six | 411 |
| Epiloge | 420 |

# Prologue

Cara leaps from the bed, squealing. A crash of thunder vibrates through the brickwork of the manor and moments later, lightning flashes across the troubled skyline, exposing the heavy storm clouds.

"Holy crap! Did you hear that?" she says to her best friend on the other end of the phone. "Count yourself lucky. At least you're in a house that was built this century. This old place shudders with every rumble."

She bounds over to the large sash windows and stares out at the rain lashing against the glass, her finger tracing the streaking patterns.

"Yes, I'll talk to her. Don't worry, I'll get her to change her mind. There's no way I'm missing Jake's party. Uh-uh, I can't ask her now. Trust me, not even this storm can drown out their arguing."

A sudden flash lights up the darkening sky, illuminating the nearby trees surrounding the estate. Branches bend in the gusting wind, their spring leaves battling for survival.

"This storm is crazy—I'd better check on Elena. She'll be awake and hiding under the covers. Sometimes I wish we lived in the village like you—storms are so much wilder up here. Sure, I'll see you tomorrow. No, I can't wait for the party either. Uh-huh, I'll talk to them, promise."

Cara ends the call with a sigh, wishing her parents weren't so strict. She slips out of her room, making her way down the stone hallway while rehearsing a compelling argument in her mind. A red carpet running along the centre swallows up the sound of her light footsteps, her bare feet cushioned against the ancient flagstones.

Before she can reach her sister's room, the lights flicker, plunging her into near darkness.

"Holy crap!" she says, coming to an abrupt halt. She counts aloud, hearing the slight tremor in her voice as she waits for the generator to kick in. "One—two—three..."

With growing reluctance, she pushes ahead down the lofty hallway, portraits of long dead relatives to her left, windows that reach all the way to the high ceiling on her right. The dull glow of the emergency bulbs is barely adequate to light her way, and she peers out from one of the narrow windows just as a fresh gust of wind slams against the walls of the manor. The force vibrates through the floor, causing her to jump back in alarm.

Heart racing, she makes a hasty dash to her sister's bedroom, catching her breath before peering her head round the doorframe.

"Hey, you okay in here?" She addresses the pyramid mound of covers on the bed. A whimper sounds from underneath. Cara tries again. "Look, I brought you these—" she says, stepping into the room.

# THE GRAYSTONE KILLINGS

Each bedroom in the manor has its own fireplace and floor rugs so soft it feels like walking on feathers. The crackling embers leave a pleasant woody smell in the air, and despite the storm's best efforts, there's a cosy feel to the room.

Cara approaches the bed and holds out a pair of white headphones—her prized possession that took weeks of convincing her parents to buy. A set of wide, tear-filled eyes peek out from under the covers. Through the material, a toy reading torch casts distorted shadows on the nearby wall.

"Not able to sleep, huh?" she says in a soothing whisper.

Her sister shakes her head, long chestnut hair tumbling around her shoulders. Elena's eyes dart to the nearest window and Cara follows her gaze. A branch suddenly whips against the glass with a crack, and she jumps back with a squeal. Her hand flies up to her chest, the beat of her racing heart like a drum against her hand.

"Bloody hell! No wonder you can't sleep—and never repeat that—sit up and I'll pop these on for you."

"Headphones! Can I keep them?"

"Just for tonight. I'll want them back in the morning. And no squirrelling them away, hoping I'll forget."

"Can I listen to music?"

"No, it's late. But they'll help to quieten the noise from outside. I'm going to check on Harry, then I'll be back to tuck you in."

"Mummy's shouting."

"I expect she's annoyed at father for cancelling the Hollies trip again. We'll still have fun, though," Cara says, trying to keep her voice upbeat.

"Don't leave me! I'm scared—" Elena grabs at her arm.

"The storm can't hurt you. It'll soon pass and everything will return to normal. Now, slip these on over your ears and settle down. I'll be back before you finish your book."

Cara lets out a heavy sigh as she steps out into the hallway, knowing it's going to be a long night. As she creeps along the hall towards her younger brother's bedroom, she hears her parents' voices louder than ever. They sound like they want to tear each other apart.

A rapid succession of flashes, followed by a lethal-looking fork of lightning, makes her scream out.

"What the hell?" She flinches at the deafening crack as the electric bolt contacts with the ground right outside the window.

Almost immediately, the hall fills with the boom of another loud crash.

Different this time, coming from somewhere up ahead.

A rush of cold air blasts past her as she realises the noise is coming from inside the house. She glances back at the arched doorway of Elena's room, half expecting to find the girl trailing behind her. Confident she's alone, she crouches low and sidles up to the balcony overlooking the twin imperial staircase. Without making a sound, Cara positions herself behind one of the wide pillars.

From her viewpoint, she can see the front door lying wide open. It slams against the wall with each blast of wind. Debris, blown in from outside, swirls around the black and white checkerboard floor, while a small table lies toppled on its side. The showcase antique vase—once a family heirloom—smashed into a million pieces on the tiles.

Cara's first thought is that someone has broken into their home.

If she can just reach the curving mid-point of the staircase, she can peer through the balusters and see what's happening below.

With a rising feeling of uneasiness, she grips the bannister for support.

After reminding herself that she's fifteen—practically an adult—and that her parents might need her help, she takes a deep breath and checks her back pocket for her phone.

Cara's heart sinks. Instead of feeling the reassuring solid casing, there's nothing but an empty pocket.

"Crap! Where did I leave it?"

There isn't time to run back and look. The voices are rising louder over the noise of the storm. It's true her parents argue a lot—but never like this.

Cara's instincts are crying out that something is seriously wrong, that whatever is taking place downstairs is escalating out of control. She wishes there was someone she could run to for help.

But out here on the exposed hillside, miles from the nearest village, they're completely isolated.

On tiptoes, she descends the red-carpeted steps and crouches low to peer through the balusters. She glimpses her mother's pink silk blouse in the gloom, but her movements appear erratic, causing her to fall in and out of view. As the confrontation escalates, her mother's voice becomes so hostile that she shrinks back into the shadows.

"I'm calling the police. I want you to leave this house now!"

Cara's brow crinkles. Her mother would never threaten to set the police on her father—there must be someone else with them.

Weighed down by dread, her hands trembling, she inches over to the bannister again. Over the sound of the front door banging and the rain drumming off the tiles, she hears the low rumble of a man's voice, cool and menacing.

"I don't think so, do you? You owe me, and now it's time to collect."

Fear shrouds Cara in an ice grip. She backs away, almost too scared to breathe, sensing danger is close by.

"I owe you nothing. Get out of my house!"

"Are you refusing me?"

"Yes! You're insane. I'm calling the police unless you leave right now."

"Then you give me no choice."

"What do you mean? Wait—where are you going?"

"What happens now is on you. Remember that."

Movement from below sends Cara scurrying back up the stairs. Before she can reach the upper hallway, she hears her mother scream, a high-pitched shrill sound that paralyses every muscle in her body. Her heart thumps in her chest as she sees the blurring motion of her mother's pink blouse racing past, climbing the opposite staircase, chasing after the dark figure of a man.

As more screaming and shouting fills the hall, Cara clamps her hands over her ears. Too frightened to move, she watches from her crouched position as her mother clambers to grab hold of the ascending figure.

She misses, tripping on the step, landing face down on the stairs.

He reaches the upper balcony—the floor where their bedrooms are situated.

"I'm taking back what's mine..."

"W-what's that—a knife? My God, what are you doing?"

Her mother's words slam into her like a physical blow, propelling her into action. Cara races up the stairs, her body driven by a primal need to keep her younger brother and sister safe. When she reaches the balcony, the air leaves her lungs in a sharp gasp; for in that moment, she knows she's too late.

On the opposite side, Harry pads down the darkened hallway towards them, a bewildered expression on his eight-year-old face. A comic book clutched to his chest.

She screams to warn him, "Harry! No! Go back!"

"Cara?" Her mother spins around, fear in her startled eyes. "Oh, dear God, no. My babies. Get out of here—keep Elena safe! Run!" Her mother looks back to where Harry has stopped to stare at the chaotic scene before him, not yet aware of the danger. "Run, Harry! Back to your room. Now!"

Cara sees the knife the same instant her mother lunges for the weapon.

Another flash of her pink blouse.

The glint of a blade.

All around them is the sound of the howling wind, its destructive force blasting through their home.

With every nerve in her body screaming at her to run to Harry, Cara hesitates, torn between helping her brother and keeping Elena safe.

A piercing scream jolts her into a run and she stumbles on shaking legs back to her sister's room. With a stifled sob, she bursts into her sister's room and slams the door behind her, turning the old key in the lock. She leans back against the door, swiping at the tears and trying to stop her legs from collapsing beneath her.

·········

"Quick, get up—we have to go!"

A crash on the other side of the door makes Cara's heart leap. Frantic with fear, her eyes dart around the bedroom, searching for the nearest item of furniture to use as a barricade. She pulls at a bookcase full of Elena's favourite stories; the pink stained wood too solid and heavy to move on her own.

"Why is mummy crying?" Elena asks, slipping off the headphones. Her bottom lip quivers and pulls downwards, unshed tears shining in her wide eyes.

"Help me!" Cara says, no time to give her sister the comfort she needs.

"I'm scared." Elena's small voice wobbles, the tears spilling over and cascading down her pale cheeks.

"I know, but I need you to be a brave girl. And that means no crying, okay? I can't move this bookcase on my own. Come over here and help me."

Elena nods, the fear etched on her youthful face. Before she can jump from the bed, a fist slams into the door, and she shrinks away, too terrified to move.

"Elena, please! Just bloody help me!"

Cara instantly regrets raising her voice, but time is running out; the door won't hold against the heavy blows for much longer.

Elena jumps down off her bed and runs over to her older sister, placing her small hands next to hers. Together, they pull at the bookcase, their knuckles white, faces flushed with the effort it takes to drag it across the floor.

"That's good," Cara says, panting as it shudders into place. Almost out of time, she kneels down to hold her sister's hands, snatching a few precious seconds to reassure her. "I want you to listen carefully. Take the torch and Bunny, and go to our secret place. Can you do that for me?"

Elena's lip wobbles. She nods, curls bobbing about her tear-streaked face, then runs back to her bed to grab the soft toy and reading torch.

"We're going to pretend this is a game, okay? No matter what happens, don't make a sound, understand? And whatever you hear, do not turn back."

Elena's face crumples as she throws herself into the arms of her sister, and fighting back a sob, Cara hugs her fiercely before pulling back.

They're out of time.

Her stomach lurches as the sound of splintering wood confirms her worst fears.

"Hurry now, and remember, brave girls don't cry. As quiet as possible—like when we sneak out to see Patch. Only use the torch if you must. This is important, Elena—you need to run as fast as you can to the stables and hide. Don't stop until you get there, do you understand? I'll be right behind you, I promise. But first... I have to help mother."

"Why can't you come with me? What's wrong with mummy?"

"There's no time, my sweet, sweet Elena—go! I love you." She places a hurried kiss on the girl's head and spins her round to face the wall. "*Remember, brave girl—no matter what.*"

She reaches over Elena's head and presses a small metal button hidden in the intricate carving of the wall's panel. A square shaped door springs open to reveal a hidden passageway running along the length of the upper floor. Cara knows that a set of stairs will lead her sister to the ground floor and out into the courtyard. Elena's walked the route a hundred times before, but never on her own.

She takes her sister's trembling hand, squeezing tight before pushing her through the gap. The air is frigid and musty; walls built of thick, rough stone, making the darkness virtually impenetrable. When Elena tries to resist, she pushes the door shut on her.

As Cara turns away from the fake panel, a sense of menace charges the air all around her and her stomach knots into a tight ball.

She gulps down the rising hysteria.

Her family needs her.

Harry's injured. Possibly even her parents, too. Elena is out of immediate danger, but she still needs time to reach safety. Whatever happens now, she mustn't lose her nerve.

"Open the door!" A voice outside the bedroom.

Cara recoils, edging as far from the doorway as possible, scanning the room for something besides stuffed toys to defend herself with. Why has she neglected to take up a martial art like all her friends? Can she even throw a punch? She clenches her fists until nails dig into her flesh.

A sharp blow to the lock causes the wood to splinter further. The heavy door slams repeatedly against the bookcase, shunting it outwards with each thud.

"Open. This. Fucking. Door!"

"Stay away!" Cara screams, panic spilling over so that her words sound choked.

"Dear God, no! What are you doing? Get away from my children!"

An overwhelming sense of hope washes over Cara. Her mother is here. Somehow, it's going to be okay. She won't let anything bad happen to them. Harry is going to be okay, too. He has to be.

"You made me do this! I warned you. I fucking *warned* you."

"Please don't hurt them. I'll do whatever you want!"

"I don't believe you."

"No! No, I'm telling the truth. We'll say it was an accident. Take what you want—I'm begging you, please, stop this!"

Cara hears her mother scream, followed by the sound of a hard thud.

Then silence.

With a final blow to the wood, the door flies open, toppling the bookcase with a crash.

A voice booms across the room at her. "Cara, don't run! I won't hurt you."

She hears footsteps scrambling over the fallen furniture, kicking at the scattered books on the floor.

And then she sees it; the flash of a blade glinting in the firelight—the same knife used against Harry, his blood still staining the metal.

Cara shakes her head, eyes fixated on the knife as she tries to back away.

This is a mistake—it has to be.

"Why... why did you hurt Harry? Is... is that his blood?" she says, bile rising in her throat. "Why are you doing this?"

"Ask your mother. I didn't mean for it to be this way. There was a plan! She's messed everything up—left me no fucking choice. Can't you see?"

Her mother staggers into the room, swaying and clutching her head. "No—stay away, don't you touch her!" she says, slurring her words. There's a gash to her temple, blood running down the side of her face.

She looks defeated—but more than that; she looks crushed.

In that moment, Cara realises she won't be going to Jake's party, after all.

A loud, guttural cry fills the room. Her mother's scream?

A blur of motion and she feels herself fall backwards onto the bed.

What's happening? She can't breathe.

Her skin turns cold and clammy. And then the pain hits her. An intense searing pain in her stomach that makes her gasp. Her body convulses, her eyelids too heavy to hold open.

"We could have avoided this, Caroline. You are the one killing her, not me. Your greed and your selfishness. *This is all on you.*"

"You're a monster—" her mother whispers, her hand trying to stench the bleeding. Cara's eyes flutter open. She sees the anguish and heartbreak reflected in her mother's face.

It's okay. The pain is fading now.

They're all going to be okay.

A clap of thunder rumbles. More distant now.

Good, the storm is passing.

Elena hates storms, and she'll be alone outside in the dark.

Lightning flashes across the room. Just before the darkness claims her, her fading vision falls on the pale, frightened face of her sister, staring out from behind the panel door.

With her final breath, Cara utters a single word.

So faint, the storm almost steals it away.

"*Run.*"

# Chapter One

## Twenty Years Later

"Morning, sweetie," says Suzy, her head peeking round the door. "I'm pleased to say there are no alarming reports of violence, natural disaster or threats of war. So, you're basically good to go!"

I smile with satisfaction as Suzy disappears again. This is going to be a good day. I turn off the alarm and, jumping out of bed, pad over to the wardrobe to pick out today's outfit for a run. Every choice I make is deliberate and calculated, and it drives my flatmate nuts. It can't be helped though, I need order and predictability. Sorry Nietzsche, but I prefer to skip the chaos and jump straight to the order.

Today I'm giving an art class so my day needs to start as harmoniously as possible. This is easier said than done when you live bang smack in the middle of central London. A mere stone's throw from Kensington, I rent Apartment 1A, Winford Street with Suzy, my closest and dearest friend.

Suzy's a model, as beautiful inside as she is out and we've been friends since... well, forever. I'd do anything for her. Anything except attend her glitzy A-list parties, where the rich and famous get to behave badly, and not worry about their antics being splashed across the tabloids by morning. For me, these events are to be avoided at all costs. Order is the key to my world and without it, my world crumbles.

Literally.

I can sense when a panic attack is about to strike. The first warning signs being shortness of breath, light-headedness and unsteady legs. Nausea and trembling are my points of no return. From there, I follow a rapid decline into the murky depths of irrational paranoia, perceiving everything around me to be a threat. That's on a bad day. I'm optimistic that today will be just fine.

Each morning, Suzy reviews the latest news, updating me with a *"good to go"* or *"hold back"* status. Sure, I could check myself, but scroll through any news app and you'll find the positive stories in the minority. Today I got the *thumbs up,* so bursting with zest for the day ahead, I tug on my running gear, tie back my long hair and stretch out my stiff muscles.

"I'm off, Suzy. I'll bring you back an iced flat," I say, calling out as I pop in my headphones.

"Thanks, I adore you!" Suzy's voice comes from deep inside her dressing room, where the intensive pruning and preening ritual of her glamorous six-foot body is well underway.

I set off on my run at a respectable pace, my long legs pounding the pavement to music selected solely on its number of beats. The carefully chosen routes offer the best views of Kensington; from the Churchill Arms, where every square inch is embellished with blooms, past Kensington Palace with its subtle grace, to the swanky grandeur of Harrods. I drink it all in like a drug as my feet pound the pavements.

The artist in me desires beautiful things, whereas the paranoia lurking within wants to be around *busy*. It's comforting being surrounded by people going about their everyday routine. There's safety in numbers and I engineer everything such that I melt into the background with ease.

I may be neurotic, but I'm not stupid—I know that the best avoidance measure to being stalked, mugged, or attacked is to adopt a varied routine. As this equates to chaos in my world, I compromise and have set routes for set days of the week. So far, I'm confident this strategy is effective.

Today's route takes me to Portobello Market in Notting Hill. Saturday brings the bustle of antique stalls displaying collectables from all around the world. I come this way to feel the vibrant buzz of the stall vendors as they set up their treasures, ready for the influx of novice collectors and tourists who will descend upon the street in their droves.

There's no cheerful waving good morning as I run by, no smiles or nods to the vendors I see every week. That's not me. I'm the faceless jogger. The girl with the unremarkable mousy brown hair tied back under a nondescript cap covering her eyes. I wear running leggings, but never brightly coloured, and a running jacket that reaches over my bum. Whenever I attract unwanted attention, my 'spidey' sense tingles and I donate my ensemble to charity, the route abandoned and switched out for the next replacement.

It's on the approach to Notting Hill Tube station that a loud bang booms out over the sound of my music, the ground beneath me shuddering. A cannonball of black smoke erupts into the sky from a few streets away.

*What the—holy shit!*

The unthinkable is happening.

There's been an explosion.

I stop dead and instinctively crouch low to the pavement, apocalyptic scenarios playing out in my head—*what if an underground train has crashed? Or worse, a bomb? Is this a terror attack? Am I about to be attacked by extremist fanatics wielding knives in the street?*

I look around and people everywhere are motionless, like statues. Stunned looks of disbelief and shock on their faces, chins titled up towards the bellowing black column of smoke. As it disperses in the wind, a sinister blanket covers the waking city below with its unpleasant, acrid smell. It leaves an unnatural metallic taste in my mouth. With a sense of detachment, I watch the activity erupting around me.

People jolt into action, running and screaming in all directions.

I'm unable to do either.

Heart racing in my chest, each beat brings with it a stabbing pain. My laboured breathing comes in successive quick gasps.

This is definitely not good.

With shaking fingers, I tap my earpiece.

"C-call. S-Suzy," I say, wheezing out the instruction to my mobile. She picks up on the second ring.

"Hey, sweetie, let me guess—pastries? For which you need me to talk you down from temptation?" Suzy's melodious voice cuts through the chaos surrounding me. "Wait—Ella? What the fuck is going on? Is that screaming? Why is someone screaming in the background? What's happening?"

My mouth is uncooperative in all attempts to form words. Finally, I manage an unintelligible rasp.

"Talk to me, Ella. Where are you? You're having one of your scares, aren't you?"

"Uh," I grunt.

"Okay, sweetie. We've got this. Now, breathe with me, and inhale…" Through the headphones I hear her deep inhale of breath. "And hold… perfect. And exhale. Excellent. Again, inhale…"

I try to match my breathing to Suzy's, to draw an inner calm from her soothing tone. We're on the third repetition when a young woman dressed in black leather with a red scarf, jeans and high-heeled boots comes running past me, sobbing. She lets out a piercing scream and stumbles into a nearby doorway as the *snap, snap, snap* of what sounds like gunshots resonates through the air.

"What the actual fuck was that?!" Suzy's outburst is directly in my ear. Coupled with the hysterics of the 'red scarf' lady, it does little to ease my anxiety levels.

I scan the chaos and listen for the shots getting closer.

*So much for this being a good day…*

# Chapter Two

A therapist once suggested I learn a martial art to help ease my feelings of stress and anxiety. With enthusiasm, I threw myself into Krav Maga defence classes, working my way up the grades. I'm fairly confident I could disarm an assailant if the circumstance arose.

But I'm in no rush to test that hypothesis out.

"For God's sake, Ella, you're basically freaking me out now! Where are you?" Suzy's rising voice—tinged with a fringe of hysteria—comes through my headphones again.

Before I can strangle any more words, I pick up on a new sound and hold my breath, listening for the faint *whoop* in the distance as it grows nearer. Sirens. Coming from all directions.

"I'm... alright," I say, my lip quivering with the effort it takes to hold it together.

"Too fucking right you are," Suzy says, a thickness in her voice as she tries to hold it together for my sake. "Focus on your breathing and tell me what you see. You need to tell me what's happening."

I glance around me in a daze.

"There's—"

A blare of sirens and screeching tyres drowns me out. Emergency vehicles race past in a blur of motion and sound. Police cars and trucks follow behind the bright red of the fire engines with their florescent yellow and blue markings. A long line of ambulances, too many to count, fill the street with a cacophony of sirens and flashing lights.

Within minutes, armed police officers are cordoning off the road and ushering pedestrians behind a barrier.

At the reassuring presence of the first responders, a wave of relief floods my body and for an awful moment I think I'm going to be sick.

"Where the buggery are you, Ella? What the fuck is going on? All I can hear are sirens and screaming!"

Suzy may be beautiful inside, as well as out, but when she's stressed, angry or scared, she curses better than any drunken sailor. It's her coping mechanism. Much like myself, she's a contradiction in so many ways. "You know what? Forget it. Whoever is standing next to you—hand them the fucking phone."

"What—?"

"The phone, sweetie. Hand the phone over. And keep up your fucking breathing until I tell you to stop—deep inhale, deep exhale."

With a quick glance over at the person next to me, I disconnect my headphones and hold out the handset.

"For you..." I say to the man in his late twenties, standing to my right and filming the chaotic scene on his phone camera.

The man frowns, glances me up and down with bemusement, then takes the mobile from my hand. I barely register him, my eyes glued to the growing number of responders, congregating like a swarm of bees from all directions. Most wear high-vis jackets, others are in black with armoured vests. A police helicopter circles overhead.

"Uh, no—I don't know what's happened, but yeah, your friend is here beside me and she's fine."

I ignore the stranger talking with my best friend, because right now, all I can focus on is the terrifying scene before me.

"No kidding? Yeah, I can do that. What number? Yeah, I know it. We'll be there in, like... twenty minutes."

With a tap on my shoulder, the man hands me back my phone. Scrawny and pale, he has a beanie hat pulled down to his spotty brow. His eyes are wide with adrenaline. I pigeonhole him to be a gamer geek, most likely living out of a dingy basement somewhere, playing video games late into the night while existing on takeaway pizza.

"I'm gonna walk you home. You know, like, make sure you're safe."

"Thanks, but—um—I'm alright. No need."

"Your pal's promised me tickets. I've to take you back and to not take 'no' for an answer—she told me to say that. Besides, you don't look so great—you're kinda white, like you're gonna pass out."

"Tickets?"

"She's a model, right? Gonna be lots of babes at this show, an' she's promised me VIP tickets." He grins at me. Great, this is all I need.

I snatch back my phone, but Suzy's already ended the call and reluctantly I fall into step with my would-be escort, grateful at least to be leaving the chaos and mayhem behind me.

……·……

"Basically, the news headlines are reporting the incident as an explosion and not terror related, so that's a relief. There's mention of a prisoner escaping and what appears to be some kind of breakout while being transported. I can't find any info about who they are, though. Details are still sketchy at best. Oh my God, I was so worried about you!"

Suzy leans against the kitchen counter and refreshes the news website on her phone for the hundredth time.

"I won't pretend it wasn't terrifying. Thanks for this, it's really hitting the spot," I say as Suzy swaps out her mobile to hand me a second cup of steaming coffee. "It was the confusion, you know? First the loud bang, smoke everywhere and people scattering in all directions. The entire time I kept thinking, any minute now I'm going to come face-to-face with one of those crazed fanatics." I take a tentative sip from the mug, enjoying the burning sensation as I swallow the near scalding coffee. "Tell me, did you honestly give that bloke tickets for *Fashion Week*?"

She nods. "VIP front row seats for him and a nerdy friend. I'll ask a few of the girls to pay them 'special' attention," she says, sporting a mischievous grin. "They are so going to piss their pants when they see the girls in their outfits."

It feels good to laugh again, and I reach out to squeeze her hand. "Thanks for being there when I needed you."

"Darling, I'll always be here for you." She crosses her heart with a manicured nail.

From my stool, I lean across the kitchen counter and hug her tight. "And I love you for it. Ugh, I have to hurry. I'm going to be late!"

Suzy eyes me with suspicion and raises an eyebrow.

"You think it's wise to go in today? After what's just happened?"

"The gallery won't run itself," I say, padding towards the bathroom to get ready. "Besides, I've got a class this morning. I'm not letting my students down because a prisoner makes a run for it. I've already survived the worst that can happen."

"Well, just be careful!"

"I will. They've most likely re-captured him by now, anyhow." I toss a smile back at Suzy and hope my tone is convincing enough to stop her from worrying. I don't tell her my spidey sense is on high alert, and that a niggling doubt about leaving the apartment lies heavily across my chest. If I give in to it, I'm likely going to spend the rest of the day hiding away in my bedroom.

And I won't let that happen. Not on a class day.

# Chapter Three

"**M**orning, Wynter. Sorry I... um... got held up. Thanks for opening."

"Oh, sure, no probs. Morning," says my assistant, reaching for the laptop and spinning it round until I can see the screen. "So I've gone through incoming, there's a couple of inquiries for commissions, also a late cancellation for today's class—flu—so I pinged the wait list and have a confirmed attendee. Social media, there's two requests: UCA Canterbury Creative Arts wants you to do a talk—already sent your apologies—and the Paris Museum of Modern Art requests five pieces for an Art and Life exhibition they're planning. I've printed off the list for your approval and I'll get a White Glove order sent through for crating."

When she momentarily comes up for breath, she flicks shut the laptop before continuing with her rapid fire update.

"I'm just about to prep the studio for class. Any requests before I begin? The agency is sending over one of their new girls to model today. Oh, and your mother called. Several times. She said to call her back the minute you arrive. Coffee?"

"Hmm, please, that'd be great, thanks. Will you send the new model to me when she arrives? I'd like to get to know her a little, make sure she's comfortable with everything beforehand."

She scribbles notes in her pad with one hand while pouring coffee with the other.

She's extremely efficient.

I met Wynter one morning three months ago after finding her sleeping outside my art gallery, The Verandah. From her youthful, dishevelled appearance, I could tell that she was a runaway; dried tear streaks down her cheeks and inadequate clothing.

"Hey there, are you in trouble?" I'd asked, keys jingling in my hand in readiness to open up the gallery.

"Sorry miss, I didn't mean to—"

Before I knew what was happening, her head bent low, and she was sobbing into her backpack.

I ushered her inside to clean up in our small customer toilet before taking her to a nearby cafe for breakfast. She was famished and visibly upset, but also there was a troubled look in her bloodshot eyes. Between mouthfuls of Full English, with all the trimmings, she told me of the life she felt compelled to run away from.

A life with her parents up North.

*"Let's start with names. I'm Ella. Ella Mills, what's your name?"*

*"Wynter Day. Mum's sense of humour."*

*"Well, Wynter, you have a beautiful name. How old are you?"*

*"Sixteen. But I'll be seventeen in a couple of months."*

"And where's home? I can hear an accent, but can't place it."

"Leeds, but we move a lot."

"Would you like to tell me why you've left home? Perhaps I can help."

"You can't. Nobody can. Mum's an addict. Dad too; only he's better at it, more careful, you know? Mum overdoses at least once a month and dad's normally too drunk to notice, so I call 999 and they come sort her out."

"That can't be easy for you. What about school or college?"

"Mostly I'm self-taught. Not that I mind, I don't like school. Kids are mean, always teasing for not wearing the right clothes, or not having the right hairstyle—my name doesn't help either. They always find a reason to bully."

"What about Social Services? Have they ever been involved?"

"I doubt they'd be able to keep track of us, even if they were. We get evicted from one place to the next because my folks never pay the bills. Sometimes we'll squat in empty buildings until we're moved on."

"Tell me more about your parents. Are they... physical towards you?"

"Well, they fight all the time. Mostly they hit each other, but occasionally they'll have a go at me. They get me to steal alcohol for them, vodka from small shops, corner stores, that sort of thing. The big supermarkets have the best surveillance cameras and fast security guards, so I don't go near those places unless they force me. Small shops are easier, that's how I never get caught, although sometimes they give chase and then I throw the bottle and run. I hate when that happens, because then my folks beat me for being sloppy and for coming back without the booze."

"I'm so sorry, Wynter. What you've described is horrible. So you just left? What prompted that decision?"

"They were off their heads as usual. Dad hit mum, she was screaming at him and clawing at his face. He knocked her out cold. I thought he'd storm off to the pub, but he took a swing at me instead. I was quicker, of course—dodged the punch and he fell and hit his head on the table. They were both lying on the floor unconscious, blood, vomit and... mess everywhere. Didn't want to hang around for the beating when they woke, so I packed a bag and got on the first train here. I am sorry, miss—I didn't mean anything by sleeping in front of your shop. You seem like a nice person."

"No harm done. I'm only sorry you had to spend the night outside in the cold. Hey, and call me Ella, okay?"

"What d'ya sell anyhow?"

"I'm an artist, specialising in portraits."

"Wow! I've never met an artist before. It must be awesome."

"It is, and sometimes I teach, too. Would you like to see inside? I can give you a guided tour, and then we can figure out what we're going to do about you sleeping in my doorway."

"You'll show me around? I've never been inside a gallery, but I'd really like that. All those fancy lights and artsy paintings; always seemed too posh for someone like me."

"That's the pompous galleries you're describing. My gallery, The Verandah, is definitely not pompous, I can assure you. Art should be for everyone, regardless of wealth or education. But I will need you to do something *for me first. I'm going to need your parents' contact details. Is there a mobile number, perhaps? I'll have to call them to let them know that you're alright."*

"You won't tell them where I am, will you?"

*"Of course not. You have my word. I know you won't think so, but they're probably worried about you."*

With great reluctance and much coaxing, she finally agreed to let me phone her parents.

It's not a conversation I'll forget in a hurry.

Before making the call, I showed Wynter around the gallery, inviting her to stay in the flat above, at least until she figured out what she wanted to do next. Although I've never lived there, it comes with the lease and provides ample space to keep my equipment. I helped her settle into the bedroom occasionally used for overnight stays, usually after late night events at the gallery, and after clearing away a stack of painting paraphernalia into cardboard boxes, I made my way down to the office to call her parents. I closed the door firmly behind me, not wanting her to overhear what needed to be said.

*"Um... Mrs Day? Good morning. Um... you don't know me, but I'd like to talk to you about your daughter Wynter."*

*"Another feckin' do-gooder, that's all I need. How d'ya get this number? What's that bloody little bitch been doing now? Well, I ain't paying for jack-shit so ya can piss right off. Feckin' interfering, busybody."*

*"Mrs Day, please, hear me out. I'm calling to tell you that your daughter is safe. I'm sure you must be worried about her?"*

*"Do I sound like I'm feckin' worried? Constantly draggin' me down, that one. Feckin' always wantin' summit. Take, take, take. Well, good riddance, I say. Keep her!"*

"You misunderstand me, Mrs Day. This call is a courtesy, one that you clearly don't deserve. Wynter will be staying with me from now on where I will care and provide for her. You and your husband will not look for her. You will not try to contact her. If I hear you have made any attempt to insert yourself back into her life, I will bring the full weight of the law down on you. Be assured that I will not stop until you are behind bars for the neglect and abuse you've put her through. Do I make myself clear?"

There was a brief silence before she hung up.

In the three months since that call, Wynter has gone from strength to strength. She runs the gallery when I'm not around and is a tremendous hit with the clients. As for Suzy, she adores her and treats Wynter like the younger sister she never had, giving her the affectionate nickname *Whackey Wynter*. Suzy's influence shows in her outlandish choices of hair colour and clothing, all of which somehow flatter her. Wynter's smart, with limitless potential. Now enrolled on a business course, she's thrown herself into it with the enthusiasm only those with a passion for knowledge can display. Sometimes I wonder what would have become of her, left to fend for herself on the city streets. Perhaps I saved her that day—I like to think so, anyway. There's one thing I know for sure. She's destined for great things and one day she will outgrow this tiny corner of London.

"Mother, you called! Several times I'm told. Are you and father okay?"

"Sweetheart, we're fine. It's you we're worried about. That awful incident this morning, right on your doorstep. We called your mobile and left a message, and the apartment, too. Thank goodness Suzy doesn't avoid our calls... She told us what happened, and that you'd already left for the Verandah. So we called the gallery, and that sweet young girl, what's her name? Summer? Or is it Autumn? Anyway, she said you'd be arriving soon. And I said to your father, 'that'll be just like our Ella, out running only to find herself in the middle of all that upset.' The police haven't released details yet. Please, sweetheart, be careful until they have more information. Do you think it's wise to open today?"

"Mother! Please! Calm down. I'm fine—just a scare. No harm done."

"No harm? Is that what we're calling it? Suzy told me you had one of your episodes again this morning. I don't think you should be at work today."

I roll my eyes, cursing Suzy for opening her big mouth.

"Listen, mother. I have to go. Busy day. I'm taking a class soon, but I promise I'll be over to see you and father soon. Maybe make that cheesecake that hates my hips so much?"

"Of course, dear, I don't want to hold you up. Your father and I would very much like that. You will be careful, though, won't you? We worry about you."

"Yes mother, I know. Love you and I'll visit soon. Tell father I said 'hi'."

"Goodbye, sweetheart."

"Bye."

# THE GRAYSTONE KILLINGS

I hang up and pinch the bridge of my nose, feeling the building tension dissipate. An involuntary shiver sends a tingle rippling through me as I shrug off a sense of foreboding. All this talk of escaped prisoners has got me jittery again.

I tell myself there's nothing to worry about.

Nothing at all.

# Chapter Four

"I'm heading out, Wynter. Won't be long."

The stress from this morning's incident, coupled with the demands of my students, has left me feeling drained and I need to clear my head.

I hold my portraiture workshops once every six weeks and they always book up months in advance. Today's class has been another resounding success, thanks to the model being easy to work with and the clientele keen to learn. Even so, it's exhausting having a dozen people looking to you for guidance in improving their craft.

The idea of the classes first came about when a passing art student spotted one of my most popular paintings displayed in the gallery—*Avant que la prochaine larme ne tombe* (Before the next Teardrop Falls)—and wanted to understand the creative process behind its creation.

Although the model in the painting has remarkable blonde hair and elfin-like features, it's not her beauty that stops people in their tracks. Clients describe standing before the portrait as an otherworldly encounter. A soul-searching rollercoaster of emotions that takes their breath away.

First, an intense locking of the eyes draws them in, followed by a surge of despair at the stark hopelessness staring back. When their gaze drops to the watery abyss—a world locked for eternity within a teardrop—their heart soars with a fresh burst of hope. Until ultimately, there comes a very individual and overwhelming sensation of longing.

After completing the portrait, several collectors approached the gallery, offering to buy the piece. But I'm reluctant to part with it, despite it holding no particular sentimental value. And so it remains on display, mesmerising those who come to gaze upon it.

"I'd grab a brolly just in case. Looks like rain," Wynter says, calling out from the general direction of one of the windows. She's working on a new display and has a natural flair for drawing passers-by into the gallery.

A quick glance outside confirms the crisp blue sky from earlier is rapidly disappearing behind gathering clouds.

"Good call, thanks. I'll take my camera too. Might be an opportunity to get some interesting mood shots for the next workshop."

Not to mention a welcome distraction from the anxiety that's circling the fringes of my mind.

After fetching my camera, I head out into the blustery street. My unremarkable ensemble of navy blue raincoat blends perfectly into the background, and I melt seamlessly into the busy throng of people.

The swollen black clouds overhead sag under the weight of their arduous burden, confirming that my flimsy brolly will be no match for the scale of the blackening sky. With determined stubbornness, I decide the much needed serenity of the Rose Garden in Hyde Park is a worthwhile trade-off for the potential drenching.

After grabbing a flat white to go from the nearest Costa, I enter the park via a set of wrought-iron gates and walk beneath the metal arches of the pergola. Despite the threat of a storm, there's enough people around to keep my nerves in check. The autumn half-term brings families and tourists out in their droves, and they're not to be put off by Mother Nature's threat of a deluge. With each fresh gust, the wind carries the squeals of delight from children chasing fallen leaves across the grass.

I inhale the atmospheric air, enjoying the earthy, fresh scents. The simple pleasure of the crunch of bronze coloured leaves beneath my shoes soothes my jaded nerves as I follow the path to the Rose Garden. Everything seems far less intense in this tranquil setting. The botanic displays that line the winding pathways are perhaps not as spectacular as the spring and summer blooms, but their strong floral scent brings me a natural comfort.

When a woman walks past in the opposite direction, she throws a friendly smile my way and I instantly recognise her as a regular visitor to the park.

"Good afternoon."

"Afternoon." I acknowledge her without slowing.

Strangers pose a challenge for me. I have an inherent distrust of them and yet crave their presence around me like a comfort blanket. The smile feels awkward and tight on my face, and it's not until she's gone past that I let my shoulders relax again.

As I approach the Boy and Dolphin fountain, dozens of leaves floating on the surface race around the circular marble bath like little golden boats in the wind. Almost mesmerising, I stare at them, forcing my mind to expel the clutter still rattling around inside my head.

With all the benches around the fountain empty, I choose one that gives me the best view of the park and set my bag and drink down while I fiddle with the camera settings. The sky is a dramatic stage, every bit as threatening as it is awesome, and since the display is about to kick off at any moment, my intention is to capture the raw energy of the scene. I just need the rain to hold off a little longer.

After firing off a few shots, a high-pitched yelping nearby distracts me so that I lower the camera to see what all the fuss is about. A teenage girl tugs on the lead of a small terrier dog, all the while glancing at the clouds and urging her pet to keep walking.

"Stop that, Miss Beazley. We're gonna get soaked. Come!"

*Miss Beazley?*

With a name like that, it's no wonder the animal is giving her a hard time. Perhaps she's right, though. With every second that passes, the storm is intensifying. The bronzed leaves in the fountain's bath are now thrown about in a frenzy, whipped up by the water's swell as the wind picks up momentum.

The little dog continues to bark frantically at the large rose bush opposite until eventually the girl, agitated and impatient, bends down and swoops the unsuspecting ball of fur into her arms. She stomps off, uttering words of annoyance.

Paranoid, I scan the surrounding greenery, pointing my camera lens past the fountain towards the bushes. I adjust the focus and sweep from right to left.

There! At my eleven o'clock. A black shadow—too big for an animal or a bird...

I adjust the lens to bring the image into focus.

Alarm bells go off in my head, but before I can listen to the warnings, the focusing ring hones in on its target.

A gasp leaves my lips.

A man stands behind the bushes, his menacing gaze staring back down the lens at me.

My instincts tell me to run away, to leave now.

Before it's too late.

The camera almost slips from my grasp as I snatch the eyepiece away. Only fifteen metres from the bench, he stands tall and motionless, dressed entirely in black, arms hanging casually at his side. A dark scarf and baseball cap cover his face so that only his eyes are visible.

And right now, those eyes are staring straight at me.

With slow, deliberate movements, he raises what looks like a mobile phone to his ear. At the same time, my phone rings beside me. A sickening dread twists my stomach into a tight ball. I ignore the jingling sound, knowing with uncanny certainty he will bear down on me if I look away for even a second.

But the muffled ringing coming from my bag is persistent, and with his stare making me increasingly restless, I reluctantly glance down.

The ringing stops.

I snap my head up, eyes searching the bush where the man was standing just seconds ago.

He's gone.

Almost too scared to breathe, everything around me blurs, and the fuzzy cotton-wool feeling in my head is quickly followed by a tightness across my chest. I fish my phone out from the bag, all the time my eyes darting over to the bushes. Each slight movement, every rustle of a branch in the wind, catches my attention as I desperately search for a glimpse of the man's black cap.

I didn't imagine him, I'm certain of it.

My body shaking, I sweep up my belongings and make a hasty retreat towards the park exit.

Few people are around now, and feeling more vulnerable than ever, the first heavy splodges of rain hit the ground as I reach the gate. With a last backward glance, I scramble my thoughts into some sort of coherent order and attempt to recall as many details of the man as possible. The police will want a description when I report the incident to them.

But first I need to call Suzy.

I quickly scan through the notifications on my mobile, hoping to see a missed call from someone I know. Instead, a withheld number from moments ago glares back from the screen.

A chill passes through me.

"Call Suzy," I say, almost screaming into my phone. She picks up immediately. "Suzy! Oh, thank God you answered!" Unable to hide the tension in my voice, I sound pitchy and highly strung even to my own ears.

"Ella? Are you okay? Has something happened?"

"I-I'm not sure," I say, trying to shout above the noise of the rising wind. "I think someone was watching me in the park."

"Sweetie, people watch people in parks. That's what they do." She gives a light laugh, but I hear the nervous tremor behind it.

"Wait—what was that laugh? What are you not telling me?"

"Nothing. Are you about to have one of your episodes?"

"No. No, I'm alright."

"Good. Head back to the Verandah—I'll meet you there in twenty minutes."

Suzy hangs up before I can quiz her further.

It's a skittish half walk, half run to the gallery. Whenever I turn to glance over my shoulder, the sideways rain hits me in the face. But even if the umbrella weren't to blow inside out, I would still be too nervous of it obstructing my view. There's no way I can risk leaving myself open to an attack.

When I finally see the welcoming lights of the Verandah up ahead, I take one last furtive glance behind me and rush to the entrance, grateful to be leaving the eerie gloom of the storm behind.

After practically falling in the door, Wynter looks up from where she's fussing over a display. She stops what she's doing and stares when she sees me.

"So, brolly no good, then?"

I'm a sodden mess, a puddle forming on the floor at my feet as I stand trying to catch my breath. I don't even want to think about my ruined shoes.

"Sorry, forgot to get lunch."

Wynter gives me a curious look.

"No probs," she says, approaching and helping me out of my drenched coat. "Let me get you a towel. I'll nip across the road in a sec. Cheese wrap be okay?"

As I stand dripping by the counter, she heads off towards the customer toilet to source me a towel. I take a deep breath and puff out my cheeks, trying to relax the tightness in my shoulders.

# THE GRAYSTONE KILLINGS

A printout placed next to the laptop grabs my attention and I spin it around to read the catchy title.

**THE UNVEILING OF ROBIN H-ART**

MODERN DAY ROBIN HOOD

OR

COMMON CRIMINAL?

WE UNCOVER THE FACTS TO REVEAL ALL!

"Thought you'd be interested," Wynter says, returning with a towel and nodding at the sheet of paper. "I spotted the article while checking for updates on that escaped convict. Sort of admire him in a way—the thief, not the prisoner. When you think about it, they're only stealing back what's already stolen.

"It's like me stealing booze from my folks, you know? They've nicked it—well, I did, but it was for them, so the same thing. This Robin H-art..." She muses over the name for a moment, letting it linger on her lips. "Do you think they're male or female? Robyn with a 'y' works, too. Anyway, *this person* is stealing back art that originally belongs to someone else. The best bit is—and I truly love this part—the people they're stealing from can't report it because it was never theirs to begin with! Anyway, thought you might like to read it." She looks up from the article, her eyes wide with admiration. "What d'ya think of them?" she says, handing me the piece of paper.

The individual Wynter refers to has made the news headlines on numerous occasions. Therefore, I'm familiar with the thefts and, in all honesty, it annoys me that the press are predisposed to romanticise a common thief, no matter what they are stealing or why. I have many opinions on this phantom vigilante, and I could debate for hours on the ethical morals of returning lost or stolen art, but right now there's a far more pressing news article I want to discuss

"Well, he—or she—is still breaking the law," I say simply. "You mentioned the prisoner from this morning's incident... has there been an update?"

I want to know what the police are doing to locate him.

And if they haven't captured him, what are the cosmic odds of me having just encountered him in Hyde Park?

# Chapter Five

"Well? Any updates...?" I say, pacing the floor of the gallery, waiting for Wynter to pull up the news website.

"Two secs, just checking now." Wynter pins me with a curious stare. I suspect Suzy asked her to keep a close watch on me today, so I force myself to stop pacing and get my neuroticism under control. "Right, here we go... oh, that's not good... they've released a name; Victor Malden. Says here that he raped, tortured and killed his victims, was caught four years ago and given a life sentence. When he escaped this morning, he was being transported for medical treatment—doesn't say what—but confirms treatments are normally given at the prison, unless a specialist procedure is required... blah, blah, blah... prisoner had help on the outside... launched a rocket at the patrol escort—that'd be the explosion you heard. He got away in the chaos and confusion. Two guards confirmed dead at the scene... several people injured... shots fired. Says details remain sketchy, but—"

The gallery doors burst open and Suzy blows in on a gust of wind. With a quick shake of her head, golden hair falls in natural waves around her shoulders. Somehow, even her immaculately applied make-up has remained in place. She smells fresh and floral, like she's just stepped out of a salon, the polar opposite of my sweaty, steaming state. How is it possible that she can stay looking glamorous in this weather? One thing's for sure, I don't need a mirror to know I have black mascara streaks running down my face.

"Bloody hell, it's lively out there—" she says, before catching sight of my dishevelled appearance. "No umbrella, huh?"

"Yeah, funny." Nostrils flaring, I attack my hair with the towel again.

"You sounded spooked on the phone. Are you okay?"

"I'm alright. Probably just being paranoid after this morning. I'll be a lot happier when this prisoner is back behind bars, though. Have you heard anything? Wynter was just reading through the latest updates. He's a nasty piece of work and I don't like the idea of him lurking around out there," I say, trying to keep in check the impulse to resume pacing.

"That's what I was coming to tell you. It's all over the news. They've just released his photograph and—"

"There are photographs? Show me—"

'Oh, sure, no probs.' Wynter flexes her hands together, cracking her knuckles, before sliding the laptop closer to her. 'Lemme just see...' she says, muttering and fixing her glasses with a quick grab of the lens frame before pushing them back in place. I wait as she taps around the screen with the trackpad before swivelling it round to face us.

# THE GRAYSTONE KILLINGS

The display shows the image of a man in his mid-forties being escorted into a white police van. He's clean shaven, shoulder-length black hair peppered with grey, and except for the odd strand across his eyes, it's swept back from his pale face.

A killer with good hair and good looks only adds to his deadly appeal.

In the photograph, he's looking over his shoulder towards the waiting journalists. They stand on the other side of a metal fence that would easily tower a double-decker bus. His head tilts down at an angle, hooded eyes burning with intensity at the cameras.

Such are his strong psychopathic features that I have no trouble picturing him luring unsuspecting victims to their deaths.

In his hunting ground, I'm certain that very few women could resist his dark and sultry looks.

"Are you able to zoom in on him?"

With a quick movement of her fingers, Wynter enlarges the image, cropping out everything except for the prisoner.

Taken after his initial arrest, he has a metal chain around his waist, as well as his wrists and ankles, attaching him to one of two flanking officers. He wears the standard bright coloured jumpsuit of the convicted, even though the image is taken before his sentencing—this was one prisoner nobody wanted to see escaping. Despite the jumpsuit, the restrictive chains help emphasise his slim waist, chiselled chest and wide shoulders.

It's obvious that when not hunting women, this man likes to work on his physique. With his looks, strong build and a well-practised charm, he would have no trouble attracting the attention of any woman he wanted.

Wynter is the first to speak. "He's kinda cute, in a creepy, vamp sort of way."

Suzy nods in agreement. "Cute, but still a fucking sociopath."

"What about victims? Does the article mention how many?" I ask.

Wynter scans the text. "Twelve women. Of those... oh, not good... he killed five."

"Shit," I say under my breath, as a familiar tightness creeps across my chest.

This is the man from the park. I'm sure of it.

Why would an escaped prisoner have my number? Or is it just an unhappy coincidence that my phone rang at the same time? I don't believe in coincidences—I'm way too paranoid for that.

What if he followed me back to the apartment this morning after his escape? The explosion was so chaotic that I wouldn't have noticed. But if that's true, then why me?

My spidey sense is off the fucking charts right now.

"Tell me he's apprehended, or at least that they're near to catching him?"

Wynter gives me another curious glance, then scans the rest of the article.

"Says here they're following leads... mentions Dover ferry port... remain cautious... do not approach... extremely dangerous... um, you want me to carry on?"

"A ferry port? So, they think he's skipped the country. Where do the boats go, France?"

As much as I would never wish a fleeing killer on the French population, I'm in desperate need of some assurance right now. I need to know that he's not the person who was watching me only half an hour ago.

When silence falls between us, it hits me that Suzy's been suspiciously quiet until now. I realise I haven't asked her why she's here. I tilt my head to the side and pin her with an expectant look. It's only when she clears her throat and sucks in her bottom lip that I take a step closer.

"Speak—"

"The thing is, sweetie—now, please don't freak out..."

As soon as the words leave her lips, my body tenses.

"What the hell, Suzy? You do realise that when you tell me 'don't freak out', that's exactly what I'm going to do!" I give her my most incredulous glare.

"Sorry—look, you've had a shitty day. I absolutely do not want to make it any worse. Only... shit, I'm going to just come right out with it—"

"Oh my God, Suzy, spit it out! What is it?"

"The prisoner... he's still here in the city. The port was a decoy. According to my source, Victor Malden is basically still in London. Of course, until it's verified that he hasn't fled the country, the authorities don't want to alarm the public. It's bad for business to admit you have a volatile psychopath on the loose in the capital."

I shudder involuntarily.

*Shit! It's more than just bad for business!*

# Chapter Six

"Who-who told you the prisoner is still here?" So far, all attempts to calm me down have only served to fuel my anxiety. Restlessly, I pace the length of the counter, sceptical of the gossip circuits that Suzy moves in. We're talking fashion world after all, not Scotland Yard.

Suzy plants her hands on her hips and glances at the ceiling, the trauma of split loyalties causing her obvious anguish.

"I'm not supposed to breathe a word of this to anyone... only, you're not just *anyone*, are you, sweetie? So, it's not like I'm breaking a confidence, not really." She sighs, the gesture exaggerated and worthy of an Oscar. "Somehow you always prise secrets out of me. It's not like I'd even consider telling anyone else, but you're my best friend. We're basically family! I'm sure he wouldn't mind... Oh, sod it—I'll tell you! It's Tom. He's extremely well connected and personally knows The Commissioner and The Director General of Security Service."

Tom is Suzy's new boyfriend of one month and counting, and of course, she's in love. Like the many other aspects of her crazy, whirlwind life, I've come to accept that my friend falls in and out of love on a regular basis. She is to love and happy-ever-after what the Grim Reaper is to a long and healthy life.

I've yet to meet Tom.

Although I'm sure he's a terrific guy, their three-month anniversary is still weeks off—the milestone I set for meeting Suzy's boyfriends over dinner. Few of her love interests make the distance, so it's a target I'm pretty comfortable with.

"What did Tom tell you? I want every last detail."

"Well, basically, he told me the prisoner was wearing one of those ankle accessories, you know, a tracker? The last known signal was somewhere on the M20 heading towards Dover, but it stopped transmitting around Ashford. The police are crawling all over the International Eurostar, as well as the ferry port, in the event he makes a run for Brussels or Amsterdam or any of the other European cities."

"Then why d'ya think he's still in London?" Wynter says, looking doubtful.

"Because, sweetie, this was a sophisticated attack. They blew up a truck with a fucking rocket, for heaven's sake! You really think the people behind this left to chance a tracking device to signal their location?"

"No, they wouldn't," I say. "Still, that's not to say he's in London. He could be anywhere by now, couldn't he?"

Suzy shrugs. "It's surprising just how much of a ball buster it is to get out of the city unnoticed. For a start, there are cameras on basically every street—Big Brother yada yada yada. Then you have the checkpoints on all major routes out of London. Airports are being monitored, too. Believe me when I tell you that the authorities would know if he left. And they don't. So we can assume he hasn't."

"France isn't out of the question, though?" I say, still clutching at straws.

*I need him to be anywhere but here.*

"Sweetie, I know what you're thinking. That's why I came straight over," Suzy says, holding up her hands. "Can you describe the man in the park? Was he anything like this photo?" She tilts her head towards the laptop screen.

Wynter looks with suspicion at the news article, then back to us.

"Yeah, so d'ya wanna to tell me what's going on?" She raises her dark, sleek eyebrows high above the rim of her glasses.

"It's nothing," I say quickly, not wanting to alarm her.

"Well, it sounds like something to me."

Wynter's quips can be ferocious when she wants. Not much gets past her, and although my default impulse is to shield her from the scary stuff, she's had to deal with a lot worse than anything either of us could imagine.

"Look, there's not much to tell. When I got to the park, there was a person staring at me. A man—hiding behind the bushes."

"Ew, d'ya think he was one of those flashers?" she says, scrunching up her nose and pulling a face.

"No, Wynter, I don't! He seemed more interested in freaking me out than waving his todger at me. Unfortunately, he was wearing a baseball cap, and a scarf pulled up around his face, but I got a good look at his eyes."

"Only his eyes...?"

I can tell Suzy is skeptical.

"Yes, but not only was he staring at me, he called my mobile, too. It started ringing as soon as he raised what looked like a phone to his ear."

"What did he say?"

"Well, nothing. I didn't answer it. I, um, sort of panicked. Here—"

I reach for my rain-soaked handbag and pull out my mobile, handing it to Suzy. Her brow pinches as she unlocks the home screen with my password and checks the call log.

"Three missed calls; one from a withheld number around twenty-five minutes ago, and two from your folks since then. But it's basically too late to recover the caller's number now. Pity. I have a theory, though, so hear me out for a sec—" Suzy says, handing back my phone.

This is where my friend becomes the voice of reason. She swoops in to bring balance to my wild conspiratorial theories, that very often have no foundation and seldom hold any weight. They are formed in the murky depths of my paranoia, and guiding me back to a place of security is what Suzy does best. I'd be lost without her.

"What you experienced this morning was awful, sweetie. I don't know what I would have done if something terrible had happened to you." She pauses and becomes misty-eyed at the mere thought of how differently events could have played out. "And although you're absolutely fine—thank God—I suspect you may still be suffering from... well, shock."

"So, you're saying... what are ya saying? That Ella sees threats where none exists?" Wynter says, blinking as she grapples with this aspect of my personality.

"Exactly!" Suzy says with a quick nod. "There are cameras in Hyde Park that would have picked up this person's movements. Anyone lurking about bushes while the city is on high alert is going to draw attention. If it had been this Victor Malden character, the entire Met Office would have descended upon your idyllic Rose Garden in an instant.

"But let's play devil's advocate for a moment. Assume the person you saw is the escaped prisoner. Why would he be there watching you? Why would he have your number? You've never even met this person, for heaven's sake!"

"Oh! What if Ella was his next intended victim...?" says Wynter, prompting Suzy's eyebrows to disappear into her hairline. "And now he's escaped, he's picking up from where he left off? Have you ever spotted him following you before?"

She has a point. Fuck. Perhaps this isn't the first time he's followed me!

A cold sweat prickles my skin and I hold on to the counter for support. Suzy's hand reaches out to squeeze my arm. She may seem like a delicate, beautiful butterfly, but inside is a lioness, and right now she's protecting her own.

"A valid observation, thank you, Wynter," she says pointedly. "But highly improbable. Malden liked to charm his victims. Even went to significant efforts to wine and dine them at the swankiest restaurants. After inviting them back to his place, they basically screwed all night. By all accounts, he's a very attentive lover—as well as being a sadistic bastard. He filled their hearts with the promise of being the man of their dreams, and then he would drug them. When they came to, they found themselves tied up in an empty room, where he viciously took back every promise and more.

"To compare the man I've just described to a stalker hiding in bushes is nonsense. So unless you've been wined and dined, made love to by the Prince of Death, or he has an obscure A to Z of victims that has your name on it, then I'd say it's highly unlikely that Malden is your man in the park."

I slouch against the counter, my chin cupped in my hands, defeated and confused.

Suzy also makes a valid point.

"Good. That's settled. We can all agree that the person you saw was not Malden, and that the withheld number was most likely a cold caller, probably hoping you'll need replacement windows because of this bloody storm!"

The muscles in my back and shoulders relax, and I puff out a sigh of relief. "Alright. Agreed."

"How d'ya know all that stuff about him, anyway?" Wynter says, scrutinising the website for photographs of the missing psychopath.

She's precisely the impressionable, starved of affection, sort of girl who would fall under his deadly spell, and I feel a surge of protectiveness for this young, vulnerable girl I've taken under my wing. I push shut the lid of the laptop.

"Tom, of course," announces Suzy, with a coy smile.

I laugh, despite myself. If I've taken anything away from this day, it's that my friend ought to rethink her pillow talk.

"Well, I don't know about you, but I'm starving! I'm gonna fetch us some lunch," Wynter says, sliding off the stool and grabbing her jacket.

A few minutes later, a customer blusters his way through the doors, a flurry of leaves and debris fast at his heels.

"Good afternoon, ladies." He beams a smile that could part clouds. "Phew! It'll blow you right off your feet out there today. Perhaps one of you lovely ladies would be kind enough to direct me towards your *Life on Canvas* collection? I'm looking for a wedding gift… best man."

Suzy nudges me with her elbow and I feel the rush of heat to my cheeks. After giving her my best scathing look, I head over to assist the customer, trying to smooth out my still disheveled appearance.

It's business as usual, just how I like it.

# Chapter Seven

"What the bloody hell, Ella?"

"What?" I say, completing my sales order and preparing delivery for the following week.

Suzy has tracked me down and is strategically blocking the doorway to my office. She will not let this go, and I can guess precisely what's coming.

I hear the hiss as she takes a sharp intake of breath and jabs her manicured nail in my direction.

"Anyone with a smidgen of perception could see that he was basically hitting on you, and *you* shut him down! If frigid ice-queen is the approach you were going for... you nailed it, sweetie."

With a shrug, I screw up my lip.

"Don't do that!"

"What?" I say again with another shrug.

"THAT! That thing with your shoulders. You're basically flipping me off. What *is* your problem? You complain about your mother's attempts to marry you off to her friend's son—the hellishly dull actuary, in case you've forgotten—yet here you are turning your nose up at a demigod who practically lands in your bloody lap."

"Wasn't my type." I keep my head lowered and pretend to check over the order. The truth is, I can't think of a single justifiable reason for ignoring the demigod's obvious flirtation. Before I can come up with any more lame excuses, I glance up to see the dreaded flash in her eyes.

Game over. She's moving in for the kill.

"You, Ella Mills, are going to end up a lonely old fussbudget!"

More finger jabbing in my direction as I sit there and solemnly nod. Although I've never heard the word *fussbudget* before now, I'm fairly certain it's not a compliment.

The frustrating part is, she's right. I did shut him down. Not because he wasn't cute—he really was—but because when it comes to mastering the dance steps of flirtation, I have two left feet. Clumsy and awkward is the best I can hope for, so I really don't need to add humiliation to the growing list of today's dramas.

"When did you last fuck someone?"

"Are you serious?!" I say, spluttering with as much indignation as I can muster, which isn't a great deal because I'm honestly trying to wrack my brain. And... well, shit.

"You can't even remember! That hot guy would have had you on this desk if you'd let him—" she steps forward and places a palm on the glossy surface of the white desktop. Her eyes take on a faraway look, like she's... no! She's remembering?

*What the actual...?*

"Tell me you haven't?" I shut my eyes, hands pressed to my lips in silent prayer that my best friend has not violated my office space.

Suzy gives me a wide grin and wriggles her perfect eyebrows.

"He was into his art and I was just showing him round the place when one thing led to another. It happens, sweetie—*if you let it.*"

"Enough! I'm trying not to think it about," I say, holding my hands up in utter distaste. "On my desk? Really?"

"Anyway, stop changing the subject."

Her fired up eyes bore into mine, and hitching a hip with ease up onto the corner of the desk, she crosses her long legs and leans on toned arms towards me.

Cornered with no escape.

"Go on then, say it—"

"That man was basically crazy about you, Ella. Although God knows why! You put more effort into hiding your looks than most people do trying to enhance them. Plus, you have his number right there in front of you, on that invoice." She stabs at the piece of paper on the desk with her long nail. "Call him and ask him out. We'll sort your hair and makeup, find you a nice sexy dress and heels to wear. There's still a chance we can salvage this." She gives me a wide beam—all teeth and glossy lips—as she looks at me with expectant puppy eyes.

For the love of God, make her stop already!

I purse my lips and lean back in the chair, folding my arms across my chest. It's hard not to notice when a grown woman behaves like a sulking child, but I honestly can't help myself. If she pushes me any further, I swear my bottom lip might jut out to complete the sulky pout.

Suzy leans in, closing the gap between us, evidently holding nothing back on the intimidation front.

"No, Mills, you do not get to pull that face!" She throws her arms up in frustration. "Nobody expects you to marry the guy. You don't even need to talk to him. It's very simple—drink, eat and fuck—and in no particular order."

She springs off the edge of the desk and begins pacing the room, arms making wild gestures as the rant picks up momentum. I swallow carefully as she hovers near the glass shelves on the farthest wall. I'm very fond of the sculptures displayed there.

When the pacing finally stops, she pivots to face me. Her face is lit up with enthusiasm.

"Why don't you come out with me and Tom instead? He'd love to meet you and you'd genuinely like him. What if we get him to bring a friend, someone far hotter than the waistcoat-wearing-actuary? And don't say no—you *always* say no. Remember, you don't need to marry the guy, you just need to—"

"Alright! I get it—" I jump up out of my chair and move across the office to link arms with my friend and lead her away from the exquisite art pieces.

Just to be on the safe side.

I walk her towards the office door and out into the main viewing gallery, where the rain now comes down in sheets across the glass.

"I will meet Tom. After the three months, as we agreed." I do my best to ignore the heavy sigh that she throws my way. "And I love that you care. Really I do, but—"

"There's always a *but*..." she says, cutting me off with accusing eyes.

"But... I have Krav this evening, and after the day I've had, working off some of this tension will do me good.

As adorable as your boyfriend may be, I'm going to take a pass. Final word."

A cloud of defeat falls across her face. Not wanting to squander the window of opportunity, I pluck her coat from the stand and extend it to her with the warmest smile possible—under the circumstances.

She rolls her eyes.

"Have it your way, sweetie, but don't come crying to me when you wake up one morning to find it's basically closed up down there from lack of use!"

"I won't. Promise."

With a frown, she takes her coat from me and, shrugging into a sleeve, says, "There's no happy ending for fussbudgets. Just remember that."

Mental note—Google term *fussbudget*.

Almost resigned to Suzy's disapproving scowl for the rest of eternity, she surprises me by showering me with a full-on radiant smile. My immediate reaction is to check whether there's a customer standing behind me.

"Anyway, sweetie, I was really hoping you'd meet Tom sooner rather than later," she says with a conspiratorial wink. "Don't take it as gospel, but I think he's going to ask me to move in with him!"

She shrieks and jumps up and down on the spot, hands flapping.

"Wow!" Once again, I'm lost for words.

I really expected this day to go so much better.

"Tom's been dropping hints about how his place is too big. And not only that—I basically caught him glancing at my ring finger the other day. Although how I'll find the time to arrange an engagement party is anyone's guess. Just the thought of it is overwhelming! Of course, I'll need to make a short-list of magazines to discuss who'll get the rights for exclusive access. And there's the venue, I was thinking, perhaps the East Wintergarden. What do you think? I mean, what could be more perfect than celebrating a promise of lifelong love beneath a glass fucking dome? There's simply so much to consider, I basically can't decide where to start!"

"This all... um... sounds fantastic. But you've only known him four weeks, Suzy. Perhaps... you know, slow things down? Get to know him better before you think about weddings?"

The radiant smile vanishes as quickly as it appeared, the scowl returning.

*Ah shit.*

"I should have guessed you'd be like this. When will you stop trying to protect me from being hurt, Ella? Sometimes you have to take a leap of faith and just go with your instincts."

"I'm not being like anything," I say, more defensively than I intend. "As your friend, I'm pointing out that you're considering getting engaged to a complete *fucking stranger!*"

Yeah. *Too far.*

"A stranger, eh?" Her voice rises several octane higher. I really should have kept my big mouth shut. "How would you know when you refuse to meet him because of some shitty three-month rule you impose? For fuck's sake, live a little, would you? Your love life is non-existent. You cut yourself off from new experiences all the time. Stop hiding behind these bloody paintings, for once."

"I have a life, thank you."

She tugs at her coat zip with more force than is necessary.

# THE GRAYSTONE KILLINGS

"Really? Because when you're not here..." She waves her arms around the Verandah theatrically. "You're beating the shit out of a punchbag, basically preparing to fight the whole fucking world. If you haven't yet noticed, the world isn't fighting back, sweetie. Just try embracing it for once. What are you so afraid of that keeps you hidden away, living this half-fucking-life?"

"That's not fair, and you know it. I don't want to argue with you, Suzy, but you can't expect me to stand back and watch my friend rush into a lifelong commitment to a man she barely knows! Do you even know what he does?"

"I—"

"You say he's well connected? Why is that?" I say, cutting her off before she can answer.

Unable to stop myself, I launch into a rant listing all my concerns about her would-be fiancé, making an elaborate show of ticking each one off on my fingers.

Hah! Suzy's not the only one with a flair for drama around here.

"Do you even know where he lives?" A flick of my little finger.

"Has he been married before?" I pinch my ring finger—*how ironic*.

"Long-term relationships?"

"Does he want a family?"

Lastly, sticking my thumb out, I say, "What does he do for a living?"

When I pause mid-rant, her wide, baby blue eyes stare back at me playfully. Then her mouth quivers in a lop-sided grin.

"Sweetie, are you quite finished?"

My shoulders slump in defeat. "You're still going to say 'yes' if he asks, aren't you?"

She nods. "Yep."

I love Suzy to bits and although she always falls in and out of relationships way too easy for my liking, the thought of her being taken advantage of by a morganatic man—scratch that, *husband*—if he gets his way, is something I won't let happen without a fight.

This Tom character has somehow slipped past my three-month safety net. It means I'll have to uncover his true agenda before he hurts my friend.

"Fine, let's make a pact," Suzy says, reaching out and squeezing my arm affectionately. "I promise to get answers to every single one of your questions, and in return, you'll agree to meet him. With an open mind. Deal?"

For now, it's the best I can hope for.

"Fine," I say, giving her a quick hug and kiss on the cheek before she steps out through the doors in a flurry of leaves and howling wind.

# Chapter Eight

Come three o'clock, it's obvious that the ferocious storm outside is keeping most people away. Kensington High Street is eerily quiet for a Monday afternoon, deserted except for a few die-hard tourists leaning into the rush of the wind.

The Met office has given the storm a name. Why? I do not know, but the public has voted in their thousands for this year's storm-naming-list, therefore we only have ourselves to blame. They named the one now raging war on us after a particularly mischievous feline who tears through the owner's home like a tornado; Storm Ruby.

Cute name for such a force of destruction. The storm—not the cat.

A bleak oppressiveness replaces the normal vibrant atmosphere of the street. From the comfort of the Verandah, with its oak beams and warm lights bouncing off colourful art panels around the showroom, it almost seems like the hues of grey and muted blue are reflecting my solemn mood. Rain bounces off the floor to ceiling windows, distorting the scene further.

The contrast to my immediate surroundings is unnerving and I glance up at a sky in turmoil, menacing clouds gathering and rolling over each other. The earlier weather warnings suggested the storm might pass us by, but that's looking extremely unlikely now. From what I can see, it's only picking up in intensity.

From the gallery, it's a mere fifteen-minute walk to the apartment. After all the upset of earlier, I'm about ready to call it a day and so flip the closed sign on the door.

"Unless there's anything else, Wynter, we should close early today," I say, throwing a glance over my shoulder at my protégé, who's busy plotting new ways to attract visitors to the gallery.

She joins me in front of the window and hands me a form.

"Only your signature, please. We're negotiating the loan of some paintings with the Tate Gallery for an event I thought we might hold next summer. I want to focus on Impressionist Henry Scott Tuke's depiction of the body, just a small exhibition, nothing too elaborate. If we're able to exhibit *August Blue* in particular, we can set up some scheduled talks for you to discuss colour and technique in relation to the human form, and how sunlight affects the skin. Of course, I'm getting quotes for a catering company too, canapés and prosecco. Thought we could make it a ticketed event. Six days should be enough, although I still need to work out the granular details; like how many talks per day, cost of tickets and how big a group, etcetera, but I checked your diary and these days suit the best—if you're happy to sign?"

After scanning through the paperwork, I nod with approval.

"You're a quick study, you know that?"

A smile tugs at my lips and I feel a burst of pride at how far she's come. When she offers me a half chewed ballpoint pen, I laugh and scribble my signature against the request.

Wynter beams at me with eyes twinkling. I mentally add 'lack of nurturing' to her parents' long list of inadequacies; they have no idea how intelligent and extraordinary their daughter is.

Another gust of wind slams into the large panes of glass, and they shudder under the force.

"Will you be alright in the flat tonight? Perhaps you should come and stay with me and Suzy?" I say, concerned at the prospect of leaving Wynter here on her own.

"Oh, I'm good, thanks." She waves a hand as if swatting away the ridiculous notion of her needing comfort during a storm.

From what I've seen, I'm sure she's right. It's doubtful she's ever needed comfort from anyone in her life. With time, I'm hoping that will change, that I'll become her go-to-person, as Suzy is for me.

"If you change your mind, you know where we are. Our door's always open for you."

"Thanks. Why don't you head off now? I can lock up."

When I hesitate, it's not because she isn't capable—she's more than proven herself in that respect—but because so few people are around now that it's making me skittish.

"I don't—"

"Honestly, I'll be fine. I'm gonna finish up here while it's quiet. After I'm done, I promise to lock the flat door—if you're still worried about that flasher?"

Sometimes the girl reads me like a book.

"Sorry, Wynter—you're absolutely right. I was just, um... I'm going to leave now," I say, grabbing my things from the office. "And for the record, he was not a flasher!"

After insisting that Wynter calls me if she needs anything, I step out into the colourless canvas of the storm and, buffeted by the wind, wait for her to lock the doors behind me.

As I hurry along the empty pavements, I struggle to walk at a normal pace; gusts slamming me from the side and propelling me along at odd angles. Litter blown from the waste bins race across my path, while swirls of airborne dirt and grit force my head down. My ears are deaf to everything except the rushing howl of the wind.

It seems every one of my senses is under attack.

Despite wishing I'd taken a less exposed route, the more sheltered backstreets are out of the question after today's events. Out here on the main street, the overwhelming urge to check if I'm being followed weighs down on me almost as much as the force of the wind. It would be easy to succumb to my fears; to imagine the man from the park walking a few steps behind, ready to ambush at any second.

I wouldn't see or hear him until it was too late.

But if I let the seeds of paranoia take root now, they'll spread like Knotweed and take me down into an all too familiar darkness, where it might be days before I find my way back again.

As much as possible, I try to centre myself, calm my breathing and my mind, and press onwards. I think back to Suzy's words and repeat them over and over in my mind until I might finally accept them as the truth... *the person I saw in the park was not Victor Malden... not the prisoner...*

We all agreed it couldn't have been him. Didn't we?

After one last scan of the area for threats, I square my shoulders against the storm and, with renewed determination, power ahead. My new resolve helps to quash the unnerving sensation of being followed. I will not scurry home like a frightened little mouse.

At the sound of a loud bang close by, my feet lift off the ground, heart pounding furiously in my chest.

"What the—"

A wheelie bin lies on its side to my right. The fright is enough to shatter my fleeting resolve and I give in to the urge and sneak a surreptitious glance over my shoulder.

In what would normally be a bustling street, I count only ten other people. They appear as washed out and weather-beaten as their surroundings, each battling to stay upright against the storm's wrath.

One person in particular catches my eye, and in that instant, all warmth drains from my body.

He wears a black jacket and jeans, complete with a baseball cap and scarf.

Just like the man from the park.

*Oh shit! Shit, shit, shit! This cannot be happening!*

I blink hard, but when I open again, he's still there—walking purposefully towards me. In a state of panic, I will him to cross the road, or turn around, or disappear into a shop, anything but be on the pavement one hundred metres behind me and closing.

In the late afternoon gloom, I squint at the advancing figure in the streetlight, trying to make out his features. It proves an impossible task, with the relentless wind and rain stinging at my face. All I achieve is to close the gap between us as he swallows up the distance with his long strides.

Fifty metres.

*For the love of God, do not panic.*
*Do not fucking panic.*
*Do not let him smell your fear.*

An anxiety attack now would render me defenceless. The last thing I need in this uncontrolled and unpredictable situation. By pushing everything else from mind and focusing only on my well-honed instincts—tuned through years of Krav—I know with absolute certainty that I can rely on them to keep me safe.

Like the flip of a switch, my mindset shifts gear and adrenaline pumps through my body.

First, I'll need a weapon. The encounter could quickly turn from one of self defence to, at worst, survival and retaliation. I make a hasty mental inventory of the contents of my purse. No handy anti-rapist pepper spray in there, but I have keys and an umbrella—stick-like enough to serve a debilitating blow. And coins that I can throw to distract and confuse.

Ten metres.

*I am in control. I am trained to survive exactly this situation.*

I flick out the key to the gallery and grip the circular end in my fist. It will slash and stab in the right hands. I clutch hold of my bag that the wind is trying to rip from my shoulder, and root around for my coin purse, prising it open with surprisingly steady fingers and grabbing a small fistful of coins.

Armed and ready, I stand tall, shoulders squared, and wait.

Five metres.

I make eye contact. His face remains impassive, but he doesn't look away or falter in his stride as he continues bearing down on me.

My grip on the key tightens.

Of similar build to the escaped prisoner, he's tall with broad shoulders and the same dark hair peaking out from beneath his cap.

When we're almost shoulder to shoulder, I anticipate his next move; a sudden lunge? Walk past then spin and attack? Or will he try to charm and catch me off guard, like his other unsuspecting victims?

But he does none of these things.

Instead, the man gives me a curious look—like I've grown two heads—and comes to a halt, looking back round at me.

"Lady, are you okay?" He has to shout to be heard above the howling noise.

Unable to respond, I stand rooted to the spot, not wanting to break eye contact.

He shrugs his shoulders.

"Do I know you?"

I jerk my head in the negative.

"Well, sorry if I made you nervous."

He carries on striding down the pavement against the wind, glancing every few steps over his shoulder to see me still fixed to the spot.

A sigh of relief escapes my lips.

Not the fugitive, then.

*Not about to be attacked.*

I gather what's left of my composure, cross the road and hurry along the pavement towards my apartment, still gripping the keys and coins.

Today's events have got me even more rattled than I thought. Until they catch the escaped prisoner, I expect I'll be seeing threats around every corner.

My life is going to be hell until he's back behind bars.

# Chapter Nine

On impulse, I stop at the off-licence on the corner of my street. After today, I'm going to need something a lot stronger than the bottle of wine chilling in the fridge at home.

The metal framed glass door makes an electronic buzzing noise as I enter, announcing my arrival. The store is owned by a middle-aged Scottish couple who moved down to London four years ago to be near their grown-up children. Stuart is a jovial personality, both tall and gangly, while Betty is small and petite. She talks—a lot—and clucks around, fussing after everyone.

Visits to their store are always a welcome addition to any day. And not just for the alcohol, but for the warm hospitality given. Even on the grimmest of days, this couple will bring an unexpected smile to my face.

At first, their overwhelming attention horrified me, but now I look forward to their lilting, sing-song Edinburgh accents and their uncanny ability to make me feel I've known them my entire life.

When they moved here, their friendly enthusiasm seemed alien to this busy borough street, where normal city cultural prevails and people pass you in the street like you don't exist. For me, it's a perfect environment and makes being invisible all the easier.

But nobody is invisible in this store—far from it.

Summoned by the buzzer, Stuart comes out from the back storeroom, weighed down by a cardboard box labelled *fragile*.

"Oh aye, lass, good to see you! C'away inside. What an awfy dreich day. You'll be wanting something to warm you, nae doubt?" He pronounces it 'doot' and I find myself smiling as his gentle dialect soothes me.

After placing his burden on the counter, he crosses the store and ushers me into the warmth. His long arms and legs sway in perfect unison as he moves in a gliding motion.

"Afternoon, Stuart. God, it's horrendous out there!" I say, shaking my head to get the rain off. "I'm after something to take the edge off a very challenging day. What do you recommend?"

"Well lass, *as it's you—*" A playful wink of his eye sends his wiry, greying eyebrows doing a jig across his face as he reaches out to one of the upper shelves. "This'll dae the job... Monkey 47 gin, slice o' grapefruit rind, add a wee tonic and we'll soon have the colour back in that peely-wally face o' yours. Made from forty-seven botanicals, that counts as medicinal in my book."

I raise a brow, and he chuckles. Never one to wear much make-up, I can only imagine how deathly pale my light tone skin might seem after this latest emotional meltdown.

"Thanks, that's an interesting choice." I take the old style pharmacy bottle and nod with approval. "Alright, I'll try it," I say, handing back the copper coloured bottle, even though I'm tempted to pull the cork from the neck and take a swig right here and now.

Such is the state of my nerves.

"Aye, lass, you'll be right as rain by the 'morrow with this inside you."

Once he's finished wrapping the gin in tissue and placing the bottle in a brown paper bag, he says, "Betty w'be sorry she missed you, lass. She's been blethering on that phone for a good hour now. She and her cronies got all worked up o'er the shenanigans of that escaped prisoner. Ah didnae ken what all the fuss is about—that convict w'be long gone by now!"

I fumble for my purse, but can't seem to control the shaking in my hands at the mere mention of the prisoner.

"Come now, lass, you're frozen half to death. Didnae bother yourself wi' that, I'll stick it on your tab," he says with a look of concern and placing the bottle in my hands. Although I'm not a big drinker, right now all I want to do is curl up in a ball with a glass of Monkey 47 and feel warm and safe again—I clutch the bag as if he's thrown me a lifeline.

"Thanks, Stuart. Tell Betty I said 'hi'."

"Aye, lass, ah will—if she ever gets off that blasted phone!" He smacks his palms down on the counter and laughs, shaking his head in amusement. "Now, you take care wi' this weather an' we'll be seeing you."

With a grateful smile, I brace myself to head back out into the storm.

There's still one more essential stop I need to make before going home. Head bowed low, I fight against the ever-increasing gusts to our local convenience store a few doors down. After completing my purchase of a sandwich, hot coffee, and pouch of dog food, I place a twenty-pound note with the bundle and battle my way along the last few blocks to my apartment. I immediately spot who I'm looking for, sheltering at the bus stop a stone's throw from my front door.

The huddled shape of a man perches on the thin narrow bar that runs the length of the shelter, convenient for waiting passengers to take the weight off their feet, but offering little comfort to someone exposed to the elements and seeking respite. As I lean on the bar next to him, I hand him the package of items just as a small black head with pointed ears pops out from beneath his raincoat.

Winston first appeared in this patch around six months ago. Homeless people are invisible without even trying. Although we see them as a society, we do our best to pretend they're not there, to not think about the events that led them to be living on the streets. Instead, we like to believe this existence was of their own doing, poor life choices made by the less fortunate. And so we go about our day, barely registering the person huddled on the ground, silently blaming them for their immorality and weakness.

Yet there are some of us who can't pretend that the homeless amongst us don't exist. Nor do we blame them for their misfortune. While I'm sure there's an element of misjudgement amongst the destitute, I'm equally sure bad luck could lead anyone of us towards a similar fate. For that reason, I'm compelled to see this man and look beyond his predicament to the real person.

Over several weeks, I observed Winston as he first took up residence in our neighbourhood. My home studio looks out over the high street and I've watched him get moved from the nearby park to the street, and the street to shop doorways. Never left in peace for long, he is continually driven from pillar to post. He never begs, although those who acknowledge him sometimes drop loose change in his lap with a sympathetic, yet wary expression.

When he thinks no-one is watching, I've seen him smile and laugh, sob and shout. I've witnessed his compassion for his four-legged companion, and often wonder how their paths crossed. What has led them to be abandoned on the streets of London?

Occasionally, whilst working in my studio, I've witnessed acts of kindness towards him, with people bringing him blankets and clothing, even the odd toiletry. Likewise, I've also observed acts of cruelty. Winston is no stranger to being spat on, pushed, or worse. This behaviour is not restricted to specific demographics; I've seen our so-called respectable neighbours being unkind towards him.

It would seem his presence offends age, gender, and status without bias.

One day, as I was walking past, I gave him a brief nod and he nodded back. We chatted, and he introduced me to his dog before going on to tell me how much he admired my art. Loosely speaking, we've been neighbours ever since.

I'm certain Winston has a fascinating and tragic story to tell, and perhaps one day he'll trust me enough to share it; such is my desire to paint this man with his life story etched so firmly in his features. If I were to place Winston in a setting, it would probably be a bank or a lawyer's office. His clean-shaven face shows great intelligence behind gentle, brown eyes. I like to think that if our roles were reversed, he would be someone I could rely on to show me compassion.

"Hey, how have you been? Are you going to be okay out here?" I say, raising my voice above the sound of the storm. The shelter is doing a good enough job of protecting us from the rain and wind, but the deafening howl in the air is unnerving.

"We'll be just fine, Ella. Me and Jambo, we're not fazed by a spot of blustery weather. We'll hunker down here for a bit."

*For a bit...* until he's moved on by the police, he means. As much as I admire his independence, I wish he'd let me help more.

"You know you're welcome to wait out the storm at mine, don't you?" I say, nodding towards the apartment. "Both you and Jambo. Anytime you need."

"That's awful kind of you, and I appreciate the gesture. But Jambo and I have no business being in that nice place of yours. Thanks for this—" He glances down at the food and cash and points his chin towards the now sodden bag containing my gin. "—of course, if your generosity could stretch to seeing your way to sharing that there bottle..."

"Drink your coffee, Winston." I give him my best eye roll for dramatic effect and get up to leave. "And use the cash for a hostel if it gets too bad out here, alright?"

"Don't you worry that pretty head about us." He fixes me with a stare, his soft eyes reflecting a look of concern. "Take good care of yourself, Ella. No good ever blew in on a storm such as this."

The smile fades from my lips as I walk away, the now familiar tension returning to my neck and shoulders.

# THE GRAYSTONE KILLINGS

I clutch the paper bag and hurry home.

# Chapter Ten

I fall through the door with such relief that I pause and throw my head back, squeezing my eyes shut before kicking off my ruined shoes and shrugging out of my dripping coat. Apartment 1A, Winford Street, has never felt so welcoming, and right now it's possibly the most desirable place in the entire world. As I head down the hallway towards my bedroom, I peel off layers of wet clothing that cling to my skin with a chilled dampness.

"Rita, lights on," I say, instructing the built-in artificial intelligence system wired throughout the apartment.

Suzy's nicknamed the software 'Rita' after her all-time favourite American actress, Rita Hayworth. After the initial strangeness of talking to software, she's come to grow on me.

Our apartment is modest by London standards, but spacious and homely. There's a large lounge with all the latest gadgets technology can offer, and a well-equipped kitchen leading to a snazzy dining room that Suzy often entertains from. When caterers come to the apartment to serve up their delicious menus to her modelling guests, I'm not too proud to scrounge an extra serving. There's also a small but well-stocked home gym, and a study that we share.

But the best part about the apartment is that we each have our own indulgence areas. For Suzy, this is a spacious walk-in wardrobe that would compete hands down with any of the luxury top-end stores. For me, it's an art studio. But unlike the studio at the Verandah, this area is solely for my personal use.

By the time I reach my bedroom, I'm stripped down to my underwear and holding a pile of sodden clothes to throw in the wash. After snuggling into a white bathrobe, the tension eases from my body and my shoulders begin to relax. Guaranteed to purge the day from my stiff and aching muscles, I take the bottle of Monkey 47 and head off to the kitchen to fill a copa glass with an unusually generous measure of gin.

"Don't let me down, Stuart—" I mutter, adding a token splash of tonic water and dropping in a slice of grapefruit rind into the glass.

After taking a large swig, I let out a deep sigh of pleasure. Fragrant and complex, I feel today's tension wash away with the smooth liquid.

*Bliss!*

Conscious of having a Krav class in a couple of hours, I push the bottle aside.

With temptation safely out of reach, I pad on bare feet to my studio, determined to get in a couple of hours of creative outpouring to help centre my psyche.

The workshop is spacious and light, with eight large arched windows monopolising two of the walls that overlook the street below. Each one has a cushioned window seat, enabling me to sit and draw whilst being inspired by the people passing outside. The walls are painted white to capture and reflect light around the room, but with this afternoon's turmoil sky, I resort to the LED floodlights that stretch the length of the ceiling. Another indulgence on my part as they're as close as it gets to simulating daylight, enabling me to see true colours more effectively.

"Rita, switch studio lights on."

As I enter through the white double doors, I take comfort in the faint smell of linseed oil and soap that blend with the delicate floral scent of autumnal flowers in oranges, limes, and purples.

The pleasing visual symmetry of the easels, tables, and stools brings me a much needed sense of peace. The supplies wall on the left has custom made units that hold colour coordinated tubes of paint and a canvas selection stacked in order of size. If I were to close my eyes, I'd most likely be able to reach for every item in this room.

There's a natural coolness to the studio that means it never gets too hot or cold and I throw off the robe for my old painting shirt. With everything in order, there's no chaos in this space, allowing me the serenity to lose myself in creating beautiful art.

"Rita, play music list *Ella Meditative*."

After a few seconds the room fills with the relaxing tune from a baritone horn, and balancing an armful of supplies, I head over to the furthermost easel. From here, I have an unobstructed view overlooking the bus shelter, for I'm still worried about Winston and where he'll go if conditions continue to deteriorate. I take a seat on the circular wooden stool facing the easel, its height adjusted perfectly for my five foot six frame, and set about mixing the paints in the pallet.

Far removed from the sound of the wind and rain outside, I focus on the music and take another sip of gin before applying the brush to the canvas. The calming rhythm helps me concentrate on bringing each inhale of breath into sync with the brushstrokes, the paint swirling in one direction across the canvas, then another.

*Much better...*

When a persistent drumming sound against the window pulls me out of my reverie, I stare at the canvas with its array of colour sprawled across it.

The youthful face of a girl with forlorn eyes glances over a raised shoulder, her head tucked down. The backdrop is a swirl of dancing light that radiates an amber glow, giving the painting a surreal, otherworldly sense. She looks fearful, lost, and enchanting all at the same time.

I stare at her for a long minute, until, on impulse, I lean forward and whisper, "*How will you find your way back?*"

Goosebumps cover my flesh and I shake my head, as if awakening from a trance.

What the actual fuck?

Confused and feeling slightly disoriented, I drop the brush and turn to check on Winston. The shelter is empty, and he's nowhere to be seen.

Moved on, no doubt.

Even on this wildest of days there are vagrancy laws to uphold. I only hope the officers involved have secured him with a place to wait out the worsening conditions.

Almost time to change for Krav class, I perform a quick cleanup of the brushes and make my way back through the apartment. The sound of Suzy humming along to a catchy tune fills the hallway and I find her in her walk-in wardrobe, sitting crossed legged on a circular sofa and wearing only a pair of finest lace knickers and stockings.

When I enter, she looks up with a smile and continues to rub a delicate smelling lotion across her tanned arms, shoulders and small, exquisitely shaped breasts. I smile back, trying to mask the apprehension I feel at the prospect of another argument over tonight's date with Tom.

"There you are, sweetie! I didn't want to disturb you. I was hoping you'd help zip me into this dress. Isn't it adorable?" she says, excitement bubbling over.

Confident I'm nearly off the hook over joining them for dinner, I reach up and take an emerald green sequin dress off its hanger. Where I expect it to be weighty, it actually featherlight and shimmers under the bright lights. It's stunningly beautiful and crafted to perfection.

"An Italian designer, basically looking to make a name for himself on the London circuits," Suzy says as I let the dress glide through my fingers, watching it glisten like a thousand jewels. "We got chatting, and he asked me to wear a few items around town from his autumn collection. So talented, don't you think?"

I nod and slide the dress from the hanger, unzipping the back, before helping her slip into the delicate material. It clings to her body, almost as if designed exclusively for her. Perhaps it is. She lifts and adjusts her breasts into a fully shaped cleavage, then spins on her toes for me to zip her up.

"It's beautiful. How does it feel on?"

I can't imagine what it must be like to have this material pressed against my bare flesh. A far cry from my cotton tops and sports lycra.

"Like the hand of an Italian lover, caressing me all over!"

She giggles and falls back onto the sofa, kicking her legs playfully in the air.

"God, I'd never be confident enough to wear a dress like that."

"Oh, but you must, sweetie. You're gorgeous! I bet you'd stop the heart of basically every man in town if you were to put this on."

At the laughable image, I shake my head. "Sometimes I wish I were more like you, you know? You're always so self-assured. Look, um, sorry I was shitty with you earlier about getting engaged."

"Already forgotten, silly."

Relieved to have cleared the air, I turn to get ready for class.

Although I haven't forgotten our pact, I seriously doubt she'll get the answers she's promised me. I may not trust this new enigmatic boyfriend of hers, but for now, I'll go along with the fairytale. It's hard not to when she really does look every bit the princess.

I truly hope that one day she gets her fairytale ending.

"Hey—" Suzy says, and I turn as she throws a ruby red dress across the room to me. "In case you change your mind about tonight." She winks mischievously, a playful sparkle in her eyes. "I'm serious. You're a modern day Leonardo, sweetie—you just don't realise how awesome you are. You're the most amazing, kind and talented person I know. And even if you refuse to step inside a nightclub with me, I still love you."

She's incorrigible and I can't help but laugh at the analogy.

"Well, my crazy best friend, I love you right back. Thanks for the dress… and the vote of confidence."

I leave her humming once again to the music, and step out of the room, wondering whether I'm being too cynical. Perhaps she really can find the happiness she's looking for in Tom.

With a quick glance down at the dress in my hands, I give a snort and dismiss her ludicrous suggestion—the idea of me glammed up in this vibrant, skimpy outfit is absurd.

Besides, I don't want to be late for Krav.

# Chapter Eleven

The walk home from Krav is another nervous and vigilant one. Although pumped on endorphins from class and feeling like I could take on the world, in reality, my game is off. I took one too many blows I should have easily blocked. Few of my sparring partners get that opportunity, but their sense of having kicked my arse will be short-lived.

Next time I'll come back stronger.

Now almost 6pm, the storm rages on with relentless persistence. With most stores closed for the day, few people are venturing out for the evening. When I see Stuart from the off-licence waving frantically and trying to catch my attention, my immediate concern is for him and Betty.

*Something must be wrong.*

He struggles to keep the door from slamming shut in the wind as he continues to make beckoning gestures.

"Over here, Ella!" he says, shouting over the noise of the howling gale.

When I finally battle my way over to him and volley through the open shop door, a lashing of rain follows behind me, soaking the entranceway.

"What's wrong? Is—is everything alright?" I say, trying to catch my breath.

"Aye, lass, didnae fret. Everything's fine. Except, we thought you should ken that your cousin was in here earlier asking efter you."

Confused, I stop shaking the rain from my drenched hair to stare at him.

"What do you mean?" I say, looking from him to Betty, as she bustles out from behind the counter.

"A tall chap. Said he wis a relative and that he'd been away for a while. Something about reuniting. Aye, that's the word he used... reunite. Betty here spoke to him, isnae that right, hen?"

She gives me a solemn nod.

"But—but I don't have a cousin!"

Stuart shakes his head as Betty takes a sharp intake of breath.

"Is that so? I said to our Betty he wis up to nae good. Didnae you worry, we sent him packing," he says, his eyes wide and shining.

"What—did he say anything else?"

Betty steps forward and rests a reassuring hand on my arm.

"He wanted to ken whether we knew you, dear. At first, I didnae think anything of it because he had a photo of you and said you'd lost touch."

"A photo of me?"

I feel the blood draining from my face.

"Aye, dear. He wisnae pushy, though. Bit of a charmer, really. But my Stu here, he didnae like the look of him—smarmy he called him—and when he asked for your address, we showed him the door."

"I don't suppose he gave you a name? A way to contact him?"

They shake their heads.

"Nothing like that, dear," Betty says. "He wis polite all the while, thanked us for our time, but even so, we kept a wee eye on him until he left. Hand on heart, ah cannae say we saw him snooping around efter that."

"Betty's right, lass. He stood there looking up at the buildings for a while, seemed a wee bit jittery, but next we looked, he wis gone."

"Are you able to describe him?"

"Aye, lass, tall fellow, well built. Older than you—forties I think. Dark hair but he wis wearing one of those baseball caps, so cannae say for sure."

"And, um… did he resemble the um… prisoner who escaped this morning?" I shift my feet and drop my gaze to the countertop.

Stuart and Betty glance at each other.

"Wit are you saying, lass? That the chap in here wis this Victor Malden that Betty's been nattering to her cronies about? Ah didnae think so!" he says, laughing nervously.

Now that I've said it out loud, it sounds incredible, even to my own ears. Yet despite how deranged I must sound, I still have an uneasy feeling hanging over me. A sudden thought hits me.

"Would you mind looking at a photograph for me? See whether it's the same man you spoke to? It'll only take a minute to fetch it back here—it's on my camera."

"Of course, dear, whatever you need. Isnae that right, Stu?"

Stuart nods and walks across the shop floor to open the door for me, the simple action taking significant effort as the wind tries to slam it shut again.

Lost in my thoughts, I step back outside onto the street. If I'm right, my camera could help confirm whether our separate encounters were with the same person.

First the park and now my home—it feels like he's closing in.

And I still don't know why.

At a sprint, I cover the last few blocks to our apartment and charge up the communal stairs to the front door. It's not until I try to thrust the key into the lock and it swings open, do I realise the door's been left ajar.

Tentatively, I push it wide open. The apartment is in darkness. In her excitement and anticipation of a wedding proposal, has Suzy left without shutting it behind her? I don't think so. My gut is screaming that something's not right.

*Fuck! Now what?*

"Suzy, are you home?" I call out, my voice wobbling.

No answer.

Indecision roots me to the spot. Do I go inside or should I call the police and wait for them to arrive? If Suzy's simply forgotten to pull shut the door, they won't appreciate me wasting their time. On the other-hand, what if it's a burglary or something more sinister?

The stalker might lurk inside the darkened apartment waiting for me.

My mind made up, I reach out to grab an umbrella from the holder in the hallway. Long and made of wood, it's one of Suzy's designer accessories. Ideal as an improvised weapon.

"Rita. All lights on."

The AI follows my command, and the hallway illuminates. I breathe a sigh of relief.

*Electrical circuits not tampered with.*

Hand clammy on the wooden handle of the make-shift weapon, I hold the umbrella across my body, my other hand firm around the material of its centre so that the metal tip faces outwards. Despite trying to stay calm, my heart is ready to beat out of my chest as I creep down the hall, warily pushing open each door with my toe, all the time expecting someone to jump out.

Poised for an attack from an intruder, I check each room, fighting back the paranoid urge to probe behind sofas and under beds—instinct is telling me I'm alone.

Even so, my hackles are up.

Someone's been here.

I can sense it. No, more than that, *I can smell it*—very faint—a woody masculine essence lingering in the air.

When I'm sure there's nobody hiding in the apartment, I check all the windows to confirm they're still locked before returning to the hallway and examining the door's latch. There's no sign of a forced entry. It's possible Suzy mistakenly left it open, but unlikely.

No longer in need of the weapon, I slot the umbrella back into its holder and make my way to the kitchen. I'm really not sure how many more scares I can handle before anxiety gets the better of me. Given that the signs of a panic attack are already in play with my mouth dry and hands shaking more than I'd like, I stumble on unsteady legs to the kitchen for a glass of water.

A niggling doubt that I'm missing something leaves an uneasy tension in my muscles, but I can't put a finger on it until I turn from the sink and notice the bottle of wine and two glasses on the countertop.

My stomach clenches into a knot.

Suzy was getting ready to go out for the evening. There's no way she would have invited someone over for drinks beforehand. Not unless Tom met her here first?

As though it might shatter at my touch, I tentatively reach out to the bottle and brush my skin against the transparent glass.

Still chilled.

Snippets of our conversation spill into my mind from earlier until I'm almost certain she was planning on meeting Tom at the restaurant. Which one, though, did she say? Frustration bites down as I try to remember where they were going. The red dress she threw at me—she wanted me to join them. But where?

Why did I not pay more attention?

There's nothing else for it. I'll have to phone her and hope I don't screw up any marriage proposals. With so many disturbing events unfolding today, I'm prepared to take the chance—I have to know she's alright.

"Rita, call Suzy," I say, hoping her mobile isn't on silent as it connects and starts ringing.

It takes a couple of seconds for me to register that the jingle isn't coming from the built-in speakers in the apartment, but from somewhere nearby. With a gripping fear clawing at my stomach, I spin around, scanning the kitchen until I spot the handset discarded on the floor.

The screen is smashed.

It switches to voice-mail and her bubbly voice instructs me to leave a message.

# THE GRAYSTONE KILLINGS

In that moment, my legs collapse beneath me and I fall to the ground, the room spinning.

# Chapter Twelve

I lunge across the kitchen floor towards Suzy's smartphone, fighting back the urge to be sick. All around me is a blur as I scramble over the tiles. No longer any doubt in my mind that something is wrong—Suzy never goes out without her mobile.

*Oh shit! Shit, shit, shit!*
*What the hell do I do now?*
I need to stop panicking for a start.

Think, think, think... Yes! Her social media! She always tags herself in updates, especially when out.

Even though she set me up with accounts for several platforms, I don't have the first clue how to use them, which is why Wynter manages all the Verandah's social marketing. I can ask her to check Suzy's status.

"Rita, call Wynter."

On the second ring, she answers.

"Wynter, it's me. Listen, I need you to do something for me." I hear the breathless panic in my voice and try to lighten my tone. "Suzy's gone out without her phone and it's important I speak with her. Are you able to check her social media to see if someone has tagged her in a post?"

"Okay, sure, no probs. I follow her on most media so it won't be any hassle to get her latest status. Gimme a sec to check... is everything okay because you sound really—"

"I'm fine. Everything's fine. Just... just find out if she's been tagged, please."

"Sure. So, she posted on her Twitter account about three hours ago. It's an eco video—she and a bunch of other celebs talking about the environment. I watched it earlier when she first posted. Pretty cool, but there's been nothing since then. Lemme check some others... on Instagram she posted a selfie forty minutes ago... another eco theme on TikTok... but nope, nothing on Snapchat or Facebook. Nothing here that would help to pin down her location."

"What about her boyfriend? How do I contact him?"

"I can leave Tom an instant message to call you?"

"Yes! Yes, do that. Tell him it's urgent that I talk to Suzy and leave him my mobile number."

"Okay, sure, no probs. I'm typing it out now."

"Can you tell when he's read it?"

"Oh, sure. He's showing as online... now reading the message... typing a reply... okay, he says he'll call you."

"Thanks, Wynter. Speak soon."

"No probs. I hope you get hold of her, and if you need anything else, call me."

After ending the call, I wait for Tom to ring. Long seconds pass as I stare at my mobile on the counter. When it lights up with an incoming number displayed on the screen, I snatch it up and put the device on speakerphone.

"Tom? Thanks for replying to my message."

"Hi, yeah, Tom Bankes here. How can I help?"

"I'm Ella, Suzy's friend. We haven't met, but I need to speak with her urgently and she's left her phone here at the apartment. Is she with you? Can you put her on, please?"

"I'm afraid I can't do that. She's not here."

"But... but she was getting ready to go for dinner. With you!"

The words sound like an accusation, but I don't care. Right now, I've no reason to hide my distrust of him.

"She stood me up. I waited almost an hour and then came home."

"What? Wait—she stood you up? Has she done that before?"

"No. Although she has cancelled on me once before, after I arrived at the restaurant, but she called to let me know."

"She didn't call you tonight?"

"No. I've tried ringing her mobile. It goes to voicemail."

"And you didn't bother to find out where she was? My friend is *missing* and you don't seem at all concerned!"

"Ella, please, I'm sure there's a simple explanation. Maybe she's bumped into friends and got sidetracked—it happens. She's a sociable and extremely popular young woman, as you know. When she calls to apologise for missing our date, I promise you'll be the first person I notify. Now, if there's nothing else—"

From his tone, I can tell he's growing impatient and considers me to be irrational. Perhaps I am, but I need to be sure that my friend is safe. Even if I am veering into neurotic territory, he seems keen to end this call.

Why isn't he concerned about her not turning up at the restaurant or calling him?

"The *second* you hear from her..."

It isn't a request.

"Of course, goodbye," he says, hanging up before I can think of anything else to ask him.

I stand staring at the two half-filled glasses of wine, irritated by Tom's lack of concern.

The bottle is not one of ours, that much is evident. There's a tinted smudge on one glass and so I move in closer to examine it—Suzy's lip-gloss—I'd recognise the bright red shade anywhere.

*God, this could be evidence of a crime.*

The notion hits me like a physical blow and I recoil back.

Not only has Suzy not got her phone with her, she left the front door open, and according to Tom, stood him up.

I dial 999 and ask for the police.

As I wait to be connected, I pace up and down the kitchen, eyeing the wine bottle.

Evidence. Fuck.

"*Hello, metropolitan police. What's the emergency, please?*"

"My friend is—my friend's missing. Something's h-happened to her."

By verbalising my fears, the words make it all too real and I stumble through the dispatcher's request for personal details. Filled with frustration at the mundane questions, I want to scream down the phone. In reality, it only takes a few seconds.

"*And how old is your friend?*"

"Twenty-six."

'*What's your friend's name?*'

"Suzy Sands."

"*When did you last see Suzy?*"

"This evening, around five. We share an apartment. She was getting ready to meet with her boyfriend."

"*How would you describe Suzy's mental state? Was she upset about anything?*"

"No! She was excited. She was looking forward to a night out."

"*What makes you believe she's missing?*"

"Suzy never turned up at the restaurant for her date. And her phone is here. I found it smashed on the kitchen floor. It looks like someone's been here, inside the apartment. I mean—there's an open bottle of wine with two glasses. And the front door wasn't closed properly when I got home."

"*Is there any sign of a struggle?*"

"Other than the phone? No. No, I don't think so."

"*And has anything been stolen?*"

"No, nothing's been taken."

"*So you believe Suzy had a drink with someone in the apartment that you share, and she left without closing the door—*"

"Yes. No. I, um, there's more to it than that. Before, when I was in Hyde Park at lunchtime, I noticed a man watching me."

"*Can you describe this person?*"

"Tall, broad shoulders and, um, dark hair. The thing is… he looked like the escaped prisoner from this morning. The one that's been in the news all day?"

There, I've said it. No going back now.

"*I see… so you're reporting a sighting of the fugitive?*"

"No. Yes. Um, I'm not sure. Yes, it could have been him. I couldn't see his face clearly."

*"Did this person approach you in the park?"*

"Not as such, no. He was watching me, but it was more than that—it felt intimidating. And he called my mobile."

*"He called your mobile? So you knew this person? Did you speak to him?"*

"No! That's the whole point! And just now, on my way home, I was told that a stranger's been asking around the neighbourhood after me."

*"Who informed you of this?"*

"The couple who run the local off-licence."

*"You were in the off-licence—"*

"Yes, but not to buy alcohol. Well, earlier I was, but—" I pause and pinch the bridge of my nose, trying to organise my jumbled thoughts. This is not going as expected. "Look, I know how this sounds. I'm... I'm not explaining things very well, but something is wrong. I feel it. My friend's missing, and I believe she could be in danger."

*"I understand your concerns, miss. We've had several reported sightings of the fugitive and I assure you we're taking each one seriously. I'm going to give you a reference number. Do you have a pen and paper to hand? Someone will be in touch shortly to take a report."*

"But—but my friend needs help now!"

*"I understand, and once we've made a risk assessment, we'll keep you fully informed if we open a missing person's investigation. Should anything further occur, please make contact and quote this reference number."*

I grab a pen and scribble the six-digit number down on a message magnet against the fridge before hanging up. Anxiously, I pace the floor, frustration screaming from every pore.

## CJ HORNE

I'll be damned if I'm going to wait around here for the police to call.

Fuck, fuck, fuck!

*Where are you Suzy?*

# Chapter Thirteen

A sudden clap of thunder booms out with an ominous crash as the noise of the rain hammers relentlessly against the apartment windows.

Suzy's out there, somewhere amid this violent storm. She could be frightened and hurt. As much as I want to believe she's gone of her own free will, the unsilenced paranoia in my head is screaming that's not the case.

For the next twenty minutes, I pace the length of the apartment, calling each of her friends. It's a frustrating and futile exercise that brings me no further to finding her.

Desperate for news, I message Wynter, asking her to keep checking social media for any updates. Then I check my call log and messages again, for what seems like the hundredth time.

Still nothing from the police or Tom.

Out of my mind with worry, I want to jump up and down screaming in frustration. If I thought it would help, I would.

"Please be alright, Suzy. Wherever you are, please, *please* be okay," I say, holding her damaged phone against me and willing it to carry my words to wherever she is. Deep down, I know she would never have missed her date tonight, especially not when she believed Tom was about to propose.

I run through all the likely scenarios in my head.

Suzy's had fanatical fans in the past—it comes with the territory and from being a model in the public eye. But she tells me whenever there's a problem and we always look out for each other. There have been no recent incidents; no overly concerning letters, no stalker, no death threats. Besides, she would never invite an over enthusiastic fan into our home to share a bottle of wine. Not a crank, then.

Not a friend either; I've checked with all of them twice now and none of her usual social circle has heard from her. It's possible she's with someone I don't know, but why arrange to meet Tom only to invite a friend over? And why keep it a secret? I dismiss the scenario as implausible.

With no credible explanation for her absence, I briefly consider searching for her around town in the clubs and pubs. Nothing about this situation is simple, but even in my agitated state, I can see that a search would be an impossible task, and unlikely to result in finding her.

Likewise, I can't just stay here pacing the floor, waiting for someone to call. What if Tom is lying? What if they've had a fight and Suzy's injured in some way?

I decide I need to speak with Tom in person. If he's not hiding anything, then he won't object to meeting with me. Also, I need to see for myself that she's not with him. I have his number in my contact list from our earlier chat, and so I type out a quick message:

**Need to see u re Suzy.**


**Pls send me ur address.**


**Leaving now.**


*Ella*

After hitting send, I head back through the apartment to get changed and wait for Tom's reply.

Not forgetting that someone is out there stalking me, I need to be invisible when I step outside—more so than normal.

While I strip off my clothes, I instruct 'Rita' to switch on the news channel as I pull items of dark clothing from my wardrobe. Amongst the daily roundup of bulletins and weather forecasts, there's only one story I'm interested in and, pulling a black jumper over my head, I hear the news anchor report on the prisoner escape from this morning.

> *"... and tonight a man who escaped from Belmarsh prison during a medical transfer has been named. Victor Malden, forty-seven, escaped earlier this morning during an attack*

> *on his convoy. Two guards were pronounced dead at the scene and a third is being treated in hospital for non-life-threatening injuries. Two officers in the police escort vehicle also sustained injuries but were treated at the scene. A Met spokesperson confirmed that attempts to secure the prisoner back into custody are being hampered by Storm Ruby. Members of the public are warned not to approach the fugitive, as he is dangerous and could be armed. Police urge anyone with information about his whereabouts to contact the number on the bottom of the screen. The following special report contains graphic images some viewers may find disturbing..."*

I watch with a sense of numb detachment as images of Malden's stalking ground flash up on the screen. Some restaurants and clubs have since changed hands, adopting a new look or name, while others are boarded-up. Only a few have bounced back from the stigma.

After another brief commentary, the screen cuts to a reporter who stands on the front lawn of a boarded-up house, an earnest expression on her face as she talks into the camera. Filmed earlier today, Victor's house of horrors makes for a macabre backdrop, hitting home the urgency of the situation. The commentary is laced with dramatic pauses. They seem unnecessary when every viewer knows this shit is dramatic enough without the need for embellishment.

# THE GRAYSTONE KILLINGS

As I watch the chronological sequence of events, a growing sense of alarm fills me. I stop what I'm doing to stare at the photographs of the young women, their sparkling eyes and white smiles filling the screen—no notion of the brutal fate that awaited them.

Equally disturbing is that each victim looks exactly like Suzy. Every one of them blonde, slim, and stunningly beautiful.

*Oh fuck, fuck, fuck!*

The reporter walks up the short driveway to the boarded-up front door as she recounts the details of the crimes committed inside. I'm transfixed, not wanting to know but unable to tear my eyes from the screen.

> *"... Malden admitted during his trial to targeting his victims and luring them back to his home. After drugging the women, he then brought them here—to this house behind me—where he subjected them to hours of horrific abuse, before disposing of their naked and bound bodies in remote woodland located around the South East. Police made the harrowing discoveries less than twelve hours after the victim's reported disappearance..."*

Crime photos of Victor's home are shown. An otherwise ordinary-looking house in an unsuspecting street. Except for one room. I shiver at the image of a door; a menacing lock and bolt on the outside. Despite being on the upper floor, the inside resembles a windowless basement, lit only by a bare bulb hanging from the centre of the ceiling.

It's all too easy to imagine his murdered victims haunting the shadows of this sinister-looking room.

The space contains three items; a bed, a table and a bucket. The single sized bed is metal framed with leather restraints attached to each corner. On top is a thin mattress, grubby and stained with dried blood. Blood spilled from multiple victims.

Young women, each one drugged and cuffed to a bloodstained bed.

I can't imagine the horror.

The next image is of a folding wooden table, the sort used for laptops or TV dinners.

Except this table has a more sinister purpose.

Laid out in a neat row are metal implements, comprising razor edged knives and a variety of tools. Amongst them are everyday DIY items like hand drills and saws that take on a new and menacing perspective in this setting.

Next to this are bottles of chemicals and cotton swabs, and a camera mounted on a pop-up tripod angled towards the bed. The reporter goes on to describe how Victor filmed each violent rape and murder. The last image shows a cheap bucket made of plastic. Its purpose is so harrowing that the contents have been pixilated.

The reporter continues with her disturbing account.

> *"... his early series of offences centred around rape and sexual assault, fuelling his desire to exercise power and control over his victims.*

## THE GRAYSTONE KILLINGS

*None of Malden's drugged and disorientated survivors could provide detectives with an accurate location or description of this property behind me. Only after escalating into higher, life-threatening levels of violence was Malden finally arrested four years ago and charged with seven counts of rape and imprisonment and five counts of murder. He was serving a whole-life order with no chance of parole when he escaped this morning. This is Kelly Fisher reporting on the harrowing crimes of the fugitive, Victor Malden. And now it's back to the studio for the latest news updates with..."*

The reporter's words echo in my mind.
*Twelve hours... dumped and left for dead.*
It means that if Malden has Suzy, then right now I'm her only hope of surviving this night.

I return to the kitchen and lean over the glass with the red smudge on the rim. Suzy is aware of the risks of having her drink spiked whilst out partying, but I doubt she would show the same level of caution from the safety of our home.

Because Suzy is so trusting of people, I've made it my business to make sure she knows all about the effects of Rohypnol, GHB and Ketamine as well as the recreational drugs Ecstasy and LSD. All have the ability of incapacitating a person to make them compliant. Although some drugs can be odourless, colourless and tasteless, I still examine her glass, hoping to notice or smell something unusual. Other than the aroma of a crisp wine, there's nothing to see or smell. I move my attention to the second glass. No lip-stick marks, so most likely a man. Again, nothing of notable concern.

I grab the message magnet off the fridge and underneath the police reference number scribble in red pen the message:

**DRINK SPIKED?**

**TEST FOR ROOFIE/GHB!**

The police need to know of my suspicions, even if I'm not here in person.

The sound of a ping alerts me to a message from Tom, providing me with his address. When I tap the details into Google Maps, it calculates him to be less than two miles away—I can be there in twenty minutes.

With one last task before I leave, I race through the apartment, grabbing the few items I'll need; the torch from the kitchen drawer—checking the batteries work—and my camera from the studio. A brief flick through the photos taken at the park, and I sling it over my shoulder with a satisfied nod.

The last item is a folding Karambit Fox knife I pull out from under my mattress. A moving-in present from my father. Some might consider sleeping with a weapon an unnecessary precaution, but my parents are super protective and have always encouraged me to prepare for the unexpected. For this reason, I never leave myself vulnerable, even when sleeping.

After a last look around the apartment, I shrug into a black waterproof jacket and pull on a matching beanie hat before heading out into the night.

Suzy's last media post was a selfie taken a little over an hour ago now.

The clock is ticking.

In less than twelve hours, she could be dead.

# Chapter Fourteen

With a total disregard for all weather warnings in place, I race towards the brightly lit off-licence whilst remaining alert for any potential threat. Every shadow and doorway I pass poses a risk now.

So much has happened in the thirty minutes since I promised to return that Stuart and Betty rush to the door as I enter. Their faces wear expressions of concern.

"There you are, lass! We wir getting worried about you!" Stuart says, throwing his gangly arms up in front of him.

"Sorry, it um... took longer than expected."

Keen to offer their help, they usher me over to the counter and wait expectantly while I lift the camera out from its protective casing and flick the 'on' switch. I angle the viewfinder round to show them a digital image of the park, taken right before the man behind the bushes startled me. Without intending to, I've hit the shutter button and captured his image.

I zoom in, showing the screen to Betty.

"Is this the man who came into the store asking about me? I appreciate he's wearing a hat and scarf, but if you could still—"

Betty leans in closer, lifting the glasses that hang from a chain around her neck onto the end of her nose. She peers at the viewfinder.

"Aye, dear, that's him. Ah cannae say fir sure of course... but aye, it looks like the same chap who wis in here. How did you come by this photo?"

"This afternoon when I was in Hyde Park—I suspect he was following me. I don't wish to alarm you, but I'm almost positive this man is the prisoner who escaped this morning. Will you call the police and relay to them everything that's happened? And this is the key to our apartment," I say, placing my keys on the counter. "Number 1A. I've already called to report Suzy missing."

"Wit are ye saying, lass? That this fellow has done something to your pal?" Stuart says, stepping forward and anxiously rubbing at the back of his neck.

"All I know is that she's gone and I'm worried about her."

Hot tears sting at my eyes, and I swallow back the emotional lump that clogs my throat.

Betty pulls me into a hug. "You poor dear, I didnae ken wits going on here, but my Stu will dae as you ask. If you need us, we'll be here."

As we pull apart, I notice the colour has drained from her face and I feel a pang of guilt for involving them. With no other choice, I leave my camera and keys on the counter and turn to leave.

Before I can slip away, Stuart rests his firm hand on my shoulder. "Be careful out there, lass. I hope your pal is safe, I really do. We'll sort things here. Didnae worry about that."

With a smile of thanks, I disappear out of the store.

Despite the squall conditions, I race through the streets, checking the blue pulsing locator on my phone's map. As my feet pound the pavement, it moves closer towards the red pin—Tom's address.

For once, the lack of crowds benefits me, making it easier to pick out my would-be attacker. Being hidden amongst a throng of people can't help me now—someone has already singled me out. I remain cautious and stick to the shadows of the deserted streets.

Paranoia might be the single best defence for staying safe in my search for Suzy.

The map takes me past a local church and I pause at the entrance gates, scanning the graveyard. It would be quicker to cut through than go all the way round, but it's creepy as hell with the clamour of wind chimes screeching out.

Traditionally warding off evil of the supernatural kind, I'm more concerned with the human, rapist-killer kind of evil that could be lurking in there.

Urgency overrides the scare factor and deciding to take the risk, I slip the torch out of my pocket to shine a path through the burial ground. Aware that behind each tombstone might be a person waiting to pounce, I resist the urge to run at full pelt.

After only a few steps, my pulse skips a beat as I sense I'm not alone.

Before I can spin around, a powerful hand shoots out from beside me, grabbing my arm and knocking the torch to the ground. A scream erupts from me as I'm caught off guard and stumbling, I'm pulled into the darkness—away from the streetlights and relative safety.

Quick to recover, my body goes into defence mode and I pull on my assailant's wrist, hyper-extending their arm. As I drive my body into them, I prepare to push away and run.

Until I hear the shouts of a familiar voice.

"It's me—Winston! You're breaking my arm!"

"What the—" At once releasing my grip, I jump backwards. "Shit! Winston, you scared me half to death! What are you doing here?" My heart is racing so fast I flop forward to rest on my thighs, puffing out my cheeks and exhaling hard. "Holy shit, don't ever do that to me again!"

"I saw you leave Stu's place. You looked so upset that I wanted to make sure you're okay. Could tell something was up when you came in here." Solemnly, he looks around at our surroundings. "Nobody in their right mind walks through a graveyard at night, in the middle of a storm. Not unless something's wrong. It's not safe for you on the streets tonight."

A low whimper comes from inside Winston's coat and I see a shiny, black trembling head with round, frightened eyes peering out at me.

"Jambo! God, I didn't mean to scare you," I say, straightening up and reaching out a hand to ruffle his ears.

He shrinks back, further down into the safety of the overcoat.

"Pay no notice. He's nervous during thunderstorms. And maybe a scant scared of you too, now," Winston says, rubbing at his arm.

I look around with despair at the uselessness of the situation.

"Winston, something's wrong—and I don't know how to fix it."

He looks at me with kind eyes that reflect the turbulent clouds above. "You have a good heart, Ella, so I know you'll figure it out. But you shouldn't be out here alone—it's not safe. I'm asking you, please, to stay at home."

"I can't do that," I say, shaking my head. "Suzy could be in danger and the police aren't doing anything about it. She needs me."

"Then let me help," he says, his arms held wide in appeal. "Tell me where you're heading and I'll get you there safely."

Hit with a sudden sense of relief at not having to be out here alone, I nod and show him Tom's address on the app.

"I know it. Put your map away." Winston tugs at his lapels to straighten his overcoat. "We'll use the backstreets, it'll be quicker. Plus, we shouldn't risk being out in the open," he says with a meaningful look.

After retrieving my torch, I scurry after him, his long strides covering the distance with ease. As I fall into step beside him, I glance round and notice the pinch of his brow. Concentration or concern? I'm hoping for the former.

"Why did you say it's not safe, Winston? Because of the storm?"

"No."

"Then what is it? Did you see something earlier? Outside our apartment?"

He glances across at me and shrugs. "Not sure. Might be something, might be nothing."

"I'd very much like to know what that *something or nothing* is."

Why so cagey? It's obvious he's keeping something from me.

As we keep stride, heads down and leaning into the wind, I take a different approach and ask him about Victor Malden instead. "Do you know anything about the prisoner who escaped this morning?"

He hesitates before answering, as if debating whether to respond. After a long pause, he says, "I hear things—yes."

"What sort of things?"

"Things that make it unsafe to be out here."

He doesn't seem to want to confide in me and so I decide not to push the conversation further. Winston hasn't survived this long on the streets by not being smart, and I'm confident that if he thinks it's in my interest to know, he'll tell me. Until then, I'll just have to trust him—something that doesn't come easy for me.

We cover the rest of the distance in determined silence, making our way down narrow cobbled roads and past buildings with colourful street art gracing the walls. We move unnoticed along rows of Edwardian terraced houses, lights burning softly inside, the occasional bark of a dog unnerved by the thunder.

Soon we're standing on a street lined with trees stripped of their leaves, where mansions stand tall with grand pillars guarding fancy doorways.

"This is the place," Winston says, coming to a halt outside Tom's house. "Jeez, there's money here, that's for sure."

Jambo whines, wriggling underneath his coat. Winston lifts him into his arms and sets the dog down on the pavement, where the animal struggles to balance against the wind. After several failed attempts, he cocks his leg against one of the smooth white pillars.

*Good dog.*

I race up the steps and push the doorbell—once, twice, three times—I keep pressing until a light comes on inside and there's movement on the other side of the privacy glass. The door swings open and I'm momentarily stuck for words as I stare at the man in front of me.

Sharp grey eyes look out from under dark, masculine eyebrows, while his jaw has a strong angular curve, sporting a well-groomed peppering of stubble. An insanely expensive-looking tailored white shirt hints at the well-toned body outlined beneath it. His sleeves are rolled up, exposing strong, tanned arms.

*Well, well, well... no wonder Suzy fell hard for this one!*

He stands at least five inches over me, and my breath catches as I stare up and lock eyes with his powerful gaze.

"You must be Ella. You'd better come inside."

# Chapter Fifteen

Tom Bankes is not at all what I expect.

Within minutes of meeting Suzy's love interests, I can normally categorise by whatever need they're using her to fulfil; whether that be sex, invitations to the best parties in town, a stunning beauty on their arm to further a career, or just plain old-fashioned gold digging.

However, the man stood in front of me with his guarded, striking grey eyes has momentarily knocked me off my game. This one is going to take some figuring out.

A rush of movement at my feet and I snatch my eyes away to see Jambo scampering out of the wind and rain through the open door and into the hallway. He shakes his short-haired black head and white body so vigorously he almost loses his balance before flopping down next to Tom's feet.

"Hey! And what's your name?" Tom asks, effortlessly folding his long frame to crouch down and offer Jambo the back of his hand.

Non-threatening, he knows how to handle animals. I wonder if he manages people just as well?

*Something tells me he does.*

Jambo licks his hand and offers Tom a paw.

*Ugh, traitor!*

"His name's Jambo," Winson says, stepping forward from the shadows. "He likes you."

"I'm pleased to make his acquaintance too," Tom says, shaking the tiny white paw before standing upright. "And you are—"

"Here to help. Name's Winston."

"He's a friend," I say, volunteering the information when I see the quizzical expression on Tom's face. "Helping me to find Suzy."

"Then you'd better all come in," he says, stepping aside to allow us through.

As soon as the door closes behind us, the noise of the storm becomes muffled. A welcome relief after being sandblasted by the rain. Grateful for the reprieve, I try to ignore the dull humming in my ears from the constant screech of the wind.

Tom appears gracious about us gatecrashing his home. He leads us down an elegant hallway, its walls and floor made from a marble that sparkles with gold hues in its veining.

At the sound of Jambo's claws tapping on the polished surface, I wonder briefly whether he's toilet trained.

As we pass several sleek looking chairs and sofas scattered throughout, presumably providing comfortable viewing for the many artworks mounted on the walls, I strain my ears, listening out for any cries for help. A mansion sized house means dozens of rooms to hold someone against their will.

Not that I truly believe Tom is behind Suzy's disappearance, but I'm not prepared to rule anything out just yet.

"In your message, you said you wanted to see me about Suzy? I take it you still haven't heard from her?" Tom says, glancing back as he walks us through his home.

With open suspicion, I regard him for signs of agitation—if he's hiding something, I'll know. His broad shoulders pull back straight, arms swinging in a relaxed fashion, while his long legs move with a natural confidence, so much so that I don't detect any nervous tension in his body language at all.

Our presence here has no effect on him.

"Do you know where she is?" I say with blunt directness.

"No," he replies without breaking stride. "As I told you on the phone earlier, she didn't show up for our date. You've tried her friends, I presume?"

"Several times. And nothing."

We continue down the hallway until it opens up into a magnificent open plan space, enhanced with floor to ceiling windows and an enormous skylight. The glass is so thick I can barely hear the rain bouncing off it. To our left is a marble winding staircase snaking up to a balcony that leads off into the heart of this elegant house.

Central to the curved staircase is a chandelier that I'm certain is reflecting handmade pieces of glass. Beneath that is a cut glass table with an exquisite vase of flowers that leaves a delicate fragrance in the air. I can't help but gawk, for embedded in the many recesses of the marble walls going up the stairs is soft lighting that illuminates the intricate metal sculptures displayed in each. Some are made from bronze, others from gold and silver, and each one is worth a small fortune. If I wasn't living my worst nightmare right now, I would stand in awe of this dream home.

"This way," Tom says, turning into another elegant marbled hallway. He glances over his shoulder at us, no doubt making sure we're not stealing anything. "We can talk in the sitting room, where it's more comfortable."

From somewhere nearby, I pick up the faint whiff of a mouth-watering aroma.

*Definitely not worried, then.*

Although I haven't eaten since Wynter went out for sandwiches this afternoon, the anxious knot in the pit of my stomach over Suzy's disappearance makes me queasy just thinking about food.

"You'll have to excuse me, I was fixing myself a late supper when I got your message," he says, as if reading my mind. "The notion of sticking around to peruse the restaurant's menu on my own held little appeal."

Whatever he's preparing smells sumptuous and I glance at Winston to see his nostrils flaring at the savoury aroma.

"Smells like roast duck... with sweet turnip infused with... peach," Winston says, causing us to stop mid-stride. I look at him, one eyebrow raised, and he shrugs. "I know my way around a kitchen."

*Maybe not a banker or a lawyer, after all...*

Tom bears a curious expression but says nothing.

As we come to another turn, both Winston and I stop dead in our tracks. Before us is a glass wall, and behind it a gleaming emerald coloured sports car. It's breathtaking and surreal; like we've stepped onto the set of a futuristic movie.

Tom backtracks to join us, following our gaze as we stare through the glass at the vehicle.

"Beautiful, isn't she?" he says with open admiration.

"You... you... um, have a car. In your house," I say, blurting out the obvious.

"Yes. Although it's actually part of the garage. Notice the section of floor the car is resting on?" He points to a discreet break in the smooth lines of the hardwood floor. "It lowers into a basement garage. Clever, really."

My ears prick up at the mention of there being a basement. If Suzy were being held somewhere beneath us, would I hear her shouts for help? It's proving difficult to keep my suspicions in check when presented with so many plausible scenarios.

"It's a beauty," Winston remarks. "What model?"

"Limited edition Valkyrie. Only one-hundred and fifty of these Aston Martin vehicles on the road. I try to support our British industry wherever possible. Plus, she's an exhilarating drive—hard to resist. I'll take you out for a spin in it sometime, if you like?"

"You will?"

Tom laughs. "Of course. I can see you're a man who appreciates fine cars."

"You hear that, Jambo? We're going for a ride—in that!"

The dog jumps up at Tom's legs and wags his tail.

*Oh, give me a break.*

"Quite a remarkable house you have. Suzy never mentioned what you do—" I say, keen to put an end to the admiration party.

"I run my own business, nothing very exciting. Shall we—" He gestures toward what I assume is the sitting room, but as we approach, it turns out to be a small and windowless office space. Inside is a desk and eight monitors lining the furthest wall.

"What's this?"

"Take a seat." He pulls out the chair from under the desk.

As I sit, I scan each monitor in turn, recognising the hallway we've just walked down. "Why are you showing me your security cameras?" I ask, glancing up.

"Check for yourself, Ella. She's not here. So unless you'd rather trudge around every room in the house, I suggest you use the home security to satisfy yourself I'm not holding your friend against her will."

*Busted. Smart arse.*

He moves closer, leaning across me as he reaches for a tablet sized device on the desk, brushing my arm with his upper body. On impulse, I inhale the subtle whiff of his aftershave and instinctively know he chose this scent for Suzy—her favourite; Clive Christian.

The man is suave, I'll give him that.

"So you tap this panel here to view whichever room—"

"Alright, you've made your point," I say, cutting him off and pushing back the chair to stand.

With appraising eyes, he nods and gestures with his arm towards the door.

I give a last glance over my shoulder at the monitors, and briefly wonder what it must be like to live in a house like this. Almost at once, I dismiss the idea.

Our apartment has oodles of character, whereas this luxury home looks spectacular, but lacks any soul. I'm pretty sure if the royal family had to choose between rattling around in the opulence of Buckingham Palace or cozying up with a hot chocolate at Balmoral Castle, they'd opt for the latter, too.

When we reach the sitting room, it's hard not to notice it's every bit as luxurious as the rest of the house, with hardwood flooring and spectacular floor to ceiling windows trailing the room's soft curving lines. The panoramic view spans out onto a well-lit expansive garden—presently being battered by Storm Ruby. Enormous white kidney-shaped sofas rest upon a thick silver rug with ebony streaks running through it, and between them a cluster of three tables, varying in height, and made from an actual trunk of a tree. At one end of the room is a well-stocked bar, the other... a painting that takes my breath away.

I look from the painting to Tom and back again, an indiscernible force drawing me over to it.

"A Rembrandt," I say, breathless with awe.

"Fake, unfortunately."

I shake my head in wonder. "No. The pigments and materials... this is a genuine painting. To the novice eye, you might pass it off as a copy, but I'm no novice."

*Holy shit—he has a fucking Rembrandt hanging in his sitting room!*

As I stand staring up at the work of art, I sense Tom's movement close beside me, and leaning in, his breath brushes my exposed neck.

A Rembrandt and no fucking concept of personal space.

*Who is this person?*

"*The Storm on the Sea of Galilee*, stolen in a heist from a museum in Boston in 1990. Consider it recovered," he says in a whisper, leaning in so close to my ear I can feel the warmth radiating from his lips.

"I'm aware of its history. But why—"

"It'll be going home. Soon."

"Forgive me," I say, turning to face him, "But I don't understand why it's here. This is the only seascape Rembrandt ever painted. It's worth millions, practically priceless. How did you—"

"Did you know it's believed he painted a self-portrait of himself next to Jesus? One saviour, twelve disciples, and an artist in a boat on stormy seas—not sure I see it myself. We could certainly use a little calming of the storm tonight, don't you think?"

Winston's voice from the other end of the room draws our attention away from the painting.

"Hey, if you're not going to eat that—"

I peer past Tom to see a connecting door through to a dining room with a table barely big enough for two chairs. It's cosy and intimate, and far less extravagant than the other rooms we've seen.

On the table is what I assume to be the roast duck dinner we can smell. Jambo sits at the foot of one of the chairs, nose raised, and sniffing the air.

Our reluctant host hesitates before saying, "Of course... er... be my guest. Help yourself."

Winston shoots him a beaming grin and takes a seat at the table while Tom shakes his head ruefully and crosses to the bar. He pours two drinks and motions to the sofa for us to sit. His eyes linger as he passes me a glass, and I shift awkwardly on the plush seat.

"Suzy talks about you all the time," he says, subtly shutting down any further discussion about the Rembrandt.

My eyebrows shoot up at seeing the drink and, taking a sip, I try to hide my surprise.

*Evidently she does.*

The vodka and cranberry are the best Cape Codder mix I've ever tasted. It's also my favourite drink, so right now I'm not sure whether to be impressed or just a little creeped out.

"You're not what I expected," Tom says, continuing to watch me.

"Hmm, likewise. So, where the hell is my friend?" I set down the drink and observe him under guarded eyes.

After taking a long sip of his whiskey, he leans forward, saying, "Okay, tell me everything that's happened. Help me understand why you feel this is so urgent that you have to be out in the middle of a storm looking for her."

I stare into his intense grey eyes, unsure whether to trust him.

Then, taking a deep breath, I tell him everything.

# Chapter Sixteen

An avalanche of words are tumbling from my mouth and I seem powerless to stop them. By throwing all my doubts and suspicions to one side, I've grasped at the opportunity to have someone who knows Suzy share my concerns for her safety.

Over the next ten minutes, I describe to Tom about being caught up in the morning's explosion, the stalker in the park, and Stuart and Betty's suspicions about the imposter pretending to be my cousin. And since I'm holding nothing back, I also confess how Suzy believed the man in the park couldn't have been the escaped prisoner. I even tell him about my ineffective call to the police and describe finding the door to the apartment open and the bottle of wine on the side.

Tom is silent throughout, but his brow knits into a look of deep concern as his steepled fingers tap against his lower lip. I take a sip from my drink and wait for him to process the information dump.

After a long minute, he looks up and says, "What makes you suspect that Victor Malden is specifically targeting you and Suzy? Have your paths ever crossed before? Any connection to his victims? Anything at all—no matter how insignificant?"

Aware of how fantastical this all sounds, and with no evidence to back any of it up, I fidget in my seat before finally replying.

"No, no connection I can come up with. Don't you think I've been asking myself the same question all day?"

"What about the call to the police? You say they're not taking your concerns seriously, but even accounting for Storm Ruby, I find it hard to believe they'd place a potential sighting of the prisoner and an abduction on the back burner. It doesn't make sense."

"Um, so... the thing is—well, I may have called them once or twice in the past. False alarms—" Now that I've started, I pause to flick at an imaginary speck of dust on the armrest, knowing only too well how this is going to sound once it's out there. "I... um, suffer from panic attacks—anxiety—it sometimes makes a situation seem more threatening than it actually is."

I run out of dust particles to swipe at and stare down at my hands instead.

"Ok-ay..."

"This isn't one of those times."

I glance up, expecting to see the judgmental expression I've grown accustomed to. Most people don't understand what it's like to live with a panic disorder.

Tom stands and walks over to the window without speaking. From his reflection, I watch him rub at the stubble on his chin as he looks out to the storm in contemplation.

"Okay," he says, turning to face me, "Here's what I think. I'm going to put a call in to someone who can help us. While I do this, you should return to your apartment and wait for the police. I'll make sure they give Suzy's case priority. Trust me, they will take you seriously."

I leap to my feet, shaking my head.

"No way! I can't sit around hoping someone is out there looking for her. Make your call, but I need to be looking for Suzy, not sat watching the clock while her window of survival dwindles. He will kill her, Tom. By morning, Suzy *will* be dead."

"Based on the assumption he's taken her—"

"Don't you dare. You do not get to do that!" I stride towards him, stabbing my finger at his chest.

"Look, I'm not doubting what you've told me because of your medical condition," he says, holding his hands up. "But everything you've described so far is circumstantial. Yes, I agree it's strange she didn't show up at the restaurant. And entirely unlike Suzy to be radio silent on social media. But being targeted by a serial rapist? One who's escaped from prison and—as you admit yourself—has no prior connection with either of you? It's—"

"She can't go back..."

We both turn to see Winston standing by the bar, wiping his mouth with a cotton napkin. Jambo sits at his feet, licking his lips and rubbing against his leg while Tom stands at my side, looking even more perplexed than before.

"What did you just say?" Tom tilts his head, frowning. "Whatever you know, this would be a good time to spit it out."

"All I can tell you is there's a lot of talk on the street. Don't get involved myself, but doesn't mean I don't hear things. Got my ear to the ground, if you get what I mean.

And if your friend is involved, you can't go back to the apartment. It's not safe."

Frustration enrages me and I cross the room until I'm standing face to face with Winston, our noses almost touching.

"Tell me what this is about—right now. Or take me to someone who will."

Winston wrings his hands. "These are bad people, Ella. Dangerous people."

"Not for me," Tom says, squaring his shoulders and stepping forward to stand at my side. "If there's someone who can give us information, you need to take us to them."

His tone suggests that Winston might consider his next words carefully.

If I'm not mistaken, Tom has just offered to help me find Suzy. Which means some minuscule part of him believes me when I say she's in trouble.

On the other hand, if he's lying and knows where Suzy is, then he's just found a convenient way of keeping tabs on me. Whatever Tom's agenda, Winston straightens his lapels, gives a sharp nod of his head, and agrees to help.

"Good, that's settled then," says Tom. "Wait here. I'll be back in a couple of minutes."

As his footsteps fade away, I speculate on how long it takes to reach the other end of this luxury mansion—time we don't have to waste.

As soon as he's out of earshot, Winston spins on his heels and ducks behind the bar to explore the well-stocked shelves. When he slips a bottle of something expensive looking into the pocket of his coat, I turn away, pretending not to have noticed.

After this is all over, I'll square it with Tom—I owe Winston that much for his service.

I pace the room, trying not to think of the wasted minutes that pass. My gaze falls on the Rembrandt.

*Why the hell is that even here?*

What if Tom's mixed up in criminal activity involving stolen art? Wouldn't that be another of life's ironies? The artist and the art thief together.

*Could this day seriously get any worse?*

I return to pacing the plush carpeted floor when I spot a cluster of framed photographs hanging on the wall. Five monochromes in varying sizes, taking up less space than a medium-sized painting. They hang just above eye level so that I have to tilt my head upwards to view them. As the significance of the images register with my mind, a burning rage sparks inside me.

The first image is of a woman in her mid-twenties with long blonde hair tied back in a ponytail. Attractive in a simple, fresh sort of way; long lashes with sparkling, laughing eyes and a kind, smiling mouth. I sense I would like her if she were a student in one of my classes.

A toddler in one of the other frames has the same blonde hair as the woman, and even with the monochrome effect, I can tell that her cheeks are rosy and her small tongue a delicate pink. She throws her head back in laughter, showing her newly gained milk teeth. Two further photos are of the woman and child together.

The last photograph is the one that's got my anger bubbling over.

It shows two people lost in the moment of a loving gaze—the blonde woman... and Tom. He has his arm around her in a tender embrace as she cradles their newborn baby girl.

The perfect family photo.

Now I understand why he never brought Suzy back here. The man is either ballsy or stupid, considering Suzy's high profile. Heat burning my cheeks, I spin to face him accusingly when, moments later, he steps back into the room.

"You're married—" I fire the words at him, pictures of his wife and child behind me as indisputable evidence.

Tom glances briefly at the photographs, his jaw visibly hardening.

"Not that it's any of your business, but they're no longer in my life," he says, looking down at his backpack as he zips it shut.

"Suzy thinks your relationship is serious. She thought you were going to propose to her tonight," I say with blunt directness.

Not divorced—I can tell that much. Nobody keeps photographs of their ex-wife hanging up.

"Propose—" His head jerks up. *Yep, now I've got his attention.* "I-I honestly don't know why she'd think that. Sure, we enjoy each other's company, but... I'm sorry, it was never my intention to give her that impression."

He seems genuinely dismayed and shocked by my brash statement—whatever his story; we don't have time for it now.

*But rest assured, Tom Bankes, we will revisit this when Suzy is back home safe and sound.*

"Winston, will you take us to these people who might be able to help?" I say, changing the subject back to why we're all here.

He nods—a quick, nervous movement.

Tom steps forward, saying, "Good. Then, listen up—if we're going to do this, we need to stay safe." He looks from Winston to me. "Let's not forget that a dangerous man is out there, and all the time he's being hunted by the police, he's going to be volatile. Until Malden's caught, we assume that—for whatever reason—he's targeting both Suzy and Ella."

He gives me a long stare that sends an involuntary shiver through my core. Whether it's his chilling words or simply being under the gaze of his intense grey eyes, something about him has me rattled.

"How far is this place, Winston? Is it walking distance?" I ask, keen to divert the conversation away from myself.

"Close to the viaduct on Hallow Avenue. And yes, it'll be easier to access by foot."

"Good. Ella, from now on, consider yourself to have a target on your back. That means you stay in visual contact with us at all times."

"You don't need to protect me. I can take care of myself." I throw him an indignant look.

Tom nods and zips up his jacket. His outfit is similar to my own; dressed all in black, he's gone for a turtleneck with black jeans and a military paratrooper type jacket. We could easily feature on the set of a Matrix film.

As he throws the backpack over his shoulder, the action distracts me long enough for him to swing back round—in that split second, he's behind me with a cold, sharp metal blade pressed against my neck.

"We should go," Winston says in an indifferent tone, casting his eye over us as a parent would two squabbling children.

"Dick move," I say, muttering through gritted teeth as I push Tom away and elbow him in the ribs.

# THE GRAYSTONE KILLINGS

"Agreed." He shrugs, heading for the door. "But as you appear not to like me very much—and unlikely to listen to anything I say—I've just demonstrated my point. You need to be careful out there."

I slug back the rest of my drink before following *Mister Smart Arse* and Winston back through the house. Just because he's right doesn't make him any less of an arse.

Some sixth sense tells me I'll need my wits about me tonight.

I may well have a target on my back, but I also know a lot more about Suzy's boyfriend than before; I know he's married, has stolen priceless art hanging in his home, and he can handle a knife—a strange skill for a wealthy business executive.

*So no, I don't trust him. Not one bit.*

# Chapter Seventeen

"To be clear, what exactly is the plan, once we're out there?" Tom says, as the three of us stand shoulder to shoulder facing the main entrance of his mansion.

"To find out what motivates this sick fuck and track him down." I glance at him with narrowed eyes—as if he really has to ask?

"Okay. So we get the information and locate Malden. Then what?"

"Let's just worry about finding him first. Suzy told me the police are working on the premise he's still in London. I assume that remains the case? She mentioned you as her source."

Tom's brow furrows. Suzy wasn't at liberty to repeat anything he told her, but I'd say we're long past that concern now.

"There's been no positive sighting yet, certainly no reports of him trying to get past the roadblocks or other checkpoints that are in place. It would've been challenging enough on his own, but if he's got Suzy with him—" he shoots me a rueful glance. "There's a firm belief he's still in the London vicinity."

"Then we have a chance to get her back."

"Yes, I believe we do. I'll need a minute—" Tom says, holding up his mobile.

"Fine. *One* minute."

While Tom is placing his call, we make our final preparations before heading back out into Storm Ruby.

Winston scoops Jambo up and tucks him back inside his oversized coat, and from one of the many pockets, he pulls out a trapper's hat, which he pushes down over his greying hair, covering his ears before tying it in place. Likewise, I tug down on my beanie and check my phone for messages.

I should call my parents to make sure they're alright, however, because they're like omniscient beings—impossible to hide anything from—I don't want to worry them. Instead, I send Wynter a quick message asking her to get in touch with them to make sure everything is okay.

Still on his call, Tom has his back to us while he speaks in hushed whispers. Even when pacing, he's calm and measured as he strides from one side of the hallway to the other. I'm yet to see him flustered or stressed.

Perhaps he's not capable of either.

With his minute almost up, I shift my weight from one foot to another, eager to get moving.

"That was the call I promised you," Tom says, rejoining us moments later. "Detectives are being assigned as we speak and they'll send someone out to talk with the couple who run the off-licence. Suzy's description is being sent to all patrol cars presently out searching for Malden. They're looking for her, Ella."

I nod my acknowledgement. "Good. Thanks for doing that."

Although I'm grateful, it doesn't seem nearly enough when I think of the danger my friend might be facing.

"You know, this may be your last chance to do the sensible thing. Why not stay here while I go talk to these people and I'll update you on any news?" Tom says, offering me his home as a sanctuary.

"Thanks, but that's not happening," I say with such conviction, it invokes no further discussion on the topic. "Winston, tell us about your friends. You say they're dangerous—how?"

"They call themselves the *Steep Street Vipers*. Violent bunch. Cross them and it's a visit to the hospital. The intensive care sort of visit," he says with a shudder and tugging his coat lapels up to his chin. "The person we need to speak with is called Gunner. He's been in and out of prison since a lad—not particularly high up on the food chain, but he's got solid connections on the inside. That's like currency in their world." He rubs his thumb over his fingertips in the universal money sign. "It gives him a position of power and influence over the younger members groomed by the gang. If anyone knows the word on Malden, it'll be Gunner. Guaranteed."

"How can you be sure he'll agree to speak with us?" I say, concerned we'll waste precious time if this gang member refuses to talk.

"I help them out from time to time, you know? Nothing bad. Occasionally, I'll be their eyes and ears when a turf war is underway. They shouldn't harass you if you're with me, but I can't make any promises."

"Understood." I try not to show how nervous I am and resist the urge to wipe my clammy palms.

"This gang, the Steep Street Vipers, are they behind this morning's attack on the police convoy?" Tom says.

"Wouldn't surprise me." Winston shrugs. "There's no question they have the aptitude for that level of violence."

"At least we know what we're letting ourselves in for, so let's get moving," I say, aware the clock is ticking.

··········

Winston is true to his word. After fifteen minutes of weaving in and out of empty side streets and alleyways, we pass under the viaduct on Hallow Avenue, and from there onto Steep Street; a bleak and dingy part of town, and not only because of the storm.

Most have no business being in a place like this.

Groups of homeless people huddle around fires burning in metal braziers as they shelter in an underpass. The flames light up the crumbling walls covered in graffiti as the wind howls around them, not quite penetrating their refuge. The fires burn steady, with the occasional intense gust catching at the flames to send a torrent of sparks flurrying into the air.

As we approach, I sense their wary eyes on us and for the first time, realise just how much is at stake for Winston.

This may well be where he sleeps, and if he's violated some sort of unspoken street code by bringing us here, then there's every chance they'll cast him out.

Guilt eats at my conscience, for until now I've never stopped to consider the price helping us might cost him.

Once we reach the entrance to the underpass, we duck inside out of the wind. There's an eerie quiet despite the rumbles of the storm and the torrent of rain pummelling at the concrete outside. At least three or four huddled shapes gather around each brazier. Nobody speaks, but neither do they look away. As I take in the scene, the smell of burning wood crackling in the flames nudges something at the back of my mind. Whatever memory is lurking will have to wait—this is no time for nostalgia.

"Is it safe to be here?" I ask in a hushed whisper, feeling like a deer caught in headlights. So far removed is this environment from my comfort zone of anonymity.

"Relax, nobody in here will harm you—it's not them you need to worry about. Follow me."

Tom and I fall into line behind Winston and we slowly pick our way past the various huddled groups; some standing while others sit leaning against the tunnel walls, their legs protruding out from under faded blankets. As we skirt around the discarded debris littering the ground, it provides a welcome distraction away from all the eyes following our progress.

The further into the underpass we go, the more I'm relieved that Tom is only a couple of steps behind me—even though I'd never admit that to him. There are more homeless here than I first thought. Shapes appear like shadow puppets moving inside tents, whilst others huddle in sleeping bags on a bed of flattened cardboard.

It's a world far removed from the one we just left.

A few of them watch us with the glazed look of the drugged or drunk, swaying to their own body's tune. Others are barely older than Wynter and I shudder as I picture her in this setting, vulnerable to who knows what type of predator. This is easily the sort of place she could have ended up, if she hadn't chosen my doorway to shelter in that day.

It doesn't bear thinking about.

As we near the far end of the underpass, Winston motions for Tom and me to wait. Alone, he moves forward to speak with a group of youngsters who stand around smoking and laughing as they mess around on their phones.

They're no older than school kids, except these youths have a menacing presence about them—the sort that makes people cross the street to avoid.

"We're here to see Gunner. Be a good lad and let him know," Winston says to one of the taller boys.

He turns his shaven head. Angry looking acne, along with a ridiculous fuzz-like beard, covers his face. No longer a boy, but not quite a man; it means he has something to prove, and that makes me nervous. I flinch as the adolescent steps forward and stares with open hostility.

Without warning, he powers a fist in an uppercut motion, catching Winston in the stomach. He doubles over as the wind is knocked out of him, prompting us to lurch forward in his defence. Before Tom and I can reach him, Winston looks up and holds out a hand for us to stay back. Still fighting for breath, I watch as he raises himself upright, checks Jango is unharmed, then smiles at the youth.

"Run along now, lad. You've had your fun. Tell Gunner the adults in the room want to talk."

The boy's cocky smile slips from his face as the other gang members laugh. He hesitates before sloping off into the howling wind and vanishes behind the curtain of rain.

Tom and I wait in silence, unsure of what happens next—my knowledge of gang etiquette is non-existent. Will Gunner summon us? Or will he return here with Fuzz Boy? Nobody speaks or moves as we wait inside the edge of the tunnel for word of our arrival to reach Gunner. On tenterhooks but trying not to show it, all eyes are on us.

Without question, this is the most uncomfortable wait of my life. So much for anonymity; that concept is rapidly becoming a thing of the past.

When Fuzz Boy finally appears back at the entrance, he's out of breath and his shaven head glistens with rain that drips onto his face. The bomber jacket, with a red snake coiled on the back, portrays the gangster persona, but is entirely inappropriate for the current deluge of rain.

He motions with an upward thrust of his fuzzy chin for us to follow him before he slips back out of the tunnel again.

There are no pleasantries here.

I look to Winston for some sort of sign that following Fuzz Boy is a good idea, and not an extremely bad one.

"Gunner's agreed to meet. Follow me and don't say or do anything until I've spoken with him first," he says with a solemn expression.

# THE GRAYSTONE KILLINGS

I steel myself for whatever we're about to face and surreptitiously feel inside my pocket for the knife from my father, the weight of it reassuring in my hand.

All the same, I hope we won't need it.

# Chapter Eighteen

Fuzz Boy takes us through what looks like an abandoned industrial estate, its buildings unoccupied and boarded-up. It's a desolate territory that only serves to heighten my fears for Suzy.

We crunch our way across crumbling slabs of concrete strewn with broken glass, the knee-high weeds growing between the cracks bent flat from the wind. Heads down, we skirt around the enormous rain puddles that have formed on the uneven surface.

To imagine Suzy being held in a place like this is almost unbearable.

After a couple of minutes, we stop at what appears to be an old office block surrounded by disused factory buildings. Fuzz Boy ducks between two broken doors that serve as an entrance, one of which hangs off its hinges and rests against the doorframe.

I grab Winston's arm.

"What if it's a trap?" I say in an urgent whisper.

"It's the gang's hideout. You want to see Gunner? This is where he'll be. Stay close."

# THE GRAYSTONE KILLINGS

We follow Winston, sidestepping around the door into a derelict corridor. The building is in a stark state of abandonment, with plaster crumbling from the walls and the constant splat of rain coming through the roof. With no electricity, the corridor is lit by lanterns spaced every few hundred metres on the floor. They give off a lacklustre glow that quickly fades into the shadows, and I shiver involuntarily—I can almost feel the damp creeping into my bones, the musty smell flaring my nostrils in protest. Coupled with the noise of the storm howling through the boarded-up windows, it gives the place a gloomy, sinister feeling that I'm struggling to shake off.

Corridors like this probably appear in dozens of horror movies. Presumably with the same unsuspecting group of soon-to-be-killed-by-the-madman victims, unwittingly walking to their deaths...

I squeeze my eyelids shut for a second.

*Shit, I need to get a grip!*

When my step falters, Tom's hand shoots out from beside me, taking a firm hold of my elbow. The action is unexpected but reassuring and I imagine this hand pulling Suzy into his muscular arms; her face looking up at him with adoration—and then I picture his baby daughter's tiny, chubby fist closing around his fingers.

*Bastard.*

Despite wanting to break every bone in his hand for lying to my friend, I don't shrug away from his touch. This Corridor of Doom is creeping me out, and I'm grateful for the comforting pressure on my arm. Without question, this is no place for a person with anxiety issues. What the hell was I thinking?

"You okay?" Tom whispers, leaning into me.

"Fine. The opulence is a little overwhelming but—"

He flashes me a grin.

My composure restored, we turn into what was once an open office space. With the previous occupants long gone, there are desks and cabinets stacked in a corner, along with the rest of the abandoned office equipment. A sofa that's seen better days now takes up most of the remaining space. Dark stains ruin the grey carpet tiles that once smartly covered the floor. Many of the squares are missing, revealing the concrete floor beneath where discarded cigarette butts have been ground flat. At the far end of the office is an upside-down crate with a small television balanced upon it, powered by a bright yellow generator that could be mistaken for a toolbox. I briefly wonder whose car they syphoned of fuel to power the set.

"Boss," Fuzz Boy says to the man on the sofa as he thrusts his chin in our direction. "I bring'd 'em, mahn, like you said. Whacha wanna do wif 'em?"

Two women and a man sit staring at the television screen. They make no effort to acknowledge our presence. The women appear to be high on drugs and short on clothing. The man—sandwiched between them—is in his mid-twenties, and has a similarly shaven head as our chaperone, except for a slick strip of dark hair running from his hairline to his crown. His face is a mishmash of scars, pockmarks and tattoos. To complete the gangster image, he has a pencil-thin moustache and facial hair trailing his jawline.

After tonight, I hope never to see this face again.

In one hand is a can of beer, whilst the other balances a sickly sweet smelling joint between yellow stained fingers. He wears the same style bomber jacket as Fuzz Boy, presumably with a snake embossed on the back.

I don't care much for snakes—not that our paths have reason to cross. As such, I wouldn't want a two metre reptile sprayed onto my sitting room wall.

This gang, however, thought it would be a good idea.

Above the decorative serpent is a banner that reads:

STEEP STREET VIPERS

If the intention of the giant, tightly coiled graffitied snake, drawn in a strike position around a severed human head, is to intimidate visitors, then job well done, Vipers.

Winston steps forward, but offers no form of greeting. Eyes lowered to the carpet, I follow his lead and try not to stare at the man on the sofa or the grotesque painting of the apex predator. Instead, I focus on staying calm and controlling my breathing as I scan the room.

The corner of a crate catches my eye. Tucked close against the side of the sofa, it's difficult to distinguish the contents in this low light, but appears to hold a variety of wooden bats and metal bars...

*Wait—are those weapons?*

*Fucking hell!*

*I'm to be bludgeoned to death in a shitty squat by skinheads with a predilection for snakes?*

The man with the mishmash face looks over at us before I can catch Tom's attention.

"Hey, mahn, good t'see you, Winston. Whasup, mahn? You lookin' for trouble, bringing posh pussy here, innit?" He pronounces trouble *trou-bow* and I feel my face screw up with the effort of deciphering his words.

In one fluid movement, he propels his lanky frame off the sofa and, with an exaggerated swagger, he circles the room towards us. The two women barely stir, their blank gazes remaining on the screen.

"You wanna see what a real mahn can do, bitch?" Gunner says, cupping his crotch, and I watch, horrified, as his dick grows hard under his jeans.

Were my stomach not empty of food, I'd likely be throwing up in my mouth right about now.

Winston fixes Gunner with a meaningful look. "They're here to talk, lad, that's all. They're no threat to you."

"Whasup, toff, you wanna a favah from Gunner, innit? How about I squirt that dolly face instead?" he says in a goading manner as he circles Tom.

I don't know what he means by *squirt*, but I can hazard a guess it involves some sort of acid, and from the look of his own face, I'd say it's already happened there at least twice.

Tom remains stoic beside me, refusing to respond to the intimidation. I'm convinced he can hear my knees knocking from where he stands next to me.

On reflection, perhaps we should have listened to Winston. This was a stupid and dangerous stunt. We don't belong in this world.

As I'm about to lean over to Tom to suggest we get the hell out of here, Winston steps forward and he and Gunner pull each other into a man-hug worthy of long-lost brothers.

"Good t'see you, mahn, good t'see you."

"You too, Gunner. They're looking for a friend of theirs," he tells him, nodding briefly in our direction. "She went missing a few hours ago. A model, kinda a big deal. D'you hear anything? Might be connected to that prisoner who escaped today. Word on the pave is that he's targeting this lady and her friend—don't s'pose you can tell us why?"

Gunner crooks his finger and beckons me to him. My stomach drops to the floor with a sickening plunge as I force my trembling foot to take a step forward.

Before I can go any further, Tom shoots a hand out to stop me. With a quick sideways glance, I nod to let him know I can handle this.

I have to—for Suzy's sake.

After a brief hesitation, he reluctantly lets go of my arm and I inch towards Gunner on tremulous legs.

Only mere steps away from the man who could hold the answers to finding my friend, I stand straight and look him directly in the eye with as much confidence as I can muster. When I stare into his restricted pupils, I notice they're not quite pin-points, but not far off. Hard drugs will do that. His breath smells of alcohol and weed—a nauseating combination—but I hold my ground.

Gunner slowly eyes me up and down and then circles me like a predatory wolf about to ambush its prey.

I swallow hard.

"Vic's aft-ha money," he finally says. "Old money. You gotta rich mummy or daddy, Posh Pussy?"

*Ugh, dangerous and a creep!*

Not trusting my voice, I give a shake of my head as my mind races to make sense of this information.

Suzy's done well for herself, but neither of us comes from *old* money. My father's a professor at the Imperial College, and as anyone will tell you, teaching is more of a calling than for any monetary rewards, so my parents are definitely not wealthy. As for Suzy's folks; nice house, a nice car, good pensions. And that's about it. No old money.

Unless I've got it all wrong and Victor Malden isn't the person behind what's been happening today...

"Dude's playin' this one close, mahn," Gunner says, interspersing my thoughts. "All I know is he's going after a rich family, innit."

"No, you're wrong!" I shock myself as the words fall out of my mouth.

*What am I thinking?*

*Obviously I'm not, because I'm arguing in a snake pit with a fucking Viper!*

*Fucking Christ! Why can't I just shut my big mouth?*

But it seems that particular ability is beyond me—because even more words tumble from my lips.

Apparently, I have no concept of self preservation.

"This is about me," I say with surprise assertiveness. "He came looking for me today—not my parents. I'm not rich, but I can pay you. Five-hundred pounds, right now, to tell me where my friend is—"

Before I can congratulate myself on having faced up to this scar-faced, coke-head thug, I register a movement in my peripheral vision.

Winston—backing away.

*Fuck.*

*That can't be good...*

# Chapter Nineteen

Gunner takes a step closer, stops, and smiles, tilting his head. Eyes with their tiny pupils bore into me.

Both menacing and disturbing in equal measure.

A gold dental grill across his bottom teeth glints in the poor light, reminding me of a Bond villain. My mouth turns dry as my newfound confidence flounders under his glare.

*Definitely not good.*

*Shit.*

He takes another step closer and despite being terrified of dying at the hands of this brute; I recognise the intimidation tactics for what they are.

If I'm to convince him to help us, I can't let him know I'm so petrified that I will never again shut my eyes without seeing his hideous face. He's our only lead to finding Suzy. I prepare to brace myself for whatever confrontation is coming my way.

Without warning, his hand shoots up and grabs my left breast, latching onto me like a limpet to a rock. When I seize hold of his wrist, it only spurs him to tighten his grip. Unbelievable white-hot pain explodes in my chest.

Determined to stand my ground, I shoot him a death-glare and curl my fingers even tighter around his wrist. The return pressure brings a wave of stinging tears to my eyes. Through gritted teeth, I inhale sharply and resist the counter-attack I want to inflict on this creep.

Before I introduce him to a whole new world of pain, I first need to find out what he knows about Malden.

Gunner thrusts his face inches from mine and hisses in a snake-like rasp, "I'll let you suck my dick for a monkey, Posh Pussy. Make it a 'G' and I'll fuck you ov-ah one of those tables." He laughs, tilting his head towards the stack of office furniture, his repulsive face so close it's almost touching mine.

Just the sneer on his face is enough to make me want to gag, even before his pungent and overpowering breath wafts under my nose.

"What is it you want?" I say, the steel in my voice disguising my pain and disgust.

"I told you, innit."

And even though it really shouldn't be possible for him to lean any closer, to my horror, his tongue slithers out from between his lips as he lunges forward to lick my face. Spittle clings to the corner of his mouth and I fight back the urge to be sick.

"Enough!" I hear Tom shout, and for the second time since meeting him, I absolutely fucking agree with what he's saying.

This is a step too far.

Gunner mistakingly thinks my hand around his wrist is a desperate reflex on my part—it isn't.

By underestimating my capability, it's about to cost him dearly.

One second he's trying to slobber my cheek whilst crushing my left breast, and the next, my shoulder thrusts hard into his extended hand until he becomes an extension of my own body. When I turn, he has no choice but to turn with me, sending him off balance.

With his arm now locked in an extended outstretch, I use my hand to force it to bend at the elbow, bringing him swiftly to his knees.

He's on the floor within three seconds, with a fleeting look of bewilderment before his features scrunch up in agony.

"Never lay a hand on me again or I'll break every bone in your fucking fingers," I say, spitting the words with contempt close to his ear.

Aware of the danger I've put us all in, I immediately scan the room for threats. But not before the sound of heavy footsteps reaches us. Three gang members, all with shaven heads and mean looking, stand in the doorway wielding weapons and blocking our exit.

This really isn't going as well as we hoped.

Further commotion from outside the room and another two thugs appear. With no windows and no means of alternative exit, we're trapped. Still keeping a firm grip on Gunner, I glance over at Winston before my eyes dart to Tom, hoping he has a plan that doesn't involve us being beaten to a pulp by a frenzied gang.

When Tom gives me a reassuring nod, so imperceptible I can't be sure I didn't imagine it, I act on his encouragement and increase the pressure on Gunner's arm as he kneels in front of me, grunting. Since the likelihood of talking our way out of this situation is next to none, he's now the only leverage we have.

How did I screw this up so badly? My offer of five-hundred pounds for information was a flagrant insult. What was I thinking? I offered them fucking pocket change.

*Stupid, stupid, stupid.*

Aware that I need to fix this before my mistake gets us all killed, I lean into Gunner and say, "I'm going to release your arm now. First, though, I need you to call off your attack dogs."

Although it will feel like I'm breaking his limb, other than an uncomfortable stiffness tomorrow, he'll walk away from the armlock without injury. But he's not to know that.

"Fuck you, bitch," he says, spitting with rage. "Vipes, you wanna teach these arseholes a fucking lesson, innit!"

*Shit! What just happened? Somehow, I've made things even worse!*

On his say, the three men blocking the doorway advance towards us.

In stunned silence, I watch as Tom spins and swings an extended leg far above the height of his shoulder. The side of his shoe slices the air with such momentum it makes a snapping noise as it finds its target—the shaven head of one of the men. He slumps to the floor, out cold.

A second man lunges forward with a flash of metal as he jabs a blade maliciously towards Tom.

"Tom! Watch—"

I start to shout a warning, but before I can get the words out, he already blocks the attack with his forearm as his knee makes contact with his attacker's stomach. A high kick aimed at the side of the man's head renders him unconscious in a heap on the floor.

When the third man makes a lunge with his knife at Tom's chest, he's too slow for the kick that catches his wrist, sending his weapon spinning harmlessly onto the floor. The snapping sound of bone startles him, and his eyes shoot open with horror.

He looks down at the hand that, seconds ago, wielded a blade. At the sight of bloody bone piercing through the flesh, his chin drops, leaving his face slack and pale. He falls to the floor, cradling his wrist—it doesn't need a medical professional to see that it's badly broken.

Even though I don't entirely trust Tom, for now I'm one hundred percent rooting for the guy. He's just saved us from a near-death-by-gang-slaying.

Two further gang members hover by the doorway. The nearest, a woman in her early twenties, has short blonde hair that hangs longer on one side. Her lips are pressed into a thin snarl that effectively robs her of her otherwise pretty features. She glances round the room, scanning for backup.

Quickly realising she's no match for Tom, she and her companion—a large heavyset man with muscles bulging from under a grey t-shirt—back away.

They've only taken a few steps when they stop, and with a smug look on the girl's face, she deliberately looks past Tom to rest her hate-filled gaze on me.

And then she smiles.

Too late, I hear a soft click behind me.

# Chapter Twenty

A teenage girl stands in my peripheral vision. No more than around fourteen or fifteen years old. Her blonde hair is twisted high in a bun on top of her head, with dyed pink tendrils falling down around her face. Her large hoop earrings sway, catching the light.

In her hand is a gun, pointing to the side of my head.

Behind her is an open door, positioned strategically where the coiled tail of the graffiti snake should be—the artwork having concealed the exit perfectly. The girl must have slipped through while I was distracted.

I really am off my game today.

"Check mate, innit. My girl cockin' on ya, Posh Pussy," says Gunner, slapping a thigh with his free hand and laughing.

And although I struggle to make out his words, I understand the gun pressed to my head well enough.

"Okay, let's all calm down," says Tom, raising his hands. Admittedly, he's not looking so sure of the situation as he did a moment ago.

The girl shoves the weapon more forcibly against my skull, but I have no intention of releasing Gunner's arm—gun or no gun—I'm not going down without a fight. Fear washes over me in waves and I tighten my grip on Gunner's locked wrist.

"Nobody needs to get hurt here tonight," Tom says in a commanding voice, befitting of a brutal boardroom. "We didn't come here for this. All we're looking for is information and we're prepared to pay—a substantial sum. Lower your gun and we can talk business."

Gunner looks from Tom to the three men still lying unconscious around him.

"You got some fucking balls mah-mahn, I'll give you that," he says, barely disguising the admiration in his voice. "Yo, Rach, put the mo-thah fucking gun down. And you let go my fucking arm."

The pressure of the cold metal barrel falls away and Tom nods for me to release Gunner. The second my hand slips from his wrist, he jumps up from his kneeling position.

"Okay," says Tom. "Now that we're all friends again, let's see if we can discuss agreeable terms in exchange for information..."

"I ain't ever fink on no mahn." Gunner looks Tom up and down. "But I like your style, innit—mo-thah fucking sticky, mahn. Fifty 'G's' and we talk."

"Wait—fifty-thousand pounds?" It's a lot of money, and although I can most likely raise the cash, it will take a few days—time we don't have. Still, this is good news; it means he must be in possession of information worth trading. "You know Malden, then?" I ask, with a renewed sense of hope.

"Yeah, I know him. We crossed paths in the cooler."

"Deal," says Tom, before Gunner can consider asking for more money. "We'll give you half now and the other half if your intel proves accurate. Take it or leave it. We have other sources—" He delivers the words so convincingly that even I almost believe him. He swings off his backpack and, counting out ten neat stacks of banknotes, he offers the thick, brick-like wad of money to the blonde-haired girl, saying, "Twenty-five thousand cash. I'll give our mutual colleague here the other half when we have our friend back." Tom tilts his head towards Winston.

Gunner considers the cash with narrow eyes and nods once. With the exchange complete, I blow out a heavy breath.

"Malden's missis runs a pub. Divorced, innit, after he got his stretch—feds were mo-thah fucking zanged!" Gunner laughs, his gold grill glinting.

"Zanged?" Tom asks.

"Mugged off, innit. Duped. She made a lot of noise about ditching him, kept her distance, right? Fucking twanged the dumb fed bastards and fell right off their radar. Malden got life, so he had to skate, mahn, no way was he walking out of there. Now him and his missis gonna breeze off." He waves a wad of Tom's cash in front of us. "You need a lotta gwop to disappear, innit—that's what Malden's after. No other reason he's fishing."

"I already told you—my parents aren't wealthy. Neither are Suzy's."

"Where would he hide?" Tom asks.

"Malden's not hiding, mahn. He's hunting, innit. Fishing for you, Posh Pussy, and there ain't nowhere safe. Vic's a ruthless bastard. Find his missus. Ain't no othah way you'll get to him."

"You say they're planning a high money job, then disappearing? Where to?" Tom says.

Gunner slaps his thigh, laughing.

"Nah, ain't nobody knows that, innit," he says, shaking his head. "Now fuck off outta here, Pretty Boy. And don't forget—twenty-five 'Gs'. You owe me, mahn."

"You'll get the money. One more thing. The name of the pub…?"

"The Snake Pit." Gunner throws his head back in laughter as he dismisses us, turning to drop back onto the sofa, where he sandwiches himself once again between the two women. He sticks his tongue down the throat of one while his hand slithers up the skirt of the other, all the time watching us. Neither woman responds in their drug induced state.

Apparently, that's our cue to leave—before I throw up over the already stained carpet tiles.

Somehow, I keep it together long enough to step over the men on the floor, ignoring their muffled grunts as they regain consciousness. As we make our way unchallenged back out into the Corridor of Doom, I double over and empty the meagre contents of my acidic stomach. Winston is immediately by my side, gently patting my back.

"Hey, you did good back there," Tom says, taking my arm and helping me upright.

"No, I didn't. I screwed up and put us all in danger."

I wipe at my mouth, still shaking but feeling better now the nausea has passed. The oppressiveness of Gunner's den releases its grip on my stomach.

Definitely a new low for me, to be standing here in this dank smelling corridor and feel nothing but relief as I spew my guts up.

"Don't beat yourself up," Tom says. "You assumed they'd play by the rules, but for these people, there are no rules. We're walking out of here with the information we came for. It's a good result."

"Where did you learn to fight like that? The way you tackled those men back there—"

"Life's unpredictable—doesn't harm to know how to handle yourself. Nothing showy. I keep it simple."

"And keep alive, huh?"

"Something like that, yes."

"Wow, the boardroom must be a jungle."

Tom shrugs, ignoring my sarcasm.

We start moving again, eager to be gone from this miserable and derelict place. At the exit, we pause for a series of claps of thunder to pass before stepping back outside into the storm, and I seize the opportunity to quiz Tom further about tonight's events.

"Can I ask you about something that's been bothering me?"

He gives me a sideways glance as he watches the rain lash across the concrete slabs. I take his silence as the affirmative.

"Why didn't you go looking for Suzy when she failed to turn up tonight?"

He gives me a long, intense look. If we're to rely on each other, I need Tom to give me something I can make sense of, anything that will help me trust him. Despite just spending fifty-thousand pounds on the name of a pub, something still feels off. It's frustrating the hell out of me that I can't read him as I do others.

"I'm here now. That's what's important. So let's go find this pub," Tom says, pulling his collar up and striding out into the rain.

# Chapter Twenty-One

We follow Winston's labyrinth of shortcuts and little known alleyways until we reach the *Snake Pit*, tucked away at the end of an old cobbled street in Covent Garden.

The historic streets are narrow and enclosed by tall Georgian buildings, giving us momentary respite from the strong winds and lashing rain. There are multi-coloured bollards spaced along the edge of the pavement, but even these cannot bring cheer to this drab night.

On turning a corner, we come to a halt opposite a traditional pub frontage painted a blood red. Above the doors is a sign depicting a coat of arms with a snake at its centre. It swings recklessly in the wind, screeching in protest against its metal frame. A warm, inviting light radiates from the triple pane windows, allowing us to see the throng of people inside. Despite the weather warning in place, logic dictates that there are worse places to ride out a storm.

I am not one of those people.

At the sight of the busy pub, I can't help but grimace at the idea of setting foot inside. Suzy has tried for years to drag me along to one, and now she's finally succeeded—only not in the way we ever imagined.

My anxiety rears its head at the prospect of having to walk through the double doors, into an enclosed space filled with the constant chatter of conversations being shouted over loud music and resonating laughter. The mere notion of it rattles my senses—I'm barely holding it together as it is.

"We should check around back, see if there's a way inside to search the upper floor," I say, planning our next move as we huddle close to be heard over the storm.

Tom shakes his head. "Better if you go in the front and cause a distraction while I sneak in the back. Also, see what you can find out from Malden's wife. With any luck, she'll let something slip. Maybe try to keep her in the bar talking while I search upstairs."

"Pubs aren't my thing," I say, staring at the red doors and feeling a sheen of sweat on my neck. "Why don't you do the distracting and I'll look upstairs?"

"Because the police will have been crawling the premises all day, so she's more likely to see me as a threat. And besides, Suzy told me you can read people like a book. That makes you the best person to speak with her."

"But—"

"Aside from that," he says, cutting me off, "we can't put you in any unnecessary danger. It seems unlikely Malden will risk coming here, but you should stay where there are plenty of witnesses, just in case."

"Fine, we'll do it your way. But don't say I didn't warn you... me and pubs do not go together. If I have a panic attack—"

"Stay focused on the task, not the surroundings, and you'll be fine. Look for any clues that tell us when they're planning to leave, because if Malden's using Suzy as some sort of leverage, my guess is they'll have to make their move soon. The answers are in that pub, Ella. We just have to find them."

"Alright, I'll try," I say, exhaling hard and puffing out my cheeks. "Winston, can you stay here and keep a watch for anyone leaving the pub? If we spook Malden's wife, she might decide to run."

Tom pulls out a mobile from his pocket and hands it to Winston. "This has one number stored. Call it if you need to raise the alarm. Tell the person who answers where we are and they'll do the rest."

Although I want to ask who the telephone number belongs to, I realise there's no point. Tom is as mysterious as he is secretive, and I'm struggling to figure out who this man is that Suzy's got herself involved with. We have a backup plan. That's all I need to know—for now.

After taking a moment to compose myself, I head towards the pub's red doors while Tom vanishes into the shadows down the side of the building. With one last glance over my shoulder at Winston, I try to give him a reassuring smile, but it feels more like a nervous tic on my face.

When I reach the wooden doors, I place my hands around the brass handles and take a deep breath. Just as I prepare to swing them open, a deafening clap of thunder crashes above me, and I bolt backwards with a yelp.

Shit!

*I'm so wound up, I'd jump at the sound of someone cracking a knuckle.*

As a flash of lightning streaks across the turbulent clouds, I grip the handles to try again, pulling open the doors and stepping over the threshold of the pub—straight into my worst nightmare.

······•·····

The noise of incessant chatter hits me first. How does anyone hold a conversation in this chaos? Even the sound of the storm struggles to be heard in here. A constant beat of music is playing in the background, but it's impossible to make out the tune as it vibrates through the wooden floorboards with a continuous *boom, boom, boom*. Thick air fills my lungs, its smell heavy with a mix of alcohol, perfumes and sweat. It makes me want to burst open the windows and fumigate the place.

Already my senses are becoming overwhelmed—it's hard to believe people come to places like this for fun.

I weave between the round tables designed to accommodate four people, many with several more revellers squeezed around them, and at least twice as many drinks cluttering their tabletops. A glossy black wooden bar runs along the length of the pub, and with effort, I push through the surrounding crowd, slipping into a slither of a gap.

There are four bartenders working fast-paced behind the bar, all wearing black vest tops; the men muscular and the women full-breasted. I stand taller, eager to speak with the nearest bartender despite being surrounded by patrons waving empty glasses and folded banknotes. I already hate this place.

Determined for Suzy's sake to push on with the task at hand, I pull out a note from my back pocket and wave it in front of me. After a few minutes, one of the muscular men stops opposite me.

"What can I get you?"

"Whiskey, please."

He deftly flips a glass from the shelf behind him and sets it on the counter in front of me. While he's pouring out a measure of the dark liquid, I pull up a photo of Suzy on my phone and show it to him.

"My friend is missing. Can you tell me if you recognise her?"

The barman glances at the screen and shakes his head.

"Would it be okay to show the photo around the pub? Someone might remember seeing her."

"Sure. Go for it."

I hand over my money as he slides the glass towards me.

"Thanks. Any chance I could have a quick word with the owner, too? It'll only take a moment." When he raises an eyebrow, I improvise. "Um, posters, you know, that sort of thing? It would mean a lot."

I smile and he looks back at me like I'm deranged.

"Wait here."

He says something to the bartender next to him and she rolls her eyes before he disappears out through a beaded curtain at the other end of the bar.

While I wait, my ears tune in on Malden's name being mentioned over the cacophony of voices. I realise the three men standing behind me are talking about his escape, and by focusing on their words, I commit everything else to background noise and try to tune into their conversation. *So that's how it works...*

"C'mon, mate, it had to be a professional job. The way they just disappeared like that. They were gone before the cops even knew what hit them! Fuck me, did you feel the blast of that rocket launcher?"

"Yeah, mate, woke us up. Maddy's been watching the news all day, says she's not leaving the flat until they have the bastard back behind bars. Suits me—I get a night out and she can't bend my ear about it." Raucous laughter follows.

"Do you think his missus knows where he is?"

"Nah, they're divorced, mate."

One of them belches. More laughter.

"Yeah, she dropped him faster than Mourinho can bin off his players."

"You reckon she knew about him, though? You know, like, what he was doing to those women? Relationships can be fucked up that way."

"You mean covering for him? Nah, mate, they'd have hauled her arse to prison. She kept well clear of it. Can't say I blame her for being made a fool of and not knowing; he was a likeable bastard, smooth as they come."

"Sounds like you were shagging him, mate."

"Piss off, you wanker." Back slapping and another bellow of laughter.

"I heard he had help. In prison, like. He got in with this big shot and next thing you know, he's out on the streets."

"Who's that, then?"

"No idea, mate. Some sicko prick still pulling strings from the inside of a cell, no doubt."

"Wankers. We should bring back the death penalty."

"Fucking holiday camp, that's what prisons are..."

I tune their voices out again.

It would seem local gossip ties in with Gunner's intel; Malden's wife did divorce him and she's kept her distance since the arrest.

Could she really be trying to divert police attention away while they flee the country together? If the rumours are correct, Malden had help on both the inside and out, but what do they gain from aiding his escape? Is this about more than just money?

I gulp back the whiskey, flinching at the burning sensation, and turn to face the noisy rabble in the pub.

*Time to cause a distraction.*

*Shit. I wish I'd asked for a double.*

# Chapter Twenty-Two

After a quick scan of the pub, I spot the ideal target. A group of young men who appear to be students, their casual shirts hanging open over t-shirts and jeans, and drinking reckless amounts of alcohol.

*Perfect.*

They're well on the way to becoming lairy, so I make a beeline for their table and thrust my phone out towards them, sweeping the image around the group.

"This is my friend. If you could just look, perhaps one of you might remember seeing her?" I say, hollering over their slurred conversation.

Seven sets of glassy eyes try to focus and track the screen.

"Wahey! She's fucking hot. Give her my number when you find her, love!"

"This is important, please—"

"Hey, isn't that the bird in the advert who rides the fucking horse? Fucking naked!"

"Bollocks, is that chick naked! C'mon mate, she's wearing a dick-teasing thong."

"Yeah, I bet it's crotchless! That's one fucking hot pussy and gagging for it. She'd get it."

"That ass can ride this any day—"

And that's my cue.

When a glassy eyed, horny student grabs at his crotch, I swipe a near-full glass of larger off the table and pour it over his lap.

*One distraction, as requested. Make it count, Tom.*

In order to distance myself from the disturbance, I spin on my heels and weave my way back to the bar as bouncers converge on the table. A woman stands waiting behind a row of pumps, her forearm leaning across the antique ceramic handles. Hooded eyes focus on me as I approach, oozing their contempt.

Did she watch as I caused that scene?

I'm about to find out.

With a final push past the crowd towards her, I leave behind the students, arguing over their inevitable ejection from the premises. As I draw closer, it's difficult to ignore the hard edge to her features, making her appear older than her reported thirty-seven years. The brightly coloured bar lights give her a jovial look as her long, blonde strands take on the hues of a rainbow. I stare back at malevolent eyes that regard me through narrow slits.

This is no friendly welcome.

Her mouth turns down in what I imagine is a perpetual look of disdain.

"Hi, are you the pub owner? Mel Malden?" I attempt to smile past the glare. There's no question she's clocked the scene I caused with the students... thank God for the enormous wooden bar between us.

Mel slowly rises, straightening out her arms and resting her palms flat on the counter, face angled towards me. "It's Duke. Divorced. You are…?"

"Ella. I'm trying to find my friend. She's disappeared and your husband—*ex*-husband—may be involved. This is important, so please, is there anything you can tell me about where Victor is? Has he been in contact?"

"Every man and his dog are searching for Vic. You aren't the first to come in here asking after him."

"Unlike the others, I don't give a shit about your ex-husband's bid for freedom. All I want is to find my friend."

"I'll say it again—we're divorced. You're wasting your time."

*Oh, this woman is a liar, alright.*

"Then you don't know where I can find him?"

"No." She leans across the beer taps, face hovering over me as the whiff of cheap perfume catches in my throat. "Now leave and don't come back to my pub. I'm going to tell you what I told the police; I haven't seen Vic. So piss off or I'll have you thrown out. Understand?"

"Perfectly. Thank you for your time," I say, biting back the torrent of abuse I want to throw at her. How can anyone stand by a monster such as Malden?

Still needing to draw out the conversation and give Tom more time to search the rooms, I spin back to face her, hoping to catch her off-guard. "Tell me something, Mel. Did you know Victor was a rapist and a killer when you married him?"

The well-rehearsed, hardened expression slides from her face and a glimpse of disappointment shows through the facade.

So, he blindsided her—interesting!

Maybe I can work with this and appeal to the person she used to be, and not the person her husband's actions have since moulded her into becoming.

"He murdered five women. The press refers to him as a monster," I say, pushing her harder. "Yet you lived with him. You never had the slightest inkling of what he was doing?"

The accusation causes an almost imperceptible sagging of her shoulders, and if it weren't for the fact I'm watching her closely, I'd easily miss it. My guess is she's standing by the man who lied and broke every promise he ever made to her, and now the burden of this four-year pretence of a divorce has taken its toll. She's strong, there's no question of that, but there's a crack in her resolve and I aim to exploit it.

"Vic's not a monster."

"Then how do you describe a man who's raped seven women and taken the life of five others?"

The distance between us closes as Mel leans forward. Her stance becomes less confrontational, a scrawny arm hugging around her waist as the remaining confidence in her husband comes under scrutiny.

"I'd recognise if my husband was a killer. He's a gentle and kind man and we had a good life together. The jury got it wrong."

"If you truly believe that, then why get a divorce?"

"It's complicated." I raise an eyebrow and wait for her to elaborate. "I was angry. When the judge handed down a life sentence, I found myself with no husband and left to run this place—" She gestures with a tilt of her chin towards the bouncers, still dealing with the drunken students. "What was the point? He was never getting out."

"How did Victor react when you told him?"

"How do you think? He accused me of abandoning our marriage vows, of betraying him. I'm as good as dead to him. His letters told me as much."

"He wrote to you from prison?"

"For a while. At first he insisted on his innocence, that I'd be making a mistake to file for divorce, how he was going to prove he hadn't hurt those women. But, after a while, the notes stopped."

"And you showed these to the police?"

She nods. "Taken as evidence after the police searched the flat this morning. I tried to explain how the pub is the last place Vic will head for, but they weren't interested in listening to me."

"When did you last see your husband?"

"The day I went to the prison and told him I wanted a divorce."

"So there was a scene—" I mutter to myself. What better way to convince the authorities than a public display of their marriage breakdown? "And you divorced him and took over the running of this place?"

Her eyes harden towards me. "For someone who only wants to put posters up, you seem overly fascinated with my marital affairs. Who are you? Not police, not a journalist—"

"I only want to find my friend, nothing more," I tell her, holding my hands up to allay her suspicions. "I need to understand why he's targeting her."

"And I told you, I know nothing about your friend or where Vic is."

Armed with Gunner's intel, I know she's feeding me lies, but at the same time, she has me intrigued.

Why tolerate this conversation? She could have me thrown out of the pub any time she wants.

What if abducting Suzy was never part of the plan and Malden's gone off-script?

Mel wouldn't be talking unless my presence here had thrown her off kilter, and since Suzy's abduction isn't official yet, this could be the first she's hearing of it.

Has Malden promised her there'll be no more women, no more violence?

*Now might be a good time to prise open those cracks.*

"All I'm asking is that you please look at her picture again."

I hold out my phone with the photo of Suzy, her sparkling eyes and infectious smile filling the screen.

Mel reaches over the bar and takes the device from me, a guarded expression on her face. I watch her closely, waiting to see if she recognises Suzy as a match for Malden's particular tastes. Behind the self-control, I see a world of pain and broken trust. Is she resigning herself to the possibility that whatever pledge Malden made to her, he's already broken within hours of escaping? Whatever lies she tells herself to sleep at night isn't of my concern. The fact is, her husband will always be a dangerous predator, offering false promises and deceit in his wake. Mel hands me back the phone with a deep sigh.

"What's your friend's name?"

"Suzy. Suzy Sands. I believe your husband charmed his way into our apartment this evening. I don't know where he's taken her. She's disappeared, and I need to find her."

"You don't understand, do you?" she says, shaking her head. "Vic didn't just stroll out of a high security prison.

He knows people, he's connected. Go home and lock your door. There's nothing you can do to help your friend."

She looks past me and gives a subtle tilt of her chin. Two burly bouncers wreaking of musk aftershave and stale tobacco materialise on either side of me.

In one last act of defiance, I say, "It was good talking with you, Mel. I don't suppose we'll meet again now that your *husband* is out... so you take care."

Malden's wife bristles, her skin flushing with anger as she turns and leaves through the beaded curtains. With any luck, I've got her rattled, and when she slips up, making a mistake, I'll be right there waiting.

One bouncer grips my shoulder, his meaty fingers digging into my flesh, before I can shrug his hand away.

"Get off, *swellhead!*"

I throw a last, meaningful glance in Mel's parting direction. Her retreating shadow lingers behind the curtain, as the scowling bouncers take me by the arms and bundle me through the overcrowded pub.

*You're on your own now, Tom.*

I'm pushed through a side door into a frigid corridor with harsh lighting and bare walls. Rows of metal circular kegs line the aisle, forcing us to walk in single file. As we enter the no frills world of the employee, the warm ambiance of the pub quickly vanishes.

"You know this is entirely unnecessary. I was leaving anyway." The bouncer in front grunts but continues squeezing his hulking mass past the kegs.

Every few steps, I'm shoved by a jolt to my back until, with a last push, a door opens and I'm thrown out of the pub. I stumble into a narrow alley, momentum propelling me into the side of an enormous wheelie bin.

# THE GRAYSTONE KILLINGS

As I lurch forward, my face impacts with the metal handle of the bin. Severe, red hot pain explodes through my nose, blurring my vision and filling my ears with a high-pitched ringing.

The rain makes the old cobblestones slippery, and I stumble, trying to regain balance just as a sudden sharp pain to my side forces the air from my lungs. At least one bouncer has followed me outside and is intent on introducing a fist to my ribs...

Despite being dazed, the man is no match for me, and dropping into a crouch, I link an elbow and knee together before turning my body to deflect an incoming kick. Unscathed, I stand and stare into a set of surprised eyes. Mel must have instructed her hired gorillas to use enough brutality to ensure I stay away.

Before the bouncer can get another strike in, we hear a sound over the rain drumming on the cobblestones... the lilting tune of a shanty song growing louder.

*What the hell?*

I turn to see a tall figure emerging through the sheeting rain.

**"Soon may the Wellerman come—Hic!—to bring us sugar and tea and—Hic!—rum—da-da-da-da-da—"**

Winston staggers and sways through the alleyway towards us, singing at the top of his lungs while clutching the bottle swiped from Tom's bar. I glance back at the bouncer, who hesitates before deciding I'm not worth the effort. With a grunt, he steps back inside the pub, slamming the door shut behind him.

"Thanks," I say, shaking myself off and trying to catch a breath. "Great singing, by the way."

"Your friend didn't seem to think so," he says with a devilish grin. "You okay?"

"Yeah, I've had worse." I wipe the blood from my face and tilt my chin skywards, letting the rain wash the metallic taste from my lips. With tentative fingers, I explore my nose and ribs for broken bones. "We were just warming to each other. Any word from Tom yet?"

"Exited the premises around the same time you were being thrown out of here. He'll wait for us a few streets away, just in case the police are nearby. C'mon, I'll take you to him."

"Don't suppose you're going to give me a sip of that?" I gesture towards the bottle in his hand.

"Not a chance."

# Chapter Twenty-Three

Winston and I meet Tom in the piazza outside Covent Garden. Storm Ruby has emptied the normal bustling square of people, restricting the typical lively nightlife to indoor cafes and bars instead. Even the famous street performers have abandoned their regular patches in favour of staying dry and sheltered. The earthy-musty smell of the storm replaces the usual mouthwatering aroma wafting from the award-winning restaurants.

We catch sight of Tom in his black attire, leaning against one of the floodlit white stone pillars outside Saint Paul's Church. The building reminds me of a Roman Temple and although the stone facade looks to be the main entrance to the sanctuary, I'm familiar enough with this *actors' church* to appreciate that we're standing far-side to the entrance. It offers a quiet, sheltered spot and a chance to regroup.

As we approach, my pulse races as I notice Tom is sporting a smug grin; he's found something that can help us find Suzy! I break into a run, eager to hear what he has to say, but as I join him under the imposing pillars of the church, his smile slips.

"What happened? Are you okay?" He steps forward, reaching a hand out to my face. Instinctively, I pull back, protective of my throbbing nose. Although the bleeding has stopped, the pain is still very much persistent.

"I'm fine. Just superficial." Whilst I don't mean to snap, neither do I want Tom's concern. All I need from him is his help to find my friend. "How'd you get on? Did you discover anything that'll help us?"

The smug expression returns to his face, and he puffs out his chest. It seems this mysterious man displays emotion after all, even if it is only self-satisfaction.

"I did. But first, tell us, did you speak with Malden's wife?"

With a brief nod, I tell them what I uncovered. "Mel's reverted to her maiden name, maintaining the pretext she's left him. The impression I get is that she's hoping her leopard has changed his spots. She had no idea that Malden planned to abduct Suzy and was pretty pissed off about it. When we spoke, she appeared to be genuine."

"And Mel did that—" Tom stares at the injuries on my face.

"Nope. Wheelie bin."

He frowns, but doesn't push for further details. "Think she's going to make a run for it?"

"Definitely."

"Then it seems Gunner's intel is solid."

"Now you—what did you find out from the flat?"

"For starters, she really ought to review the pub security. Way too easy. Once inside, it took me a while, but I found what she's kept hidden from the police..."

A big grin spreads across his face, and I hold my breath in suspense. Has he discovered where Suzy's being held? My friend is the single most important person in my life, and the anguish from not knowing what's happened to her is almost unbearable.

Tom pulls a key out from his jacket pocket. It looks similar to an old primitive skeleton key, with black metal loops surrounding a flour-de-lis lily at its centre. I take the key from him and examine the weighty object. Larger than the palm of my hand, the design is vaguely familiar. It reminds me of the keys my parents used to have hanging in our hallway.

"What door does this open?" I ask.

"I'm hoping this one—" He holds up his phone to show me a photograph of a rustic cottage. "The cork-board in the kitchen contained photographs from holidays around the world. But this particular photograph looked out of place, not their usual luxury destination. No drinks with cocktail umbrellas, for starters. The key was taped to the back, then the photo hid under images of palm trees and beaches. Easy to miss."

"Hidden in plain sight. Clever. Where is this place? Did you get an address?" I say, my voice breathless with the adrenaline rush.

"I'm afraid not. For now, all we have is this photo of what we can assume is their intended meeting point before they escape the country."

"What makes you think they'll meet here?"

Tom swipes his phone to display an image of the back of the photograph. "This."

We lean in and stare at a series of numbers written in black ink.

### 51.261022, -0.2030000

Winston frowns before saying, "Looks like coordinates to me. Decimal longitude and latitude to be precise."

"Or... a date and time?" Tom says, grinning widely.

At first glance the numbers appear to be map coordinates, but on closer scrutiny the digits of the first number match today's date, and those of the second could easily represent a time. Less than two hours from now.

"If you're right, we don't have long before they're due to meet. " I say, voicing my concern. "There must be something here to indicate where the property is?"

"As far as coordinates go, the area is mostly farmland with a few surrounding properties. But no cottage. I've had the satellite images checked twice."

"So, what are you saying? We've got a key to a cottage without a location...?"

My premature exuberance extinguishes almost immediately. Winston takes the phone from him and studies the picture, his brows knitting together as he squints at the image.

"Not exactly," Tom says, his puffed chest visibly collapsing. "I've got people searching every property database for a match. It'll take time, but we'll get its location."

"But—but you could have left the key there. We could have followed her! What will Mel think now, when she finds the key's gone?"

Moments ago, I had dared to hope we were close to finding Suzy. Now it seems she's further away than ever. The cottage could be hundreds of miles from our home here in Kensington.

I realise that a part of me believed Suzy would still be nearby, within our reach. I'll never accept that I might never see her alive again. The mere thought causes my chest to restrict.

Why is this happening to us?

Without warning, my breath hitches and becomes erratic, quick gasps failing dismally to fill my lungs. Before I know what's going on, Tom settles his hands on my shoulders and gently forces me back against a pillar. When did he move so close? Somehow he's standing right in front of me, his steel grey coloured eyes searching my face intently.

"Ella, listen to me. Trust me. I will get the address, okay? Mel will think the key has fallen off, possibly picked up by the police, but with the photograph still in place, she won't suspect a thing. My guess is she's still going to make that meeting. The woman's too invested in Malden not to."

With enormous effort, I try to draw long, deeper breaths.

"I know, it's just—" Disappointment slams into me, catching my breath again. A wrecking-ball hurtling into a house of cards couldn't be more devastating than the situation we're now facing. "Suzy was never"—I draw a gulp —"she was never part of the plan. If Malden intends to kill her, he'll do so before meeting Mel. How long to find the cottage?"

"I have the best people on it. They're working as fast as—"

"I know where this is," Winston says, cutting Tom off as he hands back the phone.

"What?" Tom shakes his head incredulously. "How's that even possible?"

"Jango and I pass it on our walk. Sometimes it's good to get away from the hustle and bustle, right? This is on the Chess Valley walk that follows the River Chess, one of our favourite trails, as it happens. Jango here likes to jump in the chalk stream and upset the fishermen. Scares off their trout. I can take you to it."

At the mention of his name, the little dog whines and Winston scratches behind his ear to settle him again.

"Are you positive it's the same place? Hundreds of cottages like this one must exist up and down the country." Tom eyes Winston warily.

"There's a tree in the right-hand corner next to the wall. I've been watching that old oak die for the last six years. No-one has been near the property, either lived in or rented. Nobody tends to the garden."

Tom and I examine the photo more closely, zooming in on the screen.

I hadn't noticed the tree in the photograph before, but Winston's right. The oak is in obvious distress, with its crown thinned out and bare branches exposed. There's dark weeping patches where the bark has split. It makes it unmistakable, and a much needed break for us.

"This disease? How prevalent is it? It looks like animal claw marks on the trunk, as if the tree is bleeding." I shudder at the creepy image.

"It's called Acute Oak Decline. Not a disease, in fact. It's caused by poor environmental conditions and it's not so common I wouldn't recognise this oak. Those marks are stem bleeds, weeping cracks in the bark. That ancient oak was at least four-hundred years old before stress got the better of it. There's no question it's the same cottage."

"What are we waiting for? We need to get there! Now!" I throw my hands up expectantly, adrenaline pumping again. If I could fly, my feet would be off the ground already.

"I'll call for a car," says Tom. "You'll be able to show us the way?"

Winston nods. "Yes, but we won't need a car. Too isolated. It'll be quicker by Tube, then it's only a short distance by foot. Besides, I only know how to reach there by following the river."

"Tube it is," I say, not wanting to waste time debating. Winston's got us this far, and we'd be foolish not to trust his judgement now. "As a precaution, though, can you still get hold of that car, Tom?"

"Yes, I've got a driver," he says, stepping forward, eager to help.

"Since we don't know what we'll find when we arrive, have your car head to the vicinity of Chess Valley and wait for us to make contact. How far along the river is the cottage?" I say to Winston.

"Chesham end, so about an hour from here."

"Right, let's go. We can decide how we'll play this on the way."

# Chapter Twenty-Four

By the time we alight from the train at Chalfont and Latimer, the winds have noticeably calmed and we have what we hope is a bullet proof plan.

It has to be. Suzy can't afford for us to screw this up.

"How far from here?" I ask Winston as we make our way outside the quaint, one-hundred-and-forty-year-old station.

"Not long. About a mile. We'll head out towards Latimer House on the big country estate. I know a short-cut."

Before long, we've left the village behind us and squelch our way along the river's grass verges. Jambo, free of the confines of Winston's jacket, scuttles around in bushes, nose to the ground and tail wagging. With the clouds finally clearing, the autumnal Harvest moon lights our way as we follow the rush of the river, its banks swollen from the day's downpour.

"At least the storm has passed," I say to no-one in particular. "It's so still and quiet compared to an hour ago."

"Only because we're in the eye," replies Winston.

"What? But—but we'll be too exposed out here."

"Not if we hurry."

"Shit! Ruby's a big storm, so it's a big eye, right?" I ask hopefully, glancing up at the sky.

"Nope—in fact, the opposite is true," Tom says.

"Don't worry, we'll reach the cottage before she blows again," Winston says assuringly.

"Uh-huh," I mutter, not entirely convinced and picking up the pace even more.

In the city, we had buildings to shield us from the full force of Ruby's power. Out here in the middle of nowhere, with wind speeds reaching sixty miles per hour, it's not a scenario I relish.

Under normal circumstances, I would drink in the view of our surroundings. The scenic river is no doubt serene and soothing in the light of day, complete with thick green rushes and weeping willows forming arches over the water. Although I'm a city girl and prefer the bustle of the busy streets, it doesn't mean I can't appreciate the unspoilt beauty of nature.

All around us is the gentle rattling sound of heavy boughs knocking against each other in the calm breeze that, for the time being, replaces the strong winds. As we pass several uprooted trees, it's a stark reminder of how exposed we are.

The river gradually widens, and we catch our first glimpse of the imposing Latimer House in the distance. The estate is nestled on a hillside and surrounded by woodland. Ground lighting illuminates the red-brick of the Tudor style manor, resulting in a spectacular show of architecture against the inky sky.

"Quite a sight, isn't it?" Winston says, "It's a hotel now, grade two listed building." I fall into step beside him, welcoming the opportunity to catch my breath as we slow to take in the splendour of the old house. "The Cavendish family built it almost two hundred years ago when a fire destroyed the original manor. Later, the military used the mansion as headquarters during the second world war and then afterwards for training. The Irish Republican Army set off a bomb here one morning—no fatalities—but it's hard to imagine violence in such a peaceful setting, don't you think?"

"It really is," I say, finding it difficult to picture anything ripping through the serenity of this valley. Nevertheless, I may change my mind when Storm Ruby continues her path of destruction. "Let's keep moving."

"Not far now. We'll cut away from the river by those trees up ahead," he says, pointing towards a darkened copse to our right. "There's a path we can take that'll lead us straight to the cottage."

After picking up the pace once more, minutes later, we enter the copse and follow Winston through the trees. Our torches light the way now that the tangle of branches overhead block out the moonlight.

I can see why the pathway is not well trodden; in order to get to it, we have to climb over fallen trees with their dead, intertwined branches clawing at our clothes, then down into a ditch lined with ferns and brambles, followed by an ungainly clamber up the other side.

For our efforts, we're rewarded with a narrow passage through the trees, each one of us careful to aim our torches down at our feet, not wishing to announce our arrival to anyone. Once on the path, it's a flat and easy walk and we soon emerge at the edge of a clearing, with the moonlight once again lighting our way.

This is my first glimpse of the cottage. It appears abandoned and neglected, moss growing on the grey stones of its two-story walls. Two chimneys are on either side of the building, but these have crumbled into disrepair, with tiles missing from the slate roof. A section of the garden perimeter wall has collapsed, the stones lying in disarray. I can't decide whether the cottage is charming or sinister, being tucked away in this secluded corner of the valley, accessible only by a single overgrown dirt track.

"It doesn't look as if anyone's home," Tom says in a hushed whisper. "No sign of lights or movement."

"We should still approach with caution." I glance at our light beams and snap my torch off. "Winston, you circle around the clearing like we discussed and look for tyre tracks."

"Remember, if you see anything, call it through to me straight away," Tom says. "We're looking for signs that Malden has been here, or at the very least, was in the area. Check all the clearings for his car. It's likely with the police searching for him, he'll have made extra efforts to conceal any transport."

"And Winston? Please, stay safe. No heroics, okay?" I step forward and squeeze his hand, needing for this man—currently alone in the world—to know that I care what happens to him.

"Don't you worry about us. If there's danger nearby, Jambo will soon let me know. You go find that friend of yours."

I smile my thanks.

Without his help, I don't know what I would have done. And in return for his kindness, I'm only too aware of the risk I'm putting him in.

With all three torches extinguished, Winston heads off, hugging the tree line, while Tom and I close in on the cottage. We squat low against what remains of the garden wall, because as abandoned as the building may seem, it's hard not to imagine watchful eyes observing our approach.

The cottage remains in complete darkness. Nothing stirs inside. From the cover of the wall, we strain to peer through the grime stained windows, watching for movement and listening for any sounds coming from inside.

But the house is still.

What was I expecting, a glimpse of a face at the window? The light from a torch?

We move, crouching low, along the perimeter of the wall until we reach a small rusty gate. It squeaks as it swings back and forth at the whim of the breeze. To our right stands the dying ancient oak tree Winston spoke of. Solitary and bleeding, I glance up at the thick boughs and experience a nudge of something familiar. For the second time this evening, my mind tries to clutch at the faint impression of a distant memory. With so many turbulent emotions running amok inside me right now, I let the strange feeling pass and return my attention to the cottage.

Tom fishes out the old key he found at the pub and holds it up in the moonlight.

"Ready?" There's a grim expression on his face, which I've no doubt reflects my own. The cottage may appear deserted, but we're walking into the unknown with no idea what lies behind that door.

"Ready," I say in reply. It's a lie, of course. I'm anything but ready. There is no scenario in this world where I'm mentally prepared to enter a derelict building at night, in the middle of fucking nowhere, with a stranger at my side, knowing my friend is in jeopardy and all the while a rapist-killer is hunting me.

*No Tom, I'll never be ready for this nightmare.*

Tom slips past the rusted gate and, like a ghostly shadow, makes his way up the short path of crumbling stone slabs to the ancient stable door. The paint has long since peeled and flaked away, and the small rectangular window, positioned centre-top, is boarded up. Someone once cared enough to at least make sure the interior remains protected from the elements, but not enough to keep the property habitable.

I scan the windows again, hoping to catch sight of even the slightest movement, and satisfied we're not in danger of being ambushed, I move swiftly and cat-like to join Tom. I hold my breath as he takes the key and inserts into the lock, waiting for the click. But it doesn't come. Tom's brow furrows as he tries again, jiggling the key in the hole, but it refuses to budge. Without thinking, I lean in and brush his hand to one side.

"Here, let me try," I say in a hushed whisper. "Sometimes all it needs is a slight upward pressure... and then to the left a little and—"

The key turns with a soft click.

Tom glances round at me, his eyes wide and reflecting the bright moonlight.

"You didn't tell me you're an expert in old locks as well as art."

I shrug. "Uh... YouTube, I guess."

The truth is, I'm as surprised as Tom that I knew how to work the lock. The odd sense of familiarity leaves me feeling unsettled. First the tree, now the lock... I get the distinct impression I've been here before, even though I'm positive that's not the case.

With a steady hand, despite the ever-growing feeling of dread, I count to one—two—three and turn the rusting handle. The door eases open on its corroded hinges, a piercing screech cutting through the air and causing me to cringe. The noise of my heartbeat pounds in my ears, blood pumping around my head way too fast. I glance at Tom, his reassuring and intense eyes looking back at me.

And then steeling ourselves, we step inside the cottage.

# Chapter Twenty-Five

Disappointment hits me like a physical jolt.

Suzy isn't here. If she were, I would sense her presence. The blow leaves me feeling sick and hollow inside.

Mel may be planning to meet Victor here, forsaking her pub and home for a new life on the run with her ex-husband, but it's obvious this house is not where he's taken my friend. The air is stagnant, and I suspect that nobody has been here for quite some time.

Tom closes the door behind us, plunging us into darkness. We remain still and silent, waiting for our eyes to adjust to the gloom.

The faint moonlight filtering through the windows should allow us to move through the cottage without turning on our torches, but we keep them to hand, just in case. The bluish hue reflecting on the white walls gives an eerie quality to the place and the frigid temperature is unnerving.

Unable to help myself, I furtively glance around, looking for anything that resembles the paranormal.

*There is every chance I will need serious therapy after this.*

Slowly scanning the room, I'm disappointed to find only dust sheets and disrepair. There are no belongings to show anyone has ever lived here. And less disappointing, no ghosts either.

"Suzy's not here, Tom. We got it wrong," I say in a low whisper. My breath exhales in small foggy wisps of steam, adding to the creep factor.

"We should check all the rooms to be sure." He tilts his head up to the ceiling, scrunching the muscles in his face as he listens for any sound.

"Alright, then let's split up. I'll take this floor while you check the bedrooms." I glance towards the spiral staircase positioned part way down the hall. The wooden steps and bannister look intact from where we stand, but it's impossible to tell whether they're still serviceable. It's unlikely anyone has used them for a very long time. "Tread careful, though. The wood could be rotten."

"Likewise, be careful, okay? Malden could lurk behind any one of these doors. Don't let your guard down for a second."

"I'll be sure to let you know if I find him."

Not a prospect I wish to dwell on.

"Sorry, that was a clumsy way of me saying stay safe," he adds with a sheepish look.

I give a quick nod, then turn and head towards the small living-room on my right. In the semi-darkness, the bulky shape of furniture covered in white dust sheets is visible; perfect for someone to crouch behind and launch a surprise attack. I hear the creak of the stairs behind me as Tom starts his ascent to the second floor. The cottage groans, as if objecting to our presence. Before I can explore the room, I catch another sound—scratching coming from further along the hallway. With nerves tingling, I snap my attention back to my own search. The noise sounds again.

*What the fuck was that?*

I move forward cautiously, wary not to misplace my footing on the uneven floor. The thick exterior wall beside me is cool to touch, the whitewashed stone damp and slimy with condensation. I ignore the impulse to pull my hand away and continue trailing my fingers across the chilled limestone.

As I advance down the hall, I pick up the whiff of a foul smelling odour. With each step, it grows stronger and I scrunch my nose up at the unpleasantness. The bitter, pungent air becomes so offensive I have to cover my mouth and nose to keep moving. Has an animal died in here? No, I don't believe so.

Not a putrid odour, more like the stench of ammonia.

At the end of the hall, I push open a wooden door left ajar, and pick up on a low whirring hum, interrupted every few seconds by the same scratching sound as earlier. I peer round the door into what was once a dining-room, its furniture covered in the same dust sheets as the other room. Only this time, there are mounds of black pellets littering the once white surfaces.

That's when I realise what I've been hearing... and smelling.

*Bats! Thank Goodness!*

A nervous laugh escapes my lips. I've been so blinkered on finding Suzy I haven't prepared myself for coming face-to-face with Malden. What if he's armed? And what if my flick-knife isn't enough to defend myself with? He may be all soft charm on the surface, but underneath, he's a vicious rapist who won't shy away from confrontation. I need to be better prepared. If it comes down to it, I need to know that I'll fight for both our lives—Suzy's and mine—and that I won't fail her.

With heightened caution and a sense of readiness to face any danger that is presented, I work my way through each dilapidated room.

Along the hall from the dining-room is a compact kitchen, with a small family breakfast table at its centre, also covered by a sheet. Bolted against the furthest wall is an antique wood stove, framed by units that are now rotting with mould and faded to a dull nondescript colour. Underfoot is a sticky film, the buildup of years of grime covering the flagstone flooring.

Grime... and mouse droppings. A shiver runs through me at the thought of them scurrying across the tiles.

The only other exit from the kitchen is a door to my left, leading out to the garden. Through a dirt-streaked window, the night sky with its gathering clouds is visible.

I shake off the skin crawling sensation of being around rodents and minutes later, complete my search of this end of the building. Relieved, I head back through the cottage to check the living-room. The fireplace in here is also home to a colony of bats, but they're more torpid than their neighbours down the hallway, with only the occasional scratching sound coming from the chimney breast. The lack of activity means at least they aren't flying above my head.

I shudder at the thought.

"Give me rush hour on Oxford Street any day. I'd swap you lot in a heartbeat," I mutter to the docile mammals as I complete my search and check the last remaining door at the opposite end of the room.

While bracing myself for a lunging assault, I pull open the old wooden door. No-one springs out at me and I let my tensed muscles relax and heave a sigh of relief.

The small boot room has a further door leading out to the front garden, different sized wellington boots and other outdoor paraphernalia fills the small area.

This is the first evidence I've seen of personal items, possibly overlooked when whoever stayed here vacated the cottage. I crouch to pick up a small red boot and blow the dust from the once shiny plastic surface. It's confirmation that a family with young children once stayed here.

Why did they abandon it?

And why the hell did Mel have a key to the property hidden in her flat?

I know from the news reports that their marriage was a childless one, so is Malden instead connected to the family in some way? Highly unlikely. The cottage would be under surveillance if he had any kind of history with it. And we'd know by now if police were surrounding us; Winston would have sounded the alert.

I return the red boot to the neat line of otherwise undisturbed, dust covered wellingtons and rise from my crouched position to go in search of Tom.

One burning question is at the forefront of my mind; why did Victor choose this cottage to meet Mel?

*Why here?*

# Chapter Twenty-Six

Upstairs, I find Tom in the master bedroom. If the ground floor is freezing, it's even worse up here. The missing tiles from the roof have caused dark mould patches to spread across the ceiling, leaving the room with a musty odour and a metallic taste that lingers at the back of my throat. I reach out my hand to touch the white painted stone of the nearest wall; wet and cold.

Similar to the ground floor, dust sheets cover every surface. Someone went to the bother of protecting the furniture only later to abandon the property. Why? I look around to see that Tom has removed a few of the sheets. They lay like deflated ghostly piles on the floor.

"So, what do you think this place is?" I say, his back to me as he pulls out a draw from the dresser.

"Holy shit!" he yells. "You scared me half to death!" He knocks against the unit, toppling the few items on top with a noisy clatter.

"Sorry," I say, grinning. We've not had much cause to smile today, and the action feels alien on my face. "Were you expecting Malden, or leaning more towards something otherworldly?"

"Funny! For the record, I'd take Malden any day. Don't know about you, but this house gives me the creeps."

"Totally. Although I get the impression, this was once a happy place." I step over to the dresser and set a brass candlestick upright. "Have you found anything that might help us?"

"Nothing so far. Not much in the way of personal belongings and certainly nothing that links back to our friendly publican. What about you?"

"Bats. Lots and lots of bats."

"Right. Bats, huh?" There's a note of uncertainty in his voice as he glances up at the ceiling, scanning for the little furry mammals. "Just for the record, I'm standing by my opinion that this is the creepiest house I've ever set foot in." He gives an involuntary shudder.

Finally, a chink in his armour—not a fan of flying mammals, then.

"Any word from Winston yet?"

"No. He should have looked over the perimeter by now, though," Tom says, pulling out his mobile. He checks the screen before zig-zagging around the room, trying to pick up a signal, all the time swatting away cobwebs hanging from the low ceiling. As he stops by the window, he calls the phone given to Winston earlier. "He's not picking up—"

"Give him a minute. He might not hear it if it's on silent."

"The phone's on vibrate. At the very least, he should feel it buzz."

'Uh-huh, but listen. The wind is getting up again. Just give him a minute to answer before we panic.'

I stare expectantly at the phone in Tom's hand, willing it to connect. A tingling feeling of dread creeps up my spine and I lean further forward, desperate to hear Winston's voice. Have we put him in harm's way by asking him to check the grounds?

Tom's words suddenly cut through the tension in the room. "Winston! Tom here, are you okay? You had us worried for a while there. What's the status of the perimeter? Good, good. And there's nothing that indicates Malden's hiding nearby? Okay, keep looking. Yes, we're inside searching the rooms now. Ring me if there's anything." After ending the call, he drags a hand across his face, exhaling with relief. "He says there's nothing to report, and that so far it's all quiet outside."

I nod, relaxing my shoulders slightly. "Mel will come tonight, won't she? I need to know we're not wasting our time here."

"The longer Malden is on the run, the more likely he is to be caught, so whatever their next move is, I believe they're going to have to make it soon. I'll carry on searching the rooms up here. Let's see if we can work out what he's planning. You okay to search downstairs?"

"Sure. I just hope you're right about this because we don't have too many other alternatives—Suzy needs us to figure this out sooner rather than later."

As I exit the room, I stop at the dresser and reach out to pick up a small wooden picture frame tucked behind the candlestick, knocked over in Tom's earlier collision. "Hey, what's—" I halt mid sentence and stare at the photo in my hands with bewilderment.

"Everything okay?" Tom says, glancing over in my direction.

Unable to speak or move, my hands start to shake. The frame almost slips from my grasp. I look up at Tom as he strides towards me and takes it from my trembling fingers.

"What is it, Ella? Talk to me." His brow creases as he peers at the image in the frame. "It's an old photograph of the cottage, but I don't see—"

"The tree. Th-the child... swinging. A woman pushing... sh-she's... *my... mother!*" The words fall from my lips in a choked whisper as my throat tightens. I'm barely holding back the turmoil of emotions that crash into me.

"What!" Tom peers at the photo. "How can you tell?"

"I think I'd recognise my own bloody mother, Tom!"

The shock of seeing this younger version of the woman who has loved and raised me is unnerving. What is it doing here, in a derelict cottage that I know nothing about?

"Okay, let's think this through logically. Do you remember coming here as a child? Because the front door... you knew how to open it. Perhaps as a kid you watched your parents—"

Tom tilts the frame towards me, and I stare at the photograph again.

The cottage with its colourful window baskets and the faint wisps of smoke rising from the chimneys. Taken in springtime, there are bluebells sweeping across the hills like a velvet blanket surrounding the charming brick cottage.

The ancient oak tree stands proud in the corner, its once vivid green leaves still pop vibrant even in this faded photograph. Attached to the thickest bough is a rope swing and a child—a girl of five or six years of age—perching on the wooden seat wearing red wellington boots.

My mother is pushing her.

Another woman I don't recognise stands opposite, her back to the camera as she holds her arms outstretched, waiting for the momentum of the swing to propel the child back to her.

"I've never been here before, Tom. I'd remember. There was never any mention of a cottage."

"Perhaps the picture was taken before you were born? An Aunt or friend they lost touch with?"

"Possibly. Although doesn't it strike you as odd that the trail to Suzy has led us here? Instead of finding my friend, I discover a photograph of my mother inside an abandoned property—that until this moment I never knew existed?"

"Okay, agreed. It is stretching the realms of coincidence. What do you think it means?"

"I don't know... I should call her." With hands that still shake, I pull out my phone to ring my parent's house. "No answer. Shit. Why aren't they answering, Tom?"

"They might be out. Leave a message for them to call you back."

"They wouldn't leave the house—there's a bloody storm raging outside! Fuck. They should have picked up by now."

"Look, let's try to stay calm. Do they have mobile numbers?"

I push aside unwanted images of my parents injured by collapsing trees or chimneys and listen to Tom's voice of reason.

"Of course, I should try their mobiles!" I say, nodding. I try my mother's first, but it goes straight to voicemail. Then my father's too. "They're still not answering."

Tom, now standing with his arms folded and rubbing the side of his jaw, watches me with intent eyes. I can't shake the sense that something is wrong. My stomach clenches into such a tight ball I almost double over as I clutch an arm around my waist.

"What about calling the gallery again?"

"Yes, that's good. I'll call Wynter and ask her to keep trying for me. Something's not right."

*About any of this.*

Tom removes the photograph from its frame and tucks it inside his jacket before saying, "Come on, let's find a suitable spot to wait for Mel. Or Victor. One of them will turn up here tonight, I'm certain of it."

With Herculean effort, I push all concerns for my parents and confusion over the photograph from my mind, and leaving the musty old bedroom behind, we head for the staircase.

Tom's close presence is a welcome comfort. We make a good team, even if I hate to admit it, and although I don't trust him with my friend's emotions, I know he's got my back on this.

Which is just as well, considering what we're facing.

We're about to prepare for company.

# Chapter Twenty-Seven

"We should lock the door," I say to Tom as we stand in the hallway, deciding which room will give us the best vantage point. "If Malden arrives here first, he might bolt if he finds the place disturbed."

"Or he might think that Mel has followed instructions and is waiting inside for him. She no longer has her key, so better to leave it unlocked."

"Mel runs a London pub, Tom. She'll find a way inside. If we're to leave the cottage apparently untouched, that means locking the front door."

Tom concedes and heads off down the hall to secure the entrance. Meanwhile, I peer into each of the rooms on the lower floor, assessing their suitability. From the living-room we can see the approach from the garden gate. But, like the dining-room, it's also a space occupied with bats. We can't risk being distracted by the squatters in the chimney breast.

# THE GRAYSTONE KILLINGS

Through the process of elimination, we decide on the kitchen for our vantage-ground. Not only can we see down the hall to the front door, there's a convenient range of make-shift weapons to hand. It also has a door that leads to the garden, giving us a means of escape if we need it.

With the front door securely locked again, we remove the dust sheets from the kitchen table and take up position at our new lookout post.

"Still nothing about this place that seems familiar to you?" Tom asks, glancing up from his phone as he checks for updates from Winston.

I shrug, looking around me, waiting for a pang of familiarity. But I get nothing, other than a shudder at the sight of the bugs and damp that surround us. "I can't say with absolute certainty, but I don't think so. When I first glimpsed that tree, it stirred something in my mind... just a vague memory. I wouldn't read too much into it."

"Since we're stuck here, why don't you tell me about your childhood? It might dislodge a memory or help make sense of this photograph somehow," Tom says, pulling the photo out from his jacket. He blows a thin layer of dust off the table and places the image between us. "Your mother looks happy in this picture. Do you think the child could be you?"

Without hesitation, I shake my head, confident that I've never owned a pair of red wellington boots. Vivid colours are not my thing and I'm sure I'd remember owning these. "I found the boots the girl's wearing in a side room off from the living-room. There're others as well, all different sizes. Tom, I'm an only child with no siblings and no cousins. And I've never so much as tried on a pair of wellies in my life. I'm not the girl in this photo."

"Then tell me about you. What's your earliest memory?"

"My earliest...? I really don't see how this can help."

"Okay, look, here's what we know. An escaped prisoner—and I hope to God we're wrong about this part—has abducted Suzy. There's a sighting of him near your apartment, asking questions specifically about you. We have reason to suspect this is where he's meeting Mel. And now we've recovered a photograph of what you believe to be your mother. All this we know. What we don't know is the connection between you, Malden, your mother, and this cottage. Ella, we have the pieces of the puzzle—it's just they're not making much sense yet."

"And you think poking around in my head will help?"

"Consider yourself to be the common link in all this, whether you like it or not. Yes, I really do believe it could help."

"Amazing. Not only are you an extremely successful businessman, a collector of priceless art, and let's not forget an accomplished ninja, now you're also a shrink?"

I could add cheat and liar to the list, but I try to reign in the level of snark.

"Your earliest memory...?" he says again, ignoring my sarcasm.

"Fine!" I hold my hands up in defeat. "If you must know, my earliest memories aren't even real ones. They're nothing more than imposed images. I lost my birth parents when I was three. There was a fire at our home, but I remember very little about it. All I have is a description of events as they unfolded and snap images of being wrapped in a silver blanket, but I don't recall the sounds or smells or anything about that night. The memories are mostly based on what I've been told."

"That's awful for you, and I'm sorry you had to go through that. Do you know what caused the fire?"

"Investigators determined it was because of an electrical fault in the kitchen. Fortunate for me, my bedroom was at the front of the house with the door shut. My parents' room was at the back where the fire originated. Poisonous gases filled their bedroom and killed them as they slept. They didn't stand a chance."

"How did you get out?"

"The flames swept through the house before the emergency services arrived. Fire rescuers believe the noise of the windows exploding from the heat woke me up. They said I was hiding under my bed when they found me, and being so low to the ground helped me to avoid inhaling the worst of the smoke."

"Were you injured?"

"I suffered minor smoke inhalation and... my feet were badly burned. Months of skin grafts as a result, but again, too young to recall." I shift my feet beneath the table, conscious of the scars. "A wall of flames most likely prevented me from escaping the bedroom, the theory being I ran back to my room to hide. We'll never know for sure. Soon after the fire, I started suffering from panic attacks. Truth is, I can't recall a time before the anxiety. They're part of who I am. Talk to any expert and they'll tell you it's a normal reaction to a childhood trauma. The fireman who rescued me tried to hand me to a waiting paramedic, but I'm told I screamed and held on so tight he had to wait until they sedated me."

"It must have been terrifying, especially being so young," Tom says with genuine regret in his eyes.

"Honestly, I have no memories of the event. I don't even remember my birth parents. Sure, I feel sad about what happened to them. Of course I do. But I love my adoptive parents and wouldn't change them for the world."

"How soon after the tragedy were you adopted?"

"My birth parents had no close relatives. No grandparents, aunts, or uncles to step forward and claim me. My parents took me home from the hospital a week after the accident and fostered me. Within a year, they applied for adoption and we became a family. They're the only family I have—other than Suzy. She's like the sister I never had."

"Tell me about that. How did you and Suzy become friends?"

My eyes drop to the table, pushing back the pain of having to talk about Suzy when I don't know where she is. Or even if she's alive.

As I reach for the photograph of the cottage, spinning it round to face me, I say, "Suzy was the popular girl at school, you know, the one everyone wants to be around? We attended the same primary and secondary schools. Every cohort from the sport elitists to the nerds wanted Suzy in their group. She was like a trophy they all vied for. For the most part, I don't think she even knew my name. I wasn't cool or interesting or nerdy enough. Much like all loners, I didn't really fit anywhere."

"That doesn't sound like Suzy. She's kind and caring and would never shun anyone. She's the polar opposite to how you describe her at school," Tom says, struggling to place the woman he knows in the setting I've painted for him.

I smile. He's right, of course. And I'm also a little surprised that he gets her so well.

"People assume popular girls are always mean," I explain. "Suzy's never fitted that stereotype. Yes, the universe revolves around her at times—a lot of the time actually—but she also has an enormous heart. At school she was like a bright light, always too dazzling for me to be near."

"And yet you became not only friends, but lifelong buddies?"

"Yes, we did. Kids can be mean. One in particular, Daisy Foster, was horrible to everyone, but especially to me. When I was thirteen years old, it all came to a head. One gym lesson she hid my socks and shoes, and afterwards I had to walk to the headteacher's office, my feet on show for all to see. She spread word around the school that 'Millsie-Web-Feet' would be walking the corridors.

"But where Daisy was my tormentor, Suzy was my protector. She overheard Daisy bragging about the prank and marched right up to her. It was like David and Goliath... she towered over Suzy! It didn't matter to her, though. She squirted water at Daisy's crotch and then started pointing and making a scene about her wetting herself. And *that* was much more entertaining than my scarred feet. I'll never forget the moment she handed her a tissue and whispered something in Daisy's ear. Suzy never told me what she said, but I got my socks and shoes back and nobody ever bothered me again. After that, Suzy and I became inseparable."

"She's quite something, isn't she?" he says with a soft smile. When I look up, our eyes connect across the table and I search the clear grey magnets that have the power to draw me in, hoping to find a glimmer of guilt or regret.

Tom needs to understand that Suzy and I look out for each other. I won't allow him to hurt her. She might hop from relationship to relationship, but deep down, Suzy just wants a man to love her the way she's capable of loving them.

Under normal circumstances, I doubt Tom would have lasted the three-months and we would never have met. But here I am, sharing stories of my past with him.

"Could there be a connection to this girl? The bully?" Tom says. It feels like he's clutching at straws, trying to make sense of the situation when there is none.

Although I laugh, there's no humour behind the hollow sound. Memories of Daisy Foster do not bring me joy.

"It was a lifetime ago, Tom. She left our school a couple of years after that incident. Her family moved abroad."

"Fair enough. I'm sorry for your injuries, and that you suffered because of them. What about your adoptive parents? Describe to me what they were like."

"They were—*holy shit, what was that?*"

I let out a scream, jumping from my chair.

Tom shoots to his feet, peering in the same direction as my gaze. A large black, furry body scuttles across the floor, trailing behind it a long, thin pink tail.

Fuck. Rats!

"Oh my God, it ran over my foot! Ugh!" I shiver and clutch at my bruised ribs, already regretting the sudden movement as a wave of pain hits me.

"Did you see the size of that thing?" Tom says, his eyes wide with disgust. "It could have wrestled us to the floor had it wanted to!"

As we tentatively settle back into our chairs, Tom's phone vibrates. He frowns as he checks the screen, all the while keeping one eye on the direction the rat scurried away.

"Is that Winston? Are they here?" My words come breathless, partly from the scare, but also from the anticipation of a killer's arrival.

"No, it's not Winston. It's the search I requested on the cottage. I wanted to see what information the property throws up. Not much, it seems. It's locked down. All files are encrypted and sealed."

"*Locked down*? What does that even mean?"

"That someone's gone to great lengths to keep people from snooping. To all extent and purposes, this cottage doesn't exist. No history. No paper trail. Nothing. Why would someone care that much about an old abandoned building? What could be so important that it warrants this level of secrecy?"

"So, this is another dead end? And we're sitting here digging up the past while time is running out for Suzy?" I can hear the frustration in my voice and immediately regret snapping at Tom. He's doing everything he can to help, but our options are diminishing by the second. "None of this makes any sense. Look at the place—why on earth would Malden choose this cottage? Why all the secrecy surrounding it? What makes this cottage so fucking special?"

Frustrated, I nibble on my split lip, tasting the metallic blood as I reopen the injury, seeking comfort where really there is none.

Tom turns to face me, taking my hands in his. In the gloom, I can see his eyes shining with unwavering resolve.

"I will get you your answers, Ella. Even encrypted files are accessible, if you know how. And believe me, my people know how. They just need more time. Mel will be here soon, I promise you. It's the only viable scenario. So while we wait, let's try to figure out this photograph, okay?" He squeezes my hand and smiles, his firm jaw set with determination.

Bolstered by his confidence, I send up a silent prayer that we still have a chance of getting Suzy back... alive.

# Chapter Twenty-Eight

Long seconds turn into minutes. After half an hour, with still no sign of Mel, I try ringing my parents again and get the same voicemail message. Frustration leaves my nerves frayed and so, needing to do something, I call the Verandah instead.

"Wynter, it's me. Any luck with contacting my parents?"

"Oh hiya, no answer still, I'm afraid. I've left voicemails on their phones, but I'll keep trying."

"Alright. I really need to speak with them urgently, so as soon as you hear from them, you'll call me?"

"Oh, sure! No probs. Should I check if the cabs are still running and head over there?"

"Thanks, Wynter, but I'd prefer you don't go out alone tonight. Just continue trying, please. They have to answer eventually."

"Sure, will do. What about Suzy? Have you tracked her down yet?"

"Not yet," I say, struggling not to sound despondent. "But we're onto something. We'll find her soon."

There's a long pause before she says in a soft whisper, "Please bring her home safe, Ella."

My throat closes up with raw emotion.

"Of course I will. Listen, I-I have to go. We'll speak again soon."

After ending the call, I rejoin Tom and take my seat across the kitchen table from him. The photograph of my mother stares up at me, willing a memory to surface and help make sense of everything. But all I'm drawing is a blank.

"Tom, I've tried, but I could stare at this photograph all night and it still wouldn't get us anywhere."

"Then let's try a different approach. The woman with her back to the camera. Have you considered she could be your birth mother? Even if you don't remember her, did your adoptive mother ever speak to you about her?"

With a sense of increasing frustration, I shake my head. "My parents decided it was better that we put the tragedy behind us and focus on the future. We never spoke of it."

Tom shifts in his chair. "So you weren't curious? You know, about your parents? About who they were? Whether you have your mother's eyes or your dad's nose?"

"For a short time, perhaps. But what good would it have done? They were gone. My adoptive parents never met them, so they couldn't tell me anything about them."

"What about this child wearing the red boots? She could have been a friend. Who did you play with as a youngster?"

In an exaggerated effort to recall, I lean back in the chair and glance up at the myriad of cobwebs on the ceiling, willing an image, however small or fleeting, to reveal itself.

I think beyond the early days of school, back to when my adoptive parents took me to a pet store to pick out my first pet, a hamster. And before that? Did I ride a bike or play in the garden, like the girl with the red boots? Yes... just like a fading dream, there's something there.

Echoes of past sensations flutter on the edge of my consciousness... a rush of green blur all around me, the smell of sweet grass mingled with the perfume of wild flowers on a warm breeze. The tickling sensation of fresh cut grass on the soles of my feet, stubby little toes gripping the short green blades between them. Around and around, holding hands and throwing my head back, laughing. The sky above blue with cotton-wool clouds and a big yellow sun. Yellow just like...

"Wait—yes! I remember!" My sudden outburst making Tom jump back in his chair. "A wooden playhouse. At the bottom of our garden. Bright yellow with white window frames and—and a doorbell! We used to squeal with laughter each time it rang." Surprised by the sudden rush of images, I stare at Tom and shake my head. He's grinning at me, white teeth flashing in the gloom. "Oh my God, I'd forgotten all about that little house until now. How is any of this helpful, though?"

He reaches out to grab my hand. "Follow me. I want to show you something."

As Tom trails me behind him through the hallway, I'm increasingly bemused by his sudden enthusiasm. The storm has picked up again and the howling gale outside whistles through the rotting window frames, the high-pitched shriek attacking my already fragile nerves.

I'm desperate to head over to my parents' place, where it's warm and dry, devoid of bats, cobwebs, or rats. More than anything, I want to ask my mother about the photograph. Except I can't, because we're stuck here, unable to leave for the risk of missing the rendezvous—our only chance of getting my friend back.

Tom leads us back to the master bedroom, with its dark stained walls and bitter tasting air that lingers at the back of my throat. I shrug and scan the room.

"So, what are we looking at?"

"Over here. Tell me what you see."

We stand in front of two grubby windows that overlook the garden, and with eyes already adjusted to the low light, I peer out into the darkness.

"I see an overgrown garden."

"What else?"

"Tom, I don't understand—"

"What else, Ella? Look harder."

It feels like I'm humouring him, but I lean forward anyway, until my nose is almost touching the cold glass pane.

The garden isn't nearly as large as I would have expected. Despite the house being in the middle of nowhere and surrounded by countryside, it's not any larger than the average urban garden, and certainly smaller than that of my childhood home.

The perimeter wall is in similar disrepair to the one we crouched behind at the front of the cottage, and the hedgerow looks wild and overgrown as the gale force winds ricochet its foliage back and forth. My line of vision follows the stone wall round the garden, but there's nothing to see except for an unkept lawn. I'm about to turn away and berate Tom for wasting time when I suddenly spot it.

Tucked in the far corner, its paintwork long since faded, roof and door missing, are the remains of a wooden playhouse.

Dazed, I turn to face Tom and find him grinning in an almost manic manner, his eyes dancing with excitement. "You see it, don't you?"

When I try to speak, no words come, and I realise my mouth is gaping open. I snap shut my jaw and give a simple nod instead.

"You've been here before, Ella," he says in a low whisper, turning to stare back out at the playhouse. "This memory connects you to the cottage. Which means it's not a coincidence that Malden came looking for you, and neither is it a coincidence he's chosen here for the rendezvous. The question remains, though, what connects all of you to this cottage?"

"I—I don't know."

"My guess is your parents owned this place, and still do. You said yourself that a family with children used to stay here. You were part of that family. Back in the kitchen, when you were remembering the playhouse, you used the word 'we' to describe playing. Who were you talking about, Ella? Who was with you in that playhouse?"

I fight down the impulse to scream at him that I've never set foot in this cottage before tonight. His constant needling for details I simply don't have leaves me with an overwhelming desire to get away from him, to work through the implications of this revelation on my own.

But I can't run; Suzy needs his help now more than ever.

It leaves me with only one choice; that of denial.

"Sorry, Tom, but you're jumping to conclusions. I mean, so what, I remember a playhouse! How many kids have playhouses growing up? We don't know whether the one outside is even yellow, it's so old. I get you want to solve this, really I do. But if we start making wild assumptions, we risk jeopardising finding Suzy altogether."

From the intensity of his stare, I can tell that Tom will not let this go. Before he can argue, I'm saved by his mobile springing to life and he glances down at the screen; the light illuminating his angular features. His dark eyebrows arch as he flashes me a look, the greys of his eyes luminescent in the moonlight.

Suzy never stood a chance with this man's devastatingly good looks and charisma, and I have to admit to myself that they must make an exceedingly glamorous couple.

Perfect, in fact, if it weren't for Tom being married.

He puts the phone to his ear and listens for a few quick seconds before hanging up. "That was Winston. He says there's a car heading here right now. Come on, we need to go!" He grabs my arm as we run for the staircase.

"Did he mention whether the driver was male or female?" I say, throwing caution to the wind and racing down the rickety stairs two at a time.

"A woman. Driving like the devil's on her heels."

I quash a pang of disappointment. As much as I dread confronting Malden, at least I'd know he wasn't doing unspeakable things to my friend.

# THE GRAYSTONE KILLINGS

Back on the ground floor, we sprint towards the kitchen just as the full beam from a car lights up the interior of the cottage. A million butterflies are flitting around my stomach as I press my back to the cold stone wall and listen to the engine being cut. I glance at Tom as he presses up against the wall on the other side of the doorway. He gives me a wink of encouragement and I'm hit with a rush of gratitude that he's here with me—that I don't have to face this alone.

Somewhere near the front of the cottage, a car door slams shut and I hold my breath, waiting for Mel's next move. Seconds later, footsteps approach the front of the cottage, the sound of gravel crunching beneath her shoes. The door handle rattles, but without her key, the door remains firmly shut. We listen intently as her footsteps crunch their way around the side of the building, halting every so often to rattle a window frame, searching for a way inside.

Through the kitchen window, her pale face appears without warning. I snap shut my eyes and stand motionless, hardly daring to breathe. To my relief, poor light and grimy glass prevent her from spotting our stiff shadow-like forms. Long seconds pass until we hear her continue round to the back door and try the handle there. I can almost sense her frustration.

The rapid crunch of her footsteps return to the front of the house and we wait in silence to see what she'll do next.

If it were me, I'd take a rock and smash a window.

The tinkle of breaking glass reaches us from down the hall, followed by the thud of something hard landing on the carpeted floor. It seems Mel has also gone with the rock solution. The piercing squeak of an old window frame being opened cuts through the silence of the cottage, and a rush of fresh air sweeps through the ground floor.

Seconds later, the beam of a torch bounces off the white walls.

*Mel's inside.*

*And she's heading straight for us.*

# Chapter Twenty-Nine

*Ba boom. Ba boom. Ba boom.*

The sound of my heart as it drums in my ears.

Not that I particularly fear Mel. She poses no threat. No, adrenaline is coursing through my body because she holds the answers that we so desperately need. Answers that will bring us another step closer to finding Suzy.

Wherever my friend is, I need her to believe she's not alone, that we're doing everything we can to find her. She needs to hold on to the hope that I'm coming to get her. Suzy's belief in me is perhaps the only thing giving me the strength to keep it together—to not plunge headlong into a world of despair.

The light from Mel's torch sweeps down the hallway like a swinging pendulum, and judging from the erratic motion, I'd say she's nervous. A few more paces and she'll reach the kitchen. I sneak a glance at Tom. His head is turned towards me as he focuses on the threshold, waiting for her to step into the room. Together we brace ourselves, counting down the seconds.

*Three—two—one.*

Spiders scuttle for cover as she enters the kitchen, their cobwebs glistening in the bright light of her torch. The beam darts across to one side of the room and follows the scratching noise of tiny claws scurrying across the flagstones. Mel holds a white tissue against her nose and mouth to block out the pungent smell of the bats. Her blonde hair, pulled back into a high ponytail, swishes with each step. The smart blouse and skirt from earlier is replaced by a dark leather jacket and pale blue jumper, complete with skinny jeans and knee-high boots. Dressed for comfort, just as you'd expect from a woman planning a long journey with her criminal husband.

In silent unison, Tom and I take a sidestep, drawing closer to each other until our shoulders touch and block the doorway. I switch on my torch and Mel spins on her heels; the tissue dropping from her face to reveal an exhilarating smile that vanishes in the instant it takes her to realise we're not Malden.

"Hello again, Mel," I say, remaining tall, with my chin tilted high.

"What the hell are you doing here?" A darkness crosses over her eyes, adding a new level of chill to the room.

"Sorry, were you expecting Victor—or Vic, as you call him? Must be running late. While we wait, let me introduce my friend Tom. He's the one who found the key to this place tucked away in your kitchen."

Tom steps forward and Mel's eyes dart between us, taking stock of the situation. She opens her mouth to speak but before she can say anything I cut her off abruptly, gesturing with the torch towards the table and chairs.

"Sit. You're going to tell us everything."

Mel hesitates before reluctantly stepping over to the nearest chair in a stiff and jilted motion. She glances over at Tom, his shoulders squared back as he stands tall, arms folded crossed his chest. If Mel was in any way unclear about her position here, one look at Tom leaves her in no doubt. She drops into the chair.

"Whatever you think this is, you've got it wrong," she says with a defiant glare.

"Oh, then you haven't arranged to meet your husband here? Why don't you cut the bullshit, Mel? Tell us what's really going on."

'Let's start with this divorce of yours.' Tom moves to Mel's side and towers over her, pinning her with a no-nonsense gaze.

Holy shit... the man can be intimidating when he wants. It's almost impressive.

"Here's what I think," I say with a strong and level voice. "You realised the police would be at your door as soon as Victor escaped. By divorcing him... well, they'd soon realise they were wasting their time, especially after the very public and staged bust up. Yet somehow you still managed to arrange this meeting. When did you learn of his intention to escape?"

"You've got this all wrong. I'm not meeting Vic here, you crazy bitch. I'm hiding from him! What do you think he'll do to me now he's escaped? I had the audacity to divorce him. He's not going to leave until he makes me pay for deserting him."

"Uh-huh. I see. Except now we have a problem," I say, sliding into the seat opposite her. Hands entwined in front of me on the table, I stare across at her with a piercing look. First her chin quivers, then she swallows hard, because beneath the deceit and the hard exterior are signs of panic. "Let me put this in simple terms for you, Mel. Your husband has our friend. We want her back. So start talking and tell us where Suzy is, or Tom here is going to call the police. Are we understanding each other?"

She glances at Tom, who holds up his mobile, and rolling her eyes with annoyance, she heaves back against the seat. "Fine. I'll tell you what I know. It won't do any good, though. It won't help you find your friend because I haven't seen either of them."

The house creaks and groans around us as we wait expectantly.

It's true that eyes reveal so much more than a person's words, and right now, with her pupils restricted to pinpoints, the tiny muscles beneath her eyes quivering and the frequent darting back and forth between us, she's displaying visible signs of distress.

I remain silent, waiting for her to fill the strained void with her version of events. The oppressive silence denies her the opportunity to consider her options and come up with a new plan. After a few moments, she squirms uncomfortably in the chair, until finally she feels compelled to speak.

"Vic's arrest left me devastated. Think about it, my husband... accused of being a rapist?" She lets out a scornful laugh. "No wife wants to hear those words, especially not at four in the morning, with armed police storming into your bedroom. At first, I was in denial. As far as I was concerned, Vic was innocent. I defended him against all the mounting evidence because I needed him not to have committed those terrible things. Otherwise, what did that make me? The gullible wife? The woman sleeping next to a stranger each night? Photos of me appeared all over the news, right up there alongside the victims. Whispers followed me wherever I went; 'How could she not know?' 'Did she help him?' 'What sort of person falls in love with a monster?' I would ask myself the same question; *how could I have not known?*

"The truth of it is, I married a stranger. I fell in love and never once questioned whether there was more to this attentive, caring, funny guy who swept me off my feet with his good looks and charm. Tell me though, does anyone really? When a dark side is so carefully hidden, their inner demons so completely controlled, do you question what they permit you to see? I don't believe so. Our desire to be loved makes us vulnerable at best, and gullible at worst. Were there signs that I missed? Of course there were. Every one of us would benefit from hindsight occasionally.

"So sit there and judge. It doesn't matter. You can find it abhorrent that he raped and killed, then came home to our bed and held me in his arms. Because you'd be right, and it sickens me to my stomach. Do I hate him for what he's done to me? To us? To our marriage? With every fucking cell in my body. But do I still love him? Without question. And I've had to make my peace with that. I'll do whatever it takes to be with the man I love, even if that means accepting that he's flawed. This sickness, the compulsion that drives him to do these evil things, you have to understand it's a disease. With my help, he will get better. But I can't do that when he's locked up in prison. You understand what I'm saying?"

I stay silent for fear of breaking the momentum and having her clam up on us. And because I know I'll throw up in my mouth if I try to speak.

Instead, I give a weak nod.

"All this time, I've kept the belief that he'll find a way back to me. Whatever it takes to make sure we're together again. The divorce was a necessary step to protect him, but Vic has a wide network of people he can call on, and through them we've been able to remain in contact since the arrest.

"The days became months, then years. All the time I waited for word of when Vic was breaking out. Life carried on, but it was a meaningless limbo, always watching and waiting, never knowing when I'd get my husband back. Until a few months ago. They gave Vic a new cellmate who told him about this place." She looks around as if suddenly remembering where she is. "This person told him where to find the key and that hidden inside the cottage was a large sum of money. Vic had one of his associates come to the pub and give me the key that you stole." Her gaze shifts to Tom, who's dealt a scathing look. "I was given the details of the cottage and told that Vic wanted me to come here and report back to him. It was all true. I found the cash."

"This money? Where is it now?" I ask her.

"In a safe place. It was a sweetener to get Vic's attention. There's a job—he didn't divulge the details—only that I was to confirm the cellmate was good for the money."

"After you'd picked up the cash, was there any further communication from your husband?"

Mel nods. "The message was straightforward. When news hit about Vic's escape, I was to behave as normal and wait for the police to lose interest in me and the pub. Detectives hung around the bar for a few hours this morning asking questions, but after they'd gone, I knew they would have the place watched. I waited for darkness before slipping out, making my way to Charing Cross, where a car was left for me. I was to drive here to wait for him to get in touch."

"How will he contact you?" I ask.

"He didn't say, and even if he did, it's none of your fucking business."

"A plausible story, but what is it you're not telling us?" From the way she swallows, her tongue pressing against the inside of her cheek, I suspect she's withholding something from us. So help me, I want to reach across this table and take her by the throat. Nothing will give me more pleasure than to squeeze the truth from her.

"That's it. Like I told you, I can't help you find your friend." Mel's words are clipped with impatience and she scrapes back her chair to stand, swinging her bag off the table to fit it over her shoulder. She picks up the torch before stepping away. "We're done here. I want the key back and then I want you to leave. Call the police. It doesn't matter now because you've fucked everything up by coming here. Did it never occur to you that Vic will have eyes on this place? He won't show now. All you've achieved is to waste whatever time your friend has left."

"*That's bullshit!*" Something inside of me snaps and I launch out of my seat, fists clenched at my side.

Suzy's life is hanging in the balance while this woman withholds information that could help save her. I swallow down the bitter taste in my mouth at the prospect of failing my friend.

Tom throws me a warning glance, and as Mel takes another step away from her chair, he grabs her shoulder to force her back in the seat—just as a whooshing sound fills the room behind me.

I spin around to see the kitchen filling with hundreds of brown, flapping wings.

The screech of Mel's chair legs must have disturbed the colony.

Tom's face drains of colour while Mel lets out a piercing shriek, which only serves to draw the bats in our direction.

As Tom instinctively ducks, Mel sees the chance to make her escape. She races past him and out of the kitchen, heading back for the open window.

*No! We can't let her slip through our fingers!*

With a parting glance at Tom's cowering frame, obscured by the cauldron of bats, I grab a torch and bolt after her.

# Chapter Thirty

Mel's retreating figure flies down the hallway ahead of me. In another few seconds, I'll have lost her and any chance of finding Suzy.

Although I give chase, my run is ungainly, hindered by bruised ribs and low-flying bats. She turns into the living-room, racing for the window. Even though I'm close on her heels, there's no way I'll close the gap in time. Before I can stop her, she has one foot up on the windowsill, clambering over the broken glass.

Out of options, I skid to a halt, ready to take my one and only shot. I grip the torch firmly before throwing my shoulder back, and releasing my hold, I launch it through the air. The projectile hurtles towards her as the beam of light manically bounces off the stone walls and mouldy ceiling. Upon finding its target, the metal casing contacts with the back of her leather boot just as she tries to make a leap for freedom. Mel screams as her Achilles tendon ruptures, bringing her to the floor amid cries of pain.

*I really hope that hurt.*

"You fucking bitch! You've broken my fucking ankle!"

With long strides I charge over to where Mel's collapsed, cradling her injured leg. The surge of anger I feel inside shocks me as I grab the collar of her coat and drag her back onto her feet.

"It's not broken. Not yet, at least." My voice roars over the whooshing noise of the wind through the smashed window. "But I will break every bone in your miserable body unless you tell me the truth. Believe me, I'll know if you're lying, so start fucking talking."

"What—what happened?" Tom asks, breathless, as he catches up to us.

"Mel's decided to tell us the truth. That's right, isn't it?"

"Vic will fucking kill you for this."

"Only he's not here. At least, that's what you told us. So it doesn't matter what bones I break. No-one is coming to help you."

Not knowing when to quit, Mel gives me one last defiant glare, and before I realise what I'm doing, my fist shoots out. I strike her face with a snapping style jab; the punch throwing her head backwards against the wall. Her eyes widen with the shock of the impact as blood erupts from her nose. One hand shoots up to cup her injured face while the other remains clutching at her ankle.

"You've broken my nose! I'll fucking kill you for this, you bitch!"

I lean forward, her shallow breath hot on my skin as I get a waft of mint and stale cigarette.

"The next words from your mouth better not be a lie. Or a threat. Believe me when I tell you I can hit your face all night long, Mel. Don't think I won't."

She wipes at the blood with the sleeve of her jumper, leaving a red smear across her lips and cheek. Fear replaces the earlier defiance in her eyes, and it gives me some satisfaction to see a sheen of perspiration beading on her forehead. I'd love to hit this psycho all night, but we need to get going. It's been too long already.

Based on Malden's modus operandi, we have less than four hours to find Suzy before she turns up dead.

"Fine. Stop with the fucking hitting and I'll tell you what I know," Mel says, trying to put weight on her injured leg.

Tom holds out a hand to help and places an arm on her waist as she hops towards the nearest chair. It niggles me to see his muscular arm around her microscopic waist, and not because I care who he puts his arms around—I don't.

No, it bothers me because Mel's the enemy.

If it were down to me, she'd be hobbling under her own steam, undeserving of our concern or compassion. Nevertheless, Tom pulls at a dust sheet from an armchair and helps her into the seat.

*He'll be plumping her bloody cushions next.*

"Comfortable?" I ask, failing to hide my annoyance. "Good. Then talk. And remember—no more lies."

Mel gingerly touches her nose and throws me a loathing glance. Right now, I'm probably her least favourite person on the planet.

"The other inmate I told you about," she says, speaking to Tom and blanking me, "He's the one who planned all this. The break from prison, I mean. And this cottage. Sure, Vic has contacts, but it was his cellmate who had the means to pay for the attack on the convoy."

"What cost for his freedom?" Tom's words are direct, no nonsense. We simply don't have time for anymore games.

"In return, he's to track someone down. Coerce them into doing what this person wants. He chose Vic for good reason. If they don't comply, he's to dispose of them. Make it look like they're another of his victims; it's nothing personal. When the job's done, he gets paid and we disappear for good." She directs her words at Tom, as if discussing a business transaction and not my friend's murder. She turns to me with a hard stare, a taunting sneer upon her lips. "Vic's not going back to prison, no matter what you do to me. Call the police and I'll just deny everything."

I try not to let her provoke me. Suzy needs me to be strong and focused right now, not emotional and reactive.

"Tell me, why Suzy? What has she done that would make someone go to these lengths? What do they want her to do?"

"There was a name, that's all I know. Vic knew nothing about the person or why they were a target. Only that they're in hiding. He's to track them down. Make them compliant—that's it."

"But—but Suzy's not in hiding!"

"The name given to him wasn't hers."

Mel's words take a moment to sink in. It feels as if I'm swimming against a riptide; no matter how hard I try, I can't get close to the truth. To understanding why any of this shitstorm is happening to us. If Suzy isn't the target, then why is she missing? Have I got this all wrong? It explains Mel's surprise when I showed her Suzy's photograph in the pub—Malden was never supposed to abduct Suzy.

"Who's name was he given?"

"I tell you that, and I'm as good as dead. Vic's cellmate isn't someone you get on the wrong side of."

I realise now that the fear in her eyes isn't because she's scared of us.

*It's what will happen to her if she talks.*

"Fine. Then tell me this, was 'Ella Mills' the name he was given?" My heart races as I speak my name, needing to know if—for whatever inconceivable reason—I'm the intended target.

Has Malden screwed up and taken Suzy instead of me?

Mel lowers her eyes and gives an almost imperceptible shake of her head.

Although her response helps to steady my off-the-chart racing pulse, it does little to make sense of the situation. I touch Tom's arm and motion for him to join me in the hall.

"What do you want to do with her?" he says in a low voice when we're out of earshot. "We can't just leave her here."

"With that ankle, she's not going anywhere. I'm not waiting around babysitting her until the police get here. I need to find out if my parents know anything about the other prisoner Mel spoke of. And how he's connected to this cottage."

Tom nods. "Okay. My driver can meet us here, then we'll call the authorities before heading out to your parents' place."

After leaving a less than thrilled Mel secured to the armchair, Tom unlocks the front door and we shelter by the entrance, waiting for his car to arrive.

"Why don't we just take Mel's rather than wait?" I say, motioning to her vehicle left in front of the overgrown path.

"It'll just be a few minutes. My car will be quicker and easier to navigate back to the main road. Trust me, we'll make up the time."

I glance at him, no longer trying to hide my agitation. For all our efforts, it seems we're no closer to knowing where Suzy is. Precious seconds tick away while we stand here doing nothing. The renewed urgency to speak to my parents has me pacing impatiently, Storm Ruby whipping at my face as her energy levels pick up.

A searing hot pain in my side catches me unaware as I crunch across the gravel. I let out a sudden gasp with the shock.

"Are you okay?" Tom asks, eyeing me with uncertainty.

"Yeah, I'm fine, it's nothing—"

But I don't get to finish my sentence as he tugs me back under the shelter of the doorway, and for one ludicrous moment, I think he's about to pull me into a kiss.

*What the actual fuck?*

With his hands on my hips, he turns me to face him before taking surprising care to peel my jumper away. When I make a grab for his hand, the stabbing pain catches my breath again.

"Stay still. I need to check you're not about to puncture a lung." Tom moves my hand to the side, leaving him free to push my top up even further. When he glances up, I hold his gaze, defying him to try anything inappropriate. I know his type; he probably thinks he's irresistible with those dreamy eyes, firm jaw and sexy voice. Well, he's in for a disappointment because I don't fall for married men and I certainly don't fall for my best friend's cheating boyfriend.

His steady fingers probe my side, causing me to flinch at the pain of his touch.

"Will you please keep still and stop wriggling about?"

"I'm not wriggling. You're prodding my ribcage."

I look down to where his head is excruciatingly close to my breasts. He raises an arched eyebrow up at me.

"I know what I'm doing, okay? You'll need to place an icepack on that bruise later to keep the swelling down, but I don't believe there's any danger of puncturing a lung. Most likely a small crack; painful, but you'll live." Tom straightens up so that we're standing so close I can feel his body almost touching mine.

"Thanks," I murmur as my breathing becomes short and erratic.

*That'll be the pain; I mean, what other reason could there be for finding it difficult to breathe right now?*

*Oh, for the love of God, Ella, just breathe normally for fuck's sake!*

Shit.

I don't want Tom to think for even a nanosecond that his proximity is leaving me breathless. Because it's really not.

"Well, my days, it's lively out here!" Winston announces, striding towards us. I jump back from Tom, pulling down my top. To my utter dismay, a sudden rush of heat burns my cheeks. "What's the plan?" Winston asks, oblivious to my obvious embarrassment.

I let Tom relay everything Mel has told us about Malden and his cellmate, feeling too emotionally depleted to chip in. When headlights finally approach from over the hillside, I let out an enormous sigh of relief. The car snakes its way towards the cottage at alarming speed, bright beams bouncing around the dark peripheral as the vehicle glides over potholes and races round sharp bends in the road. As the car draws closer, it's clear the driver is more than capable of navigating country lanes at top speed whilst being relentlessly buffeted by the wind. In minutes, the wheels of the car skid to a stop opposite us.

"Back in a sec," Tom says, going over to speak with the driver.

As we wait, Winston describes to me how Mel almost lost control of her car coming over the same hill, but I'm not listening; not really. Right now I'm too busy freaking out about how my parents will react to the old photograph.

*And wondering why the hell they aren't picking up the phone.*

# Chapter Thirty-One

The car Tom has sourced us is a top of the range Land Rover and feels as solid as a tank against the storm. To slide into the warm comfort of the luxury vehicle is a shock to the senses, especially after the miserable and dank interior of the cottage. I resist the impulse to stroke the soft leather upholstery.

We set off on the haphazard road surface, leaving Tom's driver to watch over Mel until the police arrive. The tyres chew up the miles of the rugged terrain with ease. In what seems no time, we're flying along the tarmac of the empty city highways, racing towards my parents' house.

I should be fearful of my life; the speed we're going is not conducive to the driving conditions outside. Tom, however, skilfully steers the vehicle, avoiding any debris that blows into our path, handling the car with a controlled confidence.

I add *'proficient driver'* to his ever-growing skill set.

Carefully turning in my seat, I glance behind at Winston. "Hey, how's Jambo doing back there? First time in a car?"

"Oh, don't you worry about Jambo. This little dog is resilient and adaptable to most situations. He'll be respectful of this fine leather. Impressive wheels, Tom."

"Thanks."

"Do you drive?" I say.

"Oh, many years ago. Not sure I'd remember how," He leans forward in the seat and smiles wistfully, staring at me with such openness I wish I could capture this moment on canvas. "You know, I don't mind if you want to come right out and ask me..."

As I shift in the passenger seat, Tom peels his eyes from the road to glance over in my direction, an amused smirk on his face.

"Sorry, Winston. I didn't mean to pry. That was rude and clumsy of me," I tell him, feeling ashamed for not being more candid. "Only I can't imagine what it must be like for you, living on the streets, no safe place to call home?"

"Not all homes are safe," he says, pointedly. He's right, of course. Our home wasn't safe for Suzy. "Jambo here, we look out for each other. I'd feel safe anywhere with him by my side. But I see you're curious how I ended up this way?"

Despite being an uncomfortable topic, I nod, grateful to this humble man for not making me squirm more than I already am.

"I made bad choices. Each day, telling myself I was doing the right thing for all the right reasons. Of course, I wasn't. It really is as simple as that."

"What happened?" I turn in my seat to look at him and see a face pained by regret.

"In the space of a short few months, I lost everything I'd ever worked for. Not only did I have a beautiful, intelligent wife, a son I idolised, I was also fortunate to have a very comfortable lifestyle. Everything from an enviable home and car—perhaps not as top end as this one—prestigious public schooling for our son… we were living the capitalist dream and thriving. Except, it wasn't enough."

"Your family wasn't enough for you?" I can never imagine taking my family for granted. Suzy may not be my sister by blood, but she means the world to me. Right now, I'd give everything I own to have her back home safe again.

"There's a saying that greed is a bottomless pit. Speaking from experience, I can tell you that is an accurate idiom. Put simply, the more I had, the more I wanted. I was piloting cruise ships around the world. Life was good; I loved my job, my family. Then I let it all slip through my fingers."

"I really am so sorry," I say, grappling to get my head around what he's telling me.

"Believe me, so am I. It took years to build our life together and, in a blink, it was gone. I was at work one evening in the staff mess, where a handful of us were taking our break. I overheard a couple of stewards talking about their share portfolios, in particular, the successes they were having. Not one for investing in the market, it nevertheless intrigued me, since bank interest rates were at an all-time low.

"The following week, I dipped my toe in the water and tried it out for myself. An initial investment of a hundred pounds here, two hundred there, and before long, I had a respectable portfolio turning over a small profit. Enough to pay for a few family treats. In no time, it seemed I was dealing in hundreds of thousands of pounds. So I began thinking, what if I had enough money to pay off the mortgage? Even buy a second house in Florida, perhaps a ski chalet in the French Alps! My job on the ships took me away for long periods of time. My wife, Lizzie, put in long hours as a vet. We worked hard for what we had. What if the portfolio made enough for us to retire early and spend more time together as a family? With dawning realisation, I understood how this investment could really change our lives."

"But your career was amazing, you said so yourself. Presumably your wife was happy in hers too? I can't imagine ever wanting to give up my art, no matter how much money I had."

"The more the portfolio grew, I'm ashamed to say I lost sight of what truly mattered. When I wasn't working on the cruise ships, I locked myself away in my office at home, researching the next big stock that would make me richer beyond anything I ever imagined. I started missing family meals and then bedtime stories with my son. By the end, I resented their demands on my time, time I could spend trading stock or researching the market.

"Then one day, I got wind of a fledgling mining company. Still in the exploratory phase, they were set to be the elusive golden ticket I was seeking. But I wasn't so reckless as to sink my entire savings into an AIM—Alternative Investment Market—company, not yet at least.

"To begin with, I sold a modest percentage of my portfolio and bought up a small holding of the company's shares. Several weeks later, the share price shot up, making me a substantial profit. I could hardly believe it. The excitement amongst investors was infectious. This was a licence to print money!"

"Let me guess… impossible to fail?"

"Exactly. I liquidated all our savings to buy more stock. The price continued to rise. The hype surrounding it escalated until it was all I could think about. I called in sick for work, ignored my family, and all the time raising capital by whatever means I could. The equity in our home, our jewellery—never once stopping to think that what I was doing was wrong. In my mind, I was doing this for my family, to give them the life they deserved. I would buy Lizzie bigger and better diamonds, we would live in a bigger and better house… I invested every penny I could get hold of. All the time, the share price kept climbing."

"Until it crashed?" I say, seeing with obvious clarity the path to ruin that Winston had recklessly followed.

"Spectacularly. The company submitted a request for a licence to mine the precious metals in the ground. Approval should have been a given, a mere formality. But the government rejected their application and the share price dropped, sinking quicker than the Titanic. In hours I'd lost everything. Unable to face up to the horror of what I'd done, I sought solace in alcohol. Lizzie's disappointment in me was too much to bear. I was a shadow of her former husband; a greedy and weak imposter. It was the lowest point of my entire life.

"We had to move out of our beautiful home, the place where my son had grown up, where Lizzie and I had built so many happy memories. The fancy school and the cars went too. We were starting again, literally from scratch. And all the while, Lizzie never once blamed me. Never accused me of being arrogant or reckless. We still had each other, and that was all that mattered in her eyes. Except I couldn't see beyond my own disappointment at the husband I'd become. Instead of dealing with the guilt, I let it destroy us. I stopped looking at her, talking to her, until eventually we became strangers."

"What happened? Did she leave you?"

"The reality is my marriage to Lizzie ended long before the arrest. By that time, I was drinking myself into oblivion most evenings. And then lunchtime drinking became the norm, and soon I was even sneaking a flask of alcohol into work."

"Your arrest? You were drink driving?"

"That would have been bad enough," he says, his eyes lowered.

"Oh, no! Winston—" My hand flies to my mouth as I realise the implication of his words.

"A three-week cruise—surrounded by beautiful tropical islands. Idyllic. Until I piloted the ship into shallow waters, grounding us on a sandbank. No serious injuries, thank God, but the police didn't need a breathalyser to confirm I'd been drinking. After my arrest, there was a court case. I received a suspended sentence. It was the end of my career.

"On the day of the sentencing, after I came home, I no longer saw disappointment in Lizzie's eyes. My actions had finally pushed her away until she could no longer tolerate being in the same room as me. That's the worst possible punishment for a husband... far worse than any judge could pass down. I walked right back out of the flat we were renting and never returned. As far as I was concerned, my family was better off without me."

"Did she ever try to find you? Lizzie must have been heartbroken to lose her husband on top of everything else."

As much as I want to empathise with Winston, I can't hide my disappointment at how his story ends. The actions he describes seem far removed from the man I've observed over the weeks.

"You don't need to say it, because I can see the disillusionment in your face. Yes, it was cowardly and appalling to treat her like that. After everything I put her through, she deserved so much better. Not a day goes by that I don't regret the poor decisions I made. As time passed, it became harder to reach out to her. Eventually, she met someone else. They bought a home together, and he's a wonderful father to our son—a far better role model than I could ever be."

"You still love your wife," I say, incredulous that he can choose this life over being with his family. My heart aches that he's resigned to watch from the sidelines as another man takes his place.

"Believe me when I say that I'll go to my grave loving her. But to have her know what happened to me? The least I can do is spare her that."

"All these months, how did I not see your pain?"

"You have a gift to see people, Ella, you do. But how can you even begin to understand what path a person has followed? I have to live every day knowing that I endangered the passengers and crew of my ship, that I gambled everything in my life that mattered to me. By fooling myself that I was going to give my family a better life, I justified every poor decision I made. The stupid part was that we already had the perfect life.

"Now, don't look so sad. It's not all bad. There are amazing support groups out there and I found help for my depression. As for meeting Jambo here, he gives me a purpose to wake up each day. Fact is, I need him more than he needs me." He ruffles the dog behind his ears. "And what's more, I've learned to live with my demons." He strains against the seatbelt, leaning so far forward that his weatherbeaten face is close to mine, before saying, "You need to learn how to live with yours too, Ella."

"I... I don't—what do you mean?" I ask, confused.

Winston gives me a sad smile, a knowing look in his eyes.

"Okay, we're here," Tom says, slowing the car. "Which house is it?"

I've been so engrossed in Winston's story I haven't noticed us approaching the village where I grew up. Visible from the car window is the familiar tree-lined street at the end of a cul-de-sac, nestled in Putney Heath. The village is rich in history, from duels to highwaymen, and famous authors to boat racing, all surrounded by an abundance of green space.

I look out at the street I grew up in, and stare at the traditional 1930s five bedroom family home. I love everything about this house. My parents refurbished it when they moved here, keeping all the original features that my mother couldn't bear to rip out. They restored the beautiful arched front doorway and oak panelling in the hallway to its former elegance, and whenever I visit, they're the first thing I see. The smell of the wood and the feel of the grain beneath my fingers always fill me with nostalgia.

Only now, as I point out our house with its gravel carriage driveway to Tom, bile rises in my throat and a tightness fills my chest.

# THE GRAYSTONE KILLINGS

The property lies in darkness. The arched door is banging open in the wind, the panelled woodwork reflecting the glow of the swaying street lamps.

I hear a scream.

*Mine.*

# Chapter Thirty-Two

On legs that are alien to me, I stumble from the car and race with a stunned dread towards my parents' house. The force of the wind relentlessly pushes me away until my legs give way beneath me. I crash to the gravel, landing on my knees, the stones digging into the palms of my hands.

The crunch of quick footsteps behind me, Tom's firm grip helping me back onto my feet. He takes my face in his hands, forcing me to look at him. I can't see for tears as they cascade down my cheeks.

"Ella, listen to me! You do not go in there. Do you hear me? Go back to the car and call the police."

In shocked denial, I shake my head furiously. When I try to speak, the only sound that comes is a wretched sob that catches in my throat, a strangled wail that has no place in this childhood setting.

"Look at me, Ella. Your parents are in trouble. Wait in the car, okay?"

All I can do is stare at him, dazed.

And then I run.

With every ounce of strength I have left, I will my legs to sprint to the arched doorway, screaming their names as I run up to the open door. I race down the panelled hallway, past the table that displays my mother's framed cross stitch. I don't stop until I'm bursting through the door into the lounge.

Like a rag doll, I crumple to the floor.

Tied to two dining chairs are my parents.

We're too late.

A loud gasp from behind me shatters the dreadful silence.

"Oh, Jesus Christ! No!" Tom utters, entering the room and dropping to his knees beside me.

I can't breathe. My vision blurs as the darkness folds in, flashing pinpricks of light in the blackness. A deafening ringing in my ears drowns out all other sounds. I gulp in lungfuls of air as I fight back the waves of nausea.

Determined to drive back the advancing blackness, I focus on the Persian rug beneath me, following the threads of the intricate pattern, trying to fixate on my breathing. But I can't ignore the stench of death that lingers in the air.

"I'm calling the police."

"No!" I push myself up, anger fuelling my body and coursing through my veins. "Don't, not yet."

With teeth clenched, I turn to face my parents' bloodied and battered bodies. Every muscle trembles as I push up off the floor and take a tentative step towards them, stifling a sob with my hand.

My mother's head slumps forward, her chin resting on her chest, jaw slack and fallen open. Blood pools onto her lap from deep cuts etched into the flesh of her cheeks and forehead. Placed perfectly central is her severed and bloody tongue.

*A beautiful and kind woman savaged by a monster.*

Somehow I force my trembling body to kneel beside her and, with fingers that are awkward and clumsy, I untie the binds holding her wrists behind the chair.

"No, don't touch her—" I stop fumbling with the knot and stare up from my mother's pale wax-like hands. "Ella, please. Step away before you destroy vital evidence," Tom says in a softer tone.

He's right, I shouldn't be touching their bodies.

But I won't leave them here like this.

Instead of moving away, I focus again on working the binds while hot tears roll freely down my face. Once free of the rope, her hands fall heavily to her side, the motion startling me.

She might somehow still be alive!

I need to check for a pulse.

Despite the gaping stab wound to her heart, I hold her wrist in my trembling hand and press down on the artery below her thumb. Her skin is cool to the touch. No matter how hard I press, all I can feel is the pulsing rush of my own blood through my veins.

*How can this be happening?*

My heart breaks with every second I spend in this room and as I look over at my father's body, a sob escapes me. Tom is standing behind his chair, working through the knots of his bindings.

Blood stains the front of my father's shirt. His head tilts back, lifeless eyes staring, unseeing, at the ceiling. His throat has been slit. The cut is deep, to the point of near decapitation. Dozens of stab wounds cover his thighs; round, red splotches seeping through the dark grey material of his suit trousers.

What pain did they suffer? Did he have to watch my mother die? Or did she have to watch as the intruder sliced a blade across my father's throat? Their bodies face each other, knees touching. At some point, they must have realised they were going to die. I hope their last words were of eternal promises to love each other in death as they have in life. My only comfort being that they died together.

"You shouldn't see them like this," Tom says gently at my side.

How does he do that? I'm not even conscious of him moving. As he tries to lead me from the room, his hand slips into mine. Warm skin against my frigid fingers. This time, I don't push him away. Instead, I grip his hand like he's the only thing in the world stopping me from plunging over the cliff-side and into the dark depths of hell.

Tom leads me gently into the kitchen. A modern room with shiny surfaces, filled with the smell of stargazer lilies that sit centrepiece in a crystal vase. My mother likes fresh flowers. The normalcy of the surroundings feels surreal after the horror we've just witnessed. I can't help but turn and stare at the door, expecting one of them to walk through it. Such is my need to wake from this nightmare.

As Tom helps me up onto a high-stool, I sway, unable to control my trembling limbs. He places a powerful arm around my shoulders, absorbing the violent shuddering of my body until the tremors ease.

"Why? Why did they have to die like that?" I ask, my voice a whisper.

"You're in shock. Let me get you a drink. Stay here and don't move from that stool."

He returns with a bottle of brandy and, taking a mug from the side, he fills it with a generous measure. His hand covers mine as I raise it to my lips and swallow the caramel-coloured liquid in one gulp.

"Ella, we have to call the police."

"Not yet, Tom. Please. If we call them now, it's over and they died for nothing."

"Believe me, you might think you're the only one who can save her, but take it from someone who's already made that same mistake—the police will always handle a situation like this better than we can. You just have to trust them. I promise they will do everything to make sure Suzy gets home safely. We should make the call. This—what's happened here tonight—we're out of our depth." His eyes narrow, waiting for my response.

"Malden was after something," I say, shaking my head. "I need to know what it was before you call them."

"Except this is a crime scene now. How will we even recognise what we're looking for?"

"Whatever he wanted, I don't think they gave it to him," I reply, slipping off the stool, bolstered by the effects of the brandy and a primal need to stop this man who has targeted my family. "We search the house. I'll start with the bedrooms. Can you find my father's laptop and try to access it? There's a study second door on the right." I point down the hall, desperately trying to keep it together.

"Okay, we'll do it your way, but promise me you'll be careful. Why don't we stick together and do a sweep of the house first?"

I shake my head, not wishing to think about what Malden's capable of doing to Suzy if he can do this to my parents. "There's no time. Now go, hurry!"

Tom rushes from the kitchen as I head for the staircase, and taking the steps two at a time, I fly up them, propelled by the fear that Suzy's time is running out quicker than we hoped.

When this nightmare is over, I'm certain I'll suffer the worst anxiety attack of my life.

Until then, it'll have to fucking wait.

"I can do this..." The words, like a mantra, fall from my trembling lips as I climb the stairs, clutching at the white, glossy bannister for support.

I couldn't save my parents, but I'm determined to avenge their deaths. Whatever it takes.

Ready to face anything, I slip the knife my father gave me from my pocket and flick out the blade.

Whoever's responsible for the murder of my parents had better watch out.

Because I'm coming for them.

# Chapter Thirty-Three

This is the house I grew up in, but despite the familiarity, I can't shake the feeling that whoever broke in has walked these rooms before me. Much like the victims of a burglary report feeling violated, similarly my childhood memories are now tainted.

And Malden's responsible, I'm sure of it.

What was he after?

Could the cellmate have given him my parents' names to hunt down? It makes no sense—what would anyone want with a professor and homemaker? I think of the photograph we found at the cottage tucked inside Tom's jacket pocket.

*We still don't know what my mother was doing there.*

There's a connection, a reason to target them.

If only I can figure it out...

Though the house is large with five bedrooms, each room is minimalist, with few places for a person to hide. With my knife held in front of me, I step into my childhood bedroom, scanning for signs of disturbance. They've kept the room pretty much as it was before I moved out, except for the fresh coat of paint. I know they hoped I'd sleep round here occasionally, especially after a late dinner, but the truth was I found it too suffocating to be here. The endless fussing from my mother and whenever my father thought I wasn't looking, I'd find him staring at me with a concerned expression. They were the most loving parents I could have wished for, but they weren't without their secrets, it seems.

A few of my old keepsakes remain on the dresser, and I cast a quick cursory glance over them. Items I didn't want to throw away when I moved out, but considered myself too grown up to take with me.

An eight inch soft bear, complete with floppy red hat and blue boots, given to me when my goldfish died, amid assurances that the little bear would never leave me, unlike the bloated, dead fish.

Next to the stuffed toy is a rocket. The school project my father helped me to make. He laughed when he came home from work to find I'd painted the shiny plastic surface with two big round eyes, reasoning how I could now see space from the rocket's trajectory.

After a swift scan of the room, I pull shut the door on my precious memories, not ready to seek comfort from them yet.

The last bedroom to check is my parents' room.

I take a deep breath to steady my nerves before stepping inside. My hand flies to my mouth, holding down a scream—the room is in chaos.

With a shudder, I bite down hard on the side of my bottom lip, tasting the now familiar blood as I reopen the wound from the dumpster.

*This is too much.*

All around me is evidence of uncontrolled rage and violence. It lingers like an echo in the air.

"How. Fucking. Dare. You!" I say in a hissing tone, looking around the room with teeth clenched to stop the rising scream within.

My grip on the handle of the knife tightens, knowing that in this moment I've never been more ready to confront Malden.

I'm certain that he's behind this home attack. He's made one crucial mistake, though. Whereas he's left the rest of the upper floor untouched, this room he's ransacked. Why? A random hunch that whatever he's looking for is hidden here? Unlikely.

I gingerly step my way through the chaos, careful not to tread on any of their belongings. Paintings litter the floor, ripped from the wall and destroyed in a frenzied attack. Each reproduction torn from its frame and vandalised. It would devastate them to know what's become of their beloved collection. Often I would tease them they must have raided the Tait Modern, the attention to detail so authentic they could pass as genuine.

Among the ruined paintings are the remains of my mother's favourite craft cross-stitch design. I run my fingers over the ten blue-tit fledglings, huddled in a haphazard nest on a branch, their beaks open, begging for the worm their mother brings them. The slashes that tear through the stitching cause threads to protrude and unravel—blows dealt by a man who's losing his shit.

The family safe, previously hidden behind where the craft once hung, is now exposed to the room. Of similar size to a small drinks fridge, it's a high-end spec model.

# THE GRAYSTONE KILLINGS

The metal door lies open and scattered on the floor are the contents; cash, jewellery, and official-looking documents. None of which it seems Malden was after.

"What were you searching for, you bastard? So help me, I'll hunt you down for this—" My threat is choked with emotion as I peer round the room.

Other than the paintings, there aren't too many other furnishings to search. The mattress has been up-ended and flung against the wall, clumps of white foam and metal springs protruding from the slashed material. Dragged from its position against the far wall and smashed into dozens of pieces are the massive bed frame and headboard. Two matching bedside tables with their lamps lie toppled and strewn across the carpet. Scattered beneath the windowsill is a vase, broken into tiny shards of crystal. The once exquisite flowers left crushed and trampled. Water from the vase leaves a dark stain on the cream carpet.

Nothing has escaped the violence that raged in this room. The chaos and destruction before me matched only by the ferocity of the wind and rain slamming against the windows.

It feels like everything is spiralling out of control.

I stand motionless, closing my eyes and trying to picture the room as it should be.

Why here? Why this room?

The answer is staring me in the face—because Malden's searching for something that fits in a safe. He pulled paintings off the wall in his search for it and then flew into a rage when the safe didn't contain what he was looking for.

"No, that's not it," I mutter under my breath. "*Think, Ella, think... what am I missing?*"

Malden knew there was a safe because they told him. And they wouldn't tell him unless...

Oh my God. Fuck.

They lied to him!

They gave him what he wanted and told him where the safe was, even giving him the combination to open it.

Only it was the wrong safe! Did he kill them before he discovered they'd lied? Or is that why he tortured them?

My God, there's a *second* safe. Fuck.

I snap open my eyes and, with fresh perspective, scan the room again.

And then I spot it.

The bedside lamps are plugged into wall sockets on either side of the bed. My gaze falls to a third socket with only USB chargers plugged into it. Curious, I squeeze myself between the remains of the headboard and drop to the floor to examine the white rectangular casing. Ordinary looking, I slip a fingernail behind the white plastic and tug. It remains firmly in place, flushed tight against the wall. On hands and knees, I scramble over to the nearest lamp and, after checking the lightbulb still works, unplug the light, transferring it to the other socket. Nothing happens.

I stare at the socket, my pulse racing.

*Malden never found what he came for.*

"Oh, they out-smarted you," I say, muttering to the empty room. "The safe was right in front of you the entire time... *but where would they keep the key?*"

Not behind a painting; too obvious.

Taped to the back of a drawer? Also, too obvious.

Whatever's in that safe was worth killing for, and for reasons I don't yet understand, it involves me. If they wanted me to find the key, where would they hide it?

Of course! I know where the key is…

I sprint back to my old bedroom, hurtling through the door and coming to a halt in front of the dresser. Without pausing for breath, I scoop up the stuffed toy and frisk the small bear, squeezing at the soft stuffing. There's nothing hard hidden inside. Frustrated, I toss it to one side and seize the rocket with the childishly painted eyes. Since it's impossible to see anything peering through the small hatch near the nose cone, I give it a shake instead. No rattling sound. Out of time and options, I raise it above my head.

"Sorry daddy," I say, with instant regret. I take the model and crash it down onto the dresser. Small pieces of plastic fly in all directions, but the largest piece drops to the wooden surface and spins to a halt.

Attached is a small silver key—this was their secret.

Whatever they were protecting, they didn't give it up.

What could be so important that they would die defending it?

My hands tremble.

Because the answer is terrifyingly simple… *me.*

# Chapter Thirty-Four

I stare at the contents of the box as it slides out from the cavity in the wall, steeling myself for whatever secrets it might contain. Almost too scared to breathe, I delicately lift the folded piece of paper nearest me and turn it over in my hands.

It appears to be an invoice.

As it unfolds, I attempt to read the scrawl on the carbonless paper. The handwriting is mostly illegible, being both messy and faded in places. If I had more time, I could decipher it, but for now, I focus on the company logo... *The Elevate Group.*

Well known for treating the rich and famous for addictions, I consider the possibility of someone in my family attending the clinic, perhaps suffering some sort of breakdown. Is this what my parents kept secret—a mental health issue? Not something people kill over.

I set the invoice to one side and lift the remaining items from the box. A black leather bound pocketbook, the pages a yellowish hue from age, and a thick stack of official-looking documents. A whiff of mothballs carries in the air, reminding me of old scrolls. The elastic strap of the little book is brittle to touch, and even when I slide it off with care, it still disintegrates in my fingers. After quickly flicking through it, I find nothing but blank pages. The sting of disappointment hits me as it becomes apparent the answers I was hoping for may not, in fact, be in this box.

I turn my attention to the other items. The documents appear so old that for a moment I hesitate. With a shrug, I unfold the first of the papers. Although I'm no historian, I doubt my parents would hide documents of historic value inside an inferior quality safe within their bedroom wall.

As I stare at the contents, the air leaves my lungs in a whooshing gasp.

I squeeze my eyes shut, open them again, and refocus.

No, this can't be right.

I unfold another. Then another. Before long, there's a small pile of papers by my side—deeds to dozens and dozens of properties. A chill runs through me as I reveal a document belonging to the cottage.

The final document—a bank transfer note—has more zeroes than I have time to count.

*Shit! Shit! Shit!*

*What the fuck were my parents involved in?*

The contents of the box leaves me with more questions than it's answered. I stare at the items laid out in neat rows in front of me, none yet willing to give up their secrets.

Frustration builds until I want to scream, to take the day right back to when none of this is happening. Instead, I fight back the disappointment and gather up the papers. A noise from behind makes me jump with a start and I spin to face the room, immediately letting my tension-filled body relax at seeing Tom standing in the doorway. The relief is short-lived, however, when I see the troubled expression in his eyes.

"Tom, what is it? What have you found?"

My parents lied to me, and despite the need to appreciate the true extent of their deception, it somehow feels like they're slipping away from me. They're not who I thought they were. What if the safe and its contents are just the tip of the iceberg?

"You mentioned earlier that your father's a professor at the university. What about your mother?"

"Involved in charity organisations. Why do you ask?"

"Because it doesn't stack up. There are items in this house that should probably be in a museum. Take the armchair in the study—a Dragon's Chair. At first, I thought it was a replica of one that sold at auction several years ago. It went for twenty-six million dollars. The fact is, I don't believe I've been looking at a replica at all. I'd stake my reputation—as a respected art collector—that it's over one hundred years old. An original. And here's the thing, Ella, what I'm really struggling to understand is how a professor of physics owns an item that could easily fetch millions at auction?"

I feel my eyebrows shoot to my hairline. I know the armchair well.

When I was little, I used to sneak into the study and curl up in the handcrafted leather and wood, taking pleasure in the earthy smells while pretending it was a throne. I'd snuggle into the chair and lose myself in imaginary adventures of my making, reading stories of timeless fables and magical worlds.

"Ella, did you hear what I just said?"

This is too much to process—all I can do is stare and nod.

"There's—ah—more. The art pieces you assumed were replicas? They're not. Every single one is a genuine original. It would be impossible to estimate the worth of the collection without doing a proper valuation, but again, we're looking at staggering amounts." He pauses, giving me a strange look. "You really never suspected, did you?" he says softly, moving across the room towards me. "I'm afraid there's something else I need to tell you. I received a text from my contact a few minutes ago. They've circumvented the security around the cottage deeds. The reason your mother is in the photograph is that your parents own it."

"Yes, I know." I hold out the documents and his brow pinches as he scans through the papers.

"Jesus Christ. We're looking at extraordinary wealth here," he says, returning them to me. "How could you—"

"What? Not notice that my parents are obscenely rich? I don't know, Tom, maybe I was just a kid, and they didn't feel the need to share their financial status with me. I've got no fucking clue about any of this!" Hysteria threatens to spill over any second.

"Ella, I realise this is confusing and a lot to take in. Your parents—I am truly sorry you had to see… that—but we're going to figure this out, okay?"

Tom reaches out to squeeze my hand, sending a warm ripple through my chilled core. The gesture threatens to dissolve what's left of my composure and I tense as I try not to lose my shit.

I can't be an emotional wreck right now. I have to stay strong for Suzy's sake; no matter what horrors this night throws at me. And that means focusing on finding the truth about what happened here, not on my world currently collapsing around me.

Tom either senses my emotional shift or notices my rigid stance. Either way, he pulls back.

But not before a glimpse of hurt flashes across his eyes.

"This is the only room to be ransacked. Whoever broke in and attacked my parents had no interest in paintings or relics."

Tom nods thoughtfully and walks past me, glancing round the room. "Mel told us that Victor's looking for someone in hiding, remember?"

"Yes. It made little sense back then. But now..."

"Exactly. This house is like Fort Knox. They kept themselves entirely under the radar. So we find out where their wealth comes from, why they had to live this middle-class lifestyle, and we'll be closer to knowing why you're being targeted. Is it possible they stole from the cellmate Mel spoke of?"

"Obviously, I didn't know my parents as well as I thought I did. Before tonight I would've laughed at that suggestion," I say, sarcasm heavy in my voice.

Tom shrugs his shoulders, cutting me some slack. "Fair enough. There is one other thing. When I say this house is like Fort Knox, that isn't an exaggeration. It has a state-of-the-art security system that's more advanced than anything I've ever seen." Tom speaks with open admiration, and after seeing the security at his house, it's clear we're not talking about a simple door alarm. "Nobody should have been able to gain entry, and yet somehow someone did. A blocking device was most likely used, but again, we're not talking about your average tech."

"What are you saying? That they were prepared for this attack?"

"Here, follow me. I want to show you something. I had my contact access the laptop in the study. They uncovered a software program that controls the security system. We activated it to reveal an entire wall of monitors hidden behind sliding panels. Each screen splits into two views, one for each room, excluding the bedrooms and bathrooms. The cameras have sensor activation, so recording only occurs when someone is moving around.

"Your parents' bedroom is the exception—a camera in their dressing room monitors the entrance to a panic room. And from the look on your face, I guess you didn't know about that either?"

"What the actual fuck, Tom? Why would they need a panic room? Are you sure?" It's almost like he's talking about someone else's family. And then a horrifying thought hits me. "The cameras... did they—is it all on tape? D-did you watch it?"

"No! God no! Whoever broke in deactivated the entire system."

I let out a hiss of breath, because as much as I want to see whoever's responsible pay for their crime, the thought of it all playing out repeatedly on screen makes me feel nauseous.

"Where is this—um—panic room? Is it really in there?" I glance over at the small dressing room on the other side of the bedroom.

I didn't know of its existence.

Fuck.

This changes everything.

# Chapter Thirty-Five

In the dressing-room, it's hard to ignore the lingering scent of my mother's perfume. I tamp down the rush of emotions that threaten to overwhelm. The realisation of never being able to see her again—it hits me like a sledgehammer.

In a bid to block the horror from my mind, I push away the images of their broken bodies and concentrate on helping Tom to locate the panic room.

The space is by no means as elaborate as Suzy's walk-in wardrobe, and the clothes are in the most part unremarkable, with only a few select designer garments for special occasions. And to think they could have afforded their own fashion designer on retainer had they wished. A curt laugh escapes from me—how could I have been so gullible?

Tom arches an eyebrow and gives me a strange sideway look.

"Just observing how understated it all seems, you know, considering the fortune they have stashed away," I say, failing to hide the resentment in my voice.

"You know, you could view them as having done a remarkable job of not drawing attention to themselves, especially if they were, as we now suspect, in hiding."

I slowly nod, the sparks in my brain igniting.

*Yes, precisely that.*

A remarkable job of living their lives unnoticed—just as I've done my entire life.

Oh my God, they trained me to stay hidden without my even knowing!

Fuck.

Unaware of my bombshell self-discovery, Tom continues his exploration of the dressing-room, his eyes dragging across each of the four white wardrobe doors that line both sides of the room. He scans the ceiling, positioning himself at different angles until finally he pulls on the handle of the last door on the left.

"This is the door the camera's angled towards. The lens is so unobtrusive you wouldn't notice it was there unless looking for it. Up there, see?" he says, pointing to a tiny black dot in the plaster coving above us.

He's right and I watch as Tom swings open the door to expose a neat row of my father's shirts, organised into colour sections from whites and blues, through to pinks and blacks. He takes the central hangers and pushes them apart; the metal screeching softly as they slide across the pole to create a gap. We lean forward together, peering beyond the clothes. A carefully concealed narrow door lies at the rear of the wardrobe. It looks exactly like the other white wooden panels, except this one has a discreet white handle.

We've found the panic room.

Tom gives a low whistle. "Nicely done."

I run an agitated hand across the back of my neck, unable to share his admiration. As a young girl I would dress-up in my mother's clothes, imagining myself grown up as I wobbled up and down the room in her high-heels. Of course, they realised I would never have looked inside a wardrobe dedicated to boring suits and shirts.

Another well kept secret got through my careful manipulation.

Was everything I ever knew a lie? Exactly who are my parents, and why the hell did they have this room installed?

I follow Tom into the hidden chamber as he pushes open the solid metal door—the wooden panel frontage a mere deception.

The space within is compact but comfortable.

Oak wooden panels cover walls, most likely also made of metal, and a deep silver coloured carpet completes the metal box's conversion into a space to wait out danger. I spin around, trying to take in the reality of this strange and unfamiliar room.

A well-stocked drinks fridge is placed beside a plush black leather sofa, with two glass tables beside each armrest. The only other items of furniture are a large, dark wooden desk and swivel brown leather chair. A computer panel next to the door displays the room's ambient temperature with a tiny red light flashing in the bottom corner.

On each wall are drawings of figures in a variety of poses. I stop in front of one, a black and red chalk drawing of a man wearing a ruff around his neck. A cloak is artistically slung over his shoulder, immediately recognisable as sixteen hundreds fashion. Drawn as if seen through a frame, the man sits in an armchair.

I swallow hard and circle the room several times until I'm left with no doubt. This morning I wouldn't have questioned their replica status, but now...

With care, I lift the gilt frame and its drawing of the sitting man from the wall. I've studied this art piece a hundred times, never imagining for a moment that hidden away in my family home, in a secret room at the back of a wardrobe, is the original drawing.

"These are Rembrandt," I say, breathless and stating the obvious. It's surreal to be in this unfamiliar room, surrounded by such a valuable collection of art. The more secrets we uncover, the more I feel like a stranger in my childhood home.

"I had no idea..." Tom utters, his voice a low whisper so that I'm sure I must have misheard him.

"No idea of what?" I ask, my brows pinched as I tilt my head round at him.

"Nothing—" He crosses his arms, rubbing at the stubble on his chin. My stomach lurches. Was I wrong to trust him? "Just thinking aloud, that's all. It's an admirable collection... and an impressive safe room. Why do you suppose they didn't use it when their attacker broke in? Seems odd," he says, quickly changing the topic.

I look at Tom with renewed suspicion as he stands, blocking the only exit out of here.

*What do I really know about my friend's not-quite-fiancé?*

Does he have an alternative agenda for helping me, one that doesn't involve getting Suzy back?

"I've stood in front of genuine Rembrandts not once, but twice, this evening. Don't you think *that's* odd?" I say, staring at him as I retreat backwards towards the desk, creating as much distance between us as I can. "You never said why you had a stolen collectable in your home. Did you steal the painting, Tom?"

"No, of course I didn't!" he says, but his eyes fail to match the conviction of his words. I stare at him, my heart racing, waiting for the truth.

"It turns out that the people I trusted the most have deceived me my entire life," I tell him, frustration stinging at my eyes. "And now you're lying to me, too. I just want the fucking truth. Did you steal Rembrandt's *Storm on the Sea*? Yes or no?"

The silence weighs heavy between us until finally Tom's shoulders slump into a shrug and his gaze drops to the carpet at my feet. "Not in the way you think." His steel grey eyes glance up, searching for mine, drawing me in until I'm helpless to react to his words when he finally speaks the truth. "But yes, I stole it."

I reach out to the desk for support as the ground beneath me sways.

What have I done?

If Tom is behind all this, am I wrong about Malden? Or have they been working together? To what end, though? Fear crawls up my spine.

"What about my parents? Were... were they art thieves as well? Is that why they died? Did you know them?"

He shakes his head. "No, Ella, I've never met them before," he says, taking a step towards me.

"Don't come any closer!" I hold my hand up, fingers spread stiff and trembling. "You're lying. What is it you're not telling me?"

Tom halts and tugs off his beanie hat, running agitated fingers repeatedly through his dark hair as he struggles to find the right words to diffuse the situation. After a moment's hesitation, he squares back his shoulders and looks at me with a naked sincerity I've never seen before, his glimmering eyes drawing me in once again.

"I'd never hurt you, okay? There's no hidden agenda here. All I want is to help you find Suzy. I can explain the Rembrandt, but not right now. I swear to you, Ella, I never knew your parents. If they were art thieves, I didn't know of them," he says, nodding at the framed drawing in my other hand. "I realise you have no reason to trust me, but I'm asking you to, anyhow."

He's right. I do need his help. But trust him? When he's lied not only to Suzy but now to me, too?

As I struggle to overcome my suspicion and fear, a glint of something shiny on the desk beside me catches my eye. After placing the framed art carefully down, I reach across to the object resting on the green leather blotter. The cold metal of a gold chain slides delicately through my fingers until the attached pendant rests in the palm of my hands. I turn it so that it's face up.

But I already know what I'm holding.

Bile rises in my throat as my blood runs cold.

# Chapter Thirty-Six

Tom's voice sounds distant and muffled to my ringing ears as I stare at the necklace in my hand. "What is it?"

"My mother's Saint Christopher—she never takes it off." I hold back the tears and swallow down the rising lump in my throat. "You asked why they wouldn't have used the room. I think they did. One of them, at least."

"Christ. Your mother made it here to safety, but not your father? And gave herself up trying to save him—"

It doesn't bear thinking about. I roll my teeth over the corner of my split lip and suck in the metallic tasting droplets of blood. The dull throb provides a welcome distraction. My eyes travel to the temperature panel by the door and the flashing red light that hasn't stopped blinking since we entered.

"That light on the screen over there—what do you suppose it means?" I say, indicating the panel behind him. "Controls, perhaps? Everything else in here is immaculate, except for that glass. There are smudges on it."

# THE GRAYSTONE KILLINGS

The room is small enough that it only takes Tom a few strides before he's standing in front of the black glass panel, no bigger than an iPad. The temperature display reads twenty-one degrees celsius in blue LED lights, the small red light pulsing beneath the numbers.

After examining the device from different angles, he turns to me with eyes that sparkle with anticipation. "She left finger marks on the glass. Your mother almost certainly accessed the panel while she was here."

He raises a hand to tap the screen with his index finger and it bursts into life, displaying the image of a purple shield. As it fades, an LED shaped hand with five digital squares positioned on the virtual fingertips takes its place.

A fingerprint scanner.

Tom places his palm in position and a thin green line moves from the top of the screen to the bottom, followed by flashing words in red:

**ACCESS DENIED**

"You try," he says, looking over his shoulder at me.

I stare at the panel and then at Tom, knowing that what I'm about to do could be a mistake. But with no other choice than to believe he's being candid about wanting to find Suzy, I move over to the scanner. Tom steps aside, giving me room to place my palm flat against the glass. The digital green line repeats the same scan, only this time it's followed by a red line moving from left to right. On completion, hundreds of tiny LED lights the size of a grain of salt scramble to fill the screen, forming the pattern of what appears to be a woman's face. Unnerved, I jump back as a female voice bursts from hidden speakers in the ceiling.

> *"Hello, Ella. My name is Cura. Do you require the police?"*

"Oh God, no!" I shake my head vehemently.

> *"What action do you require, please?"*

I shrug and stare at the digital face. That is an excellent fucking question.

After a long pause, I say, "I need information. Can you tell me when the room was last accessed?"

> *"Last access was at eight thirty-three this evening by Ann Mills."*

Tom checks his watch. "Forty-five minutes ago." His face fills with anguish. It means we arrived shortly after he killed them.

"Cura, um… tell me, what action did my mother require?"

> *"Your mother requested three actions; room lockdown, video recording access, and room open. There is one saved recording. Would you like to access it?"*

Tom's hand touches my shoulder, and he squeezes gently. "You don't have to do this."

I glance at him and nod, then turn back to the panel, saying, "Play the recording, please."

"*Accessing recording now.*"

The panel flickers, and my mother's face fills the screen. The bitter tasting bile claws higher up my throat, my stomach twisting with apprehension at witnessing the last moments of her life.

> "*Ella, dearest, it's your mother. If you're watching this, I fear we've failed you. This must be very frightening, sweetheart. I know you have questions for me and your father, and we will answer each one of them, I promise.*

> "*Before I continue, I need you to make sure you're safe. If you're alone right now, call the police immediately. Cura will assist with that, otherwise I have to trust that you are in safe hands and not in immediate danger. Someone has broken into the house and threatening to harm your father unless I go to him. I'm so sorry, sweetheart, but I need you to be brave now. Find the black notebook we've hidden for you. Everything you need is*

*in there. It will answer all your questions. I give you my word, Ella.*

*"Events are unfolding faster than your father and I could ever anticipate, but please, our dearest daughter, don't think ill of us. Everything we did was to protect you. We always knew this day would come; that someone would come looking for you. Although it might not seem it now, we did what we thought was best. We have always loved you, Ella. So much more than you can ever know.*

*"I'm leaving something of mine to watch over and keep you safe when we're gone. Whatever happens to your father and me... remember, we chose this path.*

*"And we would choose it again. But now it's time for you to travel the path you were always destined to take. Good bye, sweetheart, we love you and please know that we'll always be by your side."*

Tears spill freely down my face as my mother removes her necklace, softly kisses the delicate pendant, and places it on the desk. After instructing Cura to release the locks, the door opens, and then, with a final glance back at the camera, she's gone.

The screen turns black for a few seconds before the digital face reappears on the panel.

> *"Would you like me to replay, delete, or save the recording, Ella?"*

"Save," I say in a choked voice.

"Jesus, that was—are you okay?" Tom says, still staring at the panel. "I can't imagine what you must be feeling right now."

I glance down at the pendant in my hands, but they're shaking so hard the necklace slips through my fingers. Tom springs forward to catch it, his movement so swift it falls effortlessly into the palm of his hand.

"Here, let me—"

Unable to move, I remain statue-like while he steps behind me and fixes the chain around my neck. His hands are steady and warm against my skin, lingering a fraction longer than necessary. The fleeting touch only serves to remind me how alone I am right now.

A ragged breath escapes my lips as I take the pendant and drop it down the inside of my jumper, feeling the metal disc nestle against my goose-bump covered skin. I shut my eyes and swipe away the falling tears.

> *... need you to be brave...*

My mother's words play over in my mind. I'm not sure how much more brave I can be in the face of all this tragedy. I think back to the person I was when I woke up this morning, the person who relied on Suzy to help her through the day; she seems like a stranger to me now.

"Can I see that notebook again?" Tom says.

"We already checked. It's empty." I snap open my eyes, unsure of where to turn now. We're still no closer to knowing where Malden is keeping Suzy.

"No—I don't think it is."

Tom looks at me with a thoughtful expression, and curious, I retrieve the musty smelling book from my jacket pocket and hand it to him. After he flicks through it, he carefully examines the yellow tinged pages, holding them up to the light and studying the paper with narrowed eyes. Eventually he says, "I can have someone look at it for you. If there's a message in here, we'll find it."

I shrug, both baffled and vexed by the cryptic book.

"The notebook aside, what else do we have?" It's a rhetorical question, and as I pace the small room, I think out loud. "We could spend days driving to each of the locations on those deeds. It'll take too long. What about the invoice?" I stop pacing and stare at Tom as an idea strikes me. "What if we go to Elevate and ask them to go through their records? They could trace it back to find out who was treated and why."

Tom folds his arms and tilts his head to the side in thought, weighing up the merits of my plan. "Wouldn't work," he eventually says, shooting my fledgling idea down. "They'd never divulge that kind of information, not without going through strict protocols first. Unfortunately, we can't just walk in there waving an old invoice and expect results."

"There must be a way—that's the only lead we have, Tom. The invoice is it. Everything else will take too long." I feel my shoulders slump with deflation.

"Wait, I didn't say it wasn't a good idea. Yes, we should one hundred percent follow the invoice, but to get the information we need—it will take creative measures. And not exactly legal."

"I won't tell if you don't," I say, managing a watery smile. After everything that's happened, I'm willing to bend a few rules; the stakes are too high not to.

"Good. We should get out of here." He checks his watch, a grim frown creasing his forehead.

He doesn't need to say it; we're running out of time.

Back in the dressing room, I pause and turn to him, knowing that if we walk away from here, we'll be in all kinds of trouble with the authorities later. "If you want to call the police now, I won't stop you. Just give me a couple of minutes to be alone with them, alright?"

Tom hesitates, then takes my hand and squeezes gently. "I'll be waiting outside. But I'm not calling the police. They'll lock down this house and everything in it; that includes us. You were right not to let me call them earlier. How about we trigger the alarm instead? It'll alert the security company and they'll send a car out to check on the property."

As much as I hate the thought of leaving my parents like this, we have no choice. And so, after we make our way back through the house, I pause outside the lounge, my hand gripping the door handle so tight it leaves a dull ache in fingers.

"Thanks," I say, turning to Tom. "I... I just need to say g-goodbye to them. I'll be right behind you."

Tom reaches out as if to pull me into a hug, but instead squeezes my arm in an awkward display of concern. There's so little I know about him; I wish I knew whether I can trust him. I follow his movements as he slips out through the front door, and with a deep breath, I prepare to see my parents one last time.

This is not how I will choose to remember them. They were so much more. They took care of me when I lost everything, opening their home and their hearts to me.

And what scares me more than anything is finding out they've died trying to protect me.

# Chapter Thirty-Seven

I slip into the passenger seat of Tom's Land Rover, shaking off the rain and staring back through the window at the sombre house.

I'm convinced I'll never be able to step inside there again, no matter how many happy memories it once held.

A heavy silence settles on the car as we pull away. Winston leans forward to touch my shoulder. "Tom told me about your parents. I am deeply sorry, Ella. Will you be okay?"

I glance round and throw him a weak smile. "I can't really process it yet."

"No, I expect not. This might sound daft, but Jambo here is an excellent listener. If you ever want his company, you let me know. I guarantee you'll feel all the better for having this little chap at your side."

"It's not daft, not at all... I'd like that." Emotion knots my stomach for I know how much Jambo means to him, and I'm touched that he would entrust me with his beloved companion. I blink away the unshed tears that sting at my eyes. "Where're we going?" I ask, taking one last glance at my childhood home in the side mirror as it fades into the darkness.

Tom glances over, a worried look in his eyes. "I'd be happier if you'd let me take you back to the gallery. Stay with Wynter, and we'll keep you updated. You've just had a terrible shock, Ella, and—"

"And I'll deal with it when I know Suzy's safe. I'm not giving up on her, not now."

"Okay, if that's what you want." Tom adjusts his grip on the wheel and focuses back on the road. "In that case, to answer your question, *we* are going to break into Elevate."

"What!" I swing round to face him, instantly regretting the sudden movement as a shooting pain tears through my ribs.

"We got a hit on the invoice. And before you ask... don't," Tom says, affording me a meaningful glance as he expertly controls the wheel. Before I can respond, the car jolts to one side, buffeted by another ferocious slam of the wind. I grip the side of my seat and keep my mouth shut.

Unfazed by the near wipeout of the vehicle, Tom waves a finger in front of the dash computer. "This is a list of patients my contact has narrowed the invoice down to. Whenever you're ready, I'd like you to scroll through them. Since we're looking for a connection to your parents, it doesn't matter how obscure it might seem—anything at all—just throw it out there, okay?"

"I know you said not to ask... but might this be the less than legal means you mentioned?" Once again, I can't help but admire his resourcefulness. He arches his brow at me but doesn't reply. The hint of a smug smile twitches at the corner of his mouth.

Grateful for the distraction, I tap the touch-screen computer built into the dashboard, not sure what to expect. The screen instantly throws up images of patient photos for me to scroll through. I swipe from right to left until I've scanned all ten headshots; six men and four women. Then I scroll back to the first again. The image is of a man who was once obviously attractive, albeit not anymore; not with his puffy, sunken eyes and grey, pallid skin tone. He seems vaguely familiar—not on a personal level, so a celebrity, perhaps? I decide he might be worth reviewing further and tap on the link in the top right corner. The screen fills with his details; extremely sensitive, personal information, and I'm hit with a surge of guilt for having looked at his file.

After hastily tapping the icon to exit, I flick to the next image. This one is of a woman, early twenties with long red hair hanging drab against her freckled face. I imagine the hair trailing behind her, like some sort of macabre zombie bride. Her face is gaunt, with her eyes too far apart and disproportionate to her over-sized forehead. I shiver involuntarily and click on the link. A car accident four years ago, suffered severe head injury, comes from a wealthy and powerful family. I scroll down further but the name of her family holds no relation to ours, and so I hit the exit button again with a sigh. It's already feeling like a futile exercise. I don't know any of these individuals.

At my sigh, I feel Tom's eyes on me, but when I glance over, he quickly returns his attention to the road.

"What criteria were these ten selected on?"

"The invoice dates back over eight years, so we've included only those patients admitted during that time period. They're also limited by admittance type. It seems our invoice is for a very selective wing of the hospital, one that you won't find in any brochure or website."

"Uh-huh," I reply, distracted by the next patient. On the screen is the image of a woman with eyes so hauntingly familiar that my heart thumps in my chest. When I click on the link, my hands tremble. Despite the familiarity, it's obvious I'm not going to learn much about who she is or her circumstances for being at Elevate, since her file holds very few details. I lean forward in my seat, hitting the back button and staring into her face, hoping for a glimmer of recognition.

"Have you found something?" Winston strains at his seatbelt and pulls himself forward, using my headrest as leverage to get a better view.

"Good Lord! What is that smell?" I shriek as I almost gag from breathing in.

"Ah, guilty as charged," Winston says with a sheepish grin at my side. "I'm afraid my stomach isn't used to the rich food Tom served up—delicious as it was—and I'm not used to confined spaces either. Still, better out than in."

"No!" Tom cries.

"No!" I say, at the same time.

"Jesus. Christ." Tom's face scrunches as his upper lip tries to shield his nostrils.

"Open the windows before I throw up!" Never have I been so desperate to breathe in fresh air. The foul smelling stench is worse than even that of the bats.

"Can't. The wind will blow us off the road. Breathe through your mouth. And you—" he gives Winston a long and menacing stare in his rearview mirror, "N*ever* do that in my car again, or I swear I'll open that door and throw you to the kerbside!"

Jambo gives a low whine. It's unclear whether he's suffering like us or just upset by the shouting. Winston holds his hands in the air. "Sorry, my bad. On my life, it won't happen again. I only leaned forward because you were about to show me the file on the screen—you think you have something?"

"Hmm, perhaps..." I hold the crook of my elbow across my face in order to stop myself from gagging and return my attention to the computer. "This woman was admitted following a trauma, but the file is flagged as classified. There's no history about where she's come from or any contact details in her notes. She has a long list of treatments, though. Like expensive eye-watering treatments. I don't recognise her as a celebrity, but there's definitely something familiar about her. Who do you suppose she is?"

"Someone from your childhood, perhaps? Before your parents adopted you?" Tom suggests, his eyes still on the road.

I manoeuvre round in my seat to face him, careful not to jar my ribs this time. "Except my family perished in a house fire, as I told you. I've seen the death certificates and my adoption papers, all done through the proper channels. There are no other relatives, nobody to come forward and claim me when my parents died." I'm mindful of how defensive and prickly I sound.

"Yet some instinct made you stop at her image." Winston lowers his voice, and I get the impression he's almost trying to hypnotise me into remembering who she is. "What was it about her? Think back to how you felt when you first brought up her photograph..."

"Her eyes. She reminds me of someone. One of my paintings, perhaps?" I shrug, agitated by the niggling feeling that there's something I'm not remembering. The notion of familiarity remains strong as I look at the woman's photo.

"Yeah, I have to confess that your gallery gives me the creeps a bit," Winston says, taking me by surprise. "All those watchful eyes."

"In all honesty, I hadn't thought of it like that before. They've always fascinated me. Often there's a deep intensity of emotion that you might otherwise never experience without engaging on such a detailed level."

"Hah, now that I get. When I look into Jambo's eyes, all I see is intense mischief," he chuckles, ruffling the dog's ears. Jambo responds to the attention by licking Winston's face and pumping his little tail furiously from side to side. A smile tugs at the corners of my mouth as I watch them together.

"In her message, my mother said something strange, that she knew *someone* would come looking for me. Do you suppose this woman is also in danger? Is that why they kept her treatment hidden? To keep her safe?"

Before Tom can respond to my conjecture, a voice cuts through the speakers of the car, making me yelp and jump in my seat.

"*Sir, I have the number you requested.*"

"Excellent. What is it?" Tom replies, as if it's perfectly normal to be talking to a disembodied voice sounding out of nowhere.

I can't tell if the voice belongs to a male or female, but their tone is soft and their words clear. I picture someone like Emilia Clarke on the other end of the call, and I frown at the sudden pang of jealousy.

What the actual fuck?

I have no idea where that came from!

Shock—that'll be it. I'm obviously a melting pot of emotions right now. In which case, our destination could be more fortuitous than I thought; what are the chances that Elevate have a late night walk-in therapy session for people who have witnessed an explosion, are being stalked by a serial rapist, had their best friend abducted, walked the rooms of a creepy old cottage and now discovered the bodies of her parents amongst priceless artworks? On reflection, it seems extremely unlikely.

"*One-three-seven-six-nine, sir,*" the voice says, cutting through my reverie.

"Thank you. Anything further to report?"

"*All quiet here. I'll monitor for another ten minutes, then activate the house alarm.*"

"Okay, good. We'll speak soon."

"*Best of luck, sir.*"

A soft click confirms whoever was speaking has disconnected.

"Um—so who was that?" I ask, with uncharacteristic directness, still visualising the seductive Emilia Clarke.

"My contact," Tom replies, with barely a sideways glance in my direction and obvious reluctance to elaborate further.

"And the number?"

"That's the access code to Elevate's service gate."

"What—" For the second time this journey, I jolt round in my seat to face him. "'Not entirely legal' was a bit of an understatement, don't you think?"

He smiles, a soft chuckle rumbling in his throat.

It's a surprisingly pleasing sound.

Ugh... what the hell is wrong with me?

I shake my head and stare straight ahead, watching the dashed white lines on the road disappear beneath us as we race towards our destination, the manic windscreen wipers matching my racing pulse as they swipe away the rain hammering against the glass.

If there's one thing I've learned from being in the company of Tom Bankes, it's that he's an extremely resourceful man.

And I wonder what lengths he'll go to get what he wants.

# Chapter Thirty-Eight

Through rain streaked glass, I peer out at the imposing white building of the Elevate Institute as Tom pulls the car to a crawl on the deserted side road. The floodlit architecture is intimidating, with elaborate side wings sprawling out from each side of the three-storey building. All that's missing are the big fluffy clouds and pearly gates. I can almost picture the plush interior with its nurses wafting along in a hushed and ultra efficient manner.

"When their clientele arrive here, do you think they feel any less anxious than the average Joe Bloggs turning up at a regular busy, budget constrained hospital?" I say, thinking aloud. "However you look at it, it's still a hospital, regardless of whether it resembles a five-star luxurious hotel or not."

"I'm fairly sure hospitals don't feature on people's top places-to-visit list. Anyone stood on the other side of those high metal gates will wish they were anywhere but here," Tom replies, turning off the engine after a quick scan for security guards. "Ready?"

My stomach does a somersault as he slips an earpiece into his ear.

This is really happening.

We're going to break into a mental health clinic!

"What's that for?" I ask, hearing the slight tremor in my voice as I tap the side of my ear to indicate his earpiece.

"There have to be over a hundred rooms in there." He tilts his chin towards one of the wings. "We'd never find what we're looking for without help. Someone will be directing us while we're inside and tracking our movements through my phone." He smiles confidently, as if it's a normal occurrence to be breaking into buildings. "Don't look so worried, Ella. I won't let anything bad happen."

"But what if we're stopped and challenged by security?" Evidently, I'm not as comfortable with the plan as Tom appears to be. "We don't know who this person is. What if the invoice isn't for her? What if she's so drugged up to her eyeballs that she's practically stoic?"

"Then we'll apologise for the intrusion and promptly leave."

"And what if Malden's beat us to it? Have you thought of that? She could be in danger—we all could." I shiver.

"Once we're inside, if we're in any doubt of the situation, we'll alert security."

Before I can raise any more concerns, Winston interrupts us. "And what do you want me and Jambo to do while you're gone?" he asks, leaning forward between our two seats. His eyes sparkle with an eagerness to help.

"Pass me your phone."

Winston digs inside his coat and presents Tom with the mobile he gave him earlier.

"Under the tag 'SOS' is a number I want you to call—if you notice anything that suggests security has apprehended us, call it immediately. Explain to them where we are. They'll know what to do."

"Consider it done," Winston says, taking the phone back and deftly sliding it into one of his many pockets.

"So who precisely will rescue us in an emergency?" These cloak and dagger communications are making me jittery. "The mysterious *Emilia*?"

Tom raises an eyebrow as he pulls on his hat and zips up his jacket. "My lawyer. It's the number for my legal team."

"Oh, alright. Well... well good, then." I lower my eyes and feel my cheeks burn.

"Shall we?" he says, ignoring my flustered ramblings as he swings open the car door and disappears. I give a backward glance at Winston, throwing him an exasperated look as I duck out of the car in quick pursuit of Tom.

Within minutes of following the metal fence that's at least twice my height, we find the gate we're after at the rear of the property. The service access has a touchpad that accepts the digits Tom enters without protest. With an electronic clunk, the gate swings open, allowing us to slip into the grounds unobserved.

My heart pounds in my chest as we splash our way through puddles, keeping so tight to the shrubbery that the short branches stab at our legs and arms. Although the rain temporarily eases off, no longer coming down in torrents, the gusts of wind remain vicious and threaten to blow us off our feet.

Side by side, we run through the grounds, crouching low as we pass a set of illuminated archways leading to the grand doors of the main entrance. Four small red lights from security cameras blink steadily, alerting us to the fact that somewhere inside is a security guard monitoring the exterior. I hold my breath, waiting for the sound of sirens to wail or floodlights to swamp us, but we continue on unchallenged and make our way to the furthest end of the building and the east wing.

The prospect of creeping through the corridors of these vast premises, waiting to be discovered with each turn we take, is far from a welcome one.

"Do you suppose they'll have a skeleton staff covering the night shift?" I say, struggling to shake off the image of an oversized male nurse lumbering after us once we're inside.

"There's twenty-eight members of staff signed in. I'd say, given the size of this place, the odds of avoiding them are pretty good."

Thoughts of Suzy and my parents spur me onwards, and bolstered by Tom's assurance, I push past the wind battered shrubbery, my stride growing in confidence and determination.

One way or another, this will end tonight.

As we race across the wide gravel path circumventing the entire building, Tom skids to a halt in front of a fire door, almost causing me to collide with him. The plain door is barely noticeable against the white walls, conveniently tucked far enough away from the grandiose main entrance of the east wing. I gasp in surprise as it buzzes open on our approach.

"That would be... Emilia, as you like to call her," Tom says with a mischievous grin.

I swallow a lump in my throat.

If we're caught, we could go to prison for this—twenty-eight staff now seems a lot more than it did when we were outside—we'll be in more trouble than I care to think about.

Tom peers in the door and scans the corridor before motioning for me to follow him. I catch my breath as I step inside; the door closing behind us with a soft click.

Can we even leave again without setting off the alarms?

Fucking. Hell.

My heart has never beat so loudly. It's the only sound I can hear in the jarring silence. My breath comes in short bursts, trying to keep pace with the manic rhythm.

"This way." Tom leads us off to the right along a softly lit corridor with expensive beige carpet and luxury wallpaper. If I didn't know better, I would suspect we were in a top end hotel.

"How big is this east wing?" I ask, trying to get my bearings and hoping we don't need to stray too far from our escape route.

"Big. But we're looking for the *other* east wing."

"There's two?"

"Apparently so. Discreet and well hidden, it's also our best chance of finding your classified trauma case."

"And your contact can lead us there? Even though it's hidden?"

"They'll find themselves sacked if not," he says flippantly. I can't tell whether he's joking. "Let's keep moving. The longer we spend in these corridors, the higher the risk of us being spotted. If we take a less direct route, we can avoid most of the security cameras. Stay close to the sides and be ready to run if I tell you."

*Run? Holy shit.*

I follow close behind Tom as he listens to the instructions in his ear. We pass by widely spaced doors with brass plate numbers and empty communal areas with plush chairs and glossy magazines. Before ending up here, I imagine most of Elevate's patients would regularly feature in those pages. Oddly, there's a calm stillness to our surroundings that not even the storm can penetrate. In here it's all about serenity, from the mood lighting to the soft elevator music in the background, and the smell of ylang-ylang and lavender that lingers in the air.

Not at all how I pictured a mental institute to be.

After following a maze of left and right turns, we take a sharp right at the end of a short corridor and find ourselves at a dead end. We stand staring at a set of tiffany blue velvet curtains pulled closed. Positioned in front is a matching armchair with a small oval-shaped table offering some reading material. Convenient.

"A quiet spot to relax and take in the views?" Tom suggests, cynically.

"Or the entrance to an off the grid, and apparently non-existent, section of the clinic," I reply, pulling aside the corner of one curtain.

Unsurprisingly, there's no window overlooking the grounds, only a sealed doorway. At the sound of a soft click, I glance at Tom, who grins back. 'Emilia' is proving herself more than capable of guiding us through what at first seemed an impossible task.

I push down on the metal handle and gasp at the sheer opulence of the space we step into. I don't know what I expected of this hidden wing; a dingy area where few ever tread, perhaps? Instead, I stare down an arched hallway with circular skylights spaced along its ceiling. During the day, they would allow a flood of sunlight through, but even at night, they give off a soft glow from the lights embedded within them. The walls are a cool white with hanging mirrors and paintings, complemented by an eggshell blue carpet. Placed on the floor near the entrance is a sumptuous display of fresh white flowers—full-bodied French hydrangeas and wild thistles, arranged professionally in an oversized vase—it's stunning.

"I'm considering moving in," I say to Tom.

"It certainly makes my place look shabby. Who do you suppose gets to stay in a setting like this? Far beyond your average medical care—I think I need a new healthcare plan!"

"It explains the astronomical fees they charge. Do you think there's security cameras in here, too?"

"Don't worry, we've dealt with those. We have fifteen minutes before they're due to come off the continual streaming loop we've set them on. Any longer and we risk drawing attention." Just as I'm about to comment on how helpful his contact has been, he freezes beside me. "Shhh—do you hear that?"

I stop and listen.

*Footsteps.*

*And they're coming this way.*

"Quick, try that door!" Tom whispers, ushering me forward at a run.

I grip the handle of the first of four doors leading off from the hallway. Relief washes over me as it moves without resistance.

No locks—no dangerous patients.

I hope.

We slip inside, holding our breath as we wait, backs pressed against the door, willing the footsteps to pass by outside. Like an electric charge between us, the tension buzzes in my ear as I watch the rapid rise and fall of Tom's chest beside me, the risk of imminent discovery bearing down on us.

He leans his head close to mine and says in a whisper, "I think they've gone. You can let go now."

I look down and see that I'm gripping his hand. With a horrified gawk, I drop it as if I were holding a red hot poker. The rising heat burning at my cheeks only serves to exacerbate my discomfort.

Fortunately, we're quickly distracted by the room we've stumbled into; a luxurious suite to rival any of London's finest hotels. We cautiously edge our way forward, taking in the supersize bed against the furthest wall. Fit for royalty, it's made up with exquisite throws and at least a dozen scatter cushions artistically placed in neat little piles. At the end of the bed is a long table, with another elaborate fresh flower display. In front of this is a small lounge area with a sumptuous-looking sofa and two armchairs in soothing greens and pinks. A second door leads off to what I assume is the bathroom.

I suck in the corner of my bottom lip and stifle a gasp as I spot the woman we came here to see.

A frail lady sits on the sofa, motionless and staring down, unblinking at the book in her hands.

*The woman with the haunted eyes.*

# Chapter Thirty-Nine

I nudge Tom with my elbow and point to the sofa where the woman remains unaware of our presence.

"Let me approach her on my own," I say in a low whisper. "We don't want to scare her."

Tom nods, quick to assess the situation, and edges back towards the door, out of view. If she screams the place down or triggers an alarm for help, we'll find ourselves cornered with no place to run. Worse than that, it would spell certain disaster for Suzy. Even Tom's fancy lawyers would struggle to get us a quick release after this stunt.

Whoever this woman is, I need to find out if she's the person my parents have been paying for to receive treatment. And why she hides in this secret wing of the hospital.

With determined resolve, I calm my breathing and carefully approach the lounge area, trying my best to avoid startling her.

Once I reach the edge of a rectangular silk rug, with only a few steps between us, I start to wonder whether she's drugged or perhaps fallen asleep. I clear my throat softly. When she finally looks up, raising her eyes from the book, she smiles. It's the most beautiful thing I've ever seen.

"Hello," I say, my voice sounding breathless. "Do you mind if I join you? My name is Ella."

"Oh, hello, I'm afraid I didn't hear you come in. Please, make yourself comfortable," she says in a silvery voice that makes my pulse flutter.

But it's her eyes that render me speechless.

I was wrong about them being haunted. Now that I'm standing here, under her gaze, I'm captivated not only by their shimmering silvery blue hue, but by the serenity that emanates from a seemingly unreachable place, far beyond the tenderness that interlaces with a heart-wrenching sorrow. A soul-touching tranquillity that literally takes my breath away.

"Th-thank you..." I step forward hesitantly, fearful of breaking the spell.

"Caroline Atkinson-Gray. You must be the new nanny?" She gestures for me to take the chair opposite.

Unsure of what to do, I drag my eyes away to glance over at Tom, who frantically bobs his head in the affirmative whilst giving a solid thumbs-up gesture.

"Um... y-yes, I'm the new nanny," I answer, feeling every bit the fraud I am, as I lower myself into one of the plush armchairs.

"So pretty—you have a kind face. Are the children asleep yet?"

I snap my head back towards Tom.

Holy shit. We didn't prepare for this.

He shrugs and moves his hand in a circular motion, mouthing that I should go along with the pretence.

"Yes... yes, th-they're all tucked up and sleeping soundly. Um... I thought we might have a quick chat, if that would be alright?"

"Of course, how rude of me!" she says, flipping shut the book and placing it down next to a small reading lamp on the table beside her. As she removes her glasses, she leans forward expectantly, and I realise she's not as old and frail as I first assumed. Although petite and fragile, with thinning, white hair down to her shoulders, she has movement and clarity of voice of someone much younger than her appearance. "Is it Harry?" she asks, smiling fondly. "Such a delightful child, but can be quite the handful at times!"

"Everything is fine. H-Harry is—he's—what I mean is..." I stumble over my words, something tugging at the threads of a memory. "He—they're all fine," I eventually blurt out, frowning and giving my head a hasty shake. What the fuck just happened? It felt like my brain turned to fuzz. I surreptitiously glance at Tom, who squints at me through narrowed eyes as he motions again for me to move the conversation along. The minutes are passing and we don't have long before the cameras drop off their static feedback. With a steadying breath, I pull myself together and try again. "Actually, my friend is missing, and I hoped you might look at her photograph to see if you recognise her?"

"I don't understand. Who are you? You're not the nanny!" Her voice rising an octave with alarm.

Shit.

Too much.

I throw up my hands, quickly back-pedalling. "I am—I'm the new nanny! The children are sleeping, they're alright... *Harry* is alright," I say, in a firm, reassuring tone. The woman visibly relaxes her slight frame and smiles again, a hand resting on her chest.

"Please excuse me, I worry about them. The children mean the world to me."

"Which is why I'm here—as their nanny—to help. But I'm also worried about my friend... the same way that you worry about your children. If I can only ask you to look at her picture—"

"Of course. Whatever I can do to help. Only you mustn't be concerned. Your friend is safe and well, as are my children."

I'm momentarily taken aback by her words. As much as I want to believe it's true, I can see that this kindly woman's mind is not well. My heart sinks, knowing that she's unlikely to be in a mentally fit state to help us.

Yet another dead-end.

Nevertheless, I show her the image of Suzy on my phone and study her expression as she places her glasses back on to examine the screen.

"No, I'm sorry. I don't know this young woman." She shakes her head.

I swallow back the disappointment and tuck the phone back into my pocket. Next, I take out the dated image of my mother at the cottage and pass it across to her. With hands that are remarkably steady despite her fragile appearance, she takes the photograph and her eyes immediately light up with recognition. My heart races, knowing we might finally be getting somewhere.

"Dearest Shiela! Of course, I know her. In fact, I believe we're meeting Shiela and Frank next weekend at the Hollies."

"The... the Hollies?"

# THE GRAYSTONE KILLINGS

"Such a lovely getaway, right in the middle of the countryside. We named it 'The Hollies' on account of all the holly bushes we planted in the garden; so pretty in winter with the berries. But this is my favourite season at the cottage," she says, tapping the image. She looks up, smiling that beautiful smile that has the power to make a person believe, for one glorious second, that nothing bad could ever happen. "I simply adore springtime with the children running amongst the bluebells. And lambing season at the farm, the Hasselhoffs are so good, letting the children help care for the newly born. I hope you'll love it there as much as we do."

"Yes, I'm—I'm sure I will." I realise she's talking to me as the nanny. "The woman in the photograph, you called her Sheila? And her husband... Frank?" I say, keeping my voice steady. My parents' names are Anne and John. Could she be confusing them with someone else? There's no question that it's my mother in the photo.

Oh, dear God.

*Were they lying about their identities, too?*

"My dearest friends in the entire world. It will be so lovely to spend the weekend with them! The children simply adore them. Now, if you'll please excuse me, I'd like to check on the children and kiss them goodnight."

She makes to rise from the sofa, but before she can do so, I skirt around the table between us and take a seat next to her, placing a reassuring hand on her arm. She smells of honey and fruit, a sweet and delicate scent.

"The children are sleeping. We probably shouldn't disturb them. Besides, I'm enjoying getting to know your family, and if I'm to care for them I should learn more about their circumstances, don't you think? Can I be direct and ask why you're here?"

She stares at me blankly, before she relaxes back into the cushions of the sofa and looks around her slowly, as if seeing her surroundings for the first time. "You mean this old loft room?" She laughs, a soft, tinkling sound. "We're refurbishing. No need to be concerned, dear. Our rooms will be available again soon. I trust that Mrs. Wilson has shown you to your temporary accommodation?"

"Um—Mrs. Wilson?"

"Our head housekeeper. She's in a frightful tizzy with all the upheaval. We'll have you moved closer to the children's bedrooms by the end of the month. I'm looking forward to seeing the old place spruced up a bit. It was my husb—" she starts to say, before pausing and staring down at her hands. When she looks up again, I see the haunted look in her eyes that first drew me to her.

"Caroline? Where is your husband now?"

"The children have picked out the most adorable new colours for their bedrooms. I must show you!"

Husband is obviously off topic, then. Interesting.

"I'd like that, thank you. I have one other question, if I may? Do the names John and Anne Mills mean anything to you? I believe you might know them as Frank and Sheila?" Although acutely aware of pushing my luck, I need to know if she's familiar with the deception surrounding my parents' lives.

"Why on earth would they change their names? What a preposterous notion."

From the corner of my eye I can see Tom gesturing harshly, signalling for me to wrap things up. I decide to try one last approach.

"This is a beautiful house you have. Does it have a name?"

"Why yes, it's been in my family for generations," she says with an air of affection and pride. "This is Graystone Manor."

I gasp, clasping my hand over my mouth as the name shakes me to my core.

# Chapter Forty

"Ella? Ella, are you okay?"

A familiar voice calls out as images swim before me, a blend of shapes I can't make sense of. And then a snapping sound, close to my face. Something cold pressed against my lips.

"Drink this."

"Is she going to be alright?" A female voice I don't recognise.

"She's fine. A sip of water and she'll feel better."

"I'm quite relieved you were here and able to help. One moment we were chatting and the next the colour drained from her face. I'm sorry, I didn't catch your name?"

"Tom. I'm—um—helping to oversee the renovations."

Images slowly come into focus and I make out Tom's concerned face as he kneels on the rug before me. He clicks his fingers in quick succession centimetres away from my face, forcing me to blink and jolt my head backwards.

# THE GRAYSTONE KILLINGS

"There you are—" he says with obvious relief. "You had us worried for a while. What happened? You began trembling, then the colour left your face."

"Are you quite well?" a voice asks from beside me.

*The woman with the haunted eyes...* a small gasp leaves my lips as I remember our conversation.

*Graystone Manor.*

I recall reading the name when I removed the deeds from the safe, but at the time, it held no significant meaning. Now a rush of disjointed images and emotions flood my mind; a face I don't recognise looking down on me, a hand extending out toward me, kind and reassuring eyes, a sudden bright light shining at my face.

My chest feels like it's about to burst with the intensity of emotions slamming into me, one after another; fear, then confusion, the sensation of being in a cold, dark corridor.

And scared.

My God, so terrifyingly scared.

A fear that claws its way to the surface; ripping my soul apart until nothing remains.

I shudder and take another sip of the refreshing chilled water as I try to shrug off the images that don't belong to me. What is this? Some sort of psychic connection to this woman? It's a powerful and emotional reaction, and it's freaking the hell out of me!

One thing I know for certain is that I can't leave here without uncovering her link to my family. One exists, I just need more time.

"Loop the cameras again," I say in a low whisper to Tom. His eyes widen in surprise and he gives me a brief shake of his head.

"Too risky."

"Do it!"

Tom frowns, but raises himself up and steps back to mutter into his microphone. He gives instructions to keep looping the security cameras, even though he knows it's unsafe; skeleton staff or not, hospital security will expect to see someone walking the hallways soon.

"Apologises, Caroline. Please, continue—I assure you I'm fine. You were telling me about the manor being in your family for many generations? I'd like to hear about it, if that's alright?"

"Well, I'm afraid it doesn't make for a particularly jovial tale. You see, Graystone's history is steeped in tragedy. Built in the eighteen hundreds by my great-great-grandfather, a man named William Gray, it was—despite its chequered past—a gesture of adoration for his beloved wife, Margaret. Its architecture was exotic for its time, reflecting the depth of his love for her. However, within a few short months of its completion, unimaginable disaster befell them.

"Lightning struck one fateful afternoon during a freak thunderstorm, striking an oak tree within the grounds and causing it to collapse onto the summerhouse. William often spent his afternoons reading and playing the violin there, and tragically, the tree collapsed on top of him, crushing him to death. Margaret was bereft, and expecting their first child, she shut herself away from society to mourn her beloved. It's told she died from a broken heart soon after giving birth to their son.

"Over the years, several guests of the manor claimed to have heard her sorrowful weeping echoing through the halls, a heart-wrenching, mournful wail. Some even recounted seeing the ghost of a woman dressed in long black skirts, holding a baby in her arms as she walks through the mist to where the summerhouse once stood. Such a romantic notion, don't you think?"

"A real-life tragic romance. Have you ever caught sight of her ghost?" I ask.

She laughs softly, shaking her head. "No, I'm of the opinion that if my great-great-grandmother wishes to roam the grounds, then we should leave her be."

"What happened to her child? After she died, I mean?"

"Ah, my great-grandfather Henry. He remained living at Graystone Manor long after his mother passed away, raised by a spinster aunt. After he married his young bride, Isabelle, they lived a rather reclusive life, preferring solitude to society. He had a brilliant mind and was quite the distinguished scientist. But tragedy was never more than a stone's throw away. There was firm belief amongst the local villagers that Henry was an alchemist. They believed him to be not only obsessed with medicine, but with seeking the answers to eternal life. It was a time when ghost stories and seances were popular, so it's no surprise that the local population likened Henry to Frankenstein. They convinced themselves that one day he would unleash upon them a terrible monster.

"One moonless night, a ferocious fire broke out at the manor, destroying a considerable section of the house. The newspapers reported it an accident, the cause being attributed to a naked flame. Local rumour, however, suggested otherwise. The story goes that a group of villagers approached Graystone Manor under cover of the darkness and set Henry's lab alight. Borne of fear, the consequences of their actions were far more horrifying than any experiment could ever yield.

"The attack occurred after midnight. Henry and his family had retired for the day, the domestic servants in bed in their quarters. The service wing was situated close to the laboratory and tragically destroyed in the fire. Eight souls perished that night, many of whom had served the Gray family for decades."

"How awful." I shudder as the horror of that night plays out in my mind.

"Indeed, it was. Distraught by their deaths, Henry rebuilt his laboratory and threw himself into his work with even more compulsion than before. When tragedy struck again and Isabelle died giving birth to their second child, he insisted on sending the children away to live with a distant relative, and dismissed all servants. In the months following his wife's death, no-one in the local community ever caught sight of him. Nor were any new scientific papers of his work printed in any journals; it was as if he had died right alongside Isabelle. However, each evening, as daylight gave way to dusk, passersby would see a flicker of light in the windows of the manor. Many a spirited child would stand at the gates of the driveway, daring one another to catch sight of Frankenstein and his monster. But nobody ever laid eyes on Henry again."

"It seems his life was just as tragic as his parents," I say, intrigued by the story. I sit up a little straighter, an idea forming in my mind. "What happened to Graystone after Henry disappeared?"

"The family had the property boarded up, and it remained that way for many decades until my grandfather Henry, named so after his father, returned to Kent. The surviving child of the birth that killed Isabelle, he fell in love with my grandmother—the daughter of a prominent banker—and began restoration work on the old building. By then it had been lying empty for many years and stories of ghosts were not in short supply, tales passed down through generations by the villagers. Along with sightings of the grieving widow carrying her baby, they say the screams of the servants who perished can be heard across the North Downs hillside, that a burning smell shrouds the village on the anniversary of the fire. Even stories of Henry, the mad Frankenstein scientist, all entwined themselves into the fabric of our folklore, and contribute to Graystone's reputation as being one of the most haunted buildings in the South East."

"It's a fascinating history. There's no question of that. What about after they restored it? I presume your family settled back in Kent and remained at Graystone Manor?"

"Yes, dear, that's correct. And as you can see, we're all safe and well, with no tragic family curse befalling us. It was a privilege to grow up in this house, as my ancestors did before me. My children are the next generation of Grays to live here, but they're still young and are yet to appreciate the beauty of the old place. Cara would sooner swap our family home for one with modern architecture and all the latest technologies. She's teased at school, you see, for living in the 'haunted' house. And yet despite all her remonstrating, I think she's really quite fond of the place."

"Cara's a beautiful name. Is she your eldest child?"

"Yes, such a charming girl. She's fifteen. Then there's Harry, he's eight and our youngest daughter, Elena, who has just turned six. I'm so pleased you'll be assuming the position of their nanny. I know they're going to be happy in your care."

Tom's phone vibrates, and I turn to see him checking the screen. He raises his brow at the message received and pockets the device again before rejoining us.

"Mrs. Atkinson-Gray, it's been a pleasure to meet you this evening, and we've enjoyed hearing of your family's history with Graystone Manor," he says, pausing expectantly.

"It's actually *Lady* Atkinson-Gray, but please, you can call me Caroline."

Tom doesn't seem at all surprised by her title, and I suspect the message he's just received alludes to the Gray family.

"Thank you, Caroline," he says, moving a step closer until he's standing directly in front of us. "It must have been quite overwhelming for your husband to move into a building steeped in such history. Before we go, perhaps you could introduce him to us?" A dark cloud instantly falls across her face, the calm serenity of moments ago replaced with a troubled agitation. Tom places a hand gently on her shoulder as he says, softly, "Can you tell us where your husband is?"

She shrugs Tom's hand away and, leaning over, picks up her book. "I'm quite tired now. Please, show yourself out," she says, opening the pages at a leather marker.

With that, she abruptly dismisses us, returning her attention back to the book. With no alternative, I rise from the sofa to follow Tom back out towards the door. I steal a last backward glance as she sits motionless, staring unblinking at the book in her hands.

Not haunted, after all.

Only lost.

# Chapter Forty-One

"What the hell was that?" I ask Tom once we're out of earshot and making our way back down the corridor. I push past the thick curtains that conceal the entrance, no longer caring whether we bump into staff members. Such is my frustration at Tom's heavy-handedness.

"Jesus Christ, would you slow down? You're going to walk us straight into a bad situation."

When I stop and glare at him, hands firmly planted on my hips, he defiantly glares back, fuelling my anger even more until my blood pressure is racing off the charts.

How dare he accuse me of being reckless after the way he just screwed things up in there!

"Tom, she was opening up to me. And you shut her down! Why the fuck would you do that?" My words are spat with such force that he visibly flinches before grabbing for my elbow. With an irritable tug, he pulls me back through the curtain, pinning me up against the wall and boxing me in with his body.

"Whatever this is, don't kid yourself that you're angry at me. You're angry because back there—in that room—you figured out who she is. Who *you* are. So what's it to be? Are you going to remain in denial for the rest of your life or finally face up to the truth for once?" His breath is hot on my face, eyes searching mine. Almost as quick as my anger surged, it vanishes again and I slump against the wall. Tom's hands remain on either side of me, pinning me in place. "You need to talk to me, Ella."

"What would you have me say? This is fucking insane!"

He hesitates, then pulls back and slips his phone from his pocket. I wait, scowling at him, as he taps the screen before holding it up in front of me. It's an open email attachment for a newspaper article, filling the small screen with a news headline that makes my stomach shrivel and my legs turn to jelly.

**Killer Slays Family in Crazed Attack**

*Dubbed The Graystone Killings—a 34-year-old man who broke into a family home in Kent, killing a teenage girl and two young children, has been remanded in custody on three charges of murder. He is also charged with aggravated burglary with intent, possessing an offensive weapon in a public place, making threats to kill and using violence to force entry to a premises. Other charges include arson after setting fire to the property in an attempt to*

# THE GRAYSTONE KILLINGS

*destroy evidence. The man cannot be named for legal reasons.*

*At 8pm on Friday, April 23, Kent police were called to the home of Lady Caroline Atkinson-Gray after a man forced his way into their historic property, Graystone Manor.*

*The bodies of Cara, 15, Harry, 8, and Elena, 6 were discovered at the grisly scene after their mother alerted the police. The family was home alone at the time of the attack. Mr Atkinson, Lady Caroline's husband, was reported to have been out of the country on business at the time. A spokesperson for the family has described Mr. Atkinson as being 'shocked' and 'horrified' at the murders of his children. Lady Caroline is being treated for third-degree burns and smoke inhalation. She remains in a critical condition. A lawyer for the family has asked that their privacy be respected at this incredibly difficult time.*

"Oh my God," I murmur, shivering involuntarily.

"And look at this." Tom swipes the screen to the left, still holding up the phone for me to see.

I cringe at the four images; death certificates.

"Why are you showing me these?"

"Just look at them."

With reluctance, I take the phone from him and pinch the screen with my fingertips to zoom into each one. Three children, three death certificates, all causes of death due to multiple stab wounds. It makes for disturbing reading. At the last certificate, I squint at the handwriting and do a double take.

Fuck.

"Where did you get this? It has to be wrong!"

"Either it's a falsified death certificate, or the woman we just spoke with isn't who she claims to be. For the record, my money's on the former. She's legit, not batshit crazy."

Undecided, I glance again at the death certificate for Lady Caroline Atkinson-Gray. Cause of death, respiratory distress, asphyxia and respiratory failure; smoke inhalation.

"I... I don't understand—"

"Only, I think you do, Ella. Someone falsified Caroline's death certificate and I suspect they falsified Elena's, too."

"What—what are y-you saying?"

"That all evidence points to *you* being that six-year-old child." Tom shakes his head, dragging his hand across the back of his neck. "Jesus Christ, I think you might be Elena. She didn't die in the fire. But someone went to a hell of a lot of trouble to make it seem that she did."

"You realise you sound like a crazy person, right?"

"Do I, though? Even putting aside the obvious family resemblance between you and Caroline..." His gaze softens as he looks down at my face. "Come on, you must have noticed you have the same shaped face and almost identical features?"

I shrug, not wanting to admit he might be right. Caroline's oval-shaped face, cupid-bow lips, and almond-shaped eyes are the mirror of mine.

"I'll bet they adopted you around the same time of the attack. How old are you?"

"Twenty-six."

"The article was published exactly twenty years ago. You would have been six."

"I was only three years old when my parents adopted me."

"Were you? Or was that what you were told? No-one would expect a younger child to have any real recollection of their early formative years. On the other hand, a six-year-old who's blocked out a traumatic event—? That's harder to explain away. You would have questioned why you had no memory of your life before they adopted you."

"Except I've seen my adoption papers and my actual parents' death certificates."

"And did they look like this fake death certification, right here?" he asks, tapping the edge of his phone.

*Fuck. He has a point.*

The certificate I'm looking at right now could easily pass for genuine.

"At the cottage, you told me you have scars on your feet from the house fire that killed your parents. My guess is that was another lie. I believe you got those burns when the intruder set fire to Graystone, the same fire Caroline's fake death certificate purports to. And if you still need further convincing, I've watched you react to sights and sounds that seemingly hold no obvious meaning to you. Back there in the room, you reacted to Lady Caroline mentioning the name Graystone Manor. Do you know why? Because I do. It was your *home*, Ella."

I heave a long sigh before saying, "This is insane. You expect me to believe I simply erased my brother and sister from my memory? Wiped my entire family from existence?"

"No, not erased—not exactly. Suppressed. They're in there, waiting for when you're ready to handle the truth of what happened."

"You really believe that, don't you? You actually think that woman is my birth mother?"

I'm starting to suspect he's crazier than she is.

Even so, the niggling doubt in my mind makes me wonder if he's onto something. I felt it myself when I was talking to Caroline; a deep connection I couldn't explain. A familiarity that felt of belonging.

I push Tom aside and, annoyed, duck back through the curtain into the main wing. Talk such as this won't help us find Suzy. He's persistent though and follows close behind, all the while still trying to make his point.

"What about your panic attacks? A deep-seated traumatic event such as that night would have repercussions for any child, especially one so young. You said you've had them for as long as you can remember. What if that night at Graystone is as far back as your memory goes?" Tom matches my stride, remaining rigidly dogmatic in his efforts to get me to accept his version of the facts.

I spin on my heels to face him, clenching my hands into fists with frustration. "Enough, Tom! It's enough. Say, for argument's sake, that I am Elena—what then? It still doesn't bring us any closer to finding Suzy. We need to focus on her. Not this—whatever *this* is."

"Okay, fine. Have it your way," he says, throwing up his hands with a shrug. "So, what are you thinking? Where do we go from here?"

There can be only one answer to that question, and as I walk away, I throw a glance over my shoulder at Tom. "We go to Graystone Manor, of course."

Tom raises an eyebrow and lets out a low whistle as he follows behind me.

If he's right about all of this, then whoever attacked my family that night... *they're back.*

# Chapter Forty-Two

I look across at Tom's serious face as he scowls at the road ahead, his jaw clenching and pulsing with pent-up frustration. The knuckles of his hands turned white the second he gripped the steering wheel. And this time, it's not just because of the storm.

He hates the new plan.

*My plan, to be exact.*

"I can't thank either of you enough for everything you've done tonight, I mean it," I say, glancing behind me to where Winston sits holding Jambo on his lap. His face is also furrowed into a scowl.

"Huh," he says with a grunt.

It doesn't surprise me when my words are met with continued silence; they've aired their objections with feeling since leaving Elevate. I try a different approach to bring them onboard.

"Look, I get it. You think there's a better way—a safer way—to get Suzy back. But she's almost out of time. How much longer can she survive at the hands of that monster? In less than two hours, it'll be midnight. If he sticks to his known MO, he'll dispose of her, dead or alive, before sunrise."

"Say you're right and Suzy is being held at Graystone," Tom says with a stiffness to his voice I've not heard before. He doesn't wait for me to reply. "And say, for argument's sake, we agree that you *are* Elena. That a young Victor Malden broke into the manor that night, committing those atrocities to your family. What if everything that's happened tonight is his way of luring you back there?"

"Except there's no plausible reason for him to lure me, as you describe it, back to Graystone. Besides, the police apprehended the person responsible for the attack. He went to prison—you showed me the news article yourself."

"We don't know that for certain. The perpetrator's identity was protected. We already know Malden's a ruthless rapist and murderer. It's not that much of a leap to accept he started his killing career by attacking vulnerable children in their home. He serves his time, finds himself released from prison back into society with a new identity. Only he's apprehended again, this time for crimes against single women. With no chance of parole, he escapes, traces you to your apartment and abducts Suzy. He tracks down your parents, attacking them and luring you back to Graystone, your ancestral home, and the scene of his original crime."

"Oh, come on, that's ridiculous, Tom."

"Unless it's not. Are you really prepared to risk walking into a trap?"

"For Suzy? Yes… yes, I would. Besides, your theory doesn't stack up. Why would Malden wait until now? Why didn't he go after me when he was first released?

And why go after my parents? To get to Caroline? She supposedly died from her injuries, remember? Without the invoice, how could he know about the hospital?"

"Malden presumed everyone had died that night—Cara, Henry and Elena—from the wounds he inflicted, and afterwards Caroline from her injuries. But what if he discovered your parents had lied? That they'd covered up the truth about you and your mother surviving. Say it was more than just a random attack. What if your family was deliberately targeted and their closest friends stepped in to pick up the pieces? It puts them in similar danger and forces them into hiding, assuming new identities. Do you remember the names that Caroline referred to them by?"

With a nod, I think back to our conversation. 'She called them Frank and Sheila.'

"So, Frank and Sheila become John and Anne and they adopt Elena, changing her name to Ella. A similar enough name so as not to confuse a six-year-old. As for Lady Caroline, well, she's obviously suffering from some sort of mental breakdown, so they hide her away—safe and cared for—because as far as the outside world's concerned, she died shortly after the attack. Her husband, either distraught by events or encouraged to keep away, never returns from his trip abroad."

Holy shit.

What started as a fanciful notion of Tom's is actually making perfect sense.

*Holy fucking shit!*

But if everything he's saying is true, how do I tell what's real and what's not?

Situations like this don't happen to people like me! I run an art gallery; I teach an art school. I pay my frickin bills on time—I barely make a ripple in the fabric of life.

How can I be the daughter of the woman with the haunted eyes? No. I'd remember having an entire other family.

*It's not something you just forget.*

Would my parents really have lied to me about my past? I don't wish to believe it of them, but then what am I supposed to make of the panic room? Or the priceless art displayed right under my nose, posing as reproductions? I own an art gallery, for fuck's sake! Except these were my middle-class parents and never once did I stop to question the authenticity of their art collection. We actually laughed about the meticulous attention to detail, making it impossible to tell apart from the real artworks.

*Oh my God, what an idiot I've been!*

Unless Tom has got this all wrong, even the over protective childhood makes perfect sense now.

Fuck, fuck, fuck!

They built our lives around a spectacular lie I bought into hook, line and sinker.

I stare out the passenger window into the dark night, willing myself to feel something other than the numbness that shrouds me. Should I be feeling anger? Gratitude? Fear? I experience none of these things.

If this is the truth of my past... then it's too much. This day has turned my world upside-down and I don't know how to regain balance.

Tom's voice pulls me back from my despair, his tone having lost the harshness from before, his words sounding strangely distant to my muddled mind.

"Sorry—what did you say?"

"The police? We should call them now and tell them everything. Let them handle it from here. If Malden's at Graystone, laying in wait for us, then we're in way over our heads."

"No police," I say, shaking my head firmly.

"You're in danger, Ella. Hell, so is Lady Caroline."

"Suzy could die tonight because of me, Tom. That isn't an option. I have to do everything possible to keep her safe. If we call the police now, they'll surround the property, and then there's no telling what he'll do. Malden might panic and try to end this, taking Suzy down with him."

"And if we try to end this ourselves, we could compound the situation. People could get hurt—or worse. Trust me... I know."

"I need to see this through. Everyone wants something; I just need to understand what it is he's after."

"And if he's not there? What then?"

"Then we go to the police. I promise."

Tom shakes his head and I know he's frustrated by my continual refusal to involve the authorities.

"Okay, and what about Lady Caroline?" he asks. "If Malden knows the truth about you, it stands to reason he'll try to track her down as well. We broke into the hospital undetected. What's saying he won't do the same?"

Of course, he's right. With my parents gone, she's my responsibility now and I need to protect her. I sit up straighter in my seat, mind focused no longer on the past, but on what I need to do now.

"Earlier you had access to Elevation's security. I need you to do it again. Have the corridor leading to Lady

Caroline's room monitored. My parents wouldn't have told Malden where she is, but let's be certain."

"Ok-kay, consider it done." Tom looks at me with a mixture of surprise and approval. He stabs a finger at the console, and after the first ring gives instructions to the disembodied voice on the other end. No longer caring who the contact is, for the next hour I just need them to be on my side.

I will not let Malden take anyone else from me.

"We're twenty minutes out—into the lion's den..." Tom says as we race down the M20, passing a sign for Ashford International station. He glances at me, pressing his lips tight, a look of anguish in his eyes as he gives me a pointed stare before focusing back on the road.

Who is this man, really? After all, we only met a few hours ago. Yet he's been with me through this most horrific of nights. Perhaps I don't know the person, but the connection we've forged goes far beyond the everyday familiarity. Which is why I can't bear the thought of him coming to harm because of me.

"Not the lion's den, Tom. I'm not his prey—not this time. Victor Malden has no fucking idea what I'm capable of."

Just as a warrior prepares for battle, I don my emotional war paint.

I'm ready to face my childhood monster.

# Chapter Forty-Three

Fat splodges of rain hit the windscreen as we pull into the small country road overlooking the North Downs. A streak of lightning cuts through the sky, illuminating the sinister-looking clouds that gather above us. Out here on the open coastline, we're exposed to the full force of the storm and the vehicle shudders with each crash of thunder. The unexpected closeness of the thunderclaps is unnerving not only to us, but poor Jambo too, who yelps and whimpers from the back seat.

There are no streetlights here, not since we passed through the last village a few miles back. Our headlights carve a path through the blackness to show us the way along the single lane country road.

I stare out at the flimsy wire fence that runs along the ridge of the chalk landscape, grateful for that at least. Motorway lights glow in the near distance—far below the steep drop on the other side of the wire. I imagine that on a calm day the views across the English Channel out towards France must be breathtaking, but tonight there are no sweeping vistas to admire. Instead, there's only darkness and the violent rush of storm Ruby.

My breath catches as I get my first glimpse of Graystone Manor.

Through the rain streaked windscreen, the dark imposing structure looks every bit as tragic as its history. Hairs on the back of my neck bristle as a sense of foreboding clenches at my stomach.

"Fu-ck," I utter under my breath. "That's really it?"

"Impressive," Tom says, releasing a low whistle.

"How could anyone live there and not get lost?" Winston asks, leaning forward and gawping.

The three-storey manor house sits on a hilltop overlooking the Channel. Its sprawling ornamental architecture, designed by William Gray for his beloved bride, has a romantic medieval appearance, with thick walls, round arches and towers. The silhouette against the darkened sky is indeed impressive.

But all romantic notions instantly evaporate as we draw closer. Each bright flash of the storm strips Graystone of its shroud of darkness, revealing the charred black brickwork and boarded-up windows.

Before us stands the devastating result of a deadly power struggle between innocent and evil.

Tom pulls the car up in front of two ancient looking stone posts, their surface blackened with age. A rusting metal arch reaches across the two metre gap between them, baring the crest of an anchor, with words in metal scripted around it. The tall gates lie ominously open, daring the bold or foolish to step within the property's boundary. What remains of a driveway and gardens are as overgrown and abandoned as the house itself.

"What does the writing say?" Winston asks, trying to peer between us through the windscreen, the wipers struggling to push the hammering rain to one side.

"The words are *Anchor, Fast Anchor* I think. Probably some sort of family crest," Tom says, leaning forward in his seat, the headlights illuminating the old ironwork.

"It's a sign of hope. It means to stay true and hold fast to what you believe," I say, staring up at the arch. Tom and Winston glance round at me with curious expressions. "Look, I just know, alright?" I say with a shrug.

It's not alright though, because I also know that I once swung on the tall, iron gates that guard the approach to the setback manor.

Images of my younger self gripping the shiny black iron bars.

One foot pushing off as I throw my head back towards the sky.

Cotton clouds speeding past in a blur of white and blue as I laugh with exhilaration.

Oh God, what's happening?

It's like a crack is appearing in this strange mental wall I've built to protect myself. Memories belonging to a six-year-old girl named Elena are trying to squeeze through the gap. But I mustn't let them—Suzy needs me to stay focused. She needs me to find her.

A voice deep inside my head whispers faintly... *you already have...*

"Are you remembering something?" Tom says, his tone mirroring the concern etched on his face. He reaches over and gently touches my arm. When I turn and connect with his steel grey eyes, I see reflected there a look of reassurance. And hope.

"It's Suzy," I say, holding his gaze. "She's here."

Tom nods, accepting my words. Despite the boldness of my statement, he doesn't doubt or question me; I think because he feels it, too.

"Then let's go get her and bring her home," he says, turning off the car's engine without hesitation.

"No. Wait! If this is a trap to lure me back, as you suggest, Tom, then I can't risk anyone else getting hurt. I have to do this alone. Fifteen minutes, and if I'm not back, you can make the call and tell the police everything."

Tom grabs my hand and I recoil at the sudden forcefulness.

"Not happening. I won't let you go in there alone. For what it's worth, I love Suzy too, perhaps not in the way she'd like, but I care about her. I honestly can't imagine a world without her in it, dazzling us all with her beauty and humour. I need to know I have done everything possible to bring her home safe. And I can't do that from back here."

The fire burning in his eyes renders me speechless. I've never seen such passion in a person before; it's both stunning and shocking, but above all it's powerful and beautiful, all at the same time. He does indeed love her—in his own way.

"Well, you needn't think I'm waiting back here, either. I've done as you asked of me all night and stood watch, but not this time. This time, we face the bastard together," Winston says, tugging at his lapels in a defiant stance.

Jambo gives a low growl of agreement.

And with that, I know when I'm outnumbered.

"That's settled. We go in together. Wait here a sec." Tom lets go my hand to open his door and climbs out, slamming it shut behind him. We watch through the rain distorted glass as he runs to the rear of the car, the reflection from the red lights giving him a devilish glow. He quickly returns with a black duffle bag and jumps back into the driver's seat, his breath coming in short pants as he wipes droplets of rain off his face. "Okay, take one of these each—"

He hands Winston and me robust looking torches and I'm surprised by how little it weighs, much lighter than my cheap camping torch. When I switch it on, the bright beam reaches out, searching across the desolate garden and bouncing off the charred bricks of the manor.

"Wow! Where did you get hold of these?" Although I'm no expert on covert operations, I recognise a custom made device when I see one. And I very much doubt you could stroll into your local hardware store and pick one of these gadgets up.

"There's no point of failure, meaning you could drop it to the bottom of an ocean and it would still work. And there's a brightness control on the side. Set it to your own preference. They're lightweight, as you can tell, but don't let that deceive you. If you wield one of these as a bludgeon, the recipient will be out cold before they hit the floor." Tom removes three more items from the bag and hands one to each of us. "Two-way radios. I set the frequency to group function so we can keep in contact with each other at all times." He fires a quick series of instructions at us on how to use them. "And one more thing, only press the orange button in an emergency. If you locate Malden or Suzy, or just get into difficulty, push it. It alerts the rest of us you need help and we'll make our way to wherever you are. Questions?"

# THE GRAYSTONE KILLINGS

With considerable restraint, I bite back the inappropriate questions that are swirling in my head—such as why does Tom have access to such high spec covert items? He's a businessman. What conceivable use could he have for an indestructible torch and powerful radio?

"Got it," I say with a nod instead, as I pocket the items.

"Ditto." Winston transfers an assortment of items from one of his many pockets to another before placing the radio inside the topmost pocket.

"Unfortunately, we'll have to walk from here," Tom says, glancing out at the driveway strewn with debris and fallen tree trunks. The approach to the house is practically impassable.

"Then let's move. We'll stick together until inside, then split up and search for Suzy." The plan may lack detail, but right now it's the only one we've got.

I step out of the car, bracing myself against the exposure to the elements up here on the hillside. As I stand flanked by Tom and Winston, we stare up at the dark, menacing outline of the manor.

Above us is the gated entrance and its symbol of hope. I send up a silent prayer; for right now, my hope is that I've done the right thing in trusting Tom.

And that we're not too late.

# Chapter Forty-Four

We make our way across the desolate grounds towards Graystone Manor, weaving around fallen trees with their snapped branches. As we pick our way past long since dead tree stumps, we're careful not to trip over their old knobbly roots, spreading out like bony fingers in the ground. The powerful torch beams are a godsend, enabling us to avoid the flying debris, presumably left by the curious passerby. We dodge jagged broken bottles and drink cans, even an old umbrella with its spokes sticking out at awkward angles.

It seems all that is touched by Graystone becomes ugly and warped.

As we push onwards against the wind and rain, I wonder whether a building can really be cursed? Even as the thought enters my mind, the moon peaks out from behind a break in the clouds, casting a creepy blue light on the manor with its jutting towers.

We're less than one hundred metres away when I glance up to see a stream of water cascading to the ground. It pours down from a hideously ugly gargoyle, perched high on the roof. The creature is in good company, for there are other gargoyles just as hideous, staring down at those who dare to approach.

"They have a superstitious purpose to scare evil spirits away," Winston says, shouting over the roar in my ears. He stays close, following my gaze. "But really, they're just there to project surplus water away from the masonry."

"They're grotesque," I shout back over the screeching of the wind.

Winston shrugs indifferently, causing me to suspect he's witnessed a lot of unpleasantness living on the streets. I've no doubt there are people far more ugly on the inside than the stone masons have portrayed these creatures to be.

As quick as it appeared, the moon vanishes again behind dark, angry clouds. I'm glad, because I much prefer the less creepy light of our torches to that of the moonlight. Graystone Manor looks about as inviting as the bat infested cottage.

*I'm really starting to miss the creature comforts of our apartment.*

United in our bold determination, we purposefully climb the steps leading to the enormous weatherbeaten doors, our torches lighting up the night. This time, we don't dim our beams or hug the shadows. We want Malden to know we're here, that we've come for our friend.

More than that, we want him to see we're not afraid of him.

When we reach the last step, I feel for the small pendant beneath my jumper; the talisman left by my mother to keep me safe on this journey back to my old life. Was she aware of the obstacles I would face? I palm the flick knife in my pocket and a smile touches my lips. It seems my father was.

It strikes me I'm returning to Graystone not as Elena—the child who once lived here—but as *Ella Mills*. I've been preparing for this day my whole fucking life... I just didn't realise it until now.

Tom pushes open the old wooden doors, the lock no longer working. From the number of dead leaves littering the black and white checkerboard tiles in the hallway, the house has seen its share of curious visitors over the years. With heightened caution, we step inside and shut the doors behind us.

I hold my breath and listen to the cacophony of whistling, rattling and banging as the wind finds its way in through broken windows and missing doors throughout the manor. A low whimper comes from Jambo, his small body trembling from inside Winston's coat.

Arched doorways lead off in all directions from the spacious entrance, but it's the sweeping Imperial staircase opposite the main doors that commands our attention.

Wide steps lead up from either side in a 'U' shape, curving towards each other to merge into a large balcony set beneath arched pillars.

It's breathtaking.

William Gray did indeed create poetry from architecture for his beloved.

But as stunning as the craftsmanship is, the beautiful design is not what captivates us.

"Jesus, what happened here?" Tom says in a whisper by my side.

Left in the wake of a ferocious fire is a charred trail, its path of destruction clear from the black soot stains on the walls and arches, the metal railings of the bannisters warped by the extreme heat. This is a fire that raged and devoured everything in its path.

With a shudder, I sniff at the air, expecting the charred smell of burning to accompany the devastation before us, but all that remains is the musty stink of mould and mildew.

"We should search down here first," I say, noting the precarious condition of the upper floor, where the most fire damage has occurred. "Tom, you go left towards the kitchen and dining room, and Winston, head right to the lounge and library. I'll check the basement."

The words have barely left my lips when I realise the enormity of what I've said. My eyes snap wide, darting between the two men who stare back at me in stunned silence.

"Fucking hell. I know the floor layout, don't I?"

Together, they nod.

Nobody moves or breathes, both men expecting me to hyperventilate at any second.

But I don't. Instead, I stand tall, square my shoulders back and shrug.

"Uh, you okay?" Tom squints at me, releasing his breath and searching my face in the torchlight.

"What are you both waiting for? Go!"

"That was extraordinary," Tom says, shaking his head before moving off in the direction of the kitchen. With a parting glance over his shoulder, he pointedly looks at me and says, "You're the most extraordinary person I've ever met, Ella Mills. You really are."

Access to the basement is via a narrow door, disguised to blend in with the now faded blue and silver decor of the walls. Easy to walk straight past if you don't know it's there.

Except I do know.

I glance cautiously in all directions before coming to an abrupt halt beneath the balcony overlooking the stairs. The door I need is to the right of the ballroom's grand entrance, but first I place my hands against the carved wood of the enormous doors, my fingertips trailing the still visible rose shaped patterns in the oak. I steal a moment to close my eyes and let the memories float to the surface of my mind.

Music and laughter once heard from behind these doors. The excitement in the house leading up to those magical events was almost tangible.

"Oh my God," I whisper to nobody but the ghosts of the past.

I remember her.

I remember Cara—my sister! Only vague images, but I *remember*.

Too young to attend the glamorous events, I would watch with anticipation as Cara transformed from my elder sister—a girl who perpetually lived in jeans and jumper—into an enchanting vision, straight out of my princess storybooks.

On the night of the parties, I would sneak from my bedroom and sit on the balcony, peering through the metal balustrades to watch the guests arrive—glamorous women in their shimmering cocktail dresses, escorted by men who looked every bit like real life princes. Dreams of one day walking through these doors, wearing a dress of red silk, escorted by a prince so handsome that everyone would stop and stare at us, filled my young and fanciful mind.

A silly childhood wish.

The only item I possess that's red and stunningly beautiful is a tube of artist paint. I'm conventional and uninteresting to look at. I could walk through a crowded room and nobody would remember me.

Would my six-year-old self recognise the woman I've become?

I can't shake the feeling that she'd be disappointed with my choices.

And what of Cara? Might she have lived a full and vibrant life, in contrast to my own? Have I let them all down?

I cling on fiercely to the memory of Cara, terrified she'll slip away and I'll lose her all over again. The urge to walk through the doors of the ballroom is overwhelming, and before I realise what I'm doing, I slip through the double doors to stand staring at the room beyond. With my torch, I sweep the light across all four corners of the expansive room, as large as any concert hall, and stifle a sob at seeing the empty shell that remains.

Enormous floor-standing candelabras remain standing sentry beside each arched window frame, their shiny gilt long since tarnished. A few have toppled on their sides. The crystal candleholders smashed into what resembles a dull sea of glass shards. There must be at least twenty windows reaching from floor to ceiling—a once spectacular sight. Similar decorative arches mirror the frames on the opposite wall, complete with matching candelabras.

A grand piano lies abandoned and covered in the dust and debris from the fire that raged above. It rests lopsided, two of its legs having rotted and buckled beneath it. Littered across the once luxury hardwood sprung floor are large chunks of plaster and the remains of shattered chandeliers that have crashed to the ground. Water damage from the fire has collapsed the vaulted ceiling in places, with large gaping holes encroaching on the trompe mural of cherubs flying around a blue sky. Soon, they too will join the pile of rubble beneath them.

I spin around, desperately searching the ruined room, willing my friend not to be broken and destroyed like the scene before me.

"Suzy!" I cry out her name as loud as I can above the roar of the storm. Whilst holding my breath, I listen for any sound that's out of place; a sudden movement, a yell or scream. But the only sounds I hear are the wind and rain hurtling through the broken windows.

Images of the room where Malden kept his victims replay in my mind, and I realise the ballroom is too exposed for his liking. Far better to have a room where light can't penetrate and expose the horrors harboured within.

A room much like a basement.

As I step back out into the hall, I pull the double doors shut behind me and turn to face the basement door. With deliberate care, I run my hand down the side of the raised panel moulding, feeling for the metal catch that will release the door mechanism. When my fingers make contact, I apply a slight pulling pressure, and I'm instantly rewarded with the sound of a latch springing open.

It feels as if the house knows I'm back and is somehow helping me. A silly notion, but a comforting one, never the less.

A surge of renewed confidence fills my chest as I pull open the small door. An eerie silence greets me as I step forward, disturbed only by the sound of my heart drumming loudly as adrenaline courses through my veins.

"Oh Victor," I mutter under my breath. "You should never have come back here…"

I pause at the top of the wooden steps leading down to the basement, shining the light on each one to make sure they're intact. The last step is at least five metres beneath the mansion—a long way down. A frigid, damp smelling air seeps out through the open doorway and I watch with a shudder as clusters of insects scuttle away from the light, scarpering for cover and the safety that the dense blackness affords them.

The insects have nothing to fear from me—it's the monsters that should be worried. I hastily pat my pocket, checking for the knife. Then, gripping the handrail, I step inside.

With a deep, steadying breath, I descend into the basement.

# Chapter Forty-Five

The cold is biting. So chilled I can see my breath forming little clouds that quickly dissipate into the stale air. I try to ignore the cobwebs and the scurrying of rodents as I invade their territory, sweeping the powerful beam of light from left to right, determined not to leave myself vulnerable.

This time, I can't afford to make any mistakes. I won't allow Malden the opportunity to surprise me. Every nerve in my body is on high alert, every muscle ready for the call to action.

At the bottom of the stairs, I step down onto an earth floor. Footprints are visible in the dirt, small animal pad marks scuffed across them. But it's almost impossible to tell if they're fresh or not. As soon as I pass through here and darkness once again stakes its claim, I'm certain my footprints will have scuff marks too—I can almost feel the dozens of rodent eyes on me.

Further ahead, the beam picks up three pyramid shaped wine racks, all standing in line on top of a square concrete platform. The bottles are dusty, the corks within them having turned mouldy. I shine the torch all around me, but there's no sign of anyone having been here. So far, other than the footprints, it appears as if nothing's been disturbed.

A sudden loud bang reverberates from the other side of the basement.

*What the hell was that?*

I spin on my heels, shining the powerful beam into the darkness, and watch as it slices through the shadows, illuminating everything in its path. My breath catches as the dazzling light reveals a dark shape up ahead. It takes a few seconds before I realise that it's not moving, that it's some sort of brick structure built smack in the middle of the floor. My nerves tingling and mouth dry, I carefully approach it with a sweeping motion of the torch. With caution, I pass by the rusted floor to ceiling steel supports that form a straight line in equal intervals. Not wide enough to conceal a person—I check behind each one, anyway.

When I reach a haphazard pile of furniture next to an old iron furnace, I sidestep around it, realising what the thud was. Something has knocked an old wooden ladder to the ground, most likely a rodent fleeing in panic.

As I get nearer to the brick construction, it appears circular and at once I recognise it to be some sort of well. I hesitate, my foot poised in the air—I've been here before. I scan the basement, frowning. This isn't the sort of place you allow a child to play, so why do I know about the hidden latch at the entrance and recognise this water well?

I edge towards it, remaining keenly alert of the danger it poses—I already know the water is deep. Easy for someone to sneak up and push me in. I feel myself drawn to it; a sense of awareness washing over me as my memories claw their way to the surface.

It didn't scare me to be down here.

"What the hell was a six-year-old doing in a place like this?" I murmur to myself, feeling frustration at not being able to fully expose the memories.

I tentatively peer over the edge of the well and shine the torch down on the water below. It's dark and stagnant, the light struggling to penetrate through the murkiness. The brick sides are green with mildew as they approach the water level.

I look around and reach down to pick out a small stone from the soil by my feet, and extending my hand out across the top of the well, I let it tumble downwards. It hits the water with a subdued *plop* and sinks out of sight. Even with the powerful torch, it's impossible to see the bottom of the well. I step away and exhale a deep breath. Why would anyone let a child play near such a death trap?

Determined not to be distracted by the past, I continue my search of the basement and swing the beam of light up ahead. My heart sinks to find the space splits into two separate tunnels. Now what? I shine the torch down both. They're identical, except for the one on the left having a couple of wine racks lining the walls.

I venture inside the tunnel to examine the bottles and find them also covered in dust, but this time there's no mould on the corks. It means that air must be circulating through here and I hold out my hand to feel a soft breeze coming from inside the passage.

If I follow this tunnel, will it lead me to another exit? Or will I find myself cornered in a dead end with nowhere to turn? As I weigh up the risks of my next move, a cold draught unexpectantly touches the side of my face.

I turn to the wine rack beside me, but before I can investigate, my hand automatically shoots out to hold the wooden frame. I stare at my white knuckles like they belong to someone else. Every instinct is telling me to push against the frame.

And that's when I hear it.

A scream that freezes every muscle in my body. The sound piercing, coming from a place far above.

*Suzy!*

In a flash, I race through the basement as fast as my legs will go, flying up the steep wooden steps back into the main hall. As I burst from the doorway, I frantically throw the torch beam in all directions, trying to decide where the cry came from. Frustration fills my chest and I pace in circles, not knowing which way to turn.

Another cry rings out. A man this time, from the direction of the lounge.

*Winston's in trouble!*

Without hesitation, my thumb hits the orange button on the radio to alert Tom. Too late, I realise my mistake—he'll think it's me who's in trouble and head for the basement. I quickly hit the button to speak instead.

"Tom, are you there? Winston needs help. I'm heading over to him now. Come quickly!"

"Copy that. On my way." His words come back at once. The sound of heavy breathing tells me he's already breaking into a run.

A series of high-pitched barking resonates through the manor, and just like Tom, I sprint into action. At a race, I take the corners too quickly so that I almost lose my balance. As I approach an arched doorway, the cries become louder.

I tear past the entrance to the lounge and head towards the library, a room I remember to be crammed full of books, all different sizes and colours, old and new—someone holding me in their arms as I reach up for a storybook. Still going too fast, I take the sharp turn in the dilapidated hallway, slamming my shoulder against the opposite wall as I try to right myself.

Just as I pick up momentum again, I spot two figures up ahead and come to a dead halt.

Winston is easily identifiable from his tall stature and signature overcoat—the other man I recognise as Gunner, the gang member we paid for information. There's no mistaking the coiled snake motif on the back of his jacket, or the sleek of hair on his otherwise shaven head.

*What the fuck is he doing here?*

I watch in horror as Gunner pins Winston up against the wall and reigns powerful blow after blow into his body. I'm too far away to help, and before I even realise I'm moving again, my feet are pounding down the hallway at a charge. The light from my torch bounces around the walls as my arms pump the air, propelling me forward ever faster.

I hear Jambo before I see him. For a small dog, he has a ferocious growl; a deep and menacing rumble that belongs to a canine at least three times his size. He approaches Gunner with lips pulled back, baring his teeth, and his hackles raised—the hairs on his neck standing so vertical that he looks electrified. His small body is tense and poised for attack.

"No, Jambo! No—" To reinforce the command, my hand shoots outstretched towards him, palm facing out in the universal stop gesture. But Jambo focuses only on the man attacking his beloved owner and ignores my cries. With a final growl of warning, he launches from his hind legs into the air and sinks his teeth into Gunner's arm. The man yells out in pain, however it's obvious Jambo is no match for this brute. Heavily cursing, Gunner swings his arm with force away from him and slams the dog hard against the nearest wall.

Jambo's body crumples to the floor with a whimper, his small white legs twitching until, after a few seconds, he grows still.

Winston lets out a cry so primal it sends a shiver through my core. Without warning, he throws himself at the other man, barreling into him with such force he knocks him off his feet. They land with a loud thud on the floor in a heap.

"Oomph!" The air is knocked from Gunner's lungs, leaving him momentarily winded.

Winston lunges at his throat and squeezes until his hands tremble, all the time shaking and slamming the other man's head against the remains of the threadbare carpet.

I run towards them.

Ten metres, five… before I can reach them, I see it.

The glint of a metal blade.

# Chapter Forty-Six

"Winston!" I scream out his name to warn him.

But I know I'm too late.

The knife plunges into his flank, and falling sideways, Winston rolls onto his back. Gunner is on top of him in a flash, pulling the knife out—ready for another attack. Blood pours from the wound, staining the old faded carpet beneath them. Gunner turns to me, his lips curled in a chilling sneer as he raises the knife above Winston's chest.

"Don't... come any closer!" he says, through short pants, trying to catch his breath. His face shines with beads of sweat from the physical exertion of the fight. Blood trickles down the side of his face from an open scalp wound. He's taken more powerful blows than he's dealt.

Bile rises in my throat at the sight of the knife hovering above my wounded friend's chest.

"Don't do it," I say in a placating tone, dropping to my knees so that I'm level with him. He clasps his hands firmly around the handle of the knife, confident that I'm powerless to stop him. "I'm the one Malden wants. Let my friend live and you can have me. I won't fight you."

Winston makes a feeble move to grab Gunner's hand. Too weak, his arm drops back to his side again.

Gunner laughs, a hollow sound that sickens me to my gut.

"Whasup, Posh Pussy? Ain't you pleased to see Gunner?"

"Let him go." I stare back at him with open disgust and loathing.

"Ain't nuffin personal—business, innit?" He wipes the sweat from his face, the knife still hovering in the air. "Malden's aft-ha you. Gonna fuck your brains out, then slit your throat—just like all the othah bitches. Ow 'bout you come over 'ere and suck my dick, maybe I'll fink 'bout not shanking our pal?"

My eyes narrow towards him as my chin juts forward in defiance. Winston is in serious trouble here—I'll need to act quick, before it's too late.

Like the accomplished adversary I am, my mind races through the potential scenarios of the scene before me, selecting, without hesitation or doubt, the one with the highest probability of success.

First, I need to make a show of not being intimidated by Gunner's threats and crude words. The crazed glint in his eyes warns me our violent situation is feeding his desire for power—escalating his level of aggression. With the flick-knife positioned and ready in my hand, I have one shot at this. Any sudden movements will most likely result in him killing my friend.

I smile slowly, keeping perfectly still, and in a deadpan tone say, "Gunner, let's be real. We both know I won't be sucking your *needle* dick."

Confusion instantly clouds Gunner's face. In the same moment, I swing back my wrist, adjusting and lowering my aim as he drives the blade of his knife down towards Winston's chest.

The air leaves my lungs as I watch my weapon hurtle through the distance between us, catching Gunner's hand mid-swing and knocking the knife from his grasp. With a string of expletives, he yells and falls backwards, clutching his injured hand.

"Ella!" I turn to see Tom sprinting down the hall towards us. "Are you hurt?" he asks, slowing enough to avoid colliding with me. In a frantic dash, I spring to my feet to check on Winston.

"No, I'm alright. But Winston's been stabbed." I throw myself down beside his still body. We're too exposed out here in the hallway—I can't protect him like this. "Where is he? Where's Gunner?" I say, concerned about a second assault and sweeping my torch around with urgency. "He's been helping Malden this whole time. We need to stop him!"

"He did this?" Tom's face flares with rage. "I'll go after Gunner while you see to Winston. Apply pressure to his wound and try to stem the bleeding," he shouts, already in a run and following the trail of blood leading off to the library.

Tom disappears out of sight and I realise he's left me alone with Winston, and no medical training.

Holy shit—I'm way out of my depth here.

With hands that tremor as if I've just overdosed on a truckload of caffeine, I place my torch facing upwards on the floor beside me and gingerly lift Winston's bloodstained shirt. It exposes a gaping gash in his side, where thick, dark blood is flowing from the wound.

Already he's lost so much—an almost black pool forming beneath him. Desperate to stem the bleeding, I tear off my jacket, holding it against the wound and applying gentle but firm pressure. Winston's eyelids flutter and I feel an overwhelming surge of relief that he's not dead. I angrily blink away the tears that sting at my eyes.

How could I not know that Gunner was working with Malden? Tom tried to warn me this was a trap. And instead of listening, I trusted the scales of justice to tip in our favour. My naivety has put everyone I care about in danger.

*It was a mistake to come back here.*
*I thought I was ready.*
*I'm not.*

"Vic—" Winston's ragged voice snaps me out of the despair that threatens to overwhelm me.

"Shhh, don't try to speak. I'm going to get help."

My mobile—I need to call an ambulance, but I can't reach the phone inside my jacket without first releasing pressure on the wound. The knife must have hit a vital organ because I haven't been able to staunch the flow. He's still losing too much blood. Shit.

"F-family. Th-this house. Not... safe. Go!"

His stilted words reach something in the dark recesses of my mind.

*Someone shouting.*
*A storm raging outside the window...*
*I'm being told to leave...* "Go!"
*No, wait—that's not it.*
*Oh my God!*
*I was being told to* "RUN!"
Someone was telling me to *run*!

My face is wet with tears as I look down at Winston. "I know what happened here that night," I say in a whisper. "It's alright, I know."

"You... have... to g-go."

My whole body trembles from the shock of the violent flashbacks. Hot tears stream down my cheeks as I shake my head, choking back a sob. "No, I'm staying with you. I won't leave you."

*I ran all those years ago—not this time.*

Waves of nausea hit me one after another as my stomach clenches in on itself, like physical blows to my body.

Winston's eyelids flutter, his blood still seeping through my fingers.

I've never felt so scared or helpless.

When he moves his lips, still trying to speak, I lean forward, careful to keep steady pressure on his wound. His voice is barely a whisper, floating on a shallow breath. "Trap..."

Startled, I pull back.

The familiar icy grip of fear and anxiety reaches out to pull me in. But I won't let it—no more—I've spent my entire life being fearful.

"Shhh, I'm not leaving you," I say with conviction. "Don't worry, we know it was Gunner who attacked you. Tom will find him. Just stay with me, alright?"

Winston's breath is coming fast and alarmingly shallow. Even if I get to my phone and dial 999, deep down I know they'll never make it here in time.

His lips move again, and I inch closer, scared to miss even a single syllable. "J-Jambo—"

It takes every ounce of control to swallow back the sob as I peer over to where the dog's crumpled body lays motionless. Instead, I plaster what I hope is a reassuring smile on my face.

"Jambo's going to be fine. You don't need to worry about him. Just a little shaken—he's going to be alright."

"W-where…"

"Soon. You'll see him soon. I promise." I gently squeeze his hand, hoping to bring him some last comfort. His skin feels so chilled against mine.

As my chin drops to my chest, I screw my eyes shut tight and listen as Winston takes his last breath. Salty tears roll off my face, cascading down like the torrent of a burst dam.

At the noise of urgent footsteps approaching, I look up to see Tom striding back into the hallway. There's no sign of Gunner with him.

"What happened?" I say, searching behind Tom into the darkened doorway as I swipe at the tears with my sleeve.

"Gunner won't be bothering us again for a while. How is he? Have you called for an ambulance?" Tom moves in closer to get a better look at Winston's wound, and I shake my head.

"He's gone."

"Jesus Christ. Fuck. I'm so sorry, Ella… there was nothing you could have done."

"I'm responsible for bringing him here. Winston's dead because he was trying to help me. Don't sugar-coat it by pretending otherwise." Blood is everywhere—my hands, clothing, shoes—and desperately tamping down the impulse to heave, I clench my fists and squeeze my eyes shut, hoping that when I open them again, all the horror will be gone. "He said something about my family—or me—I'm not sure," I say, rambling and struggling to process what's just happened. "This house—he said it's a trap, that it's not safe. Do you think he was trying to tell us about Gunner, about him selling us out to Malden?"

"Perhaps. Shit, why the hell didn't he radio for help?"

"There was a woman's scream... I ran from the basement and that's when I heard fighting. They were shouting. Jambo was barking—" I look over at the shape of the little dog's body.

Tom follows my gaze and shakes his head wistfully before saying, "Yeah, I heard the scream, too. Sounded like it was coming from the opposite side of the building. I was just racing back when you called." He crouches beside me and reaches over to run his hand over Winston's eyes, gently closing them for the last time. As he turns to me, he takes my hands in his and uses his sleeve to wipe the blood from them. "Suzy's alive, Ella—we know that much, at least." Determination and hope reflect in his eyes.

I swallow hard, replaying the scream in my head. She sounded hurt. But he's right—she's still alive. "We don't give up..."

"Never." He lets go of me and drags a hand across his jaw, a worried frown pinching his face. "What I still don't understand is why Winston would face Gunner alone. Why not raise the alarm immediately?"

Tom eyes up Winston's overcoat. Back in the car, we both watched as he made a fuss of putting the radio in his top pocket. I give Tom the nod to check his coat.

By the time he's patted down the many pockets, it's clear the radio is gone.

"Perhaps he dropped it in the struggle?" I say, scanning the surrounding floor.

"Or Gunner's taken it. Or Malden."

At the mention of his name, the memories from earlier rush once again to the forefront of my mind. "Oh my God, Malden... I remembered, Tom! That night when I was six—I remember all of it..."

He reels round, searching my eyes with his. "Jesus. Are you okay? Are you able to tell me about it?"

"I will. But first, let's check out your theory and find out if Malden's got Winston's missing radio."

Before rising, I straighten the lapels of Winston's jacket then tenderly touch his cheek. I lean in close, whispering in his ear inadequate words of gratitude before taking my torch and pushing myself upright. My legs feel stronger than I expect.

"I threw my knife at Gunner—"

Tom searches around him, spotting it laying close to the wall. When he bends down to retrieve it, he uses the sleeve of his jacket to clean Gunner's blood from the blade before handing it back to me.

"You shredded his hand, you know. That's a pretty impressive aim you've got."

"Good. He deserves a lot more." I stare down at Winston's lifeless body, then pocket the weapon back in my jeans and hold the radio up to my lips.

Tom looks at me through wary eyes. "What are you planning on doing?"

"This—" I press down on the handset button of my radio to speak. "Victor? Victor Malden? I know you're listening. I know who you are and what you've done. I also know that you've been looking for me since your escape this morning. You killed my parents, didn't you? They didn't deserve what you did to them."

I release the button and wait, staring at the device in my hand.

"What the hell do you think you're doing?" Tom moves to take the radio from me, but I shrug him away and press the button again.

"I'm here now, Malden, so let Suzy go. That's what you want, isn't it? Here's the deal. I'm going to meet you at the top of the stairs by the balcony. Let Suzy's boyfriend take her somewhere safe and then you and me can talk. Help me understand what it is you want—why you're doing this? Come to the stairs, Malden. I'll be waiting."

I release the button and hold my breath. The radio crackles, then falls silent.

"Okay," Tom says, crossing his arms firmly in front of him. "What you just said? That's not fucking happening." His brow pinches in a deep scowl.

Tucking the radio away, I give him a brief wink. "Too fucking right, it's not. Back stairs, let's go!"

# Chapter Forty-Seven

The discreet passageway at the top of an ancient set of stairs has the same musty smell as the rest of the building, but with no windows, the air is stale and dank. It leaves an unpleasant earthy taste in my mouth.

They built these narrow hallways that run the length of the manor for servants to move about the house unseen, a network of corridors hidden from view. I'm keen to keep moving, to be out of this claustrophobic space, because although I have vague memories of playing and running through here as a child, for an adult, it's a far less appealing environment.

We move silently in the opposite direction of the main hallway and balcony where I promised Malden I'll be waiting. I'm hoping this plan will buy us the precious time we need to get Suzy to safety.

"Sorry about back there with the radio," I say in a hushed whisper to Tom as he follows behind me. "You probably think it was impulsive and reckless, but Malden's been sitting in a cell planning his every move. The best weapon we have against him is to be unpredictable—force him to react to us."

"And offering yourself up as bait does that how?" His voice is low, a distinct edge of annoyance to it.

"Look, he expected me to come here alone. What he didn't bargain on was me having help. When Gunner told him about you and Winston, he reacted by bringing Gunner here. Then, when we arrived, he knew that Suzy screaming would send us into a panic, and that makes us vulnerable. Which is exactly what he wants; panic and confusion. Now he has the radio, he can listen in on our comms and no doubt try to manipulate us. This is a game Tom, we're playing Cat and Mouse. Malden thinks he's the fucking cat."

"Then why let him know we're on to him? Isn't that just going to piss him off more? He's a volatile psychopath. You really want to push his buttons and hope he doesn't take it out on Suzy?"

"That's exactly what I'm trying to avoid. Now that I've remembered what happened here that night, my hunch is he'll be holding her in the place where the tragedy ultimately played out all those years ago—my old bedroom. If we can distract him, entice him away from there, then we'll have the upper hand. I suspect he plans to kill her in front of me. I'm certain of it."

"Jesus Christ! Why would he do that?"

Tom's footsteps falter, and stopping, I turn to face him.

"Because whoever was behind the attack all those years ago, they smashed their way into my bedroom and killed my sister in front of our mother—on my bed."

"Fucking hell... that's what you remember?"

I nod, grimly.

"Until we know otherwise, we have to go with your theory that it was Malden behind the attack, and that he sacrificed Cara to coerce my mother into giving him what he wanted. He didn't get what he was after, and my family has been in hiding from him ever since. Now Malden's back, and he has Suzy. If we're not careful, history will repeat itself. So we lure him away from my old bedroom. That's the only way to keep her safe right now."

Tom reaches out to place his hand on my arm, a firm but gentle grip, reminding me I'm not alone in facing the enemy. As he lets his hand slide down my arm to take my hand, his eyes lock on mine, and instantly I forget about our cramped surroundings. My heart races as he purposefully steps closer, leaning his body towards mine. For a brief second I try to pull back, but something stops me, keeps me rooted to the spot—his eyes—I feel as if I'm falling under a spell every time I look into them. My breath catches as Tom gently runs the back of his finger down my cheek.

"Okay, I'll go along with your plan, but this time, we stick together. There's no way I'm letting you out of my sight again."

I nod, even though his actions and words have left me confused.

*Why am I behaving like a love-struck teenager?*

Tom shouldn't care about what happens to me. He's here for Suzy, not me. Tomorrow he'll go back to lying to my friend about his wife and child, leading her on and letting her believe he's going to propose marriage. He'll break her heart, just as all the others have done before him, and she'll rebound straight into the next relationship—call me cynical, but I know how this works.

I pull my hands away. "Fine, whatever you want," I say, flustered with embarrassment. "We can stick together."

Not knowing what else to do, I turn my back on him and continue creeping down the corridor.

Now that I've met Tom and got to spend time with him, I can tell he's far from an ideal match for Suzy. Not only has he deceived her about being married, he's also in possession of stolen art. His fighting skills, along with the torch in my hand and radio in my pocket, would suggest he's more than just the businessman he portrays himself to be. So what if he appears physically perfect with intense eyes and a toned body that flexes in all the right ways?

That aside, I really can't trust him.

No, he had absolutely no right to touch me the way he did.

Why then is my skin betraying me? It tingles at the lingering feel of his touch on my cheek and I lift my hand to my face before I realise what I'm doing.

*Fuck! What is wrong with me?*

I pretend to tuck an imaginary strand of hair behind my ears and keep moving. I will have to deal with my perplexing reaction to this exchange later.

The servants' corridor quickly leads to a similarly claustrophobic staircase, with crumbling plaster and cobwebs in equal measure. The stone steps show signs of wear from the constant footfall that once passed through here—servants bustling backwards and forwards all day long. Like the rest of the house, it's now home to the creatures that dwell here.

"Remember, as quiet as possible. We're almost there," I say as my torch beam picks out the shape of the narrow staircase.

"Okay, right behind you."

We ascend, taking care to keep our tread light on the steps and our torches dimmed. All around us is the scratching noise of nearby rodents and the rasping flutter of moth wings as the insects react to the unwelcome intrusion.

At the top is another corridor, this one with obvious signs of fire damage. Parts of the wall and ceiling have collapsed, the fallen masonry littering the floor. Still keeping as quiet as possible, we navigate our way over the piles of rubble, ever conscious that we mustn't alert Malden to our whereabouts for our plan to work.

When we finally come to a wooden door at the end of the passage, not even the restricted light can obscure the hideous black scorch marks around the framework. I take a deep breath, hoping I've led us to the correct part of the house.

Although snippets of my childhood are emerging from the dark recesses of my mind, they're just that—snippets. So, until my memory gives up all its secrets, I have no choice but to rely on my instincts.

Right now, those instincts are telling me this is the door across the hallway from where we need to be.

"Ready?" I say, with a backwards glance at Tom. He nods, his eyes round and shining in the gloom. "You should know that once we're through this door, the hallway is wide and straight—exposed. It puts us in a vulnerable position. Across the hall from here is my old bedroom."

"Understood. I'll keep eyes to the right and you keep a watch behind us as we make our approach."

I nod in agreement, steadying my nerves as Tom inches past me to turn the handle. Gently, he pushes the damaged door open a fraction, just wide enough for us to scan the immediate area.

"Clear," he whispers, "Quick, let's move! Stay close to the wall. If you see anything, get down. No heroics, okay?"

"Okay," I say in quick agreement. We can't blow it by being reckless. The more covert we remain, the better chance we have of reaching Suzy. Going in guns blazing would be a mistake, no matter how desperate we are to get her out of here. Together, we step out into the hallway.

What was once elegant architecture with exquisite carvings is now a charred shell of its former grandeur. I nod towards what remains of a scorched black door.

My childhood bedroom.

*That currently emits a flickering light from inside.*

We move towards the room using quick side steps, our knees bent, ready to run or duck at any moment. I keep my eyes scanned behind us, the faint light from my torch sweeping in steady circles.

As we draw closer, I catch sight of a wavering glow through a jagged hole in the door. All around the room are dancing shadows from the light of a candle.

I crouch low, preparing to peer inside.

# Chapter Forty-Eight

Destroyed by the fire, black soot covers every inch of the bedroom's walls and ceiling. Scraps of scorched curtain hang pitifully at the side of the boarded-up windows, where wooden slats, long since rotted away, provide little resistance to the wind that howls through the gaps. What remains of the furniture is now unrecognisable, charred shapes of twisted wood and metal. Soot and dust cover every surface.

With one exception.

An icy chill passes through me. I screw my eyes shut for a fleeting second, trying to comprehend the scene in front of me.

When I open them again, the horror remains.

In the middle of the room, placed upon the fire and water damaged floor, is a large circular Chinese rug, the colours now faded with dozens of bare patches where the once tightly bound weave has weakened. The rug doesn't belong to this room. At its centre is a chair, the gilt carvings and faded seat covering too elegant to be part of this macabre scene. It doesn't belong here either.

*And neither does my friend.*

With disbelief, I stare at Suzy, bound to the chair with plastic cable ties. Blindfolded, gagged, and naked, she's so still I can't tell whether she's alive or dead. At her feet is a single candle, the flame emitting a soft light that exposes angry purple bruises on her arms and legs. Blood seeps from open wounds on her flesh. So many cuts.

"Sh-she's not m-moving! Why isn't she moving?" The words tumble from my mouth, barely coherent to my numb mind.

It feels as if my heart is being squeezed as my world shatters into tiny pieces around me.

*Suzy can't be dead!*

"What. The. Fu-ck?" Tom's body grows tense next to me. He leans closer to the hole in the door, his head level with the blackened wood, peering into the darkened room. "Wait, Ella! I think she's still breathing."

"Out of my way—I need to go to her!"

Before I can barge through the door, his hand shoots out to hold me back. "Remember what you told me? By stepping into that room, you'll only be putting both your lives in danger. Stay here. Signal with the orange SOS button on the radio if you see or hear anything. Do not draw attention to yourself. Okay?"

"Okay—just be quick!" I can hear the fringes of hysteria in my voice. Tom hesitates, concern etched on his face as his eyes dart repeatedly from me to Suzy. He's torn between going to her and leaving me here. I take a deep breath and give a sharp nod. "Go to her, hurry! I'll be fine." Urgency now replaces my earlier panic, my tone invoking no further hesitation from Tom.

"If something happens, you run and don't look back. Get to safety, then call for help."

His words set my nerves on edge. What if Malden isn't making his way to the balcony as we hoped? What if the plan has failed, and he's still here, lurking in the shadows? Could he disarm Tom if pitched against each other?

Almost forgetting to draw breath, I watch as Tom pushes open the remains of the damaged door and cautiously steps inside. The beam from his torch hastily sweeps all four corners of the charred bedroom, and seeing no signs of Malden, he treads carefully towards the centre of the room. The noise of his footsteps must reach Suzy, for she at once stiffens and I breathe an enormous sigh of relief.

She's alive.

Only then do I realise a small part of me was already mourning her, that I couldn't imagine a single scenario where she comes back from this horror.

My relief is short-lived, however, because the closer Tom moves towards her, the more agitated she becomes. Her head shakes from side to side as she struggles against the restraints. The tape across her mouth muffles her cries, but the noise is still loud enough to draw attention to us.

*She thinks Malden's returned for her.*

"Talk to her, Tom," I say, in an urgent whisper through the gap.

He looks over his shoulder at me and nods.

"Suzy, it's me! Tom. You're going to be okay—you're safe now." His voice is calm and reassuring as he tries to penetrate her terror. But his words have the opposite effect than intended. For a moment Suzy pauses, becoming quiet and cocking her head as if listening intently. Then, like a frenzied animal caught in a trap, she becomes hysterical. She shakes her head even more vigorously than before, jerking her body in the chair, until it almost loses balance. Her suppressed cries pitching higher and higher as she tries to scream.

*Oh fuck, fuck, fuck, fuck!*
*Have I got it wrong?*
*Is it Tom she's terrified of?*
*What if I've been trusting her abductor all this time?*

A single thought races through my mind—I need to go to her!

I propel myself into the room, determined to prevent Tom from reaching her. My heavy footsteps immediately alert him to my presence and he spins to face me, his face contorted into an aggressive scowl; eyes narrow and lips pulled back into a snarl. I lurch to a halt, noticing his fists clenched tight, feet spread wide—prepared for attack.

Despite the intimidating confrontation, I stand my ground. Tom does a double take, his eyes widening with confusion.

"Jesus Christ, what are you doing, Ella?"

"Stay the fuck away from her." I edge closer, circling the rug with the chair holding Suzy. He ignores me and takes another step towards her. "I mean it!" I say with conviction and reaching for my knife. "Back off—now!"

Tom gives me another perplexed look as Suzy's muffled yells suddenly break off, the room falling silent except for the sound of the storm and our heavy breathing.

She stops moving, no longer fighting against her restraints. I glance over to the chair and see that she's cocked her head to one side, her body rigid.

She's listening… to my voice.

"Suzy, I'm here. It's Ella. I won't let *anyone* hurt you," I say, staring pointedly at Tom.

Suddenly, the chair precariously tilts backwards as her body jerks in another violent spasm. Her reaction to my voice is so unexpected that it catches me off guard and I scream out, immediately clamping a hand over my mouth.

"Stay here," Tom says, taking control of the rapidly deteriorating situation. He takes another step towards Suzy, all the while holding his palm out towards me. I stare helplessly, the shock of seeing my friend like this leaving me paralysed.

I don't know whether to run to her or tackle Tom away.

All I know is that something is seriously wrong with this picture.

Why is our presence invoking such a violent reaction in her…?

"I'm going to cut the restraints and pass her over to you. Okay?" Tom's words somehow penetrate through my disorientation. "Ella, you can trust me, I promise."

But I can't shake the overpowering sense that something's not right. My mind races as Tom moves another step closer to the chair, immediately causing Suzy's movements to become even more frenzied.

And that's when I realise what's happening.

She's trying to tell us something.

*She's trying to warn us.*

"Wait!" I scream out, throwing my hands out towards Tom.

Already committed, he takes another step before turning towards my voice, his reaction to the warning a fraction too slow.

The rug beneath him crumples, and I watch in horror as the ground swallows him up. His eyes snap wide, features frozen with shock. His hand shoots out to grab at the side. The hole is too large, his fingers snatching at the empty void. He disappears with a loud thud, followed by the most awful silence.

He's gone—just like that.

Dust rises through the hole, the glow of Tom's torch lighting up the swirling particles. One half of the rug remains dangling from the edge, swinging slower with each oscillation. I can see now that Suzy's chair is balancing precariously close to the jagged, gaping hole in the floorboards.

Somehow, she's miraculously stayed upright.

Silver tape across her mouth muffles Suzy's deep, wrenching sobs. I realise my hand is covering my mouth; I don't recall the movement, but I'm grateful for the pressure tamping down my own screams.

Too scared to move or speak, I stand rooted to the spot, knowing that somehow I have to convince Suzy to stay still. If she fights the restraints like before, there's every chance she and the chair will plunge down after Tom.

"Suzy, listen to me," I say softly, fearful of her reaction to my voice, but not knowing how much longer the damaged floorboards will support her weight. I try to keep my tone level after the shock of seeing Tom fall through the floor. "I know that you're scared right now.

But I need you to stay extremely still for me. I'm going to get you out of here, I promise. First, though, I need to approach the hole in front of you and check on Tom, alright? Nod slowly if you understand."

I wait, hardly daring to breathe. Suzy's sobs quieten to little more than whimpers and then she nods with a slight jerk of her head.

"That's good, Suzy, you're doing great. I'm stepping forward now. The footsteps you hear will be mine."

Another nod of her head.

With each step, I tentatively apply pressure to the floor, checking it will support my weight as I advance towards the edge of the hole. When I'm close enough, I crouch low and shine the torch into the dust filled void. Tom isn't moving, but neither is he crumpled and broken on the floor, as I feared. A banquet table has broken his fall, its once polished wood now littered with rubble from the ceiling collapse. Tom's legs rest haphazardly on the remains of a chandelier, his boots entangled in the shattered crystals.

As I move the light beam along his body, my premature sense of relief evaporates and my throat constricts, allowing only a small gasp to pass my lips.

A large piece of wooden splinter is sticking out from Tom's chest.

I blink my eyes, the sight of the bloodstained, jagged tip rendering me stunned with disbelief.

On my knees and leaning over the edge, I desperately scan his empaled body for any signs of breathing, all the while gaping in horror at the scene beneath me.

"Tom!" I call out as loud as I dare, choking back the bile rising in my throat. First my parents and Winston, and now Tom. This can't be happening.

No response. Not even a flicker from behind his closed eyelids. Blood trickles from the corner of his mouth, but more worrying is how deathly pale his face looks in the torchlight. There could be internal bleeding or worse—I have to reach him.

When I glance up at Suzy, she's shaking uncontrollably, and I quickly triage the situation. First, I have to get her away from the edge and to safety, then somehow find my way down to check on Tom. As I drag my eyes from his motionless body, I pull back from the hole and freeze.

Too late, I sense a presence behind me.

A sudden sharp pain shoots through my neck as a needle plunges into my flesh.

The breath leaves my lungs, just as a terrifying darkness rushes towards me.

# Chapter Forty-Nine

Relief washes over me, a still calmness that soothes the weariness in my bones. Back in my studio, secure, safe and warm—I don't want to leave. In fact, there's nothing I desire more than to stay here shrouded by the comforting smells of the paints and canvas. Beside me, Suzy is wearing the shimmering green party dress, and I turn, smiling, as she slips her hand into mine and squeezes.

But she doesn't smile back. Because silver duct tape secures her mouth.

I scream and try to reach for the tape, but I can't move, can't breathe, and as I frantically search around for someone to help us, rising panic shuts down my ability to function. My body becomes a prison going into lockdown, doors slamming shut. When I turn back, Suzy has gone and Wynter is in her place.

No longer in my studio, a calmness once again settles upon me as I watch Wynter from across the Verandah's floor, fussing with the displays, thriving with the opportunity to leave her past behind—the past...

Wait—*no, no, no!*

This isn't right.

I look down and Suzy's grip is on my hand again, only this time she's holding so tight it causes a bruising pain. When I turn to her, we're sitting on a white leather sofa—Tom's sofa—and a deep, bellowing laugh resonates from across the room. Winston is standing opposite us with Tom, slapping him on the back as he hands him a drink from the bar. They turn to face me, Tom rubbing his strong stubbled chin in powerful silence, his mouth firm and eyes staring.

But his eyes are all wrong.

The familiar striking grey, once with the power to hypnotise, are now empty, shallow pools of black glass. Fearful of being trapped, of finding myself looking into the eyes of the devil himself, I glance away.

The picture of Tom's wife and daughter hangs beside me. Suddenly she moves, swinging her blonde ponytail across her shoulder as she stares down at me from within the frame. Uncomfortable, I shrink under her accusing gaze, and as her hand rises to point at me, she says, "*You did this. You killed them.*" The child with her starts to cry.

Suzy's grip on my hand now throbs with an unbearable pulsing pain and I try to pull my hand away. But she won't let go, and tightens her grip even more. I turn to her, shocked to see that the green sparkling dress has gone. Instead, her body is naked beside me, blindfolded and gagged, blood from deep knife wounds seeping into the white leather.

The thick, red liquid pools next to me and when I glance down, blood coagulates in rivulets around my feet. The air is heavy with the metallic odour of blood, and I look up to see Tom and Winston standing in front of me, their clothes stained red from the gaping holes in their torsos.

They point at me, saying, "*You did this, Ella...*"

When I try to scream, the only sound that escapes is a raspy cough.

My tongue feels swollen and alien in my mouth, throat sore and burning—dehydrated.

I gag.

Oh my God, *I'm suffocating*!

I struggle to fill my lungs with air, but my breathing is alarmingly shallow. The smell filling my nostrils is not the metallic scent of blood, but the harsh, acrid stench of ammonia.

What's happening? Where am I?

When I try to move, my head feels drowsy and heavy.

Fuck! Why can't I move?

Fear rising, I try not to succumb to the panic. Instead, I compartmentalise the sensations my brain is struggling to process.

Arms. I have restricted movement—pinned behind me, fingers tingling. Too tight. The squeezing isn't from Suzy's grip, but from some sort of ligature pinning my wrists together.

Oh dear God, where am I?

*No, do not panic—process.*

Not in my studio at home—the air is too cold and the smell unfamiliar. Nor am I in the gallery—I spend too much time in there not to recognise the surroundings. Definitely not at Tom's house with its climate controlled atmosphere and 'elegant' aromatic air.

I have to open my eyes.

At first my eyelids seem glued shut, but after several attempts I prise them open and try to focus on the nearest object. Blurred images swim in and out of view.

A constant drumming and whooshing sound pricks at my ears with relentless insistence. It's a familiar sound I've been hearing all day... the sound of storm Ruby raging outside.

All at once, everything comes flooding back.

Now I remember *exactly* where I am.

That son of a bitch stabbed me with a fucking needle!

I shake my head, trying to shrug off the effects of whatever drug is in my system. By picking out a bright, flickering movement in front of me as a focal point, I zero in on the light until my vision clears. In my peripheral, I make out the fuzzy shape of a person walking away from me. The dancing light gradually comes into focus, sharp enough now to recognise it as the flame of a candle.

Just like the one at Suzy's feet.

I snap my head upwards, ignoring the searing pain as my brain slams into the back of my skull. Malden is standing over Suzy, the glint of a blade catching the candlelight. No longer blindfolded, she stares at me through wide eyes filled with terror.

Is this another drug-induced psychosis?

*Oh dear God. Anything but this.*

"Ah, there she is. Welcome your friend back in the room, sweetheart," he says to Suzy, leaning close to her ear and resting the steel blade against her tear stained cheek.

An involuntary shiver runs through me at the chill in his voice and the knife touching her flesh.

"Stay away from her, you sick bastard!" I try to say, but the words tumble from my mouth in little more than a raspy croak.

Malden laughs, the same deep, bellowing sound that touched my unconscious mind moments before. Only now I'm able to place it. Not my friend Winston, but a deranged and dangerous killer, the menacing undertones easily recognisable. Like a switch being flicked, the sound ignites in me a survival instinct; the same instinct that kept me alive in this room all those years ago.

In defiance, I raise my chin and stare into Suzy's terrified eyes before saying, "Don't be scared. I won't let him hurt you." Only this time, my words come strong and clear.

Malden laughs even louder, waving the knife at me.

"I do believe you are seriously misreading the situation here," he says, puffing out his chest and winking playfully. If it wasn't for the threatening darkness lurking behind his eyes and the weapon brandished in his hand, he could almost pass for charming.

That's what makes him so dangerous.

Despite the odds stacked heavily against our survival, a fierce determination rages inside of me. I hardly recognise myself. The Ella of old would have crumpled with fear at the hopelessness of our plight; Suzy bound to a chair, me slumped on the floor, trussed up against the wall—*but I don't crumple*. I keep my chin raised and stare into the black abyss of his eyes.

"Let. Her. Go."

"Sweet, sweet, Elena. Back once again in the family home—" He sweeps his hand in an arc around the fire gutted bedroom. "It must be upsetting for you, seeing your friend like this. Being helpless to save her... to save *any* of them—" he says with a grin as Suzy whimpers at his side.

Great, he really is a fucking psycho.

I need to buy us some time and keep him talking until I can figure a way out of this.

"Don't call me that... my name is *Ella*. I know it was you following me in the park this morning, and that you went to my parents' house tonight intending to kill them. What I don't know is what the fuck you want from us? Why are you doing this?"

"Really? You haven't worked it out yet? Well, that is fascinating. Ah, your parents. A pity, but they really left me no choice. I have a job to do, and not a lot of time in which to do it. All I needed from them was their cooperation. A simple request they refused."

"You wanted to know my mother's location."

Malden raises his eyebrows. "Very good, Elena," he says, slowly clapping his hands while circling the back of Suzy's chair. Each smash of his hands makes her jump and, with a shake of my head, I implore her to keep it together. She needs to keep still until I can get her away from him, or risk toppling over the side. "But your mother is an unexpected loose end, nothing more. I'll deal with her in due course. Nothing I can't handle, as you'll soon find out."

Apparently, the challenge isn't getting Malden to talk, after all. It's getting him to shut his narcissistic mouth long enough to answer my question. His inflated sense of self-importance is fuelling an obvious need for my admiration—he's using me to stroke his fucking ego. I feel the heat of rage and contempt flush my cheeks.

"A loose end to what? You haven't answered my question. What do you want from us? You know about my birth mother—are you the reason my parents felt they had to keep her safe?"

He stops pacing and stares across the room at me with his creepy eyes. I fight the impulse to look away and as a chill cuts through me, my anger gives way to a deep felt sorrow. Sorrow for all the women who stared into those eyes with their dying breath.

"Do you know what the greatest advantage of prison is? I'll tell you. You get to meet the most interesting people. Ruthless, fascinating people." He steps towards me, his soulless eyes boring into mine. "Do you remember what took place here all those years ago, sweet, innocent Elena?"

He's searching my face, but for what? Recognition?

"Did you kill my family? Was it you who broke into our home and attacked us?"

"Why, you flatter me," he says, laughing. "Indeed, I was a child prodigy in many respects, but what happened here—not of my hand. My tastes lean more to young, beautiful ladies; the unattainable and the exquisite. Not families with their snivelling off-spring." Malden glances back at Suzy before adding, "She's perfect, don't you think?"

"Don't you dare fucking touch her!"

Tears well in my eyes as he ignores me and steps back to the chair. Suzy's eyes widen with fear, her body visibly trying to shrink away from him. As he runs the blade of the knife across her shoulder, blood spills from the wound until the only sound I can hear is my screaming.

"Shhh... Elena, you're killing the mood—such flawless skin, quite magnificent. We've been getting to know each other, haven't we, my beauty?" Suzy's breathing, restricted by the duct tape, comes in short, terrified gasps. When his hand drops to follow the trail of fresh blood, each stroke as tender as a lover's, her body shudders violently in response, as if his touch scalds her skin. With abruptness, he folds his hand around her neck, applying such force that his fingers form deep indentations and her eyes roll back in her head.

"Let her go!" I cry out, tears of frustration stinging at my eyes. But my words have the opposite effect and he grins, tightening his grip around Suzy's long, beautiful neck. Unable to watch as he kills my friend, I drop my head and let the tears cascade down my face.

"Look at me. Or your friend goes over the side—"

Forced to drag my eyes back, he releases the pressure on her neck as I comply with his demand. The respite is short-lived. Malden moves with deliberate menace to stand at Suzy's side. Slowly, he wets his lips before crouching down next to her, his face level with her bare breasts, all the time glancing over to ensure I don't look away. In the most grotesque display of dominance, he leans in close, flicking his tongue as he explores her flesh, pausing to circle and glide across her breast, up to her neck where angry red pressure marks are already appearing.

She tries to fight him, but the restraints restrict her so that she's barely able to put up any resistance.

Suzy's defenceless—I need to help her.

"Victor!" I scream his name, just as I see the glint of his knife move towards her thigh. "Just tell me what you want!"

Without acknowledging me, his eyes follow the trickle of blood as he runs the tip of the blade along Suzy's inner thigh. Images of his mutilated victims swirl around my mind.

Desperate to help my friend, I try again to divert his attention.

"Tell me about your cellmate, Victor. Who is he? Why has he sent you crashing into my life like this?"

*Like a great big fucking wrecking ball!*

Malden pauses and Suzy's body shudders with relief. It's working.

He might be feeding his dark impulses, but I'm certain it's not Suzy they've sent him here for...

# Chapter Fifty

Victor raises himself up from his crouched position beside Suzy and turns to face me. With his attention no longer on her, an inaudible sigh of relief escapes my lips.

"Cara died in this room, did you know that?" he says with morbid adulation. With the blade of the knife, he points to the charred remains of what had once been my childhood bed. "Right over there."

"Who told you that? Was it your cellmate? Was he the one to attack our family?"

"Oh, Elena, he didn't just attack your family. *It was his family, too.* You really don't remember, do you?"

His words trigger a memory hidden and buried for so long that my heart leaps in my chest, the sound of rushing blood drowning out everything else.

*Oh my God. No, no, no—it can't be true!*

The dark, menacing figure smashing through my bedroom door.

Twice the size of a normal person.

Features contorted with rage—*the face of a monster.*

Lady Caroline's refusal to acknowledge the horrors of that night.

The night her *husband* took everything she held dear from her.

My father... he did this!

I remember now—all of it.

Malden's hollow laugh penetrates my shocked mind. His eyes squint, peering out from beneath long black lashes, and he lets out a low whistle. This was his plan, to bring me here and have me remember—but for what purpose? With his gaze still on me, he moves to the bed where he places the knife down, and rubbing his hands together, he strides back across the room towards me.

Instinctively, I sense we've just crossed a line. We're now in the next stage of this macabre game—whatever that might be.

"Finally, we're getting somewhere," Malden says with a chilling smile, leaning in so close that his stale breath is on my face. "On the same page at last. I'll be honest, the confused and lost girl look was growing a little tiresome. Of course, you won't know this, but your father is an extremely powerful and resourceful man. He's the reason I'm standing here in front of you. For weeks we planned this operation, and when finally we tracked you down, he sent me to find you."

The grin on his face tells me I need to choose my next words with care. I can't afford to make a wrong move.

"You're his confidant, I can see that."

*Flattery*—play to his narcissistic ego—whatever it takes to survive.

"We would talk for hours. He told me about his life here at Graystone, how he met and married your mother—so gullible and privileged, never stopping to question his sincerity or motives. More than cellmates, we understand each other on a level ordinary people never can.

"Remarkable really, just how simple it is to convince someone of a lie they desperately want to believe. All the women I selected, each one of them seeing only what they wanted to hold true. Had they looked closer, past this—" He waves a nonchalant hand at his sculpted face and body. "They would have lifted the veil, seen the truth and ultimately saved their life. I gave every one of them that chance, the opportunity to discover the real me before I took from them. Not one could see past their own desires; lovesick and naïve, just like your mother."

He laughs at the notion of any woman surviving an encounter with him, his amusement sickening me to my stomach.

*The mask of the devil.* A shudder runs through me, thinking of the women he romanced to their deaths.

"My mother wasn't naïve, she was in love."

"But your father wasn't—he was simply playing his role," Malden says, relishing his captive audience. "By biding his time and giving your mother the family she wanted, he manipulated her. Made himself indispensable, isolating her from her family and friends—he became her world. He spent her money and controlled her fortune—his fortune—right until that last night.

"What you need to understand is that relationships... they're little more than petri dishes for lies and distrust. Your mother was having an affair, you see. Even to this day, your father didn't think she had it in her. Despite everything he'd sacrificed, Caroline was going to cast him out and cut him off without a penny. There were legal documents, as you'd expect. If the marriage ended in divorce, he would receive what amounted to little more than a pittance. That's when the situation became untenable. He tried to reason with her. She could have her divorce and he would allow her to leave with the children, but she would have to sign over the estate to him. Essentially, her life for her inheritance.

"But she refused, telling him he was delusional, that he'd never see another penny of her fortune. She was going to cut him off, with immediate effect. And that, sweet, sweet, Elena, is when he took back all that was his—the family he had given her."

"No, you're wrong!" I blurt out. "Our father loved us. He would never have deliberately harmed us. This is lies, all of it," I say, blinking away tears. The horror of his story sets a sharpness to my voice that I immediately regret, and my chest tightens with dread as I watch for his reaction.

Malden leans over me, and placing a finger under my chin, he forces my head upwards until I'm looking into his sinister black eyes. The proximity repulses me, and I fight back the urge to shrug off this hand of a rapist.

"Another outburst like that and your friend goes over. No warning. You will accept the truth, Elena. That's the only way we can all move on from here."

When I lower my eyes and turn my head to the side, his hand falls away.

*No more mistakes.*

I know what I have to do to save us.

"Tell me about my brother and sister—how they died."

Malden pulls back and nods. For now, at least, content with my compliance. He stands and turns, striding back across the room to where the steel metal of the knife glints in the candlelight amongst the ashes.

Whilst his back is to me, I push my shoulder blades against the wall, lifting myself off the floor, just enough to create a small gap to slide my hands under. Hands no longer behind my back, I sneak a glance down at the cable tie securing them together.

*Shit, shit, shit!*

The locking mechanism is positioned over my left wrist. To break free, I'll need to reposition the lock until it's central to where my two wrists meet.

Desperately wriggling my hands, I try to slide the plastic strip round before Malden reaches for the knife. The hard plastic cuts into my flesh, but I barely notice the pain as my eyes dart between my wrists and his retreating figure.

At first the strip is stubborn and refuses to budge, but with each step Malden takes, I work it harder, pushing with my thumbs until eventually the lock inches into position.

Now I'm ready.

*When the time comes, I'll make my move.*

I glance over at Suzy and wink. For the first time, there's hope in her eyes. When I told her I wouldn't let him harm her, I meant every fucking word.

Unfortunately, though, Suzy's not going to like my plan. Not in the slightest.

Malden reaches for his knife and turns to face me again. I drop my hands to my lap, not wanting to draw attention to the lacerations from turning the cable tie.

*Nor do I want him noticing my hands are no longer tied behind my back.*

# THE GRAYSTONE KILLINGS

"Harry was first. Your father told me about the look on your brother's face when he attacked him with the knife. Didn't see it coming. The boy was as gullible as your mother. I know... I know, you're probably thinking, how can a parent harm his own child? But you see, your father never wanted, loved or even *liked* any of you. That's what made it easy for him to destroy you all when the time came.

"The demands he made were simple. Although too late for Harry, he gave Caroline one last chance to save you. All she had to do was sign over her fortune and leave with you and your sister. But instead of seeing the situation as a business transaction, she became hysterical and ultimately sealed the fate of her remaining children."

"Our father underestimated Cara, though, didn't he? Harry was only a young boy, but Cara—she fought back."

"Right here in this room, in fact. I've heard so much about that night. It's surreal to be finally standing here, in the same spot where it all happened."

"The dresser—I helped Cara pull it in front of the door. It didn't stop him, though," I say, with equal measures of bitterness and sadness.

Slowly turning my head in the door's direction, the emotions of that night are surfacing almost too fast for me to control.

Only six years old, it had been too terrifying and distressing for my innocent mind to deal with. Alone and traumatised, I had erased all memory and associated emotions. Now, with the floodgates open again, I remember the raw fear like it was yesterday.

"Tell me, how did you survive?" Malden asks, curious. "Your father has never worked that part out. You should have died that night, yet here you are… and he's been searching for you ever since. Without question, we can all agree that Frank and Sheila did an excellent job of staying under the radar. But not quite good enough." He points the blade at me, rupturing into laughter.

It takes a few seconds for me to realise that he's referring to my adoptive parents by their real names. I knew them as John and Anne, but in reality they were my mother's friends who selflessly turned their lives upside-down to keep me safe. And because of the man standing in front of me, I'll never get the chance to tell them how grateful I am.

"I don't remember how I escaped," I say, shaking my head as if trying to dislodge the memory.

But I do remember.

Every last detail.

# Chapter Fifty-One

Cara. A beautiful and brave guardian angel who died protecting me.

Instead of saving herself, she faced my monstrous father, sacrificing her life to give me the chance to live mine.

Earlier tonight, I believed I was guilty of forgetting my siblings. Shamed by the idea that I could so easily wipe their existence from my mind.

But I didn't forget Cara or her sacrifice, not for a second.

Without knowing, I've been filling my studio with her portraits. Paintings of the girl who lived on in my subconscious, despite the trauma playing out in my fragmented mind. The Verandah has become a shrine to her selfless soul, where the clientele gaze upon her face, enchanted by her mesmerising eyes.

It's the reason I can never sell the *Tear Drop* portrait. It wasn't the model I was painting—it was Cara.

All this time I thought my art was a remarkable gift, an extraordinary talent that enables me to create images that connect me with my audience, evoking powerful emotions. Except it's more than that; *it's been an outlet for my grief.*

For the first time in my life, everything makes sense; the hypnotic-like trances while painting—most likely my mind tapping into the secret chamber of my heart where Cara and Harry continue to exist. The panic attacks for which I could never fully understand the cause of, when my memories are of a happy and balanced childhood—not so balanced after all, as it happens. How else was a six-year-old child to cope with the horror that played out here?

Unbeknown to me, I've spent my life preparing and waiting for the Graystone killer to re-emerge from the shadows—and now he's here.

My father has found me.

"What does he want?" I ask Malden, who stands once again behind Suzy's chair. I'm desperate to understand his motive; money certainly, but how does he mean to get it? It will determine my next move. Suzy's odds of survival are considerably better if they need me alive.

"Business first, eh? No piecing together of what went wrong that night and your unlikely escape? Okay, as you wish. It's the reason we're here, after all." Malden looks from me to Suzy, grinning wildly.

He moves to the side of the chair, taking a wide stance and casually slipping his hand to rest inside the pocket of his jeans.

This can't be good.

He looks way too fucking confident. Self-assurance is rolling off him in waves that turn my mouth dry.

"You have a message for me, don't you? From him?"

"More of a proposition. Your old man's getting out soon. He set the wheels in motion the minute we received news of your whereabouts. When he walks from that prison, you can either be a part of his plan or a casualty of it. All he's asking of you is to perform a role—be the front person—if you will. You'll become the face of the empire and take over the business. Be the good, obedient daughter while he controls everything from behind the scenes. Please, don't look so disdainful; it's nothing personal and you'll be generously rewarded. So, immediate thoughts?"

It sounds fucking delusional, but I don't tell him that.

"What do you mean by 'the face of the empire'? Since you seem to have all the answers, why don't you tell me precisely what it is my family owns?"

Malden lets out another low whistle. The man really is pissing me off and I can't wait to wipe the smirk from his face. "Interesting. Still in the dark, eh? Then let me enlighten you, Elena *Atkinson-Gray*, heir to Gray Industries—"

What the actual fuck?

I stare at Malden, speechless.

Gray Industries is a multi-national conglomerate corporation, worth millions. Probably more. Despite not following business trends, I know that it's a household name providing food, clothing and construction, alongside innovation and mineral exploration.

*Gray Industries is my family organisation?*

This morning I would have thought it an absurd notion, but now...

A giant corporation worth killing over—no wonder my adoptive parents changed my name to Mills.

"I see we're back on the same page again. Good. Questions? No? Excellent. Except you're wondering why you should agree to his terms?" he says, pointing the knife at me and smirking. "Simple, really. She dies if you don't." Malden turns the knife in Suzy's direction. At his threat, her eyes widen, looking like they'll shoot from their sockets any moment. "Think about it. After you give your father control of the company, you'll never live in fear again. Refuse and you'll spend the rest of your life looking over your shoulder. He'll come after every person you care about. Don't doubt for a second that his influence is that far-reaching. You'll never feel safe again, because he will destroy whatever life you build around you again and again, just as he has tonight. There's nowhere to hide, Elena, not anymore. He will always find you. Frank and Sheila understood the risks."

"That's why you killed them? Because they protected me? You're a monster!"

"As I told you before, they always knew there would be consequences. He sent me to dispose of them as retribution for hiding you away. They begged me not to harm you. Told me you were of no use to your father because his wife was still alive and that he'd never find her. That put a bit of a spin on things, as you can imagine… they wouldn't give up her location, though. But I'll deal with that little detail later. Well, this has been fun," he says, glancing at Suzy. "And as much as I'd love to stay and chat, I have places to be. So, will you agree to your father's proposal?"

Malden believes he has the upper hand.

And in so many ways, he's right.

Sure, I don't care about wealth and power; those things aren't important to me. But if I refuse to be exploited by my father, then what sort of existence will I have? Already having spent most of my life in hiding without realising it, he will never give up hunting me, until fear and paranoia are all I know. *A life of not being able to trust anyone again.*

The alternative? Agree to his terms and reclaim my identity—my ancestry. I can become the person I was always supposed to be; confident and taking charge of my life—not someone who relies on her best friend to say when it's safe to get out of bed. Perhaps *Ella* has served her purpose, and it's time to take back my identity. But knowing I can never be in charge of my own destiny? Is that something I'm ready to accept? My father's threat would always hang over me. I'd always be a puppet in his control.

Somewhere below us I hear a faint noise—almost imperceptible, but there nonetheless.

It seems there is one other alternative, after all...

"I have an answer for my father," I say, raising my eyes in defiance. "Tell him to go fuck himself." I practically spit the words at Malden as his eyebrows shoot to his hairline in surprise. I motion towards Suzy. "*She* is my family. And unlike my father, that means *everything* to me. He should never have come after the thing I care about the most. Now that I know what he's after and how he means to get it, it also means I know you won't push that chair. Not when Suzy's the only bargaining power that you have over me—the only insurance you have left. Oh, there's no question you've been clever. But not clever enough. In all your planning, you missed one vital detail. I tried to tell you, but you wouldn't listen."

"And what would that be?" Malden's eyes are blacker than ever, his voice low with hostility. No longer playing the role of the charmer, the mask has finally slipped.

"*I'm not Elena.* Not anymore, you fucking sicko!"

## CJ HORNE

Suzy whimpers as I stare at the man that I'm going to kill. The smokey candle at her feet flickers, as if sensing what's coming.

# Chapter Fifty-Two

Malden's face darkens, his body visibly stiffening until his teeth clench so hard I expect he might break his jaw.

A rage is surfacing.

Good. I am so fucking ready for this. I'll see him and my father in hell before I let them take anyone else from me. Defiance isn't something Malden's prepared for, and while he hesitates at this deviation from his plan, I make my bold move.

With my teeth, I tug at the end of the cable tie around my wrists, pulling the nylon strap as tight as it will go. It makes a satisfying zipping noise as the serrations lock in rapid succession; the tension cutting into my already bruised flesh. After raising my bound hands high above my head, I swing them down to strike against my stomach, elbows deflecting outwards off my hips. The momentum is enough to snap the taut plastic strip from my wrists.

*Just as I knew it would*; we've practised it a hundred times in Krav class.

The second my hands are free, I waste no time pushing myself upwards. The movement feels sluggish at first, the drug Malden injected me with yet to work its way through my body. But adrenaline soon takes over and I shrug off the heavy feeling in my legs, sprinting for the far corner of the room.

Inside of me, a battle rages. I'm escaping an evil monster whilst leaving my friend behind—every fibre of my being is telling me to run to her. But I can't. If I take Malden on now and fail, he'll kill her for sure. Everything now rests on my prognostications being correct—that he won't harm her until she's served her purpose.

As I race across the room, I pause for a second and glance down to where Tom fell through the hole in the floor.

My heart leaps in my chest.

The table is empty.

Tom is alive, just as I'd hoped. The noise I heard moments ago was him moving beneath us.

*It's game on.*

I make it to the corner of the room, where I abruptly skid to a stop. Malden shouts, his footsteps growing closer as he flies across the room after me.

"I have you cornered, Elena! There's nowhere to run. Don't make me hurt your goddamn friend!"

His eyes stray to where my hand gropes at the charred wall. Only now does he realise he's underestimated me again; I was never cornered.

With fingers still tingling from lack of blood supply, I search for the discreet button on the panel's ornamental carving. Even as a surge of panic rises at the idea of the fire having damaged the secret mechanism, the tips of my fingers make contact and push down.

# THE GRAYSTONE KILLINGS

The latch releases with a low clunking sound, and the panel door pops open just enough for me to hook my fingers around. I swing back the door, briefly faltering as ghost-like memories from the past rush out from the darkness.

This is the secret den Cara urged me to hide in all those years ago. How is it I'm back here again, in the same fucking situation as before? Once again, running for my life.

Only this time is different.

*This time, I want the psycho to chase me.*

After shaking off the memories, I pause and turn, ensuring Malden has taken the bait. The dark eyes that connect with mine reveal his fury, tight lips compressed into a thin, mean line.

The face of a dangerous killer.

He gives one sharp shake of his head and the message is simple; there will be consequences if I take another step.

All our lives depend on him following me, and although the prospect is terrifying, I can't let fear control me now. In order to give chase, Malden will have to mimic my actions and find the release mechanism. But will the delay be enough of a head start? *It has to be.*

I look beyond Malden to Suzy and see her cheeks shine wet in the candlelight as tears now flow freely. To leave with her thinking I've abandoned her—even if it costs me precious seconds—is too much of a burden to bear. With a nod, I raise my finger over my heart, tracing the symbol 'X'; our special bond to let the other know we'll always be there for them.

Suzy shuts her eyes in acknowledgement, and I duck my head low as I dive into the passageway, pulling shut the panel door behind me.

Once inside, I listen to Malden's rage as he kicks and punches at the door.

"I'll kill her, you bitch. I'll fucking kill her! Come out or I'll slit her fucking throat. I swear I'll do it!" Through the panel, his voice booms loud, becoming increasingly exasperated as the door refuses to yield to his strength.

On the other side, I stand in the darkness, squeezing my eyes shut and biting down on my bottom lip—anything to stop the scream from escaping.

Was it a mistake to attempt luring him away from Suzy?

I make a silent plea to the universe.

*Please let her live...*

·····•·•····

The last time I set foot in this secret passage, a raw fear froze me to the spot. I remember staring out from my hiding place through a small gap in the panel door, watching the man I believed to be our loving father. I watched him smash his way into my bedroom, grab hold of my sister and throw her backwards onto the bed. The crashes of thunder amplifying his monstrous roars of rage. My mother's screams of anguish drowned by the sound of the rain pummelling against the glass.

How could I have forgotten his expression as he pinned Cara down by the throat? She had clawed and

# THE GRAYSTONE KILLINGS

fought our crazed father, confusion and shock in her terrified eyes.

Then a loud gasp, and she stopped fighting. Her head falling backwards, eyes filled with tears as her empty gaze fell towards my hiding place.

One last word left her lips. Carried on a whisper to me, despite the shouting and screaming and noise of the storm.

*Run.*

Twenty years later, I sense my big sister all around me, encouraging me to push aside my self doubts, urging me to keep going, and ultimately put as much distance between me and Malden as possible.

This time I'm no longer six years old and paralysed with fear.

This time I listen to her voice echoing in my ear—I run.

The passageway is low and narrow. The top of my head brushes against the roof of the tunnel while my hands easily touch the cold, rough stone walls on either side. There's a faint breeze on my face where the air from outside has found its way in. It's a reassuring sign that a collapse hasn't blocked off my escape.

Although the space is smaller than I remember it to be, it's still every bit as dark. As children, we would shine our toy torches to light the way, our faces flushed with anticipation at sneaking outside after bedtime to the stables. Instantly regretting having lost the torch Tom gave me, no doubt dropped when Malden injected me with the drug, I rely instead on my instincts and sense of touch.

Under normal circumstances, finding myself alone in here—an oppressive, dark and confined space—would have triggered a panic attack for certain.

Except, I don't feel alone or scared.

Somehow, being back here at Graystone and reclaiming my buried memories has empowered me. My family's memory lives on in the fabric of this manor. Their voices echo in the air, as much a part of this house now as they were two decades ago.

Cara's very essence propels me onwards.

*Run, little sister, run!*

I know every twist and turn of this tunnel. Even when I hear Malden's thundering footsteps pounding the concrete floor behind me, and his torchlight pierces the surrounding blackness—I don't falter or panic.

Because my plan is working.

By enticing him away from Suzy, I have to believe that Tom will find his way to her, despite the injuries he's sustained.

"You can't run from this, Elena, don't make me chase you," Malden shouts through the tunnel behind me, his voice thick with anger.

Whatever promises my father made him in return for my cooperation, they're rapidly slipping through his fingers. But more than that, he sounds desperate—panicked. Their well executed plot is unravelling around them, and I wonder what the cost of failure will mean for Malden.

When I come to a break in the wall on my right, I slide my hand down the stone, dropping it to waist height until touching a wooden rail.

The steps leading to the basement.

I pause for a second. If I carry straight on, it will take me out to the courtyard and the stables. Once outside, I can run back to the village we drove through earlier and get help.

Would I even reach safety before Malden caught up with me, though? Out here on the exposed hillside, the storm is ferocious, and his strength against the gusting wind will give him a distinct advantage.

With no time to waste, I make my decision.

I take the stairs back down into the basement.

# Chapter Fifty-Three

The impulse to sprint down the concrete steps is strong as Malden's footsteps and laboured breathing grow louder by the second. The light from his torch intensifies as he closes the gap between us.

Fortunately, these tunnels are not designed for tall, wide men like Malden, otherwise he would be upon me already. Calmly, I descend the dozen or so steps, trying my best to ignore the advancing sounds behind me. It would be end game to fall and suffer an injury now.

The temperature plunges the further down I go until the chill of each breath stings at my lungs. My fingers inch carefully along the ancient wood, reaching for the end of the bannister. When I approach what I hope is the last step, I hold out my hands and feel for the wooden door that will lead into the basement. A sigh of relief escapes my lips as my fingers make contact with a long metal handle, and I push down until the latch releases.

As soon as the door levers open, its rusty hinges screeching in protest, I launch myself through the gap and step down onto a soft earth floor.

# THE GRAYSTONE KILLINGS

I reach out and feel for the disguised wine rack, recognising it immediately. The earth floor... I know exactly where I am. Earlier; I stood here and felt the breeze from the tunnels on my face. Then Suzy had screamed and everything changed.

I don't waste time closing the old door behind me. There's nothing to barricade it shut with, and the sound of the hinges squeaking will only draw attention to my location. All I can hope for is that Malden continues down the tunnel and outside to the courtyard.

Despite the complete darkness surrounding me, I still have my bearings and know that I'm in the left most tunnel after the basement divides. If I turn left from this point, I'll find another disguised door that will take me to the other wing of the manor. Go right and I'll find myself back in the basement as before. From there, I can make my way up the set of stairs I used earlier and come out into the ballroom.

Without a torch, I know I'll never outrun Malden, and besides, I won't leave my friend behind. I have no way of knowing for sure that Tom's reached Suzy, unless I backtrack on myself.

Decision made, I resolve to return to the bedroom. First, though, I have to scavenge some sort of weapon, and I reach out to grab a bottle of wine from the rack. Not ideal, but lethal enough if I have to use it.

This time, as I pick my way through the basement, the layout seems familiar. Although not moving as quickly as I'd like, I'm mostly successful at navigating around obstacles, even holding in a scream as rodents scuttle across my path. As I circumvent the well, hands trailing over the stone circular structure, I'm careful not to bump into anything that will alert Malden to my whereabouts.

Eventually, after what feels like long minutes, I reach the staircase on the opposite side. I take the steps two at a time, my hands trembling with an eagerness to be back in the main house and free of this impenetrable darkness.

Hands outstretched, I reach for the handle and pull hard.

*Nothing happens.*

I pull again, this time putting my weight behind it, but the door remains stubbornly in place.

Jammed. Shit!

It means I'll have to go back.

I spin round to face the basement. Still no light piercing through the darkness—a good sign. Perhaps Malden is already heading towards the courtyard, giving me the opportunity to take the alternate passageway to the farthest wing. It's a longer route and may well be blocked, but there's no other choice if I'm to move through the house undetected.

The quickest route would be to double back the way I've come, but I can't risk bumping into Malden.

With ears primed and listening out for the slightest sound, I cautiously make my way back through the basement to where the tunnels split.

The sudden noise of footsteps running in my direction stops me in my tracks.

I hold my breath, straining to listen over the thump of my racing heart.

He's found me.

# THE GRAYSTONE KILLINGS

The steady thud as he descends the concrete steps is enough to jar my nerves and send me into a blind panic. I spin round in a circle, despair crashing down on me.

*Think, think, think! What do I do?*

Then I remember the Saint Christopher hanging around my neck—my mother's last gift to me.

A blinding beam of light spilling out from the doorway tells me I'm almost out of time.

Any moment, Malden will reach the bottom step and we'll come face to face. I need an advantage and quickly. With a desperate bolt towards the disguised doorway, I tug the gold chain from my neck until it snaps in my hands. As I sprint through the shadows, past the open door, I let it drop to the dirt.

A bright light bounces off the walls of the basement just as I dart behind the false wine rack. On the other side of the door, I can hear Malden's laboured breathing.

A trickle of cold sweat runs down my spine. My situation couldn't be any more dire; alone in the basement of my family's abandoned old manor house, with a convicted killer and nothing but a dusty old bottle of wine as a weapon. My hands tremble as I think of the death and carnage he's caused. All the lives lost and ruined. So much heartache and all for something as crass as money and power.

Now I'm the only one standing in my father's way, and the enormity of that knowledge is terrifying.

This needs to end tonight.

All sacrifices will have been for nothing if I don't stop him right here and now.

*Run, little sister, run!*

No, Cara, not this time. No more running.

I square back my shoulders and tighten my grip on the glass bottleneck—this is what I'm trained for. I am one of the best fighters in my club. Years of training have come down to this single moment—this one battle for survival.

And I'm ready to fight to the fucking death.

Malden shines his torch around the walls, sweeping in large, searching arcs. The sound of his footsteps makes a soft thud in the dirt. The light is dazzling after the absolute blackness, but I don't avert my eyes or move a single muscle. I keep my breathing steady and silent. The beam swings abruptly to the ground, hovering over the spot where I dropped the necklace. I hear the rustle of his clothes as he steps forward into view, crouching low to pick up the gold pendant. In one hand is his torch, and in the other... the knife.

When Malden reaches down to hook the chain with his little finger, I make my move. Carefully edging out from behind the door, I raise the bottle above my head, pulling my shoulder backwards to increase momentum.

My tread is so light that he doesn't hear me approach from behind. I watch as he examines the pendant, then looks up and shouts into the cavernous basement, "I know you're down here. It doesn't have to be this way. I'm a reasonable man. We can talk this out, Elena. Stop fucking around and show yourself!"

"—Right here," I say, behind him. His head snaps round, eyes wide with surprise.

With disciplined motion, I angle my left foot outwards and jump, loading my right leg ready for impact, knee bent as I rush through the air towards him. My foot stretches out in a strike as he tries to pull up from his crouched position.

In that second, nothing else matters. A sense of weightlessness takes over, stripping away the burden of the day and replacing it with an awareness of righting all the wrongs.

The timing of my kick is perfect and I catch his jaw, sending him falling backwards into the dirt. The knife flies from his hand, landing a short distance behind him. I stand tall as Malden rolls over onto his hands and knees, frantically swinging his torch as he searches for the weapon.

For a brief moment, I glance towards the door—*my only means of escape.*

If I run away from this fight, though, it will never be over. Suzy will never be safe. They will keep coming for us until my father gets what he wants. And so I turn my back on the door and charge towards Malden, just as he makes a dive for the knife.

Glass versus steel blade—not ideal.

I swing the bottle against the wall, hearing the loud smashing tinkle of glass as the bottom breaks away. It arms me with a weapon of long, jagged edges. The red wine sprays like blood down the wall, staining into the soil.

*Now the playing field is even.*

I approach Malden cautiously, keeping far enough back as he swipes the knife towards me in wide, sweeping movements.

"Put the knife down, Victor. It's over."

"I say when it's over," he says in a snarl.

"Police are on their way. Soon you'll be back where you belong—behind bars." I keep my body low, each step calculated to stay clear of the lunging distance of the blade.

"You think I'm worried about their man-hunt? They're not coming, Elena, we both know that. It's just you and me. All your friends are dead, so what's it to be? Is Suzy to join them or are you going to agree to your father's terms?"

"That's where you're wrong—seems we're still not on the same page. Tom didn't die in that fall, and the only reason you're here is because I wanted you to follow me. Suzy's safe now. Evidently, my father should pick his henchmen with more care."

A flash of uncertainty crosses Malden's dark eyes, just before the rage boiling inside erupts and the basement fills with his spine-chilling roar. This time, there are no taunting threats as he lunges at me, slashing with the knife.

Too quick and too skilled for him, I reach back on my right foot, arms locked in front of me to block his swing. My fingers lock around his forearm, controlling the recoil as I pull his arm underneath mine and apply upward pressure, forcing Malden towards the ground. With my free hand, I secure my thumb and fingers over his and easily flick the weapon from his grip, swinging it across until I'm holding the lethal tip close to his face.

"Enough, Victor. Don't make me hurt you," I say, staring down into his hate-filled eyes.

"Stop—fuck!" The pain in his voice is unmistakable. Although tempted to break his arm, I clear the knife from his reach and push him to the ground instead. No sooner does he hit the dirt than he looks up and says, "Dumb move, Elena."

My heart sinks as he looks up with a triumphant grin.

For the second time this evening, a gun is pointing at my head.

I stand facing him, hands dropped to my side, but still clutching the knife.

"So, what now? You're just going to shoot me? Except I don't believe you will, because you need me alive, don't you? All of this is pointless if you kill me. You'll never see a penny of the Gray fortune."

"True. But daddy didn't stipulate whether I deliver you to him with or without bullet holes. Right now I'm swaying towards the former. Perhaps a knee-cap, prevent you from doing another of those fancy bullshit kicks. Or how about the shoulder?" he says, waving the gun at me. "Pity you're not my type—too drab—but I might make an exception and teach you some fucking manners. Drop the knife and move over there, against the wall. Hands on the ridge where I can see them. No ninja shit or I will shoot." He waves the shotgun again, motioning for me to move past him.

I walk calmly to the well and lean forward to place my hands on the low wall. Malden comes up behind me and I shudder as he presses up against me, kicking my legs apart, his hand pressing on my hip. I feel the hard muzzle of the gun jab my bruised ribs, and I choke back a cry as the pain forces tears that sting at my eyes.

"Don't get your knickers in a twist, sweetheart. I'm saving myself for your friend. But I am going to frisk you, and if you so much as move a muscle, I'll shoot. Understand?"

I nod slowly.

As Malden's hand expertly flies across my body, apparently no novice to frisking, I wait for an opportunity to disarm him. When he reaches for my inside leg, the pressure from the gun eases against my ribs, and I make my move.

The ledge enables me to thrust myself upwards and, turning on my heel, I pivot my body round to grab his hand and elbow. In the same instant, my hand flies up to take hold of the barrel of the gun, ensuring I'm out of the line of fire, while my knee propels upwards, contacting with his groin. I slide to the end of his hand and force back his wrist, pulling the weapon from his hand and striking him on the side of the head with as much force as I can.

Malden staggers, lurching to one side. I try to leap out of his way—too late—his hand shoots out, desperate fingers grabbing at my belt.

*Oh fuck.*

I know what's about to happen.

And I'm powerless to stop it.

# Chapter Fifty-Four

Malden's body disappears over the side of the well, his outstretched arm yanking me off my feet after him. I scream, an alien guttural sound, as I'm pulled head first downwards.

In my fall, I slam into the wall, knocking the air from my lungs as my already injured ribs explode with pain.

Together we hit the water below and I gasp with the shock. Freezing cold water rushes into my lungs, filling them with equal measures of icy cold liquid and fear. What started as a scream turns into a coughing splutter, and my fingers struggle to find purchase on the smooth sides.

Green and slippery with algae, there's no grip.

*I can't get out!*

My breathing quickly becomes erratic, shallow breaths that I instantly recognise as a sign of my body going into shock. Suzy's voice rings in my head; always there to talk me down from a heightened state of panic in an anxiety attack.

This time I have to do it without her. Or risk blacking out and drowning—in a fucking well, of all places.

Oddly, it's not how I imagined my life would end.

Determined to concentrate more on my increased rate of breathing than my demise, I tread water and focus on taking deeper, longer breaths of the sulphur smelling air. With pursed lips, I exhale slowly, until eventually I'm expelling more of the stale tasting ground water than I take in.

But I'm still not out of the woods yet. To prevent as much heat loss as possible, I try keeping my arms and legs still, using only slow motions to keep treading water. After what feels like a long minute, my skin gradually adapts to the lower temperature, and with my breathing under control, I sense the immediate risk from cold water shock has passed.

There's still one other life-threatening danger I need to contain, and so, treading in a circular motion, I scan the surface of the water and listen for any sound.

*In the fall, I've lost track of Malden.*

Confident that he's nowhere beside me, that leaves only one place he can be—under the water. I take a deep breath and prepare myself for a tug on the leg that will pull me down into the icy depths. Long seconds pass, but it doesn't come.

Not knowing how much visibility I'll have, I duck my head under the surface and peer through the murky water. There's a glowing light at the bottom at least three metres down. It has to be Tom's torch that Malden took from me. After scanning the water, I spot a dark shape floating downwards, arms reaching lifelessly outwards with his head slumped forward.

Out of breath, I pull up and fill my lungs with as much air as they can hold. I dive after him, kicking through the water towards the man who wishes me only harm.

To do nothing while he drowns isn't something I want on my conscience. Because I'm nothing like him... I'm not merciless.

The closer I get to Malden, I can see he's not moving. The impact of hitting him with the gun would have only dazed him, not render him unconscious. He must have hit his head in the fall, and although it would be easier to let him sink to the bottom, that's too good a fate for this evil predator. Victor Malden deserves to be back in prison, paying his debt to his victims and their families. Faces from the news report float in front of me, propelling me to keep kicking downwards until my fingers wrap tightly around his collar.

Despite the water's buoyancy, my legs burn with the effort of dragging him back up to the surface, and the exertion leaves me gasping for air. As we resurface, I gulp in oxygen greedily and hook an arm under Malden's, supporting his back. With his head tilted against my shoulder, I place my other hand across his forehead and hold him securely against me. My legs will have to work harder to keep us afloat, and already feeling tired and heavy, I don't know how long we could be stuck down here. I take the only course of action left and start shouting for help.

"Help! We're down here. Please, someone help us!"

Every few seconds I stop shouting to listen, hoping to hear something that tells me I'm not alone at the bottom of a well, with a killer in my arms. But each time my cries are met with silence.

"Help!" I scream louder. "Help us!"

Tom will find us. Somehow, I have to believe that he will come.

Down here in the darkness, it's impossible to tell how much time passes—minutes, hours—the cold continues to creep into my bones. Every kick of my legs depletes my energy further. There's no way I'll be able to stay afloat for much longer. Almost ready to give up hope of being rescued, I try to call out one last time, but my voice is hoarse and the sound fails to carry.

For what must be the hundredth time, I give another kick of my leg, but instead of remaining buoyant, I roll over without warning. There's no time to draw breath before my head is forced under the water.

Malden's arm is around my neck!

Before he can get a proper grip, I fight back, but he's so much stronger and it's clear I'm no match for him. While my efforts to keep us afloat have taken me to the very limit of my endurance, Malden has regained consciousness and seems determined to pursue his goal. I hear his distorted grunts through the water as we wrestle and sink further down into the depths of the well.

Down towards the murky glow of the torch.

Almost depleted of all energy, I make one last attempt at survival as my lungs burn, desperate for oxygen. I hook my hand around the front of Malden's face and clamp it across his mouth, pushing back with every ounce of strength I have left. The unexpected move throws him backwards and I grab the back of his thigh, upthrusting his leg to increase the momentum. The manoeuvre works, sending him off balance, and disorientated, he releases his hold on me.

I aim a final blow at his neck before kicking away, swimming back up towards the darkness, and away from the light.

# THE GRAYSTONE KILLINGS

I break the surface, gasping for air and throwing my head backwards, coughing as I try to gulp in as much oxygen as I can. He'll be back for me, I'm sure of it. Any moment he'll find me and drag me back under.

"Tom! Suzy! Please, someone help!" I half cry, half choke in desperation as time and energy run out.

I'm not sure how many minutes pass before I realise Malden's not coming for me. The kick to his neck... Even if I wanted to—which I don't—I couldn't save him now. I can barely save myself.

"Oh dear God, thank you," I say through tears, my voice a pitiful croak as I take a moment to marvel at still being alive.

However, the immediate threat that exhaustion poses me quickly extinguishes all feelings of relief. The top of the well isn't very far from reach—if only I could get a proper grip on the slick sides. But I don't have the energy to waste trying, and with nobody coming to help, I'm in actual danger of drowning. With each intake of water, I lose what little strength I have left to stay afloat, and risk slipping beneath the surface.

Soon I'll no longer be able to shout for help.

*Think, think, think!*

I try to remember my training, to visualise the moves we practised in water. Anything that will help me stay buoyant.

Buoyant—of course!

I've had a floating aid with me the whole time.

I fill my lungs with stale air and duck under the water, bending my knees as my fingers fumble to undo my boots. They come off without resistance and sink towards the bottom. When I come back up for breath,

I loosen my trousers and duck under again to slip them off.

Although I keep kicking the water, it's barely effective now. When I surface again, I tilt my head back to gulp at the air before submerging myself one last time. With numb fingers, I tie the legs of the trousers together in a knot, and pulling at the zip, I give a final push to the surface. After flinging the improvised float around my neck, I slap at the water to fill the trouser legs with air. Once inflated, I snap closed the opening of the waist and lean back, more exhausted than I ever thought was possible.

I close my eyes and let hot tears of relief roll down my deathly cold cheeks.

It worked—I'm floating.

Tom and Suzy will find me.

I have to believe they're not dead—that help will come.

As I slip in and out of consciousness, I cling to my float, hoping against hope for someone to find me.

No longer alone, Cara and Harry are here beside me, comforting and smiling, beckoning me to go with them... But something holds me back and keeps me clinging weakly to life.

I've only just discovered who I am, and I'm not about to give that up without a fight. If only I could stop shaking. Hypothermia is taking hold—too hard to stay awake. My mind begs to give in to the drowsiness—to close my eyes for just a second...

So tired.

So very cold.

Do I believe in life after death? I don't think so. Nevertheless, my siblings beckon me. And if I just close my...

Through the fuzzy confusion of my mind, I hear a faint scraping noise.

Malden! He's come back for me, climbing up the slimy surface of the well to drag me back down with him. I have no fight left. Nothing.

The sound reaches me again.

And then again.

No, wait—*it's coming from outside the well!*

I slap the surrounding water in a feeble attempt to refill the almost deflated trousers with air. Although I try to call out, the words fall from my shivering lips in a slur.

"Help! Down here! Help!"

In my head, I'm screaming so loud that the foundations of the manor shake. In reality, my words barely carry any further than the well.

Another noise. Different this time. I strain my ears, hoping I'm not hallucinating. It sounds like heavy breathing, and when all around me fills with the sound of incessant scratching, I realise what I'm listening to—claws scraping on the wall of the well. A dog is furiously sniffing and panting above me.

Suddenly there's an explosion of noise, and a high-pitched barking makes my heart quiver with overwhelming relief.

Help is here.

I'm going to live!

The barking grows in intensity. Abruptly, I'm blinded by a dazzling light as a hand reaches down, slipping under my arm and pulling me upwards; *up and up, out of the icy cold water.*

I land in the dirt, a dripping mess. Grateful to be alive, I feel the firm muscles of a warm body encasing me, holding me in their arms as I shake uncontrollably. They hold me tight and I fear that if they let go, I'll plunge back down into the freezing cold abyss. I fight to keep my eyes open, not wanting to be in the dark again, but my eyelids are so heavy. The sheer burden forcing them down...

"Stay with me, Ella. Open your eyes."

A familiar voice.

He came.

Tom found me.

"S-Suz—"

"Safe. She's going to be okay, thanks to you."

A rough tongue licks my face. Through the numbness, I feel the weight of small paws dancing excitedly on my lap.

"You found her, Jambo, good boy!" Tom says in praise.

*Jambo is here?*

I watched his little body crumple after Gunner threw him against the wall. How can he have survived the impact? Oh God, am I hallucinating? Am I still at the bottom of the well? I squeeze my eyes shut and accept the warmth of Tom's body encasing me, his arms wrapped across my chest as my head rests on his shoulder.

I'm alive... pretty sure of it. *Well, almost.*

"Ella, open your eyes. You need to stay awake. Do you know where Malden is? Ella, listen to me. Where's Malden?"

I turn my head towards the well, and Tom's torso reaches across to look over the side. His muscles tense beneath me, a twitch of restrained movement.

I can almost sense his inner turmoil; stay here with me, or try to save Malden?

"Leave him," I say, gripping Tom's arm with more force than I realise I had. I won't let him risk his life, not for that worthless bastard.

"Okay, okay, he's gone. He can't hurt you ever again. It's over."

Tom shrugs off his jacket and drapes it over my half-naked body. My buoyancy trousers lay beside me, discarded in a sodden pile. I feel myself being lifted, powerful arms wrapping around me as I'm carried from the basement. When Tom flinches in pain, I place my hand gently on his chest, remembering his impalement on the table beneath the rubble.

Gradually the surrounding air becomes less chilled, and although I mostly lose the battle to keep my eyes open, I sense we're back in the secret tunnel and making our way outside to the courtyard.

Jambo gives a low whimper as we move through the darkness, leaving the house—and his master—behind us.

The breeze in the passageway grows stronger on my face with each step Tom takes, until soon the wind is rushing past us, chilling my already frigid body. Jambo is barking again, his frenzied yap almost lost in the storm's roar.

"Over here, help us!" Tom's voice cries out.

Now voices are all around, instructions shouted out, hands lifting me from the warm safety of Tom's arms. I try to protest, but my voice is barely a whimper. Blue lights flash, dazzling me through the narrow slits of my eyelids, forcing them shut again.

But not before I catch sight of Suzy. She's wrapped in a silver blanket, paramedics tending to her wounds at the back of an ambulance.

## CJ HORNE

It's finally over.
At last, we're safe.

# Chapter Fifty-Five

Hatred. Resentment. Fear. Love.

*All emotions that I'm currently not feeling.*

Suzy begged me to let her come with me, but I refused to drag her through any more of my personal shit. Besides, I *need* to do this alone.

I'm about to face my demons—my father, to be exact. Why? Because I have to convince him he holds no power over me. Only then can I believe it for myself.

As I walk purposefully into the lift, flanked by two guards, my only emotion is of mild curiosity. Will he be as I remember him? The man I once looked up to with adoring eyes. Or will I see him for what he is?

There's no way of knowing. This will be the first time in twenty years that I'll be in the same room as him. The last time we were together, he was smashing his way through my bedroom door, hellbent on destroying our family.

My stomach flips, and I squeeze my eyes shut for a brief second before regaining my composure. I glance up at the cctv in the corner of the stainless steel car, hoping no-one has noticed.

The nerves are not because I'm meeting Simon Atkinson, my murderous father. It's the memory of what he's done that is making me want to throw up over the two guards' shiny boots.

I'm not sure I'll ever get used to the images he's left me with. They replay in my head without warning. For me, what happened the night of the storm all those years ago feels like only yesterday. The memories are fresh to me, not old and faded as they should be, and somehow I have to learn to live with them.

After a brief ride, the lift doors open. We step out onto a floor that could easily be mistaken for a regular office block... if it wasn't for the metal bars at either end of the corridor. With highly polished tiles, the space has many doors leading off from it, and I'm ushered through the nearest one into the governor's office.

The man whose job it is to keep his prisoners in check rises from behind a large, dark wooden desk to greet me. His face is sombre, sweat beading along his silver hairline.

"Miss Atkinson-Gray, thank you for being here today," he says, offering me his hand. His pale blue eyes are serious looking, and I notice he struggles to maintain my gaze.

It seems I make him uncomfortable.

Good.

After shaking his clammy hand, I hold on a few seconds longer than necessary, forcing him to look into my eyes. "It's Mills... Ella Mills," I say, correcting him.

"Of course, my apologies. P-please, ah, take a seat. Can I offer you any refreshments?"

"Coffee, black. Thank you."

He nods to someone behind me, and I hear the door shut quietly.

"I wanted to take this, ah, opportunity to tell you personally, Miss Mills, how profusely sorry I am for the unthinkable events that took place last week. Be assured that lessons, ah, will be learned. Please accept my deepest regret for your loss."

I nod graciously, but I'm not here for his platitudes. I've heard them already via my lawyers. Simply put, I'm here to see my father. Nothing more. And after what this prison put me through, we made sure the man sitting opposite me couldn't refuse my request.

I have left nothing to chance.

This part of our family story ends here, now.

I smile my thanks as a young man wearing an ill-fitting suit places a coffee in front of me, the cup rattling on its saucer. He steps back and hesitates, rocking slightly from side to side, watching me closely through wide, nervous eyes. The tension in the room is palpable.

"Tell the guards to bring the prisoner in," the governor says to the young man, who turns on the balls of his feet and rushes off, his nervous energy finding a much needed outlet. "Are you, ah, quite sure about this, Miss Mills?" he asks when his assistant has left the room.

I steady the slight tremble in my hand and square back my shoulders, sitting taller in the upholstered seat and tilting my chin upwards. I'm confident in my decision. "Yes, Governor Roberts. Quite sure."

As we wait, I reflect on my ability to be sitting calmly in this office. A week ago, I needed the anonymity of London's busy city life to feel safe and secure. Now, sitting here in the 'Number One' governor's office of a high security prison, for which I have Tom to thank—he really does know people in high places—I need no such assurances. I glance down at my hands. The most I have to deal with is a near imperceptible tremor.

In my defence, it has been quite a fucking week.

·····•·•·····

The day following the abduction, Tom brought Suzy home from the hospital. At least, his driver did, since Tom's injury means he won't be driving anywhere for some considerable time. The apartment seemed constantly filled with police officers, and we were all just going through the motions on auto pilot. Statements had to be given, detailing everything that happened the day Malden abducted Suzy.

Well, almost everything.

What Malden told me about my family's wealth and being an heiress—we left that part out. First, I need to process that detail for myself.

Annoyingly, it was Tom who came to my rescue again.

I was in my home studio, giving him and Suzy privacy to discuss their future. Believe me, it's hard to stay mad at a man who's just saved your life, and so I had afforded him the opportunity of telling Suzy about his wife and child; better it comes from him than me.

While he was busy breaking my friend's heart, I was keeping myself distracted and looking through the old documents recovered from my parents' safe. The pocketbook baffled me, and since Tom was yet to have it analysed by his team, I sat scrutinising every page thoroughly.

As far as I could tell, it was just a blank book.

At one point, I even considered heating the paper to see if it revealed a hidden message. Very quickly, I discounted the idea as ridiculous; my parents had kept my existence a secret for good reason, but they weren't exactly MI5! After setting the book aside for the hundredth time, I was reading over the various property deeds when Tom peeked his head round the door.

"How is she?"

"Fine. I've told her everything, and we've agreed to cool things off for now. She's in her room resting, but she's okay. I wanted to see you before I leave. How are the ribs?"

"Sore. How's the shoulder?"

"Same. So, what's all this? Are those the old documents from the safe?"

"Uh-huh, I'm sorting through them. You know, keeping my mind occupied so I don't dwell on the shit-storm that is my life right now."

"Want some company?"

"Sure, why not? Perhaps you can figure out why an empty pocketbook is amongst this lot. I'm drawing a blank on that one."

And that's how Tom, with a pair of my eyebrow tweezers, stumbled upon the concealed slip of paper hidden in the book's spine. I say 'stumbled' but I'm pretty sure he knew to look there. He didn't seem nearly as surprised with his discovery as I was. There's a lot I still don't know about Tom—but I now know I can trust him.

Inside the rolled up slip of paper was a name and number, and although curious, I was reluctant to make the call. I honestly wasn't sure I could cope with any more revelations about my family. So Tom had taken the paper from me and, with a reassuring smile, dialled the number.

Ever since then, I've been caught up in a whirlwind of activity.

The details on the slip belonged to a firm of lawyers. You won't find them on any high street or phonebook, because to the outside world they don't exist. Old school, they've been the Gray family's solicitors for over two hundred years.

For me, they have been a much needed lifeline.

Twenty years ago, after the fire that destroyed the manor, they helped my adoptive parents build a new life for me, and were integral in keeping us safe; hidden both physically and mentally from the horror until my subconscious was ready to accept what had happened.

My re-emergence has caused them considerable excitement, and as overwhelming as this last week's been, they've been fantastic in guiding me through the process of stepping back into my old life.

Which is why I'm here, waiting to meet with my father.

I have my own terms for him, and I can't wait to share.

On the desk in front of the governor are two documents drawn up by my lawyers—I wonder if I'll ever get used to that, having my own lawyers? It's fucking incredible, it really is! Sweat sits on the governor's upper lip, but his face remains neutral. That's good. I don't want Simon smelling fear of any kind when he walks in here.

A few moments later, I hear the door behind me open, followed by the jangle of chains.

Slowly, I rise from the chair, turning to face the father who sought to destroy me.

# Chapter Fifty-Six

A man with greying long, wavy hair shuffles into the room, surrounded by three guards. Almost as tall as them, he has the presence of someone far more self-assured than his situation warrants.

Relieved that he looks nothing like I remember him, I stare into the face of this evil stranger.

With a thick neck, deep, ugly wrinkles etch his leathery looking face. Or maybe they're scars? Either way, prison life hasn't been kind to him. I'd put him in his sixties, rather than his actual forty-eight years. I've read his file from cover to cover twice. Did I mention my lawyers? It seems there's nothing they can't get for me. The document makes for disturbing reading; intimidation and coercion, brutality, suspected murders, drugs and smuggled goods. And never, *ever* any witnesses. Malden was right. His poisonous influence is far-reaching.

But that's all about to change.

"Simon. It's been a long time," I say, keeping my expression neutral as he looks across the room at me. In some ways, it's like staring at my own reflection—the amber coloured eyes are undoubtedly from our shared genetics.

"Elena. Well, well, well. You got big." His voice is warm and smooth, not what I was expecting.

What do killers sound like, anyway? Is it any wonder women fall victim to men like him and Malden? *Deceptively disguised predators.*

"Despite your many attempts at filicide—yes. I got big."

"You look just like your mother."

Until now, Governor Roberts has watched our exchange in silence, but I sense his extreme discomfort. After this meeting, he will resign his position as governor and never work for the prison service again. My lawyers are handling everything.

What I feel for this man isn't sympathy, because indirectly he sacrificed my family to save his own, but neither do I want to see his life and reputation in tatters. What purpose would that serve? Only another victim of coercion.

*Another victim of Simon Atkinson—my father.*

At the mention of my mother, Roberts strides from around his desk, injecting himself between us and demonstrating his authority over his prisoner. With the threat hanging over his own family now exposed, he openly stares at my father with cold eyes of loathing.

"Officers, have the prisoner sit," he says to the guards, motioning to a chair on the other side of his office. They lead Simon across the room, his stride shortened by the chains around his ankles, so that his walk is a strange sort of shuffle. One guard places a no-nonsense hand on his shoulder, forcing him down into the chair.

## THE GRAYSTONE KILLINGS

By seating him apart from us, the chair so low to the floor that his knees rise to his chest, Roberts strips my father of any delusion of power over us. A simple yet effective technique. From his disadvantaged position, he glances between us, his brow furrowing. A look of suspicion crosses his yellow-copper eyes as the realisation of being outmanoeuvred registers.

"What's this about?" he says to Roberts, his long and meaningful stare an unmistakable veiled threat that there's a line not to be crossed.

"Miss Mills will bring you up to speed herself. She's been extremely instrumental in making all the necessary arrangements."

"Arrangements for what, exactly?" Simon's voice is laced with menace, his focus firmly on Roberts, daring him to test the validity of his threats.

It's almost too pathetic to watch.

Sent to prison for his crimes, he's now about to find out what *real* justice for the murders of my brother and sister looks like.

I take a long breath, savouring each second, then say, "As we speak, your army of thugs are being disbanded and are to be transferred to various prisons across the country, all privileges withheld. Their movements are to be restricted and monitored at all times, and I can guarantee not a single one of them will step in front of a parole board. For all this, they have *you* to thank, Simon. They believe you ratted them out, because that's what I want them to think. Should you ever miraculously find yourself on the outside again, you will never know real freedom—only fear. The fear of looking over your shoulder, of not knowing whether the person who passes you in the street is there to kill you."

His lip curls into a sneer.

"Foolish bitch—you can't stop an out-of-control freight train. Just ask Governor Roberts. He'll tell you... isn't that right, Governor?" he says, snapping his neck first to the right then the left, so that loud cracking noises fill the room.

Roberts shakes his head and reaches over for one of the papers on his desk. He hands it to me with a steady hand. In this moment, I see him for the governor he could have been, if not for the man sat in front of us.

I turn to my father, taking slow, purposeful steps towards him. The guards visibly tense, their stance ready to restrain their prisoner. When little more than an arm's length away, I stop and stare down at him, knowing I'm about to wipe the cocky smirk permanently off his face.

With the sheet of paper in my hand, I spell out why I've come.

"My lawyers drew this up—or I should say, my mother's lawyers—but we'll get to the content shortly." A flicker of doubt crosses his eyes. "Oh, you heard me right. The family lawyers have been incredibly helpful and efficient. She never shared their details with you, did she?" His shoulders drop, the confidence he walked in here with instantly stripped away at their mention. "Hmm, didn't think so. Not nearly as naïve as you imagined her to be, then? Without the knowledge of who she put in control of the family business, coupled with your repeated failed attempts to track me down, you've been unsuccessful at getting your hands on the Gray fortune. Or perhaps it's the power you crave? No, no, don't answer that. I'm not interested in your reasons for

# THE GRAYSTONE KILLINGS

doing what you did. I'm not here for any sort of closure, not from you.

"Incidentally, I met your friend Victor Malden, but you know that already. We had an interesting chat, as he held a knife to my friend's throat. Seems you've never been able to work out how I survived that night. So perhaps it's you who needs the closure."

By now, he'll have worked out that Malden is dead or apprehended. Either way, he's of no use to him now.

"Mother was leaving you, wasn't she? She told you to pack your things and leave. Sheila, her closest friend, along with her husband Frank, were waiting outside for moral support. She wanted you out of her life. No-one could ever have imagined the resentment you held towards her, the lengths you were prepared to go to. All to get your hands on her fortune.

"You really want to know how I escaped? Cara—she was the one who saved me. She witnessed you kill Harry. Knew you would come for us next, and so we barricaded ourselves in the room. What you couldn't know was that she hid me in a passageway behind the wall. It was our special place, one we kept a secret from everyone, except for Mother, of course—she grew up at the manor, too.

"Cara urged me to run, to get help, but I was so paralysed with fear... Instead of running, I stood behind the panel, peering through the crack as you killed my sister. She was fifteen years old—your *daughter*."

Simon lowers his head, eyes down-turned toward the floor. Not an action borne from shame, I realise, but from frustration. I've been the thorn in his side all these years, the one person he believes to be standing in the way of his dreams and ambitions, however warped they may be.

Unintimidated, I lean forward, wanting him to acknowledge what I say next.

"You called out my name that night, searching for me. You would have killed me too, if you'd known where I was hiding. So you did the next best thing and set my bedroom alight. I watched as flames devoured my world, felt the intensity of the heat on my bare feet, the acrid smoke seeping into the passageway where I hid.

"And still I stood there, watching as you turned and left the burning room, leaving our mother behind as she cradled Cara in her arms. You left us there to die. Do you remember at the doorway, when you turned, scanning the room to see whether I'd come running out from my hiding place? Did you know you looked straight at me? I was so sure you knew I was there—that you could hear the pounding of my heart over the roar of the flames. And that's when I ran; you looked directly at me and I ran. Through the passageway, alone and frightened, straight out into the courtyard and into the arms of Sheila and Frank.

"So desperate were you to prevent the marriage from ending in divorce and risk getting nothing, that even when terrorising us, her children, didn't have the desired result, you just left her to die. You really believed her fortune would pass to you.

"What you didn't realise is that during your time married, you were being observed. Concerned by your treatment of your wife, the lawyers put into place careful measures to protect the family interests. And whilst they were prepared to grant you certain privileges, there was never a single scenario where you would gain control of the Gray empire. Everything you did, it was all for *nothing*.

"The reason I'm telling you this, Simon, is because I want you to know that there were two of us who survived that night."

My father's head shoots up, his amber eyes clouding as he processes what I'm saying.

"Margaret didn't die—" he says in a low voice, his shoulders sinking further.

A smile reaches my lips. "Alive and well. That little chat I spoke of with your cellmate, Malden... he let slip how you thought her to be dead. Seems you've been chasing the wrong heiress all this time. Not so smart, eh?"

"But... but the obituary. She died, they... they all did—" his voice trails away, despondent in the face of obvious defeat.

"Family lawyers. They saw to everything. A false obituary in the papers, a legitimate-looking death certificate should you ever come searching. They even covered your heinous crime by locking the story down in the press. Did you never wonder at that? A man attacks his entire family and your face isn't plastered on the front page of every newspaper in the country? They swept you aside like the piece of garbage you are."

I don't add that he left both me and my mother traumatised, that the heiress—and majority shareholder of the company—now lives out her days in a mental health clinic.

Chains clink as Simon clenches his fists so tight the whites of his knuckles show through the scarred skin of his hands. The guards lean forward, poised to wrestle their prisoner into the seat should he try to lunge at me. I lean back and look down at the man I've come to destroy.

"When you realised you'd lost your only means of ever standing at the head of the Gray empire, your wife dead and facing down a long prison sentence, you started to wonder about me, didn't you? Had I died in the fire, too? Could I have made it out alive? I was your last remaining means of gaining control of the fortune you so desperately sought. When did you first realise that Sheila and Frank had seemingly just vanished? Not for many years, I'm guessing. They always supposed that one day you might come looking for me, and they made sure that when the time came, I was equipped to survive whatever you threw at me. You're a nobody, Simon. *Nothing.*"

He makes to speak, tilting his head until his eyes contact with mine.

"Don't—" I say, holding up the piece of paper in front of me so he can read the printed text. The colour drains from his face, lips pressed into a thin colourless line, his jaw set hard.

"You can't—"

"Yes, I can. My lawyers have been engaging with a team of health professionals who have been—well, no need to bore everyone with the details. The upshot is that you have been medically assessed by Section 12 approved doctors, and under Section 47 of the Mental Health Act, you are to be transferred at once to a secure hospital where you will receive treatment for your condition. And Simon, I can promise you that the treatment will be lengthy. You will never again pose a threat to me and my family. Or my friends. You are to spend the rest of your miserable existence doped up to your eyeballs and drooling into your lap. *That* is your life now."

My father looks at me, face contorted with rage; lips curled in, eyes twitching in a mean squint as his brow pulls together...

*There you are! There's the monster I remember.*

"You won't get away with this," he says in a deep growl. Without warning, he launches himself from the seat; chains clanging and guards shouting.

The office descends into chaos all around me.

I stand unflinching as I watch the guards wrestle my outraged and yelling father out of the door.

"He'll try to escape, you know that, don't you?" Roberts says, standing at my side.

"He can try. You have his gang rounded up and turned against him. We'll all be a little safer after today."

"Thank you." Governor Roberts hands me a copy of his resignation letter.

I nod as the two guards from earlier enter the office to escort me back out.

It's over.

Personal shit dealt with.

# Epiloge

## Two months later

"Oh my fucking god! You are going to look incredible tonight, sweetie."

"Can I see?"

"No! For the hundredth time, no peeking until we're done."

"Promise I won't be mistaken for a drag queen? Not that they don't look amazing, but, you know—try not to get too carried away, alright?"

"Darling, when have I ever got too carried away when it comes to glamour? You're basically a billionairess now. Which means you can't go wearing a fucking sack to the opening night of your exhibition!"

"Stop exaggerating, Suzy. It's not billions. And do I really need to wear this push-up? I have a cleavage that makes Dolly Parton look flat-chested. We're talking serious risk of spillage here. Wynter's already having a meltdown organising this event, so let's not push her over the edge, eh?"

"You are going to wear that gorgeous dress over there and your badongas are going to look fucking fabulous. Now please stop whining and let me focus!"

Resigned to my fate, I close my eyes and sigh contentedly as my best friend fusses over the final touches to my make-up.

How she convinced me to agree to tonight is still a mystery, but here I am, sitting in her dressing-room as she chooses not only my wardrobe but my entire look for this evening.

There has been a constant flow of stylists and beauticians to the apartment—from the intense to the flamboyant—all experts handpicked by my friend to transform me into a seemingly flawless deity.

Since the night Malden came crashing into our lives, Suzy has been there for me. Not as my emotional crutch as before, but as my best friend. From my adoptive parents' funeral, to tracing Winston's family, confronting my father and understanding my mother's illness—even crying over my siblings' graves... she has been by my side.

Outwardly, she seems mostly unscathed by her experience with Malden.

But I know her better than anyone, and she's not okay. Despite her strength and resilience, I worry about her.

In the first few weeks following her abduction, she pushed back on all her modelling commitments to allow her wounds time to heal. Our story dominated the tabloids until eventually bigger newsworthy topics moved into the spotlight, but there's still murmurs out there about when, or even if, Suzy will return to the catwalk. Big label sponsors are growing impatient too—I've heard her on the phone to them.

Deep down, I know she's scared—her confidence rocked. Counselling can only do so much, and it breaks my heart to see her sparkle snubbed out in this way. Ultimately, she will have to fight her way back from the dark place Malden dragged her down to. Whenever the doorbell rings, I notice her body tense, but she refuses to talk in any depth about her ordeal. Some days I let my mind believe the worst, that he raped and tortured her, on others that version is too horrific to contemplate.

When I suggested giving up the apartment, she flatly refused, adamant that we shouldn't be driven from the home we both love so much.

Two months ago, after switching out his clothes and ruffling up his hair, Malden had rung the doorbell, claiming to be a neighbour recently moved into the building. Both charismatic and easy-on-the-eye, Suzy had at once ring-fenced him as a potential love interest for me. Stood on the doorstep, holding a bottle of wine and asking to borrow a corkscrew, she had invited him in and led him through to the kitchen. Victor had insisted on pouring her a glass of wine as a way of thanks, and seeing an opportunity to find out more about him, she had decided that one quick drink before meeting Tom couldn't harm.

How wrong she had been.

I'm confident tonight will help someways in bringing my friend back to me. After everything my father and Malden put her through, the least I can do is sit in this bloody chair and let her preen, primp, polish and pluck me to within an inch of my life.

"Ta-da! All done! Now slip into this and take a peek in the mirror," she instructs, unzipping the bag hanging next to us.

"Swear to me that I don't look like someone about to step onto the set of a bad porn movie?" I say, trying to gauge the extent of damage and potential embarrassment I might face on social media tomorrow.

"Promise. All bias aside, sweetie, I'd say you're more of an 'Aphrodite' than 'Angel-xoxo'. Trust me, you are going to love it."

"Ugh. Ignore me. Just nervous about tonight, that's all." I give her a sheepish grin and take the dress she hands me. "Holy shit, this colour is gorgeous! Where did you get it?"

"That new designer on the circuit, darling. I had him make this especially for you. The reds and purples are so going to complement your colouring. Cross my heart, you'll be stunning."

The dress slides on like shimmering, metallic liquid, hugging every inch of my body. Now I understand the need for the bone-crushing corset. Alright, so perhaps I'm exaggerating, but I have never felt the need to squeeze my bum into a pair of elasticated pants before now.

They are insanely uncomfortable.

I let Suzy fasten the leather strap of the high-heeled sandals, convinced I'll rupture a vital organ if I try to bend more than forty-five degrees.

I have a newfound respect for anyone who wants to become a model. Why would someone put their body through this torture? I gaze at my friend with a mixture of admiration and suspicion as she continues fussing with the straps. Supermodel or superhero? I feel the pull of the elastic and glance down at my spectacularly plumped cleavage nestled within the sweetheart neckline of the dress; I'm veering towards the latter.

Suzy thrusts a leather tote bag into my hand and skips to the mirror—frustratingly covered with a tulle material to stop me from peeking since I sat down.

"Are you ready?"

I nod, feeling both self-conscious and ridiculous.

Why did I ever agree to this?

As the tulle drops away, I stare at my reflection and almost forget to breathe.

*Because staring back at me is Cara.*

Just as I remember her; wearing the finest gown and looking stunningly beautiful. Unshed tears sting at my eyes and my lip tremors with emotion.

"Oh my God, I'm such an idiot," Suzy cries, hand flying to her mouth. "You really hate it! Oh fuck! I'm so sorry, sweetie. Please, don't cry... I can fix this. We still have time—we can swap the dress out... I have a blue one somewhere in here. It will go perfectly with your eyes. I... I can tie your hair up. The violet streaks will be barely noticeable—"

"No," I say, shaking my head. "It's perfect."

"Christ, thank fuck for that!" She puffs out her cheeks and fans her face with her hand. "You almost gave me a heart attack, sweetie." She slides her arm around me as we both stare back at my reflection. "Never thought I'd be saying this to you, Ella Mills, but you look—awesome. Let me get into my dress and we'll get going. Don't want you to be late for your own event! And don't you dare shed a single tear and ruin your make-up. Not for the next five minutes at least, okay?"

"What happens in the next five minutes?" I drag my gaze away from the mirror.

"You'll see. It's a surprise!"

# THE GRAYSTONE KILLINGS

Suzy slips into a silver sparkling cocktail dress, intended to complement the crimson colour I'm wearing. We stare at each other in the mirror and I reach for her hand, squeezing tight.

If I try to speak, to tell her how much I cherish her, I really will start crying and destroy hours of her work.

The doorbell sounds, and for the briefest moment her body tenses before she spins on her high-heeled toes and gives me a coy grin.

"Oh good, your surprise has arrived!" she says, laughing and moving towards the door, every bit the model with her confident and natural walk.

Still staring at my reflection, I picture a six-year-old girl peering from the balcony, and as the twinkle in her copper eyes glints back at me, I know she would approve.

The rise and fall of Suzy's voice as she speaks excitedly reaches me from down the hallway, followed by the low hum of male voices responding. Curious, I venture out into the hall.

Oh shit, not a blind date!

I am one-hundred percent going to kill Suzy for this—even if the man does look remarkably like Chris Hemsworth.

*What's even more surprising is who she's invited along as her double-date.*

I haven't seen Tom for several weeks, but we've spoken on the phone a few times; mostly asking his advice on business matters and to share our concerns over Suzy's recovery. Their breakup has been an amicable one, and although they've agreed to stay friends, I'd be lying if I said I didn't have reservations about him being around her. He should be with his wife, not laughing with my friend and looking all aristocratic and refined in his perfect fitting suit, smelling no doubt of Clive Christian Suave.

"Tom, this is a surprise. I didn't know you were in town," I say, stepping forward.

"Ella? Wow! You look utterly captivating." His expression fails to hide his astonishment.

I feel myself blush, suddenly self-conscious of my cleavage and wishing I'd insisted on a more modest dress—with a much higher neckline.

The Hemsworth lookalike greets Suzy, then me, with a hand-kiss.

*For real?* I am seriously going to kill her for this.

"Ella, I'd like you to meet an exceptionally talented friend of mine," Suzy says, making the introductions. "This is Charles Peele. He owns a restoration company and is super keen to look around some of these properties you've come into possession of. I was thinking you could both get together to discuss the ideas Charlie has? He's basically the most talented person in the business, sweetie. I'm sure you'll adore him as much as I do." Suzy flashes her infectious smile.

"It's a pleasure to meet you. Thank you, I'd like that very much," I tell the hand-holding, kissing hunk.

Admittedly, I've been putting off having to decide what to do with both the cottage and Graystone Manor. They feel too personal to have their fates determined by the lawyers.

It seems Suzy has cleverly engineered me into renovating the buildings.

"The pleasure is all mine, I can assure you. And can I say how in awe I am of your work? Your exhibition is causing quite the excitement around the city. I shall very much look forward to working with you in the future. We will create magic together!" he says, and holds out his arm.

About to hook my arm through his, Suzy subtly slips past me.

"Oh, this is my date, sweetie. Charlie and I bumped into each other last week and we have simply oodles to catch up on, don't we, darling?"

I stare at her incredulously as she leaves me standing alone with Tom. With a brief pause at the door, she glances back and winks.

What. The. Actual. Fuck.

"I hope you don't mind?" Tom says, stepping close with a mischievous smile playing on his lips. His eyes lock on mine, and in that instant, we're alone in the universe. "I meant what I said. You look exquisite tonight—breathtaking. This new life suits you."

"I, um—"

"No, please, let me speak." Tom reaches out to take my hand, and my skin tingles at his touch. "I've wanted to tell you this since the night we... when I pulled you from that well and held you in my arms—I thought I'd lost you, *really* lost you. I couldn't bear it. From the minute we met, you captivated me, and the more I tried to resist, the more I fell under your spell. You are both courageous and determined, compassionate and empathetic, funny and smart. I think about you all the time. Please, stop pushing me away—it's driving me insane. These past few weeks you've done everything humanly possible to keep me at arm's length, but I'm here, right now, wanting desperately to kiss the woman I'm falling in love with."

"B-but... Suzy? Y-your wife? You—we can't—"

"My wife and daughter passed away, Ella. Two years ago—there was an accident... Suzy knows. She's always known."

"Holy shit! Ah... what I mean is—Christ. I'm so sorry. I didn't realise, she never mentioned—"

*Fuck, fuck, fuck!*

*How could I have been so stupid?*

*She never said because I wouldn't let her, not with my idiotic three month rule on her love life.*

"No need to apologise," he says, his voice deep with emotion. "When you came to my house, the photographs on the wall—you were protecting your friend. I never intended to deceive you or to mislead Suzy. Her friendship means too much to me. Speaking of whom, she called me last night, asked if I'd like to escort you to the opening of your exhibition. Of course, I jumped at the chance."

Before I know what's happening, Tom's lips are on mine and my entire world tilts on its axis once again. His kiss is so intoxicating that I want to stay in this moment forever.

But I can't...

Still reeling from recent events, I mustn't complicate matters further by giving my heart to my best friend's ex. Already regretting my decision before it's even made, I pull away.

"Tom, I—"

"Need time—I get it," he says, cutting me off before I can say the words we'll both regret hearing. "However long it takes. Just promise you won't keep pushing me away." He smiles and pulls me into his arms.

*It's the safest, most wonderful place in the world.*

When, reluctantly, he releases me again, he says, "I also wanted to give you this." Tom reaches into his breast pocket and takes out my mother's Saint Christopher. "Recovered from the bottom of the well. I had the chain repaired." Carefully, he slips it around my neck and kisses me softly on the cheek. "There, back where it belongs."

"Thank you, Tom. For everything—" My hand reaches up to touch the pendant, tears stinging at my eyes.

He smiles and my stomach flutters.

"—While we're on the topic of recovering lost treasures... I read about the recent return of *Van Gough's Poppy Flowers*—don't suppose you had that hanging on your sitting room wall, too?"

Tom cocks his head, an amused glint in his eyes. "You're absolutely right. I still owe you that explanation, don't I? Over dinner tomorrow evening?"

"You really are impossible!"

"I know," he says with an infectious smile. "Hey, where's that little Rottweiler of yours?" He looks around expectantly.

"Call him. He'll be thrilled to see you."

"Jambo! Here, boy!"

A little black head with pointy ears and white body comes racing round the corner, paws skating on the wooden floor in his haste.

Jambo launches himself into Tom's open arms.

A horn honks outside and my heart swells, a smile playing on my lips.

Thank you for reading:

THE GRAYSTONE KILLINGS

ELLA MILLS MYSTERY - BOOK 1

Ella will return in:

The Crimson Cove Killings

Ella Mills Mystery - Book 2

December 2023

Can't wait until then? Head over to my website

**www.cjhorne.com/ellamills**

**to sign up for my book updates and receive a FREE book download**

TOM'S STORY

# ENJOY THIS BOOK?

## You can make a big difference

Reviews are the most powerful tools in my arsenal when it comes to getting attention for my books. Honest reviews of my books help bring them to the attention of other readers. If you've enjoyed this book, I would be very grateful if you could spend just a few minutes leaving a review (it can be as short as you like) on the book's Amazon page.

You can jump right to the page by following the link below.

**US**
https://www.amazon.com/review/create-review/?ie=UTF8&channel=glance-detail&asin=B0C1HY4NVW

**UK**
https://www.amazon.co.uk/review/create-review/?ie=UTF8&channel=glance-detail&asin=B0C1HY4NVW

Thank you very much.
CJ Horne

## HEAR MORE FROM CJ HORNE

If you'd like to keep up to date with my latest releases, just scan the QR Code below or head over to my website **www.cjhorne.com** where you can sign up using the links provided. We'll never share your email address and you can unsubscribe at any time.

www.linktr.ee/cjhorneauthor

# AUTHOR'S NOTE

Thank you to all my family and friends for their support during the writing of this book.

Special thanks to Sally & Evi for their diligent edits and advice – I couldn't have done this without you!

The real Chess Valley Walk and North Downs are both areas of outstanding natural beauty and are well worth exploring for yourself. For the purposes of this fictional story, I have added various properties which do not exist. Likewise, all characters are fictional.

Until the next installment of Ella Mills.

CJ HORNE
APRIL 2023

# ABOUT THE AUTHOR

*CJ Horne is an author whose debut novel, The Graystone Killings, is the first in the Ella Mills series.*

Born in Scotland, she studied undergraduate Economics at university in London and has spent much of her working life in IT. Now she is pursuing her dream to write and lives with her partner, son and two dogs in Kent. She enjoys reading a variety of books, from thrillers to sci-fi, drawing and illustration, travelling and spending time with family and friends.

Printed in Great Britain
by Amazon